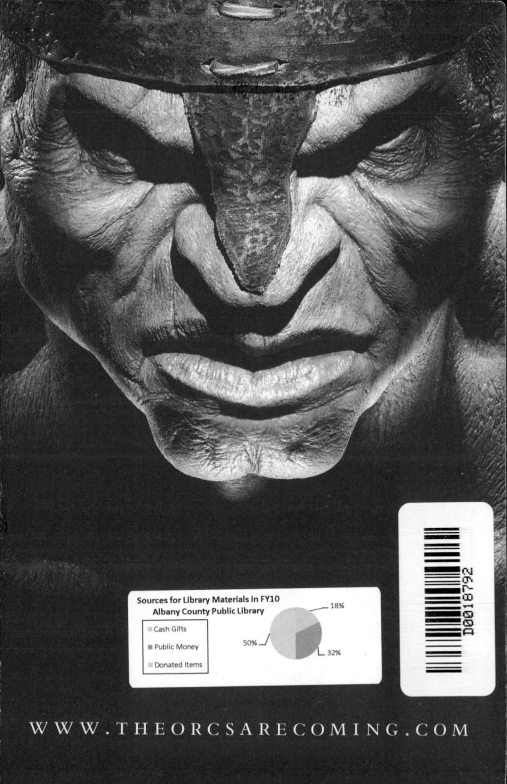

WWW.THEORCSARECOMING.COM

Praise for ORCS

"With grand-scale world building, labyrinthine plotlines, extensive backstory, and pedal-to-the-metal action, Nicholls captures adventure fantasy at its very best." —*Publishers Weekly* (starred review)

"Stan Nicholls takes his well-deserved place beside Robert Jordan and George R. R. Martin as a modern star of fantasy." —*The Independent*

"Incorporating wall-to-wall action with undercurrents of dark humor, *Bodyguard of Lightning* is a gritty, fast-paced novel with a neat twist. The heroes are orcs—though you wouldn't want to meet any of them on a dark night!" —David Gemmell

"Weirdly charming, fast-moving and freaky, *Bodyguard of Lightning* is the most fun you're ever likely to have with a warband of orcs. Remember, buy now or beg for mercy later." —Tad Williams

"A neat idea and Stan Nicholls pulls it off with great panache.... Enough weird sex to keep the tabloids outraged for weeks. You'll never feel the same about *Lord of the Rings*." —Jon Courtenay Grimwood, *SFX*

"A warning: if you don't wish to become addicted to the most impressive new fantasy sequence in many a moon, you should avoid *Bodyguard of Lightning*." —Genre Hotline/LineOne Science Fiction Zone

"Stan Nicholls tries to correct the bad press authors such as Tolkien have given to orcs. Nicholls tells his tale briskly and entertainingly.... If you like lots of hacking and slashing, *Bodyguard of Lightning* is for you!" —*Starburst*

"*Bodyguard of Lightning* is naturally full of fighting, blood-letting and double-crossing. Nicholls has created a fast-paced adventure." —*The Mentor*

"In the fantasy field, Stan Nicholls's *Legion of Thunder* demonstrates a truly coruscating imagination in its outrageous narrative." —*Publishing News* Books of the Year 1999

"Nicholls knows how to describe a battle in gritty detail, in such a way that it grabs your interest and yet still appears as unglamorous and unromantic as it should. A strange tale of magic, fantastic creatures, and mythical elder races that warps your expectations."
—The SF Site

"*Warriors of the Tempest* is, above all, a wonderful piece of storytelling: fast-paced with plenty of hairpin twists, crammed with loads of juicy battles and properly bad baddies, racing towards a carefully set-up conclusion that's both exciting and genuinely moving.... Underlying all the fun and games are a core of skillfully drawn, fully realized characters who engage your sympathy from the start and never let go....Sweet and sour orc, a feast for the most jaded fantasy-lover's palate."
—Tom Holt, *SFX* magazine

"The prose flows smoothly and the story is exciting."
—*Science Fiction Chronicle*

"Breathless and ruthless, menacing and fun. Easy to read and totally engaging."
—The Alien Online

"Stan Nicholls's excellent Orcs sequence...is a welcome counterblast to the anti-orc onslaught due with the film launch of *The Lord of the Rings*."
—*The Guardian*

"Now's your chance to catch up with one of the most unusual writers in the genre. And it's particularly wonderful not to have to put your brain to bed while reading Nicholls—unlike many of his writing peers, there's a real intelligence always at work here. Not that we don't get the requisite rip-roaring action and colorful worldbuilding—along with some cutting humor."
—Tiscali SF Zone

"It is an excellent adventure read. A good adventure story with plenty of action, humorous and well-crafted. Thoroughly recommended."
—SF Crowsnest

ORCS: BAD BLOOD

STAN NICHOLLS

www.orbitbooks.net

New York London

Orbit
Hachette Book Group
237 Park Avenue, New York, NY 10017
Visit our Web site at www.HachetteBookGroup.com

First Edition: April 2009
Originally published in Great Britain by Gollancz, 2008

Orbit is an imprint of Hachette Book Group. The Orbit name and logo are trademarks of Little, Brown Book Group Limited.

The characters and events in this book are fictitious. Any similarity to real persons, living or dead, is coincidental and not intended by the author.

Library of Congress Cataloging-in-Publication Data
Nicholls, Stan.
    Orcs : bad blood / Stan Nicholls.—1st ed.
       p. cm.
    ISBN 978-0-316-03369-5
    I. Title.
    PR6064.I1179O74 2009
    823'.914—dc22   2008051024

10 9 8 7 6 5 4 3 2 1

RRD-IN

Printed in the United States of America

In fondest memory of David Gemmell, 1948–2006

HOW THE WOLVERINES
WON THEIR FREEDOM

Maras-Dantia abounded with a diversity of lifeforms. There were inevitable conflicts between these elder races, but mutual respect and tolerance maintained the social fabric.

Until a new race arrived.

They called themselves humans, and braved unfriendly wastelands to enter Maras-Dantia from the far south. Small in number at first, over the years they grew to a torrent. They claimed the land as their own, renamed it Centrasia, and set about exploiting its resources. Rivers were polluted, forests stripped and elder race settlements destroyed. They showed contempt for the cultures they encountered, demeaning and corrupting the native inhabitants.

But their greatest crime was to defile Maras-Dantia's magic.

Their greed and disregard for the natural order of things began to drain away the land's vital energies, diminishing the magic elder races depended upon. This in turn warped the climate. Before long, an ice field was advancing from the north.

So it came to war between the elder races and the humans.

The conflict was far from clear cut. Both sides were disunited. Old divisions within the elder races resurfaced, and some even

1

threw in their lot with the incomers. The humans themselves suffered from a religious schism. Some were Followers of the Manifold Path, commonly known as Manis, and observed pagan ways. Others adhered to the precepts of Unity. Dubbed Unis, they supported the newer sect of monotheism. There was as much animosity between Unis and Manis as between elder races and humans.

One of the only native races without magical powers, orcs made up for the deficiency with their superior martial skills and a savage lust for combat.

Stryke captained a thirty-strong orc warband called the Wolverines. His fellow officers were Sergeants Haskeer and Jup, the latter the band's only dwarf member, and Corporals Alfray and Coilla, the group's sole female. The balance of the command consisted of twenty-five common grunts. The Wolverines were part of a greater horde serving despotic Queen Jennesta, a powerful sorceress who supported the Mani cause. The offspring of human and nyadd parents, Jennesta's taste for sadism and sexual depravity were legendary.

Jennesta sent the band on a perilous mission to seize an ancient artefact from a Uni stronghold. The Wolverines gained the artefact, which proved to be a sealed message cylinder, along with a cache of an hallucinogenic drug called pellucid. But Stryke made the mistake of letting his band celebrate by sampling the drug. The following dawn, returning late to Jennesta and fearing her wrath, they were ambushed by kobold bandits who stole the artefact. Knowing they would pay a terrible price for their negligence, Stryke decided to pursue the raiders.

Assuming treachery by the Wolverines, Jennesta declared them outlaws and ordered their capture, dead or alive. She also established contact with her brood sisters, Adpar and Sanara, with whom she was linked telepathically. But bad blood between the siblings prevented Jennesta discovering if either knew the whereabouts of the band or the precious artefact.

During the search for the kobolds, Stryke began to experience lucid visions. They showed a world consisting solely of orcs, living in harmony with nature and in control of their own destiny. Orcs who knew nothing of humans or the other elder races.

He feared that he was going insane.

Locating the kobolds, the Wolverines exacted bloody revenge and regained the artefact. They also liberated an aged gremlin scholar called Mobbs, who thought the cylinder might contain something that had a direct bearing on the origin of the elder races. He believed the cylinder was connected with Vermegram and Tentarr Arngrim, two fabled figures from Maras-Dantia's past. Vermegram was a sorceress, and the nyadd mother of Jennesta, Adpar and Sanara. She was thought to have been slain by Arngrim, a human whose magical abilities equalled hers.

Mobbs' words brought out a latent spirit of rebellion in the band, and Stryke successfully argued that the cylinder be opened. Inside was an object fashioned from an unknown material, consisting of a central sphere with seven tiny radiating spikes of variable length. To the orcs it resembled a stylised star, similar to a hatchling's toy. Mobbs explained that it was an instrumentality, a totem of great magical power long considered mythical. When united with its four fellows it would reveal a profound truth about the elder races, a truth which the legends implied could set them free. At Stryke's urging, the Wolverines abandoned their allegiance to Jennesta and struck out to seek the other stars, reasoning that even a fruitless search was better than the servitude they knew.

Their quest first led them to Trinity, a Uni settlement ruled by fanatical preacher Kimball Hobrow, where an instrumentality was revered as an object of worship. Seizing it, the band narrowly escaped and made for Scratch, the trolls' subterranean homeland, where they hoped a further star might be located.

Impatient with her own minions, Jennesta employed the services of Micah Lekmann, Greever Aulay and Jabez Blaan.

Ruthless human bounty hunters who specialised in tracking renegade orcs, they undertook to return with the Wolverines' heads.

The band's expedition to Scratch was successful, and a third star was secured. But Haskeer, seized by a strange derangement, made off with them. Coilla, giving chase, fell into the hands of the bounty hunters, who negotiated to sell her to goblin slave traders. Haskeer himself, convinced that the stars were communicating with him in some way, was captured by Kimball Hobrow's zealous followers, the custodians.

Having rescued Coilla and Haskeer, the band learned that an instrumentality could be in the possession of a centaur called Keppatawn and his clan in Drogan Forest.

Jennesta stepped up the hunt for the Wolverines, including more dragon patrols under the direction of her mistress of dragons, Glozellan. She also maintained telepathic contact with her brood sisters, Adpar and Sanara, queens of their own domains in different parts of Maras-Dantia. Adpar, ruler of the underwater nyadd realm, was making war against a neighbouring race, the merz. Jennesta offered her an alliance to help find the stars, promising to share their power. Not trusting her sister, Adpar refused. Enraged, Jennesta used sorcery to cast a harmful glamour on her sibling.

On their way to Drogan, the band several times encountered an enigmatic human called Serapheim, who warned them of approaching perils before disappearing, seemingly impossibly.

Entering Drogan forest, the band made contact with the centaur Keppatawn. A renowned armourer hampered by lameness, Keppatawn had a star which he stole from Adpar when he was a youth. But a spell cast by her left him crippled, and only the application of one of her tears could right him. Keppatawn declared that if the Wolverines brought him this bizarre trophy he would trade the star for it. Stryke agreed.

The orcs made their way to the nyadd's domain. Nyadds and

merz were at war, and Adpar had slipped into a coma as a result of Jennesta's magical attack. Fighting their way to her private chambers, the Wolverines found the queen on her deathbed, abandoned by her courtiers. When the cause looked lost, she shed a single tear of self-pity, which Stryke caught in a phial. The tear healed Keppatawn's infirmity, and he gave up the instrumentality.

Stryke's visions continued, and intensified, and he became preoccupied by the notion that the stars were singing to him.

The final instrumentality was housed in a Mani settlement called Ruffetts View, where a fissure had opened in the earth and was expelling raw magical energy. Once there, the band became a rallying point for disaffected orcs, many of them deserters from Jennesta's horde. Learning that two armies, Jennesta's and Hobrow Kimball's, were heading towards Ruffetts View, Stryke reluctantly allowed the deserters to join him. A siege ensued, and in the chaos of its aftermath the Wolverines made off with the last star.

When connected, the five artefacts formed a device that magically transported the band to Ilex, an ice-bound region in the extreme north of Maras-Dantia. In a fantastical ice palace they discovered Sanara, who proved benevolent, unlike her tyrannical sisters. She was held captive by the Sluagh, a pitiless race of near immortal demons who had pursued the instrumentalities for centuries. Unable to defeat the Sluagh, the orcs were imprisoned by them.

Their saviour appeared in the form of the mysterious Serapheim, revealed as the legendary sorcerer Tentarr Arngrim, father of Jennesta, Sanara and Adpar. Through him Stryke learnt that Maras-Dantia was never the orcs' world, or the natural world of any of the elder races. Arngrim's ex-lover turned enemy, the sorceress Vermegram, brought orcs into Maras-Dantia to create her personal slave army. But the magical portals she opened also swept in members of other races from their own dimensions. Ironically, Maras-Dantia was and always had been the home world of humans.

Stryke's visions were not insanity but glimpses of his race's home world, brought on by contact with the powerful energy generated by the instrumentalities.

Tentarr Arngrim, trying to make amends for what humans had done, created the instrumentalities as part of a plan to return the elder races to their home dimensions. But the scheme was dashed and the stars scattered.

The sorcerer helped the Wolverines escape, and they managed to take the instrumentalities back from the Sluagh. A portal was located in the ice palace's cellars, and the sorcerer guided the band to it. But as he prepared to send them to the orcs' dimension Jennesta arrived with her army. A magical battle with Arngrim and Sanara on one side and Jennesta on the other ended with Jennesta consigned to the portal's fearsome vortex. The sorcerer queen was either torn apart by its titanic energy or flung into a parallel dimension.

Jup, the dwarf member of the Wolverines, chose to stay in the world he knew rather than cross to his race's home dimension. He and Sanara went off in hope of escaping under cover of the anarchy that engulfed the ice palace. For his part, Tentarr Arngrim elected to stay in the crumbing fortress and hold the Sluagh at bay while the others got away. Thrusting the instrumentalities into Stryke's hands, he set the portal for the orcs' dimension.

And the Wolverines stepped into the vortex...

1

Bilkers were the second most dangerous species in Ceragan. They had teeth like knife blades and hides as tough as seasoned leather. The only thing greater than their fearsome strength was their aggression.

The bilker being stalked by two of *the* most dangerous of Ceragan's inhabitants reared on its massive hind legs. Its scabby head brushed the crest of a tree that a flick of its barbed tail would have been powerful enough to fell.

"Think we can take it alone?" Haskeer whispered.

Stryke nodded.

"Looks like a mob-handed job to me."

"Not if we're smart."

"*Shit's* smarter than a bilker."

"You should be all right then."

Haskeer shot him a mystified glance.

They were fine specimens of orc adulthood, with imposing shoulders, expansive chests and a muscular build. Their craggy faces bore proudly thrusting jaws, and there was flint in their eyes. Both had fading scars on their cheeks where the tattoos signifying their rank, the marks of enslavement, had been purged.

The bilker thudded down on to four legs. It gave a watery growl and resumed lumbering. Trampling shrubbery, grating bark from trees it rubbed against, it began moving along the bottom of the valley.

Stryke and Haskeer emerged from the undergrowth, spears in hand, and followed stealthily. They were downwind, catching the noxious odour the beast exuded.

The orcs and their prey meandered for some distance. Occasionally, the bilker stopped and clumsily turned its head, as if suspecting their presence, but the orcs took care to stay out of sight. The creature gazed back along its wake, sniffed the air, then trudged on.

Passing a small copse, the bilker waded a pebbly stream. On its far side was a broad rocky outcrop, dotted with caves. To carry on the pursuit, Stryke and Haskeer had to break cover. Keeping low, they dashed for the shelter of a lichen-covered boulder. They were within five paces of it when the bilker swung its head round.

The orcs froze, mesmerised by the beast's merciless, fist-size eyes.

Hunters and hunted stood transfixed for an age. Then a change came over the creature.

"It's bilking!" Haskeer yelled.

The colour of the animal's skin started to alter. It took on the hue and mottled appearance of the sandy granite wall behind it. All except its swaying tail, which aped the green and brown of an adjacent tree. With increasing rapidity the bilker was blending into the background.

"Quick!" Stryke shouted. *"Before we lose it!"*

They ran forward. Stryke lobbed his spear. It struck square in the creature's flank, drawing a thunderous bellow from the wounded beast.

Camouflage was a bilker's principal defence, but far from all it relied on. Its fighting capacity was just as effective. Turning head on, it charged, the spear jutting from its bloodied side. As it splashed back across the stream, its cloaking ability, triggered by self-preservation and working overtime, continued to mirror the terrain. But with concealment giving way to attack, it functioned chaotically. The bilker's upper body still imitated the rock-face, while its bottom half mimicked the water. Charge gathering pace, its hide shimmering bizarrely, the creature's lower quarters seemed almost transparent.

Stryke and Haskeer stood their ground. Haskeer had held on to his spear, preferring to use it as a close range weapon. Stryke drew his sword.

They stayed put until the last possible second. When the bilker got close enough for them to feel a gust of its rank breath they dived clear; Haskeer to the left, Stryke to the right. Immediately they commenced harrying the animal from either side. Haskeer repeatedly thrust his spear, puncturing flesh. Stryke slashed with the blade, his strokes deep and wide.

Roaring, the bilker lashed out at them, spinning from one to the other, its great jaws snapping loudly. It raked the air with its claws, coming perilously close to shredding orc heads. And it brought its tail into play.

Haskeer felt the brunt. Whipping round shockingly fast, the tail struck him a glancing but potent blow. It knocked him flat and almost senseless, and parted him from his spear. The bilker moved in to finish the chore.

Stryke darted in and scooped up the spear. With a heave he drove it into one of the animal's hind legs. That proved enough of a distraction for Haskeer to be forgotten. The bilker turned about, its drooling jaws wide open, looking to tear its antagonist apart. Stryke had hastily sheathed his sword before reaching for the spear. Now he groped for it.

A throwing knife zinged into the side of the bilker's snout

and the beast recoiled. It was enough of a sting to hinder the advance on Stryke. Haskeer was on his knees, plucking another knife. Stryke wrenched his sword free. The bilker came at him again. He saw inky black orbs floating in jaundice-yellow.

Stryke plunged his blade into the beast's eye. There was an eruption of viscous liquid and an unholy stink. The bilker mouthed a piercing shriek and pulled back, writhing in agony.

Haskeer and Stryke moved in and set to hacking at the animal's neck. They struck alternately, as though hewing the sturdy trunk of a fallen oak. The bilker thrashed and howled, its hide transmuting through a succession of colours and patterns. One moment it faked the blueness of the summer sky, the next it copied the grass and earth of its deathbed. It briefly wore the image of Stryke and Haskeer as they laboured to stifle its life with their blades.

Just before they parted its head it settled for a coat of crimson.

Stryke and Haskeer backed off, panting. The bilker twitched, blood pumping from the stump of its neck.

The orcs slumped on a downed tree trunk and regarded their kill. They breathed the pure air of victory, and relished the way life seemed brighter, more immediate, after a kill.

They sat silently for some time before Stryke became fully alert to where they were. A stone's throw away stood the gaping mouth of the largest cave. Not for the first time he reflected on how often he was drawn to the spot.

Haskeer noticed too, and looked uncomfortable. "This place gives me the creeps," he confessed.

"I thought nothing spooked you."

"Tell anybody and I'll tear your lungs out. But don't you feel it? Like a foul taste. Or the smell of carrion. And I don't mean the bilker."

"Yet we still come here."

"*You* do."

"It reminds me of the Wolverine's last mission."

"All it reminds me of is the way we arrived. I'd like to forget that."

"Granted it was...troubling." Stryke flashed the memory of their crossing, as he thought of it, and suppressed a shudder.

Haskeer's eyes were fixed on the cave's black maw. "I know we came to this land through there. I don't understand how."

"Nor me. Except for what Serapheim said about it being like doors. Not to billets, but worlds."

"How can that be?"

"That's a question for his sort, for sorcerers."

"*Magic.*" From Haskeer, it was an expression of contempt. He all but spat the word.

"It got us here. That's all the proof we need." Stryke indicated their surroundings with a sweep of his hand. "Unless all this is a dream. Or the realm of death."

"You don't think...?"

"No." He reached down and yanked a fistful of grass. Grinding it in his palm, he blew the chaff from his stained fingers. "This is real enough, isn't it?"

"Well, I don't like not knowing. It makes me...uneasy."

"How we came here is a mystery beyond an orc's grasp. Accept it."

Haskeer seemed less than pleased with that. "How do we know that thing's safe? What's to stop it happening again?"

"It'd need the stars to work. Like a key. It was the *stars* that did it, not this place."

"You should have destroyed 'em."

"I'm not sure we could. But they're kept safe, you know that."

Haskeer grunted sceptically and continued staring at the cave mouth.

They sat like that for a while, neither speaking.

It was quiet, save for the rustling of small animals and the faint chirruping of insects. Flocks of birds flapped lazily overhead as they made for their nesting grounds. With the sun going down, the evening was growing cooler, though that didn't stop a cloud of flies gathering over the bilker.

Haskeer sat up. "Stryke."

"What?"

"Do you see...?" He pointed at the cave.

"I can't see anything."

"*Look*."

"It's just your fancy. There's noth—" A movement caught Stryke's eye. He strained to make out what it was.

There were tiny pinpoints of light inside the cave. They swirled and flickered, and seemed to be getting brighter and more numerous.

The orcs got to their feet.

"Feel that?" Stryke said.

The ground was shaking.

"Earthquake?" Haskeer wondered.

The vibrations became stronger as a series of tremors rippled the earth, and their source was the cave. In its interior the specks of luminosity had coalesced into a glowing multicoloured haze that throbbed in unison.

Then there was an intense blast of light. A powerful gust of blistering wind roared from the cave. Stryke and Haskeer turned their faces from it.

The light died. The trembling ceased.

A shroud of silence descended. No birds sang. The insects quietened.

Something stirred inside the cave.

A figure emerged. It walked stiffly, moving their way.

"I *told* you, Stryke!" Haskeer bellowed.

They drew their blades.

The figure was near enough to reveal itself. They saw what it was, and the recognition hit them like a kick in the teeth.

The creature was quite young, insofar as it was possible to

tell with that particular race. Its hair was a shock of red, and its features were flecked with disgusting auburn spots. It was dressed for genteel work, certainly not for combat. No weapon could be seen.

Cautiously, they edged forward, swords raised.

"Careful," Haskeer cautioned, "might be more."

The figure came on. It didn't so much walk as lurch, and it gaped at them. With an effort, it raised an arm. But then it staggered, legs buckling, and fell. The ground was uneven, and it rolled a way before finally coming to rest.

Warily, Haskeer and Stryke approached.

Stryke lightly toed the body. Getting no response, he booted it a couple of times. It lay still. He crouched and felt for a pulse in the creature's neck. There was nothing.

Haskeer tore his attention away from the cave. He was agitated. "What's this thing doing here?" he wanted to know. "And what killed it?"

"Nothing obvious I can see," Stryke reported, examining the corpse. "Here, give me a hand."

Haskeer knelt beside him and they turned the body over.

"There's your answer," Stryke said.

The human had a knife in its back.

2

They ventured into the cave to make sure there were no more humans lying in wait.

There was a lingering smell of something like sulphur in the surprisingly large, high-roofed interior. But the gloom proved empty.

They went back to the body.

Stryke stooped, took hold of the dagger and tugged it from the corpse's back. He wiped the blood on the dead man's coat. The blade had a slight curve, and its silver hilt was engraved with symbols he didn't recognise. He thrust it into the ground.

They turned the body over again. The colour was draining from its face, making the ginger hair and freckles all the more striking.

The human wore an amulet on a thin chain about its neck. It bore symbols different from the ones on the dagger, but they were unfamiliar too. There was nothing in the pockets of the corpse's jacket or breeches. Nor did it have a weapon of any kind.

"Not exactly kitted out for a journey," Haskeer remarked.

"And no stars."

"So much for them being a key."

"Wait."

Stryke pulled off one of the man's boots. Holding it by the heel, he shook it, then tossed it aside. When he did the same with the other boot, something fell out. It was the size of a duck's egg and wrapped in dark green cloth.

The object bounced and landed nearest Haskeer. He made to reach for it, but checked himself. "What if—?"

"He doesn't look too dangerous," Stryke said, nodding at the corpse. "Same probably goes for whatever's in his boot."

"You never know with his kind," Haskeer replied darkly.

"Well, we have to find out some time." Stryke scooped the thing up.

Once the cloth was unwound, instead of some smaller version of the stars, as they half expected, they found a gemstone. Whether it was precious, or deceiving glass, they couldn't say. It covered an orc's palm, and it was weighty. One side was flat, the other multifaceted, and at first they thought it was black. Looking closer, they saw that the gem was the colour of darkest red wine.

"Have a care," Haskeer warned.

"Seems harmless enough." Stryke ran his fingers across its shiny surface. "I wonder if—*Shit!*" He tossed the gem away.

"What is it? What happened?"

"Hot!" Stryke complained, blowing on his hand and waving it around. "*Damn* hot."

The gemstone lay on the grass. It appeared redder than before.

"It's doing something, Stryke!" Haskeer had his sword out again.

Stryke forgot his pain and stared.

The gem had a glow about it. Suddenly, silently, it sent up a beam, not so much of light as something resembling smoke. Disciplined smoke, pale as snow, that flowed in a perfectly straight column, untroubled by the evening breeze. At the top of the column, taller than the orcs, the creamy smoke formed a large oval shape. It swirled and shimmered.

"It's a hex!" Haskeer yelled, and would have dashed the gem with his blade.

"*No!*" Stryke protested. "Wait! *Look.*"

The pillar of smoke issuing from the gem had changed colour from white to blue. As they watched, the blue gave way to red, and the red to gold. Every few seconds the hue changed, so that the column hosted all colours in rapid succession. In turn these bled into the egg-shaped cloud suspended above their heads, giving it a rich vibrancy.

Haskeer and Stryke were mesmerised by it.

The coloured haze took on the appearance of solidity, as though it were a canvas hanging in the air. A canvas upon which a deranged artist had hurled pots of paint. But order soon swept away the chaos, and a distinct feature came into focus.

A human face.

It belonged to a male. He had shoulder-length auburn hair, and a beard, trimmed short. His eyes were blue, his nose hawkish, and his well shaped mouth was almost feminine.

"It's him!" Haskeer exclaimed. "Serapheim!"

Stryke needed no confirmation. He, too, instantly recognised Tentarr Arngrim.

The sorcerer was of indefinite age to an orc's eye, but they knew him to be much older than he appeared. And no matter how alien a race humanity might be, the man's presence and authority were obvious to them, even filtered through an enchanted gem.

"*Greetings, orcs.*" Arngrim spoke as clearly as if he stood before them.

"You're supposed to be dead!" Haskeer shouted.

"I don't think he can hear you. This isn't...now."

"What?"

"His likeness has been poured into that gemstone somehow."

"You mean he *is* dead?"

"Just *listen.*"

"*Don't be afraid,*" the wizard's image went on. "*I realise how foolish a thing that is to say to a race as courageous as yours. But be assured that I mean you no harm.*"

Haskeer looked far from comforted. They kept their swords raised.

"*I'm speaking to you now because the stone was designed to be activated once it detected the presence of Stryke.*" Arngrim smiled, adding mellifluously, "*I hope this is so, and that you can hear my words, Captain of the Wolverines. I can't see or hear you, as should already have been explained by Parnol, the emissary who delivered this message. He's a trusted acolyte. And don't be deceived by his youth. He's wise beyond his years, and brave, as you'll find.*" The sorcerer smiled again. "*Forgive me if this embarrasses you, Parnol; I know how you dislike a fuss.*"

Stryke and Haskeer glanced at the messenger's body.

"*Parnol's role, as I expect he's already told you, was not only to bring you the gem, but to act as your guide, should you agree to my proposal.*"

"Guide?" Haskeer said.

"*What Parnol wouldn't have told you is the nature of the task,*" the sorcerer continued. "*I judged it best to present that myself.*" He paused, as though collecting his thoughts. "*You believed me to be dead, perhaps. The circumstances in which we parted must certainly have led you to that conclusion. But I had the good fortune, and the necessary skills, to survive the destruction of the palace at Ilex. My story isn't important at the moment, however. Of much more significance is the reason I've sought you out, and the point of this message.*"

" 'Bout time," Haskeer grumbled.

"Ssshh!"

"*On the principle that a picture outweighs a torrent of words, consider this.*"

Arngrim vanished. He was replaced by a kaleidoscope of

images. Scenes of orcs being whipped, hanged, burnt alive or cut down by cavalry. Orcs fleeing, their lodges plundered and their livestock scattered. Orcs herded like animals, to internment or slaughter. Orcs humiliated, mocked, beaten, put to the sword.

In every case, their tormentors were human.

"*I feel shame for my race,*" said Arngrim, his voice accompanying the imagery. "*Too often we act like beasts. What you see is happening now. These outrages are taking place in a world similar to yours. But a world less fortunate, where orcs are dominated by cruel oppressors and have had their freedom stolen, as yours was.*"

"Orcs fucked over by humans," Haskeer muttered. "What's new?"

"*You can aid your fellow creatures,*" the sorcerer told them. "*I'm not saying it would be easy, but your martial skills, your valour, might even help bring about their liberation.*"

Haskeer grunted charily. Stryke shot him a glare.

"*Why would you want to undertake such a mission? Well, if the plight of your orc comrades isn't enough, look upon something else you know.*"

The scenes of persecution and destruction faded. They were replaced by a female form, not entirely human, nor totally of any other race. Her eyes were somewhat oblique and unusually long-lashed, and they had dark, immeasurable depths. Her aquiline nose and shapely mouth were set in a face a little too flat and broad, framed by waist-length hair the colour of squid's ink. Most striking was the texture of her skin, which had a faint glistening of green and silver, giving the impression that she was covered in minute scales. She was beautiful, but her allure was just this side of freakishness.

"*Jennesta,*" the wizard supplied unnecessarily.

The sight of her chilled Stryke and Haskeer's spines.

"*Yes, she survived the portal. I don't know how. And even though she's my own offspring, my bitterest regret is that she lived.*" Jennesta was shown riding a black chariot at the head of a triumphant parade; addressing a frenzied crowd from the balcony of a palace; presiding at a mass execution. *"Let me be blunt. Her continued existence is a bigger problem than the fate of your kin, no matter how dire their situation. Because if left unchecked, she'll enslave more, of your kind and mine. Alone, I'm unable to defeat Jennesta. But it could be within your power, perhaps, to stop her, and to gain your revenge. If you choose that path, Parnol will thoroughly brief you. But he'll need the instrumentalities you possess if he's to be your guide. His journey to your world was one-way. I trust you still have them, else the enterprise is doomed before it's begun."* Arngrim smiled again. *"Somehow, I think you do."*

"Know-all," Haskeer mumbled.

A fresh image emerged: five perfect spheres of different colours, each the size of a newborn's fist. They were fashioned from an unknown material. All had projecting spikes of variable lengths, and no two spheres had the same number. *"The instrumentalities, or stars, as you choose to call them, have remarkable powers. Greater even than I was aware of when I created them. Though perhaps I should have known, given how bringing them into being drained me of so much. It was the kind of achievement sorcerers have only once in a lifetime. I could never construct another set. But note. Although rare, the instrumentalities are by no means unique."*

"Does he mean there's more of 'em?" Haskeer whispered.

"Must be. How do you think he got here?" Stryke jabbed a thumb at the corpse.

"Parnol would use the stars you hold to navigate the portals," Arngrim explained. *"For instance, to reach the place you last left, Maras-Dantia, they would have to be manipulated like this."* As he spoke, the spheres came together in a way that seemed implausible, if not actually impossible, and formed a single, interlocked entity. *"To travel to the land I showed you requires this configuration."* The stars executed another improbable manoeuvre, ending again in one piece. *"And to return to where you now are..."* They shifted

and locked together in a different but still perfect combination. *"Attempting to use the instrumentalities without having first set them causes them to act randomly, and that can be very dangerous. But you've no need to worry about how they operate. That's Parnol's job."* His voice took on a graver tone. *"Your duty is to guard them as you would your own lives. Apart from being your only way home, they must never fall into the wrong hands. I urge you to accept the task I've outlined, Wolverines. For the sake of your kind, and for the greater purpose."*

The light went out of the enchantment. Instantly, the column of smoke was sucked back into the gemstone. Evening shadows returned, and the quiet.

"I'll be fucked," Haskeer said.

"You put it like a poet."

"Greetings, orcs."

They swung back to the gem, blades ready. It was glowing again.

"Don't be afraid, I realise how foolish..."

The stone began fizzling. It throbbed with a grey luminescence.

"...a thing that is to say to a race as courageous..."

A greenish vapour was streaming from the gem. It crackled and spat.

"...as yours. But be assured—"

There was a loud report. Fragments of gemstone shot in all directions.

Stryke went over and prodded the smouldering remains with his sword tip. The dying embers gave off a fetid odour.

They stood in silence for a while, then Haskeer said, "What the hell do you make of all that?"

"It could be what we need."

"What?"

"Do you ever feel...?"

"Feel *what*?"

"Don't get me wrong; finding Thirzarr, coming here, having

20

the hatchlings...they're the best things that ever happened to me. But..."

"Spit it out, Stryke, for fuck's sake."

"This place has everything we hoped for. Good hunting and feasting, comradeship, tourneys, our own lodges. Yet, now and again, don't you get a little...bored?"

Haskeer stared at him. "I thought I was the only one."

"You feel that way?"

"Yeah. Don't know why. Like you say, life's good here."

"Maybe that's it."

Perplexity creased Haskeer's brow. "Whadya mean?"

"Where's the danger? Where's the *enemy*? I know we skirmish with other clans sometimes, but that's not the same. What we're missing is a...purpose."

Haskeer glanced at the fragments of the gemstone. "You're not taking this seriously, Stryke?"

"Wouldn't it be good to have a mission?"

"Well, yeah. But—"

"What better than to whet our blades again, and to help some fellow orcs? *And* have the chance to pay back that bitch Jennesta."

"It's crazy. Ask yourself: why's the sorcerer taking our side? Why not his own kind? If we learnt one thing, it's don't trust humans."

"He helped us before."

"When it suited him. I reckon there's more to this."

"Could be."

"Anyway, this is all so much jaw flapping." He nodded at Parnol. "He ain't gonna be doing no guiding."

"Maybe we don't need him."

"Oh, come on, Stryke. You couldn't follow all that fucking around with the stars Serapheim showed us...could you?"

"The movements that get us back here; I'm trying to keep them in my head."

Haskeer looked impressed. "What about the others?"

"Er...no."

"Not much good then, is it? He said it was dangerous if—"

"I know what he said. But something's been nagging at me."

He went over to the dead body. Kneeling, he removed the amulet the man was wearing. Haskeer peered over Stryke's shoulder as he examined it.

The engravings etched into its surface were small, and they strained to make them out. They consisted of rows of symbols in groups of five. The symbols were circles with lines protruding at various angles. Stryke studied them for what seemed like a long time.

"That's it," he finally announced.

"What?"

"See that third lot of figures? It's the same as the way the stars have to be moved to get back here."

Haskeer did nothing to hide his incomprehension. "Is it?"

"Looks that way. All these markings are different, and there's a lot more than the three Serapheim showed us."

"You mean...that tells you how to use the stars?"

"Yes. The messenger must have had it to help him remember. Like a map. I reckon this first line is how to get to Maras-Dantia, and the second gets you to that world with the orcs. The rest...who knows?"

"That's pretty smart, Stryke," Haskeer stated admiringly.

Stryke put the amulet around his neck. "Don't get too excited; I could be wrong. But I've often wondered why Arngrim gave me the stars. Perhaps we know now."

"Think he planned this? From the start?"

"Could be he was mindful of future trouble."

"And counting on us to deal with it."

"Who knows? Humans are two-faced."

"That's no lie."

Stryke adopted a pensive expression. "There was something

about the things he showed us. Did you notice? Not once were those orcs fighting back."

It hadn't occurred to Haskeer before. "They weren't, were they?"

"And when did our kind ever turn a cheek?"

"What's *wrong* with 'em?"

All Stryke could do was shrug.

Haskeer pointed at the corpse. "And who killed him?"

"I don't know. But I've a mind to find out. You game?"

Haskeer thought about it. "Yeah. If there's a fight in it."

3

The summer afternoon had softened into early evening, the quality of the light mellowing from golden to carroty. A gentle breeze brought the sweet perfume of lushness. Tender birdsong could be heard.

Eight or nine lodges stood together, along with a corral and a couple of barns.

The settlement occupied the crest of a low hill. In all directions, the outlook was verdant. There were luxuriant pastures and dense forests, and the silver thread of a distant river marbling the emerald.

In one particular lodge, a female was diverting her offspring.

"In those days," she told them, "a blight afflicted the land. It was a walking pestilence. A puny race of disgusting appearance, with yielding, pallid flesh and the nature of a glutton. An insatiable host that gloried in destruction. It tore the guts from the earth, plundered its resources and poisoned its waters. It spread disease and stirred up trouble. It threw away the magic."

Her offspring were rapt.

"It felt contempt for other races, and revelled in their slaughter. But its hatred wasn't directed solely at those who were different. It fought its own kind, too. There was warfare between their tribes. They killed when there was no good purpose to it, and all the other races were fearful of them." She eyed the siblings. "Except one. Unlike the pestilence, they didn't murder for pleasure, or wreak havoc for the sake of it. They didn't lack nobility or honour, and weren't hideous to look at. They were handsome and brave. They were—"

"Orcs!" the hatchlings chorused.

Thirzarr grinned. "You pair are too smart for me."

"We're *always* heroes in the stories," Corb reminded her.

She tossed them each a chunk of raw meat. They gobbled the treats with relish, red juice trickling down their chins.

"Are there any of those human monsters around here?" Janch asked as he chewed.

"No," Thirzarr told him, "not in the whole of Ceragan."

He looked disappointed. "Pity. I'd like to *kill* some."

"No, *I* would," Corb announced, brandishing the wooden sword his sire had made for him.

"Of course you would, my little wolf. Now give me that." Thirzarr held out her hand and he reluctantly surrendered the weapon. "It's time you two slept."

"Ah, no!" they protested.

"Finish the story!" Corb insisted.

"Tell us about Jennesta again!" Janch piped up.

"Yes!" his brother echoed, bouncing. "Tell us about the witch!"

"It's *late.*"

"The witch! The witch!"

"All right, all right. Calm down." She leaned over their couches and tucked them in, then perched herself. "You've got to go to sleep straight after this, all right?"

They nodded, saucer-eyed, blankets to their chins.

"Jennesta wasn't a witch, exactly," Thirzarr told them. "She was a sorceress. A magician born of magicians, she commanded great powers. Powers made stronger by her cruelty, which fed her magic. She was part human, part nyadd, which accounted for her strange appearance. And no doubt the human part explained her cruelty. Jennesta called herself a queen, but her title and realm was gained through deceit and brutality. Under her rule, fear held the whip hand. She meddled in the affairs of humans, supporting them one moment, battling them the next, as her self-interest dictated. She waged needless wars and relished sadism. She sowed conflict that steeped the land in blood and fire."

"*I'm back!*"

"Dad!" Corb and Janch cried. They sat bolt upright and tossed aside their blankets.

Thirzarr turned to the figure who'd silently entered. She sighed. "I'm trying to get them to *sleep*, Stryke. Oh, Haskeer. Didn't see you there."

The males sidled in. "Sorry," Stryke mouthed.

Too late. The brood were up. They rushed to their father and clamped themselves to his legs, clamouring for attention.

"Steady now. And what about Haskeer? Nothing to say to him?"

" 'lo, Uncle Haskeer."

"I think he's got something for you," Stryke added.

They instantly transferred their affections and stampeded in Haskeer's direction. He grabbed the hatchlings by their scruffs, one in each massive fist, and hoisted them, giggling.

"*What've you got us? What've you got us?*"

"Let's see, shall we?" He returned them to the compacted earth floor.

Haskeer reached into his jerkin and hauled out two slim cloth bundles. Before handing them over, he looked to Thirzarr. She nodded.

The brothers tore at the wrapping, then gasped in delight. They found beautifully crafted hatchets. The weapons were scaled-down for small hands, with polished, razor-keen cutting edges and carved wooden grips.

"You shouldn't have, Haskeer," Thirzarr said. "Boys, what do you say?"

"Thank you, Uncle Haskeer!" Beaming, they began to slash the air.

"Well, it should be their blooding soon," Haskeer reckoned. "They're... how old now?"

"Corb's four, Janch's three," Stryke supplied.

"And a half!" Janch corrected indignantly.

Haskeer nodded. "High time they killed something, then."

"They will," Thirzarr assured him. "Thanks, Haskeer, we appreciate the gifts; but if you don't mind..."

"I need to talk to you," Stryke said.

"Not now," Thirzarr told him.

"It's important."

"I'm trying to get these two settled."

"Would a bit longer hurt? I have to tell you about—"

"*Not now.* You went for meat. Where is it?"

Given the hint of menace in her voice, Stryke knew better than to argue. He and Haskeer allowed themselves to be pushed out of the door.

When it slammed behind them, Stryke said, "I'll tell her what happened when she's cooled down."

"You know, Stryke, I could almost believe you're afraid of that mate of yours."

"Aren't you?"

Haskeer changed the subject. "So what do we do now?"

"We find our mistress of strategy."

4

A bucketful of water consists of billions of minute droplets. Rivers and oceans have untold trillions.

No number could be applied to the sea of parallel realities.

Its constituent parts were infinite. They decorated the void in dense, shimmering clouds, each particle a world. In the impossible event of a spectator being present, these tiny grains would appear identical.

But a particular globule, looking like all the others, shining no more or less brightly, differed in one very important respect.

It was dying.

The imaginary observer, peering closer, would make out a world in flux. A bubble of acrid waters and fouled air.

Its surface was one of extremes. Much was still blue-green, but tendrils of aridity patterned the globe. White masses were spreading from the poles, like cream trickling down a pudding, and the atmosphere was tinted by an unhealthy miasma.

There were four continents. The largest, once temperate, now included swathes of semi-tropical terrain. At its core a dustbowl had formed, and previously fertile land was drifting to desert.

A group of militia, fifty strong, made its way across the wilderness. In their midst, two men struggled to keep up on foot.

Each was led by a horse to which they were roped. Their hands were tied.

The soldiers bore the crest of a tyrant on their russet tunics. The prisoners were civilians, their clothes stained with sweat and dust.

It was hot. With midday approaching it would get much hotter, but neither man had been allowed water. Their lips were cracked, and their mouths were so dry it was hard for them to speak. They laboured on blistered feet.

There was little between them in age. The slightly older of the two had the look of someone who enjoyed a soft life. His waist was beginning to thicken, and his reddening skin was pasty. He had quick, some would say shifty, blue eyes, and a bloodless slash of a mouth framed by a skinny goatee. His black hair showed a hint of grey and was thinning, revealing the start of a tonsure.

The younger of the pair was fitter and taller. His build was strapping. He had a full head of blond hair and he was clean-shaven, bar a couple of days' growth. His eyes were brown, and his flesh tone healthy. The filthy clothes he wore had been much cheaper to start with than his companion's.

The older man shot the younger a sour, anxious look. "When are you going to do something?" he hissed.

"What do you expect *me* to do?"

"Show some respect, for a start."

"What do you expect me to do, *sir*?"

"Your duties include my protection. So far you've made a complete—"

"*Keep it down!*" an officer barked. Several other riders directed hostile glances their way.

"...a complete cock-up of it," the older man continued in a coarse whisper. "You did precious little to stop us being captured, and now you're—"

"You got yourself into this," the younger returned in an undertone, "not me."

"*Us.* We're in it together, if you hadn't noticed."

"So it's *you* when times are good and *us* when you're in the shit. As usual."

"That insubordinate tongue of yours is going to get itself cut out." His face was growing redder. "Just you wait 'til I—"

"Until you what? Not exactly a free agent at the moment, are you?"

The older man wiped the back of a manicured hand across his forehead. "You know what's going to happen when they get us to Hammrik, don't you?"

"I can guess what's going to happen to you."

"What's good for the master's good for the servant."

"That's as maybe." He nodded at what was coming into view. "We'll find out soon enough."

The towers of a fortress could be seen, wavering in the heat haze like a mirage.

As they drew nearer they saw that it was constructed of a yellowish, sandy stone, not dissimilar to the colour the surrounding landscape was turning to. And it was massive, with walls that looked thick enough to resist an earthquake. Close to, the structure bore signs of conflict. Fresh pockmarks, nicks and cracks told of a recent onslaught.

A ramshackle township mushroomed at the fortress' base. A muddle of shacks and tents stood in its shadow, and lean-tos hugged the ramparts. People and livestock were everywhere. Water carriers, hawkers, nomads, farmers, mercenaries, prostitutes, robed priests and plenty of soldiers. Mangy dogs ran loose. Hens scratched and piglets ate garbage. There was a sickly odour of sewage and incense.

The riders barged through the crowd, dragging their captives. They passed heckling street urchins, hard-eyed guardsmen and merchants leading strings of overloaded donkeys. People stared, and a few flung insults.

They went by vendors' stalls heaped with bread, goat's

cheese, spices, meat and limp vegetables. Some offered wine, hogsheads of brandy or pails of beer. The prisoners turned particularly envious eyes on these wares. All they got was a half-hearted pelting with rotten fruit, each piece raising a little puff of dust when it struck their backs.

The fortress gates were suitably imposing, their surrounds frothing with epic statuary and heraldic symbols. But old and faded. Inside was a large inner courtyard. There was noise and bustle here too, though of an ordered, soldierly kind.

Greetings were exchanged. The prisoners were glared at or ignored. Everyone dismounted. Grooms came forward and led the horses to troughs, which was more than the captives were allowed. Left with their wrists bound, they sank exhausted to the warm paving slabs. Nobody rebuked them.

They slumped next to a small garden enclosed by a low wall. It dated from earlier, more verdant times, and had long dried out. The soil was like powder, and the pair of trees at its centre were desiccated and skeletal.

Most of the prisoners' escort dispersed. Four remained, eyeing them from a distance while they conferred with an officer.

The elder prisoner turned his face from them and whispered, "Let's make a run for it."

"Bad idea," his companion judged. "We've no allies here. That crowd wouldn't be a haven."

"It's a better chance than waiting on our fate like cattle, isn't it?"

"Not unless you want an arrow in your back." He indicated the battlements. Several archers were looking down at them.

"They aren't going to kill us. Hammrik would be furious if they denied him that pleasure."

"But I doubt they're under orders not to wound. If you fancy a couple of bolts through your legs, go ahead. Master."

The older man glowered at the fresh impertinence, then returned to sulking.

A minute later the guards were rousing them with cusses and kicks. He asked if there was any chance of a drink.

"Favours are my lord's privilege, not mine," the highest-ranking replied, jerking them to their feet.

The brief rest had made their aches more noticeable now they were moving again. They were stiff, and their muscles were knotted. But their captors treated them no more gently for it. Stinging blows from leather riding crops hurried along their progress.

They were driven to a set of double doors opening into the castle proper. The interior was gloomy to their dazzled eyes, and it was cooler, which was a mercy.

Like many fortresses that had been ᴧdded to and built on over the years, there was a warren of passages, corridors and stairways to be negotiated. They passed through checkpoints and locked doors, but saw few windows, save arrow slits.

Finally they arrived at a sizeable hall. It was wood panelled and high-ceilinged, and its drapes were drawn to keep out the heat. Light came from oil lamps and candles, and the air was stuffy. High up, where the panelling ended and a stone wall began, there had been coats of arms. But they were freshly defaced, their features smashed, revealing whiter granite beneath.

The guards in attendance wore the livery of a personal body-guard. A handful of civilian officials were also present.

There was no furniture except an oak throne on a dais at one end of the room. It, too, had been vandalised; someone had hacked away the device on its tall backrest. The prisoners were made to stand in front of it.

A minute passed, glacially. They exchanged bleak glances.

Behind the throne was a cleverly concealed door, set flush to the panelling. It opened, and someone entered.

Rulers come in a variety of guises. Those who inherit leadership can be unprepossessing. Those who seize it often have the appearance of brutish warriors. Kantor Hammrik looked like a clerk. Which was appropriate for someone who had effectively bought a kingdom. Bought in the sense of financing the bloody overthrow and regicide of an existing monarch.

Hammrik resembled a quill-pusher because, in a way, that's what he was. Early on in his illicit career he realised the efficacy of the equation between money and power. Learned it, and took it to what passed for his heart. He grew adept at using his ill-gotten riches to manipulate the greed of men without scruples, and rose on a tide of other people's blood, bought and paid for.

His build was more suited to running from a fight than engaging in one; what some called wiry framed. Any muscularity he had was restricted to his brains. He responded to hair loss by having his head completely shaved, which stressed the angularity of his skull. His raw-boned, beardless face was dominated by acute grey eyes. But woe to anybody who took him for a book-keeper.

As Hammrik swept in, the prisoners were forced to their knees. Everyone bowed.

"Ah, Micalor Standeven," the usurper uttered as he perched on his stolen throne. "I was beginning to think I'd never have the pleasure of your company again."

The elder prisoner looked up. "How delightful to see you, Kantor." He went for casual bonhomie.

Hammrik gave him a stony, threatening look.

"That is," Standeven hastily corrected, "greetings, my liege. And may I take this opportunity to congratulate you on your elevation to—"

Hammrik waved him to silence. "Let's take the fawning as read, shall we?" His gaze fell upon Standeven's companion. "I see you've got your lapdog with you, as usual."

"Yes, er, sire. He's—"

"He can speak for himself. What's your name?"

"Pepperdyne, sir," the younger prisoner replied. "Jode Pepperdyne."

"You're bonded to him?"

Pepperdyne nodded.

"Then you're equally liable."

"If this is a misunderstanding about money," Standeven said, as though it had just occurred to him, "I'm sure we can settle such a trifling matter cordially."

"Trifling?" Hammrik repeated ominously.

"Well, yes. For a man of your newly acquired status it must be a mere—"

"Shut up." Hammrik beckoned to a studious-looking old functionary standing to one side. "How much?"

The old man was carrying a dog-eared ledger. Wetting a thumb, he began flipping pages.

"A round figure will do," Hammrik told him.

"Certainly, sire." He found the entry and squinted. "Let's see. With interest, call it ... forty thousand."

"Is it *that* much?" Standeven exclaimed in mock surprise. "Well, well. Still, I'm a little puzzled as to why you should call us in over this. I can understand it might have been necessary when you were a money len—when you were providing pecuniary services. But surely, sire, you don't need it now?"

"Look around you. This hardly resembles a thriving kingdom, does it? Overthrowing Wyvell was a costly business, and though his followers were beaten, they're not entirely crushed yet. It all takes money."

"Of course."

"A debt is a debt, and yours is overdue."

"Absolutely. It's a matter of honour."

"So what are you going to do about it?"

Standeven stared at him. "Do you think I might have something to drink? We were out in that sun for an awfully long time, you see, and ..."

Hammrik raised a hand, then called for water. A young flunkey brought him a hide pouch. Hammrik rose and stepped down to the kneeling Standeven. But he didn't give him the pouch. Instead, he tilted it, so that a single drop splashed into Standeven's outstretched palm. Frowning, the prisoner licked up the moisture with his parched tongue.

"One drop," Hammrik said. "How long do you think it'd take to feed you say, forty thousand?"

Standeven was baffled, and said nothing.

"Probably no time at all," Hammrik decided, "if you had it all in one go. In a tankard, for instance."

"Kantor...I mean, sire, I—"

"But suppose you had it one drop at a time, like just now. How long would that take? Days? Weeks?" Hammrik held the water pouch at arm's length, as though studying it. "This stuff's going to be precious here soon, given the way this land's going. The way the whole world's going. I can see water being as valuable as...blood."

Standeven shifted uncomfortably. Pepperdyne betrayed no emotion.

"That's the deal," Hammrik continued. "Repay me in coin or I'll take it in blood. Forty thousand drops, one at a time." He leaned closer to Standeven's face. "I don't mean that as any kind of figure of speech."

"I can pay!" Standeven protested.

"Does he have the money?" Hammrik addressed the question to Pepperdyne.

"No."

"You're asking a *slave* about my financial arrangements?" Standeven complained. "What would he know?"

"He's smarter than you. Or maybe not, seeing as he hasn't yet cut your throat while you were sleeping. But at least he didn't insult me with a lie. That earns him a quicker death than yours."

"You can have him."

"What?"

"To settle the debt. He's strong and hard working, and—"

Hammrik laughed. "And I thought *I* was a bastard. He's not worth a fraction of what you owe me. Why would I want another mouth to feed?"

"I can pay you, Hammrik. I just need a little time to get together the—"

"I've wasted enough time as it is. I've no alternative but to have you both executed. *Guards!*"

Men came forward and took hold of the prisoners.

"There's no need for this," Standeven pleaded. "We can work it out!"

Hammrik was walking away.

"Suppose we could get you something more valuable than money?" Pepperdyne called after him.

The upstart king halted and turned. "What could you possibly have to interest me?"

"Something you've long wanted."

"Go on."

"Everybody knows about your search for the instrumentalities."

A passionate glint lit Hammrik's eyes, though his words belied it. "And many have lied about knowing where they're to be found."

"We're different. We really could help you gain them."

"How?"

"As it happens, my master wasn't being entirely untruthful when he said he could pay you. The plan was to locate them, sell them to the highest bidder and settle your debt from the proceeds. In fact, we were following their trail when your men picked us up."

"Why didn't you mention this before?"

"Would *you* in our position, and run the risk of losing such a prize?"

Standeven had looked bewildered at this turn of events. Now he was nodding furiously. "It's true. Like you, I've heard the stories, though I confess to being unclear about what the instrumentalities are supposed to actually do. But I've always thought that anyone who found them would make a fortune."

"I've no interest in making money out of them," Hammrik stated.

"You're not interested in their *value*?" Standeven was shocked.

"Not that kind of value. If they function as they're rumoured to, there's a chance me and my people can escape this stinking world."

Pepperdyne and Standeven were puzzled at the remark, but thought it wise to keep quiet.

"So what makes you think you've a chance of finding them when everyone else has failed?" Hammrik asked.

"We've come across evidence," Pepperdyne replied.

"What evidence?"

"You'll forgive us for not throwing away our only bargaining chip," Standeven said.

"You're bluffing, the pair of you."

"Can you afford to take that chance?"

"And what do you have to lose if we're lying?" Pepperdyne added.

Hammrik considered their words. "What does finding the instrumentalities involve? What would I have to do?"

"With respect, sire," Pepperdyne told him, "not you, us."

"Explain."

"The information we have indicates that they're to be found upcountry."

"How far upcountry?"

"All the way north, to the new lands."

"Centrasia? From what I hear it's full of freaks and monsters."

"They say there's magic there too, of a sort. But that makes it the logical place to find what we're seeking, doesn't it?"

"What can you do there that I couldn't achieve with an army?"

"Do you have one to spare? Besides, we have the contacts."

"Why don't I just have you tortured to find out what you know?"

"Our contacts will only deal directly with us. If anybody else turns up they'll be long gone."

A long moment of silence ensued as Hammrik weighed the options. At last he said, "On balance, I don't believe you. But if there's a chance, I'd be a fool not to take it."

It was all Standeven could do to suppress a loud sigh of relief.

"There'll be a time limit, naturally," Hammrik explained, "and I'll be hand-picking your escort."

"Escort?"

"Of *course*. You didn't think I'd let you two swan off by yourselves, did you?"

"No. No, of course not."

"If you get the instrumentalities, the debt's cancelled. I'll even reward you on top. If this is a ruse you'll just be delaying your deaths with a brief reprieve in a land of horrors. You'll be brought back here and I'll kill you. Understood?"

They nodded.

Without further word, he walked away.

Standeven turned to his bondsman. "What were you thinking of?" he whispered. "We don't know where to find those things, or even if they exist."

"You'd prefer it if they killed us? I had to come up with a story that bought us time."

"And what happens when his thugs find out we were talking through our arses?"

"I don't know. We'll think of something."

"It'd better be a damn good —"

"*Ssshh.*"

An officer approached, the same one who earlier refused them water.

"As you're in my master's good books," he announced, "at least for now, I thought you could use that drink."

Standeven looked up expectantly.

To laughter from most of the other people in the room, the officer poured the contents of a canteen over Standeven's raised face.

He shook his head, like a dog leaving a river, scattering a million droplets of water.

5

Glass was an uncommon commodity. Orc artisans knew how to make it, but rarely bothered except for specific purposes, such as casements in certain places of worship and one or two of the chieftains' grand lodges. It was occasionally found in taverns.

As Stryke and Haskeer approached the inn they sought, they witnessed why glass was so infrequently used as a building material.

With a resounding crash, an orc was propelled through one of the windows. He bounced a couple of times before coming to rest in the shards.

The tavern's door was stout. But not so strong as to resist another flying body. The battered orc that crashed through it managed to stumble a couple of paces before collapsing.

There was uproar inside. A wild cacophony of shattered earthenware, breaking furniture and yelled curses.

Stryke said, "This must be the place."

They stepped through the splintered doorframe. An orc landed on his back in front of them. He came down heavily, shaking the floorboards.

Stryke nodded to him. "Morning, Breggin."

"Captain," the orc groaned.

The interior of the inn was essentially a single, large room. There was a serving bench at one end and a storm in the middle. The storm's eye stood astride a table.

Coilla wielded an iron cooking pot. Clutching the handle, she swung at the heads of the half-dozen males struggling to reach her.

She was a handsome specimen of orc womanhood, with attractively mottled skin, dark, flashing eyes, barbed teeth and a muscular, warrior's physique. Most alluring of all, she fought like a demon with toothache.

As Stryke and Haskeer entered, she delivered a well-aimed kick to the jaw of an opponent who ducked too late. He met the floor as surely as a dropped sack of offal. The others tried to catch her legs and topple her, but she skipped away with ease. They started rocking the table.

"Should we help?" Haskeer wondered.

"I don't think we could beat her," Stryke replied dryly.

Chiming like a bell, Coilla's cooking pot caught one of her antagonists square to the side of his head. Knocked senseless, he tumbled floorward.

Haskeer spotted a half-full tankard of ale. He lifted it and started drinking. Stryke leaned against the counter, arms folded, watching the brawl.

The four remaining males finally upended the table. Coilla leapt clear, feet-first into someone's chest. He spiralled out of play. Quickly righting herself, she swiped at the next in line, flattening his nose with her pot. Driven backwards, he came to grief in a tangle of chairs.

The two still upright rushed her in unison. One was dispatched by the simple expedient of running into her raised elbow. It connected with the bridge of his nose, sending him downhill and comatose. She dodged the clutches of the last orc standing and pounded his features with the fist of her free hand, rendering him insentient.

Coilla briefly savoured the scene, then, tossing the cooking pot aside, gave Stryke and Haskeer a cheery greeting.

"What was that about?" Haskeer asked. He thumped down the empty tankard and belched.

"It started as a fight *over* me, then kind of developed into one *with* me." She shrugged. "The usual."

"Keep up these courting rituals and you'll run out of suitors," Stryke commented.

"Cosy up to *that* lot? You must be joking. Anybody who can't knock me down doesn't deserve consideration. So, what are you two doing here?"

"We've news," Stryke told her. "Let's go outside."

It was the beginning of a glorious day. The sun was up, bathing the land in balmy warmth. Birds were on the wing and bees droned.

They went and sat on a little hillock. Stryke explained what had happened, with Haskeer adding unhelpful interruptions. They showed her the amulet.

"But Jennesta's dead, surely?" she said. "We saw her pulled apart by that vortex thing."

"Maybe she can't be killed that easily," Haskeer contributed. "The sort of powers that bitch had, I'm thinking she can't be killed *at all.*"

"I'd bet on cold steel through the heart revoking her sorcery," Stryke replied.

"You reckon she's got one?"

"We don't know how she survived, but it seems she did, and she's making orcs suffer. What are we going to do about it?"

"If we leave this land, you know what we're likely going to," Coilla reminded him. "Prejudice about us, and hatred and bigotry. Sure you want to go through all that shit again?"

"We've rode out worse than words."

"It's not words that worry me. And don't count on too many allies wherever we fetch up."

"I'm not saying there isn't going to be hardship, sweat and violence."

"Just like old times, eh?"

"So where do you stand, Coilla? Are you saying no?"

She grinned. "Hell, I'm not. This is a good place, but it can get kind of dull after a while. I've been itching for a real fight. I'm tired of lightweight scuffles."

A wheezing orc staggered out of the tavern, gobbing teeth.

"You're game, then?"

"Sure."

"So what next?" Haskeer asked.

"We round up the rest of the band and put it to 'em," Stryke decided.

Haskeer wrinkled his craggy brow. "Strange to think of the Wolverines re-formed."

"If they want re-forming," Coilla said.

Nep and Gleadeg were easily found; they lay insensible in the tavern, alongside Breggin. Zoda and Prooq were fishing with spears a little way upriver. Reafdaw was helping build a long-house as part of a service to the community edict imposed by local elders, following an affray. Eldo, Bhose, Liffin and Jad were with a recently returned hunting party. Calthmon was discovered drunk on the steps of a hostelry and required dunking in a nearby rain butt. Orbon and Seafe, like Stryke, had mated, and were at their lodges, coddling offspring. Vobe, Gant, Finje and Noskaa were traced to a regional tourney they were competing in. Toche and Hystykk turned up in a felons' compound, the result of a little horseplay involving riot and arson, and had to be bailed.

Stryke explained the mystery of the human who came through the portal, and outlined Serapheim's message. There was some discussion, but a surprising degree of unanimity, despite Coilla's doubts. Much as they relished their hard-won freedom, all felt jaded and welcomed the prospect of a mission.

By late afternoon, Stryke was ready to begin a new search. Recruits were needed to replace those lost in the Wolverines' previous battles and bring the warband up to strength. He set about tracing a half dozen likely prospects he'd had his eye on.

Word got around that something was afoot. That evening, a curious crowd gathered at the clearing where Stryke mustered his troop.

Several of the Wolverines' mates were there, too. Thifzarr came, wearing the flaming crimson headdress Stryke first saw in his visions of this place. They stood away from the others.

"And you're sure you don't mind?" Stryke repeated.

"Would it matter if I did? Don't look doleful, you know you're desperate to go."

"Don't put it that way. I'll be back. It's just—"

She stilled his lips with a coarse finger. "I know. You don't have to explain an orc's instincts to me. I'm only sorry I'm not going with you."

He brightened, relieved at her reaction. "That would have been good. We've never had the joy of fighting side by side. I've always felt it's something missing from our union."

"Me, too. Couples should spill blood together."

"We will," he promised.

"Be careful," she said, suddenly serious. "Stupid thing to say. But I'd like to think the kids' father's going to be around as they grow. Don't take risks, Stryke."

"I won't," he lied. He looked round. Haskeer had got the Wolverines into a semblance of order. To one side, another, smaller group shuffled their feet and looked slightly self-conscious. "I need to get started."

She nodded, and he went to his band.

"Heads up!" Haskeer bellowed.

The company straightened their backs.

"I'm glad you all volunteered," Stryke told them. "We always worked well together, and we can do it again." His tone hardened. "But let's get one thing straight. This is a well-ordered fighting unit. Or it used to be. We've all back-slid a bit while we've been here. Got soft, some of us. Sign on for this mission and you'll be subject to military discipline, just like before. I'm in charge, and there'll be a chain of command." He shot a sideways glance at Haskeer. "Anybody got a problem with that?"

Nobody had.

"At a time like this we remember fallen comrades," he went on. "Kestix, Meklun, Darig, Slettal, Wrelbyd, Talag. They all died serving this band, and we should never forget it." He paused. "That means we don't have our full quota. So I'm bringing in replacements." He waved forward the recruits, and counted them off. "This is Ignar, Keick, Harlgo, Chuss, Yunst and Pirrak. I expect you to make them welcome. Show them our routines and get them used to our ways. They're good fighters, but not combat trained. Though they will be by the time we've finished with them."

There was laughter. In the case of the recruits, somewhat nervous.

"Somebody else we lost can never be replaced," Stryke continued. "We all respected Alfray." Heads were nodding agreement. "He was more than the band's medic and a veteran fighter; he was a link in the chain binding us to our kind's past. We can't replace him, but we need another corporal alongside Coilla here, so we'll fill the void he left as best we can." He beckoned. Someone came out of the crowd.

He was an orc of advanced years, though still in his prime and looking fit. But the light in his astute eyes owed more to autumn than summer, and of all the fighters present he was easily the oldest. He approached with assurance.

"Meet Dallog," Stryke said.

The older orc lightly nodded to them; a small gesture but amiable enough.

"Some of you might know him already, particularly if you've needed a broken bone put right." There was another ripple of laughter. "He has talent as a healer. He's steady and he's smart, and I'm making him a corporal. And he's got an important duty." Stryke raised a hand.

A youngster trotted towards them. He carried a spiked lance with a furled pennant, which he passed to Dallog. At Stryke's signal, Dallog opened it, revealing the band's standard. He held the pole aloft and the ensign fluttered in the evening breeze. The Wolverines cheered. Except for Haskeer, who wore a dour expression.

"The standard's in your charge," Stryke said. "Guard it well."

"With my life," Dallog promised. He went to join the ranks.

"We've plenty to do tonight," Stryke reminded them all, "so go about your tasks. *Dismissed!*" As they moved off, he called, "Get to know the new ones! They're Wolverines now!"

Haskeer arrived at his side. "It's not true," he complained.

"What isn't?"

"What you just said about the new intake being Wolverines. They have to earn it."

"We all started from scratch."

"We were already battle-hardened when we joined. Not like these...*civilians*."

"That's the point. We need to get the band in shape fast, which means making them feel a part of it from the outset." He regarded his sergeant. "Is that all you're in a foul mood about?"

Haskeer said nothing. But his gaze flicked to Dallog as he went off with the standard.

"Ah," Stryke said, "that's your beef, is it?"

"He's no Alfray."

"Nobody said he was."

"So why do we need him?"

"Chain of command, remember? We have to have another corporal, and a band healer. I reckon Dallog fits the bill."

"Well, I don't like it."

"Too bad. You just heard me say I'm in charge. If that's not to your liking either—"

"Oh, shit."

Stryke balled his fists. "You want to make an issue of this, Sergeant?"

"No. What I meant was, look who's coming."

The youth walking their way was barely on nodding terms with adulthood. He dressed extravagantly for an orc. His jerkin consisted of strips of different coloured material, and his breeches were lilac. He wore gaudy boots. Looped about his neck was a stringed instrument. It had a long fingerboard and a body the shape of a sliced strawberry. He cradled it as tenderly as a babe.

"Oh, shit," Stryke said. "Be tactful. Remember who he is."

Haskeer gave a weary grunt.

"Stryke! Haskeer!" the youth greeted. "I've been looking for you."

"Wheam," Stryke replied.

"What do you want?" Haskeer demanded, stony-faced.

"You're about to set out on a great adventure," Wheam enthused, "and it should be celebrated."

"Maybe they'll be time for feasting when we get back," Stryke responded. "But at the moment—"

"No, no, I mean celebrated in *verse*."

"We couldn't put you to the trouble."

"This is history in the making; it *must* be recorded. Anyway, I've already started an epic ballad about this mission. It's work in progress, of course, but—"

"Well, if it's not finished..."

"How can it be? You haven't started yet, have you?"

"True."

"So I thought I'd let you hear the opening, as a kind of inspiration."

"Must you? I mean, must you *now*?"

"It won't take long. There's only about forty verses so far."

"We're very busy just now and—"

Wheam began discordant plucking. He cleared his throat loudly and proceeded to sing off key.

> *"On battle's eve the Wolverines*
> *Whet their blades and readied their spleens...*

"It's hard to get anything to rhyme with Wolverines, but I'm working on it.

> *"Their Captain bold he seized his chance*
> *To take up dagger, sword and lance*
> *And spitting in the face of fate*
> *He marched his band to the magic gate..."*

"Gods," Haskeer muttered.

> *"With swelling breasts and hearts so true*
> *They smote the foe for me and you..."*

Coilla arrived, pulling a face behind the minstrel's back. She saw the expressions of appeal Stryke and Haskeer wore, and took pity.

> *"Upon the field of slaughter red*
> *His gallant crew he bravely led*
> *And taking up his cleaver keen..."*

"Excuse me."

"He hacked his way to—"

Coilla prodded Wheam's shoulder-blade with a bony finger.

"Ouch!"

"Sorry," she smiled, "but I have to talk to my superior officers. You know; operational matters."

"But I've barely got going."

"Yes," Stryke intervened, "and it's a pity. We'll just have to
hear the rest some other time."

"When?" Wheam asked.

"Later."

Stryke and Haskeer grasped the protesting balladeer's elbows
and impelled him towards the crowd.

Rejoining Coilla, Stryke breathed a sigh. "Thanks. We owe
you one."

"At least we won't be seeing him again for a while."

"Never would be too soon," Haskeer suggested.

"Did you want something, Coilla, or was this just a rescue?"
Stryke said.

"Actually, I was wondering how things were going with the
stars."

"We had them hidden in five locations, as you know. I've got
four of them back. The fifth—" There was a commotion at the
edge of the crowd. "Matter of fact, this should be it now."

A massively built individual appeared, a retinue in his wake.
He was elderly but still fearsome. At his throat he wore an
emblem of valour; a necklace of snow leopards' teeth, numbering at least a dozen. He was battle-scarred and proud.

"Hard to think he could have sired such a fop," Coilla
remarked.

"Best keep that opinion to yourself," Stryke advised.

The chieftain and his entourage swept in.

Stryke welcomed him with, "Good of you to come, Quoll."

Quoll snorted. "You left me little choice."

"Sorry for the short notice. We have to move quickly."

"You're leaving soon?"

"First light."

"And you've everything you need?"

"All except the item in your safekeeping. Do you have it?"

"Of course. But I've been thinking."

"With respect, Chief, what's there to think about?"

"My thought is that you could render me a service."

"We're always happy to help," Stryke replied warily, "if it's in our power."

"This is well within your gift, Captain."

"And providing it doesn't put our mission at risk."

"There's no reason it should. You know my son?"

Stryke felt a cold apprehension. "Wheam? He was just here."

"Spouting nonsense, no doubt."

"You said it," Haskeer remarked.

Stryke shot him a poisonous look. "What about Wheam, Chief?"

"I want him to go with you."

"*No way!*" Haskeer exclaimed.

"Who's in charge here?" Quoll asked. "You or your sergeant?"

"I am," Stryke confirmed. "Shut it, Haskeer. Let's get this straight, Quoll; you want your son on this mission?"

"That's right."

"Why?"

"Look at him." He pointed at Wheam, who was strumming his lute for a group of disinterested bystanders. "I spawned a popinjay. A fool."

"What's that to do with us?"

"I want the tomfoolery knocked out of him. He needs toughening."

"We've no room for amateurs. The Wolverines are a disciplined fighting unit."

"That's just what he needs: discipline. You're taking other unproven recruits, why not Wheam?"

"They've shown combat skills. I don't see that in your son."

"Then it's time he learnt some."

"Why us? There must be another way of cutting his teeth."

"None as good as an actual mission where his survival's at stake."

"And ours. We've got six tyros as it is, without carrying somebody untrained and unsuited. It puts the whole band in peril."

"Much as I hate to say this, Stryke, you and your band have had things pretty much your own way since you came here. Isn't it about time you did something to repay our hospitality?"

"Much as *I* hate to say it, you don't own this land, Quoll. You're a clan chief, and we respect that, but you're not the only one in Ceragan."

"I'm the only one in these parts, and I want Wheam signed on for this mission."

"And if we refuse?"

"If you were to do that, I'm afraid there might be some delay...some *lengthy* delay in finding the artefact I'm holding for you."

Stryke sighed. "I see."

"That's blackmail!" Coilla erupted.

Quoll glowered. "I'll pretend you didn't say that."

"Pretend what you like, it's still what you're doing!"

"That's enough, Corporal," Stryke told her.

"But he can't—"

"That's enough!" He turned to Quoll. "All right. We'll take him."

The chieftain smiled. "Good." He snapped his fingers.

One of his followers came forward holding a small wooden chest. Quoll opened it and took out the remaining instrumentality.

"I confess I'm glad to see the back of this. I've not been happy having such a powerful totem in my lodge."

As Coilla and Haskeer silently fumed, he handed it to Stryke, who slipped it into his belt pouch.

"I'll have Wheam report to you this evening," Quoll said. He started to leave, then stopped and added, "And Stryke, if anything happens to him, don't bother coming back."

The chieftain strode off, trailed by his helpers.

"Oh, that's just great, isn't it?" Haskeer moaned. "Now we're fucking babysitters."

"Calm down," Stryke advised.

"Haskeer's right," Coilla reckoned. "The last thing we need is a hanger-on."

"What else could I do?"

"Refused, of course!"

"And never see the star again?"

"We could have taken it."

"Not a smart move, Coilla. This is our home now."

"It won't be if that idiot gets himself killed," Haskeer put in.

"There's no point arguing about it. We're stuck with him. Let's just try to make the best of it, shall we? We'll put him on fatigues or something, and have one of the older hands keep an eye on him."

"It doesn't bode well," Haskeer grumbled, "having a clown on the team."

"I'm not going to apologise for it. But there's something I should say sorry to you about, Coilla."

"What's that?"

"By rights I should have promoted you, to fill the vacancy for a sergeant. You could do the job, and you certainly deserve it."

"Thanks, Stryke, but I don't mind. Really. To hell with that much responsibility. I like the level I've reached."

"Well, I said the band needed two corporals, which didn't go down well with everybody." He glanced at Haskeer. "But it needs two sergeants, too."

"Who *are* you thinking of promoting then?"

"I'm not."

"Come again?"

"My idea's to reform the band as completely as we can."

"Yeah, well, that would mean having Jup, and he's...Oh."

"Right. We're going back to Maras-Dantia."

6

"They're dangerous," Coilla whispered. "Remember what they did to Haskeer. Hell, remember what they did to *you*."

Stryke was staring at the instrumentalities. He had them laid out on a bench in a kind of order: two spikes, four spikes, five, seven and nine. Grey, blue, green, yellow, red. He found them fascinating.

"*Stryke*," Coilla hissed.

"It's all right, I'm just looking. Nothing sinister's going on."

"You know what they can do, Stryke. Or at least a *part* of what they can do. And it's not all good."

"They're just a tool."

"Yeah?"

"Long as you don't get too involved with them."

"My point exactly."

"Why are we whispering?"

"It's them." She nodded at the stars. "When they're all together like this, they make you want to."

"I wonder what they're made of?"

"Damned if I've ever been able to figure it out."

"Wish I had a blade forged from it."

"Don't get too interested. We've got enough problems brewing in the band without you going AWOL from your senses."

"Thanks for putting it so delicately."

"I mean it, Stryke. If those things start singing at you again—"

"They won't."

"You'll be carrying them. *Exposed* to them, all the time. It could affect you."

"I've been thinking about that. Once we get to Maras-Dantia, would you carry one? Maybe breaking them up will dampen their influence."

"I'm flattered. You've never been keen on parting with them in the past."

"And look what happened. Will you do it? I would have asked Haskeer, but he's such a crazy bastard."

"Rather than burden the helpless female, you mean? Don't go spoiling it, Stryke."

He smiled. "I'm no human. I could never think of you as helpless."

"Course I'll do it. But what if it doesn't work? Will you share them between more of us?"

"I don't want to up the risk of any being lost. So...I don't know."

"Great. Something else for us to worry about."

"We'll face that if and when. It's near time. We should be getting ready."

They slipped into thick over-breeches and lined boots, then donned fur jerkins. Before she put hers on, Coilla laced a sheath of throwing knives to each arm.

"Seems weird doing this in a heat wave," she remarked.

"Maras-Dantia's going to be a damn sight cooler than here, that's for sure." He collected the instrumentalities and put them in his belt pouch.

They buckled on swords, daggers and hatchets.

"Don't forget your gloves," Stryke said.

"Got 'em."

"All right, let's go."

Outside, by the mouth of the cave where they first arrived in Ceragan, the band waited, sweating in their furs. Haskeer was keeping them in order, when he wasn't shooting disgusted glances at Wheam, who'd insisted on bringing his lute.

Quoll and his usual entourage were at the forefront of the crowd of spectators. Thirzarr was there too, along with the hatchlings. Stryke went to them.

Before he could speak, Thirzarr mouthed, "We've already made our goodbyes. Let's not stretch it out, for their sakes." She indicated Corb and Janch.

Stryke knelt. "I'm counting on you to look after your mother. All right?"

They nodded solemnly.

"And be good while I'm away."

"We will," Corb promised.

"Kill the witch!" Janch squeaked.

His brother bobbed in gleeful agreement and they waved their miniature cleavers about.

Stryke grinned. "We'll do our best."

He took one last look at his brood and turned away.

"Fare well," Quoll said as he passed him.

Stryke gave a faint tilt of his head, but didn't speak.

At the cave's entrance, he faced the band.

"Conditions were bad in Maras-Dantia when we were last there," he said. "They're going to be much worse now. Expect extreme hostility, and not just from the weather. This particularly applies to you new recruits, so stick by the buddy you've been assigned. As I'm assuming we'll fetch up in Illex, in the far north, we can't take horses; they couldn't handle the conditions. Be prepared for a long, hard march south." He weighed his next words carefully. "Last time, we had to face the Sluagh." He bet more than a few of the band suppressed a shudder remembering the repellent demon race. "I don't know if we'll run into them this time. But we beat 'em once, and we can do it again if we have to. Are we all set, Sergeant?"

"Ready and eager," Haskeer replied.

"If anybody's having second thoughts about this mission, this is your last chance to pull out. They'll be no dishonour in it." He stared pointedly at Wheam. No one said anything. "Any questions?"

Wheam raised a hand.

"Yes?"

"Going through this...portal thing. Will it hurt?"

"Not as much as my boot up your arse," Haskeer assured him.

Laughter eased the band's tension a little.

Stryke checked that the crowd was held well back, then nodded.

Haskeer barked an order. Brands were lit, and jerkins fastened.

A rhythmic pounding started up. The onlookers were beating their spears against their shields in a traditional farewell for orcs off to war. There was some shouted encouragement, and a few cheers.

Stryke led his band into the cave.

It was cool and echoing inside.

Coilla caught up with Wheam. "Going through's unsettling," she explained. "Just remember we're all doing it together."

He looked pale. "Thanks," he said, and walked on.

Stryke overheard. *"Unsettling?"*

"I couldn't say terrifying, could I? He's just a kid."

They reached the centre of the cave, and Stryke had them all gather round. He studied the amulet by the light of the brands. Next, he took out the stars and began manipulating them.

For a clammy moment, he thought he couldn't do it. There seemed no sense in the way they linked to each other. He started to fumble and grow confused.

Then four stars slotted together smoothly, in quick succession, and he could see exactly where the final one should go.

"Brace yourselves," he warned, pushing it into place.

They fell, plunging down a shaft made of light.

Sinuous, pulsating, never ending. Beyond its translucent walls was blue velvet, smothered with stars.

They dropped ever faster. The starscape melted into a blur of rushing colours.

Transient images flashed by. Fleeting glimpses of perplexing otherwheres.

There were sounds. An inexplicable, discordant, thunderous cacophony.

It lasted an eternity.

Then a black abyss swallowed them.

Stryke opened his eyes.

He felt like he'd taken a beating, and his head throbbed murderously.

Getting to his knees, it took him a moment to focus on his surroundings. But he didn't see what he expected.

There was no snow or ice, though it was cold. The grim landscape seemed gripped by deepest winter. Trees were leafless. The grass was brown and patchy, and much of the foliage wasn't just dormant, but dead. Black clouds dominated the sky. It was in total contrast to the balmy climate they'd just left.

He climbed to his feet.

The rest of the band was scattered around him. Some were

on the ground, still dazed, and several were groaning. Others, recovering more quickly, were already standing.

"Everybody all right?" he called.

"Most of us," Haskeer said. He scornfully jerked a thumb at Wheam, who was being sick against a rock, with Dallog in attendance.

Coilla and Haskeer went to Stryke. They looked shaken after the transference, but rode it well.

"This isn't Illex," Haskeer pronounced.

"You don't say," Stryke told him.

"But it *is* Maras-Dantia," Coilla said. "I recognise some of the landmarks. I reckon we're near the lip of the Great Plains, not far from Bevis."

"You could be right," Stryke agreed. "Looks like the stars don't put us down in exactly the same place each time." He realised he was still clutching them, and began dismantling.

"At least it cuts the amount of marching we'll have to do."

"And with any luck we won't have to go to Illex next time we use them." He was stuffing the instrumentalities into his belt pouch. "But I'm sorry we didn't bring those horses."

"It's not morning here," Haskeer decided.

Coilla sighed. "You're an expert in stating the obvious now, are you?"

It looked to be late afternoon, going on early evening.

"And the season's wrong," Haskeer added.

"I'm not so sure about that," Stryke said. "This could be what passes for summer in Maras-Dantia these days."

Coilla stared at the terrain. "Things have got that bad?"

"It was heading that way when we left, so why not?"

Haskeer frowned. "What'll we do? Camp 'til first light?"

"I say march on," Coilla suggested. "I mean, we only got up about two hours ago. It's not as though we need the rest."

Stryke nodded. "Makes sense. If we are where you think,

Coilla, we need to bear south-west. It's still a hell of a march to Quatt, but not near as far as we reckoned on."

"Maybe we can rustle up some transport on the way."

"I'm counting on it. All right, let's get 'em organised. Haskeer, see how the new intake are faring; Coilla, secure the area. Get some lookouts posted."

Coilla went to pick sentries. Haskeer walked over to Dallog and Wheam.

The band's banner thrust into the ground beside him, the aged corporal was offering the young recruit a drink from his canteen. Wheam took it with trembling hands.

"Why the idling?" Haskeer snapped.

"He was shaken by the crossing," Dallog explained.

"He can speak for himself." Haskeer turned his glare on Wheam. *"Well?"*

The youth flinched. "Going through that…thing…really… unsettled me."

"Oh, what a shame. Would you like your daddy?"

"You don't have to be so—"

"This is no fucking picnic! We're in the field now! Get a grip!"

"Go easy, Haskeer," Dallog advised.

"The day I need *your* advice," Haskeer thundered, "is the day they can take me out and cut my throat. And it's *Sergeant* to you. *Both* of you."

"I'm only doing my job, Sergeant."

"You're nurse-maiding him."

"Just cutting the boy some slack. He doesn't know the ropes."

"You and him both. You've never been on a mission, and you don't know this band."

"Maybe not. But I know orcs, Sergeant, and I know how to mend 'em."

"Only been one Wolverine could do that, and you ain't him."

"I'm sure Alfray was a—"

"You're not fit to use his name, Dallog. Nobody matches Alfray."

"Pity you were so careless with him then."

Haskeer's face darkened dangerously. "What'd you say?"

"Things change. Live with it. Sergeant."

Wheam gaped at them.

"Being old don't excuse you from a beating," Haskeer growled, making fists.

"Whenever you want to try. But maybe this isn't a good time."

"Now you're telling me what's what?"

"I meant we shouldn't brawl in front of the band."

"Why not?" Haskeer said, moving in on him. "Let 'em see me knock some respect into you."

Somebody was shouting. Others took it up.

"Er, Sergeant..." Wheam pointed.

Haskeer stopped and turned.

A group of riders could be seen, moving their way across the sward. It was hard to gauge their number.

"We'll settle this later," he promised Dallog.

"What's happening, Sergeant?" Wheam asked. "Who are they?"

"I doubt they're a welcome party. Be ready to account for yourselves. And try not to shame the band by dying badly." He left Wheam looking terrified.

By the time Haskeer reached Stryke and Coilla, the approaching riders were recognisable.

"Oh, good," Haskeer muttered. "My favourite race."

"What do you think," Coilla said, "around sixty?"

"More or less," Stryke replied. "And they look ragtag; no uniforms."

Dallog arrived, exchanging glowers with Haskeer as he passed. "What *are* they, Captain?"

"Humans."

"They're...freakish."

"Yeah, not too pretty, are they?"

"And they're getting closer," Coilla reminded them.

"Right," Stryke said. "We assume they're hostile." He addressed Haskeer and Dallog. "Get the band into a defensive formation at that table rock over there. And keep an eye on the new recruits. *Move!*"

They rushed off, barking orders.

"What about me?" Coilla asked.

"How many good archers we got?"

"Five or six, counting a couple of the tyros."

"And you. Get yourselves on top of the rock. *Go!*"

The rocky outcropping Stryke had indicated was a slab the size of a cabin. It jutted out of the ground at an angle. But its highest point, tall as a tree, was flat.

Band members were drawing blades and discarding their heavy furs, the better to fight.

Coilla steered her archers to the rock and they scrambled up. Stryke joined the rest of the Wolverines under the tapering overhang at its base.

The humans were galloping in at speed, and a clamour rose from them. Stryke was sure he heard them chanting the word *monsters.*

He slapped the rock above his head. "We've got a good natural defence here," he told the band, "as long as we don't break ranks." The veterans knew that well enough; he was thinking of the recruits. "Let's see those shields!"

The old hands deployed theirs expertly, slipping the shields from backs to chests in a single, deft movement. The newbies fumbled. No more so than Wheam, who got himself in a tangle trying to swap his shield for his beloved lute.

"Like *this*," Stryke instructed, extricating the youth. "And hold your sword *that* way."

Wheam nodded, grinning dourly and looking bemused. Stryke sighed.

A greater racket went up from the riders.

They charged.

Coilla's unit had arrows nocked and were stretching their bowstrings. Some preferred kneeling. She stood.

The leading humans were no more than a spear throw away, horses white-flecked and huffing vapour.

"Hold fast!" Haskeer bellowed.

Coilla waited until the last possible moment before yelling, *"Fire!"*

Half a dozen bolts winged towards the charging attackers. One of the leading riders took a hit to his chest. Unhorsed by the impact, he tumbled into the path of those following, bringing several down.

A handful of the humans had bows, and returned fire. But shooting from the saddle meant most of their shafts were wide.

The orcs' next volley found three targets. Arrows struck the thigh of one man and the shoulder of another. The third grazed a rider's temple. He fell, to be trampled.

Coilla's team kept on firing.

Within spitting distance of the rock the humans slowed and their charge turned into a confused milling. Shouts were exchanged, then they broke into two groups. The largest turned and began galloping around the outcrop, hoping for a breach. The rest advanced on the orcs at ground level.

Some of Stryke's cluster carried slingshots. As the humans approached, they deployed them. The salvo of hard shot cracked a couple of skulls and fractured an arm or two. But there was no time for more than a few lobs before the raiders were at their line.

Their horses gave them the advantage of height, and flailing hooves could prove deadly. The snag was reach. To engage the orcs they had to lean and hack, making themselves vulnerable.

All was churning mounts and slashing blades at the base of the rock. Blows rained on the orcs' raised shields. They struck back, and fought to bring down the riders. A dagger to the calves was sufficient in some cases. In others, concerted efforts were needed to drag horsemen from their saddles. A grinding melee ensued.

Around a dozen raiders dismounted of their own accord, the better to engage in close quarters fighting.

One human singled out Stryke for particular attention. He was burly and battle-scarred, with an overlong, disorderly beard. Like his fellows, he wore mismatched, raggedy clothes. And he swung a double-headed axe.

Stryke dodged and felt the displaced air as the weapon skimmed past. Before it reached the end of its arc, he lunged, slashing with his blade. The human moved fast, pulling back in time to avoid contact. Then he attacked again, unleashing another murderous swing. Stryke dropped and kept his head.

The man fell to hammering at Stryke's shield, looking to dislodge it. Stryke weathered the battering, and at the first let sent back a series of blistering swipes. He failed to penetrate the human's guard. But it seemed that, for all his heftiness, his opponent was starting to slow under the effort of handling the axe. Stryke wasn't about to break the formation, regardless of that. He forced the man to come to him.

The human rushed in again, spitting fury. Another pass whistled by Stryke's skull, too close for comfort. Stryke powered forward, using his shield as a ram. There was a tussle, orc and human straining with all their strength against each other. At its height, Stryke sidestepped, wrenching the shield out of play. His balance spoilt, the man stumbled forward, losing his grip on the axe. It dangled on a thong at his wrist, and he scrabbled to bring it into play. Stryke was quicker. With a savage downward sweep, he lopped off the human's hand. The man howled, his wound pumping crimson, the axe in the dirt.

Stryke stilled his pain with a thrust to the heart.

As the axeman fell, a confederate barged in to take his place. Scowling, broken-toothed, he took on Stryke with knife and sword. Their pealing blades added to the melody of clashing steel.

The orcs' line still held. But the fights boiling at the base of the rock were making it indistinct.

Up above, Coilla's archers continued to take their shots where they could. Though as the struggle became fiercer, and friends and enemies began to mingle, their task was harder. Coilla judged the attackers to be as undisciplined and ill-assorted as the way they dressed. Not that it made them any less determined, and there was an unpredictability in disorder that could be more dangerous than facing a well-organised force.

Coilla switched to throwing-knives, which she felt she used with more expertise than a bow and were more precise in chaotic situations. Taking in the scene, she spotted two likely marks. Mounted on a white mare, a wild eyed, mop-haired human was laying about an orc with a broadsword. She got a bead on him and hurled a knife with force. It buried itself in his windpipe. He flew backwards, arms spread wide, and met the ground. As a bonus, his horse panicked and kicked out with its rear legs, downing a man on foot.

Her second target was also on foot. Bald and beardless, he was built like a stone slab privy. As Coilla watched, he broke into a run at the defensive line, a javelin outstretched. She drew back her arm and flung hard. Her aim was true, but the human made an unexpected move, swerving to avoid a fallen comrade. The blade pierced his side, near the waist, proving painful but not fatal. He bellowed, nearly tripping, and went to pull out the knife. She swiftly plucked another and threw again.

This time she put it where she first intended, in his chest.

Stryke wrenched his sword from a human's innards and let him drop. He glanced around. Bodies littered the ground, slowing the raiders' advance, but there were still plenty to deal with.

Further along the line, Wheam cringed under the onslaught of a human with a mace. The metal ball's continuous pounding was distorting the shape of his shield. Wheam simply clung on, white knuckled, making no attempt to hit back. It was left to the veterans on either side to lash out and deal with his tormentor.

Nearby, Dallog was giving a much better account of himself. The band's standard jutting from the ground behind him, he made good use of his sword and dagger. Slashing the face of an attacker, the ageing corporal followed through with a thrust to the man's guts.

Hollering at full volume, a human with a spear hurtled towards Stryke. Leaping aside, Stryke grabbed the shaft. There was a forceful, snarling battle for possession. Stryke broke the deadlock with a brutal head-butt. His adversary was knocked senseless, releasing his hold. Flipping the spear, Stryke drove it through the man's torso.

Beyond the siege at the outcrop's base, riders were still circling. Every so often, one of them loosed an arrow at Coilla's archers. None caused harm. But it was only a matter of time before somebody got lucky.

On top of the rock, Coilla stood shoulder to shoulder with new recruit Yunst, who was proving adept with a bow.

She pitched a knife. A human crashed headlong into the barren ground.

"Nice shot," Yunst said.

"Keeping count of yours?" she asked.

"Not really."

"I make us about even."

"Can't have that." He focused on a target and drew his bowstring taut. "Let's see if I can—"

There was a fleshy *thump*. Coilla was splattered with blood. An arrow had gone through Yunst's neck. He collapsed into her, a dead weight, and she went down. The impact sent her tumbling to the nearby edge. She cried out, and went over.

It was a short drop, but Coilla fell awkwardly. The jolt of landing knocked the breath out of her and jangled her senses. Lying on her side, swathed in pain, she tried to gather her wits. She was aware of fighting all around. Shuffling feet and stamping hooves. Shouting and screaming. With a groan, she rolled onto her back, then lifted her head.

Something swam into view. A shape loomed over her. She blinked and cleared her vision. A leering horseman was bearing down, his iron-tipped spear aimed at her chest. Coilla struggled to get herself clear, while groping for her blade. It was fifty-fifty whether she'd suffer the spear piercing her flesh or the rearing mount shattering her ribs.

Then someone was there, putting themselves between her and the threat. She saw that it was Haskeer. He had hold of the horse's bridle with both hands as he ducked and weaved to avoid the probing spear. Orc and beast wrestled. Several times the strength of the shying horse lifted Haskeer's feet off the ground. The thrusts of the spear came near to running him through. Finally, he lost patience.

Letting go, he jerked back his fist and gave the horse a mighty punch. The stunned animal's front legs buckled and its head went down. Yelling, and parted from his spear, the rider was unseated. As he fell, several orcs rushed forward to finish him.

Stryke appeared. He and Haskeer jerked Coilla to her feet and half dragged her to the relative safety of the orcs' line.

"Anything broken?" Stryke said.

She shook her head. "Don't think so."

"What happened up there?"

"We lost a new one. Yunst."

"Shit."

"That's what we get for using amateurs," Haskeer remarked.

"He was a good fighter," Coilla informed him sternly. "And don't hit horses, you bastard."

"No, don't bother thanking me," Haskeer came back acerbically. "I only saved your life."

"We've work to do," Stryke rebuked.

They pitched into the attackers.

The human ranks were starting to thin. But fighting was still intense. Heartened by killing Yunst, the surviving raiders stepped up their assault, and the orcs' defences were sorely tested. The otherwise silent landscape continued to echo to the rattle of steel on steel and the shrieks of the dying.

Given his shaky resolve, only luck and his comrades had kept Wheam safe. Now good fortune was put to the test. While all about Wheam were occupied, a human dashed in and laid about him with zeal. Wheam adopted his usual tactic of hiding behind his shield and letting it soak up the blows. But his assailant was determined. Wielding his broadsword two-handed, he beat the shield relentlessly, striking sparks off its misshapen surface. Then a solid swipe dislodged it from Wheam's grasp.

Wearing a look of terror, Wheam faced his foe undefended bar his sword. He gave a couple of feeble swings that barely connected with the human's blade. The volley he got back almost pummelled the weapon out of his trembling hand. A further blow snapped his sword in two. He stood transfixed and at the mercy of his opponent.

An orc careered into the human. They fought, Wheam forgotten. For a moment it looked as though the Wolverine had the better of it. But in the struggle his back was turned to the enemy. A nearby human saw his chance and buried his blade in it. As the orc went down, both men hacked at him mercilessly.

"That's Liffin!" Coilla yelled. She made to move.

"*Hold fast!*" Stryke barked. Then added softly, "There's nothing you can do."

The pair of humans had little time to savour their kill. From the rock's peak, the archers repaid the blood debt. The man with the broadsword took three arrows, any one of them fatal. His comrade caught two. For good measure, several Wolverines ran forward to add their wrath with steel and spears.

There was no let to the band's fury. Any humans venturing close were slashed, flayed, mauled, cut down. Soon, their numbers and their resolve ebbed away. With over half their company lying dead or mortally wounded, the raiders retreated. They rode off, back towards the plain.

The Wolverines expelled a collective breath. Yunst and Liffin's corpses were retrieved. The band took to binding their injuries and wiping their blades.

"That's a *fucking* good start!" Haskeer raged. "Two dead, and one of 'em Liffin!"

"We take losses," Stryke told him evenly, "it's part of the job. You know that."

"At this rate we'll all be dead before we even *find* Jup! Not an hour gone and this happens!"

"Anger won't bring them back," Coilla said.

Haskeer wasn't mollified. "We should never have lost 'em! Or Liffin at any rate. I don't care about the tyro, but Liffin was an old hand. And he threw his life away for...*what*? That...little shit!"

"He died for the band. We look out for each other, remember?"

"There's some not worth looking out for. If I had my way—"

Wheam appeared, still clutching his broken sword. "I wanted...I wanted to say I'm sorry about—"

"You cowardly bastard!" Haskeer shrieked. "I could kill you for what you just did!"

"That's enough!" Stryke cautioned.

Sheepishly, Wheam tried again. "I didn't mean—"

"Liffin was worth ten of you," Haskeer thundered, "you snivelling heap of crap!"

"Shut it, Haskeer!" Stryke ordered.

"I'll shut *him*!" He lunged at Wheam and slammed his palms

against his chest, sending him sprawling. Then he went for a knife.

Stryke and Coilla grabbed him, pinning his arms.

"*I said that's enough!*" Stryke bellowed in his sergeant's ear. "I'll have no insubordination in this band!"

"All right, all right." Haskeer quit struggling and they loosened their hold. He shrugged them off.

"Any more of that and I'll break you back to private," Stryke promised. "Understand?"

Haskeer gave a grudging nod. "But this ain't over," he growled. He jabbed a finger in Wheam's direction. "Just keep that freak away from me."

7

They should have honoured tradition and disposed of their dead with flame. But they couldn't afford the attention fire might bring. So they buried Liffin and Yunst deep, their swords in their hands. Dallog proved adept at carving, and fashioned small markers bearing the symbols of Neaphetar and Wystendel, the orc gods of war and comradeship.

By the time that was done, and some of the humans' abandoned horses were tracked down, a good chunk of the day had gone. At last, with the watery sun high, the band set out for the dwarves' homeland.

There weren't enough mounts for everybody, even with doubling up, and a third of the band had to take turns walking. The sole exception was Haskeer, whose mood was so foul Stryke encouraged him to ride alone. And he saw to it that Wheam, paired with Dallog, was as far away from the sergeant as possible. None of it made for rapid progress.

Stryke and Coilla headed the party, sharing a ride, and tried to take a route offering fewest chances for ambush. The landscape was chill and miserable, and they saw no other living creature in four hours of travelling. No one was particularly talkative, and the convoy moved quietly.

Coilla broke the silence, albeit in an undertone. "He was right, you know, Stryke."

"Hmm?"

"Haskeer. Not the way he acted; what he said. We've not started well."

"No."

"I feel bad about Liffin. He was a brother in arms, and we've been through a lot with him. But I feel worse about Yunst somehow. What with it being his first time out, and depending on us to—"

"I know."

"Don't think I'm blaming you."

"I don't."

"I blame myself, if anything. About Yunst, I mean. I led that detail. I should have looked after him."

Stryke turned his head to glance at her. "How do you think I feel?"

Silence returned for a while.

"Who do you think those humans were?" Coilla asked, steering the conversation into less murky waters.

"Just marauders, I reckon. They didn't have the look of Unis or Manis, nor the discipline."

"If they're typical, Maras-Dantia's sunk even deeper into anarchy."

"All the more reason I should do this," Stryke said, reaching into his belt pouch. He brought something out and passed it to her. "If you still want to take it."

She held an instrumentality. The blue one, with four spikes. It felt strange in her hand, as though it was too heavy and too light at the same time. And it had another, deeper quality Coilla found even harder to understand.

"Course I want it," she replied, pulling out of her reverie. She slipped the star into her own pouch.

"If it starts to trouble you, give it back."

"What about getting the band to carry it in turns, a couple of hours each? Not all of them, of course, just the true Wolverines."

"And what happens when Haskeer wants his turn? No, it just makes problems. But if you don't want it—"

"I said I did, didn't I?" Her hand instinctively went to the pouch, and she wondered how it was for him, carrying four of the things. She changed the subject again. "How long to Quatt, do you think?"

"Couple of days at this rate."

"Assuming that's where Jup's going to be."

"Well, we're not going to find out tonight, that's for sure."

The pewter moon was up, big and fat, tendrils of cloud swathing its face. Colder winds blew.

"Where do you want to strike camp?"

"You're our strategist. What looks like the most defensible spot?"

Coilla scanned the drab terrain. It was flat and mostly featureless. "Not much choice in these parts. Wait. What's that?" She pointed.

Well ahead of them, and not far off the trail they followed, there was a jumble of shapes.

"Can't tell," he replied, straining to make them out. "Curious?"

"Sure."

"Then let's head that way."

As they got nearer they saw that the shapes were ruins. A small settlement had once stood there, but now only shells of buildings remained, or just their foundations. Charred timbers indicated that fire played its part in the destruction. There were tumbledown fences and the hulk of an abandoned wagon. Sickly green lichen grew on the stonework. Weeds choked the paths.

Stryke ordered the band to dismount.

"Humans lived here," Coilla said.

"Looks like it," Stryke agreed.

"I wonder what destroyed the place?"

"Probably other humans. You know what they're like."

"Yeah."

"Let's get organised. I want sentries posted. See to it."

She set off.

Stryke called to the nearest grunt. "Finje! That could be a well. Over there, see? Go and check it."

Haskeer arrived, face like granite.

"Have this place searched," Stryke told him. "We could do without any more little surprises."

"Right," his sergeant grunted morosely, turning to obey.

"And Haskeer."

Haskeer looked back.

"What happened with Liffin and Yunst is done. Live with it. Your moods put the band off whack, and I won't have it. Save your temper for enemies."

Haskeer nodded, curtly. Then he went off to scare up a search party.

"*Well's dry!*" Finje shouted. He demonstrated by upending a shabby bucket. Only dirt and gravel came out of it.

Coilla returned. "How *are* we for water?"

"It's not a problem yet," Stryke replied. "But we could do with finding a clean source soon. Guards in place?"

"Done. But there's something you should see."

"Lead the way."

She took him to the largest and most intact of the ruins. Parts of three walls were still standing, and they could see that it once had peaked eaves. A pair of large, heavy doors lay in the debris. They showed signs of having been breached with force.

As they scanned the scene, Haskeer joined them.

"What's so special about this?" he asked.

"I reckon it's a place of worship," Coilla explained.

"So?"

"Look over here."

They followed her to a low dry stone wall. Parts had collapsed, and there was what was left of a gate. The wall enclosed about an acre of land. Very little grew in it beyond three or four gaunt trees. Dozens of stone slabs and wooden pointers jutted from the ground, many at skewed angles.

"You know what this is, don't you?" Stryke said.

"Yes. A burial ground."

"Oh, great," Haskeer muttered.

"Not afraid of a few dead humans, are you?"

He glared at her.

"But why is nothing growing in there?" she wanted to know. "Look out here; they're weeds everywhere. Nature's reclaiming it. Why not there?"

"Maybe they did something to stop things growing," Stryke suggested. "Sowed it with salt, or —"

"Why?"

"Out of respect for their dead? Who knows with humans."

"Too right," Haskeer agreed. "They're fucking crazy."

Stryke thought this a little rich coming from Haskeer, but kept the observation to himself. "This is as good a place as any to pass the night. The wall can serve as a windbreak. Get them to pitch camp, Haskeer. But no fires."

"That won't make for much cheer."

"Just do it."

Haskeer strode away, looking unhappy.

Coilla watched him go. "He's being his usual joyful self then."

"That's not our only problem right now."

"Wheam?"

"Wheam."

"What you gonna do about it?"

"Give him some kind of job that keeps him out of our faces, and clear of Haskeer. Come on."

Looking bemused at the bustle of activity going on around

him, Wheam was standing by Dallog further along the wall. An uncomfortable expression came to his face when he saw Stryke approaching.

Before Stryke could speak, Wheam said, "You're going to punish me, aren't you?"

"Because of Liffin?"

"Of course. But I was afraid and—"

"Nobody under my command gets punished for being afraid."

"Oh." Wheam was confounded.

"Only fools don't feel fear," Stryke went on. "It's what you do despite the fear that affects our survival. So you'll be trained in combat, and you'll practise what you're taught. Agreed?"

"Er, yes."

"But we don't carry non-combatants; everybody's expected to fight. That's your part of the bargain. Understand?"

"Yes, sir, Captain."

"All right. I'll work out a training rota for you. If you want to honour Liffin, you'll stick with it. Meantime you need to have a proper role. What special skills do you have?"

"I could be our official balladeer," Wheam replied hopefully, holding up his lute.

"I meant something useful." Stryke turned to his new corporal. "Dallog, what are you doing?"

"I was about to check the wounded. Change dressings, that sort of thing." He nodded to a small group of waiting orcs.

"Wheam can help. All right with you?"

"Fine. If today's anything to go by I could use an aide."

Wheam looked apprehensive.

"We can't risk kindling any light for you," Stryke said. "Got enough to work by?"

"The moon's good enough."

"Make a start then."

Dallog got Wheam to move closer, then beckoned over the

first in line. Pirrak, one of the new intake, stepped forward, a grubby dressing on his forearm.

"How's it been?" Dallog enquired.

"Bit sore," Pirrak answered.

Dallog began unwinding the bandage. "Did you know blood flows more copiously when the moon's full?" he remarked conversationally and to no one in particular.

"Course I did," Coilla replied. "I'm a female."

"Ah. Yes." There was just a hint of awkwardness in the corporal's response.

He carried on unravelling. As the layers of binding peeled away they grew more soiled, until finally the wound was exposed. Dallog absently draped the gory bandage over the graveyard wall.

"Hmm. Lot of congealed blood. Might need to sew this gash. See how the flaps of skin hang loose on either side, Wheam? And all this pus—"

There was a groan and a weighty thud.

"He's fainted," Coilla said.

The queuing orcs burst out laughing. Pirrak laughed, though he winced at the same time.

"What kind of an orc *is* he?" Using her teeth, Coilla pulled the cork from her canteen and poured a stream of water over Wheam's ashen face.

"Go easy with that," Stryke warned, "we've none to waste."

Wheam spluttered and wheezed, causing more hilarity among the onlookers.

"I'll take care of him," Dallog sighed, kneeling to his new patient.

Stryke and Coilla left them to it.

"Perhaps medicine isn't Wheam's calling," she commented dryly.

"I wonder what is."

"He should have *some* kind of job."

77

"Such as? I wouldn't trust him on sentry duty, or in a hunting party. He might cope with digging latrines and preparing rations, though I wouldn't put it past him to poison us."

"I don't think that's what Quoll had in mind."

"To hell with him. He should have raised his spawn right in the first place, rather than dumping him on us."

"Maybe that training you promised will sort Wheam out."

"Maybe."

"It's bound to be a bit of a struggle fitting new members in, Stryke."

He nodded. "What do you think of Dallog?"

"I like him. He fought well today, and he's all right with the medic thing. I know he's not Alfray, but who is?"

"I wish everybody felt that way."

Reaching the wrecked hay wagon, they perched themselves on the still intact shafts. They watched the band making camp and attending to chores. The breeze grew colder as evening shaded into full night.

Working his way through the wounded, Dallog continued to absent-mindedly deposit their bloodied bandages on the stone wall behind him. More than a dozen white strips had accumulated, fluttering in the wind. Unnoticed, a stronger gust whipped most of them away. They blew into the cemetery. One became entangled in the emaciated branches of a tree, another was caught by a wooden grave marker. The rest were scattered across the barren ground.

High above, the stars were sharp and hard, like diamonds.

"Funny to think we were born under these skies," Coilla reflected. "Do you ever feel homesick?"

"No."

"Not even a twinge of longing?"

"It was a different land then. Humans ruined it."

"That's true. But it still feels strange to be back here. Everything seems so long ago, and yet as near as yesterday. If that makes any sense."

He smiled. "I know what you mean."

They passed time in silence, surveying the scene. The band went about the business of preparing to settle for the night. Weapons were cleaned and rations passed round. In the distance, sentries patrolled.

The few grunts waiting to be seen by Dallog had seated themselves on the graveyard wall. Wheam, still looking unsteady, had been sorting lengths of bandages for the corporal.

"I've finished," he announced. "What else can I do?"

"I'm busy here," Dallog replied, intent on cleaning a lesion Wheam couldn't look at. "Use your initiative." He thought better of that and looked around. "Make yourself useful and pick up those dressings. Can't have infections spreading."

"What do I use to—"

"Here." Dallog thrust a small canvas shoulder bag at him, normally used to carry shot for catapults.

Wheam set about the task with minimal enthusiasm. Making a face, he collected the couple of bandages still clinging to the wall, lifting them with thumb and forefinger at arm's length. The watching orcs elbowed each other's ribs and snickered.

He peered into the graveyard and saw the other scattered strips. Clumsily, he negotiated the wall. Once inside, he bent, picked up the first bandage and stuffed it into the bag. Spotting the next, hanging on the wooden marker, he went to retrieve that. Slowly, he worked his way through the cemetery, gathering the grubby windings of cloth.

He stooped to a bandage lying across a grave. There was a sound. He froze, listening. Nothing. He reached for the bandage. As his fingers almost brushed it, the noise came again. Once more he paused, trying to work out what it might be. The sound had a kind of scuffling, scrabbling quality, as though something subterranean was burrowing. Wheam stared at the ground. The earth was bulging and shifting. He leaned closer.

The ground burst open. A bony hand shot out and grabbed his wrist. Wheam struggled against its iron grip. He opened his mouth to shout but nothing came.

The earth was erupting on every side, spewing writhing shapes.

Sitting on the wagon's shafts, Coilla and Stryke were savouring the night air and the quiet.

"Doesn't seem so bad now, does it?" Coilla said. "With the moon up and the stillness, we could almost be back in Ceragan."

"I wouldn't go *that* far."

"So what would you be doing if you were there on a night like this?"

"If I was at home I'd —"

A piercing scream rent the air.

Coilla leapt up. "What the fu —"

"Over there! The graveyard. *Come on!*"

They ran towards the cemetery wall. Others were dashing that way too.

There was another loud yell.

They arrived to see Wheam in the middle of the graveyard, bent over and apparently tugging at something like an oversized tree root. All around him, indistinct figures were hauling themselves out of the earth.

Coilla and Stryke moved closer, most of the band at their heels, and took in the scene. The graves were disgorging strange fruit. What looked like rotting melons or oversized, cracked eggs were pushing through the soil. It took them a moment to realise that they were heads.

Creatures rose, heaving from the loam with wriggling, undulating movements. As they emerged, their forms could be seen.

They were human. Or had been. Their bodies were decayed. Some were merely putrid, with discoloured, rotting flesh. Others were near skeletal, scraps of skin and cloth hanging from their exposed bones.

They progressed fitfully, decomposing limbs jerking and quivering, and their eyes were afire with malicious hunger. The smell that accompanied them was obnoxious.

One of the creatures scooped up a gory bandage and crammed it into its mouth. Its dislocated jaw clicked loudly as it chewed on the sodden fabric.

A score of the animated dead had surfaced, with more appearing. The orcs watched, transfixed.

Haskeer arrived, panting. "What the *fuck*?"

"That's what I said," Coilla told him.

"Snap out of it, Wolverines!" Stryke yelled. "Let's deal with this!"

Everyone drew swords and headed for the wall.

"I'm going for Wheam," Coilla announced.

"Can't we forget the little bastard?" Haskeer pleaded.

Coilla ignored him.

As the band approached, the walking corpses stopped and turned their heads as one. Then they advanced on the orcs.

The creature hanging on to Wheam was out of its grave. It was far gone in corruption, with much of the flesh on its chest rotted away, revealing the ribcage and foul innards. Wheam struggled to escape its grasp. He pawed at his sword sheath with his free hand, trying to reach the weapon. The creature dragged him closer.

The Wolverines swept to the wall. Coilla leapt over it and ran into the graveyard. Stryke and Haskeer chose its broken gate. A pair of the monstrosities were shambling through, and it seemed to Stryke that they were starting to move faster and with more fluidity. He charged at the nearest. The creature lurched to one side, but not quick enough to avoid the attack.

Stryke's sword met no resistance as it plunged into the fetid chest. The only effect was to make his target stagger slightly, and as he swiftly withdrew the blade a puff of rank dust was liberated.

Haskeer struck out with his sword, burying it deep in his foe's side. It hewed parchment flesh, and splintered bone, but hardly slowed the creature. Haskeer delivered a weighty slash across its belly. The contents spilled out, releasing an unspeakable stench. Entrails dangling, the abomination kept coming, arms outstretched, hands like talons.

More of the creatures stumbled out of the gate. Others dragged themselves over the squat wall. The orcs met them with steel and spear. But Stryke's sense that the brutes' speed and mobility was growing proved right. One of them, moving surprisingly fast, landed a powerful arm swipe to the side of a grunt's head, knocking him senseless. Ignoring menacing blades, another crashed into an orc and encircled him in a crushing bear-hug. They pair of them collapsed struggling.

Coilla did as much dodging as fighting to get to Wheam. The creatures were noticeably gaining rapidity, though still reacted slowly compared to the living. But that wasn't an issue when a hulking specimen blocked her path with arms spread wide. She skidded to a halt. The putrefying figure instantly lashed out, cuffing her hard in the face. Coilla went down.

She rolled and quickly regained her feet. Spitting a mouthful of blood, she went on the attack, sword extended. Her opponent strode forward into her driven blade. It entered a little above his heart, or where his heart should be, and exited through his back. The blade met no resistance. Nor did it do any harm. Coilla tugged it out and switched from point to edge.

Her hacking caused more damage, cleaving chunks of rotten flesh, but didn't halt the advance. Then she cursed herself for not seeing the obvious solution sooner. Leaping to one side, out of the creature's course, she stooped and swung her sword. It sliced through the creature's leg, and the limb was so desiccated that one blow was enough. Amputated just below the knee, the creature lost balance and crashed to the ground. Coilla left it thrashing about.

When she got to Wheam he was still trying to get away. And Coilla saw that his captor was female. She had straggly, once blonde hair, and a hint of almost vanished comeliness in her gaunt features. One hand remained clamped to Wheam's wrist. With the other she had hold of his jerkin front, and was drawing him to her.

The corpse jerked Wheam close to her blotchy face. Her mouth gaped open, revealing a pair of unusually long, yellow-stained incisors. Darting like a venomous snake, she buried the fangs in Wheam's neck.

Coilla rushed in, yelling and brandishing her sword. The female pulled back, blood trickling from the corners of her rancid lips. Wheam looked to be in a state of shock, his complexion ashen, a seeping wound at his jugular. Keeping hold of his wrist, the creature turned. There was a large cavity in her chest that exposed the ribcage and viscera. Wheam's blood dribbled from it.

Carving a downward arc with her blade, Coilla cut through the creature's arm. Wheam fell away, the withered hand still attached to his wrist. Fangs bared, her features hideously distorted, the female let out a guttural hiss.

Coilla swung her sword again and sliced off the creature's head. It bounced away into the darkness. The decapitated body stood swaying for a second, then fell, crumbling to a heap of arid skin, dust and bones.

"Bloodsuckers!" Coilla yelled.

They heard it at the wall. But Stryke and the others needed no warning. The undead they faced were also trying to target orc throats.

"What kills 'em?" Haskeer shouted, holding a ravenous corpse at bay with jabs from a spear.

"Beheading!" Stryke hollered, slashing at an opponent of his own.

"Right!" Haskeer yelled back. Discarding the spear, he brought out a hatchet to do the job.

"And fire!" Dallog added.

Having parted the head from his adversary's shoulders, Stryke barked an order. *"Use fire! Deploy your bows!"*

A handful of archers peeled off from the fighting. Some already had tar arrow tips, and quickly attached them. The rest used windings of cloth smeared with oil. Flints were struck.

The night air was filled with fiery streaks. Incendiary arrows smacked into the bloodsuckers, engulfing them in flame. Turned to fireballs, the creatures blundered about, wailing.

Dallog tackled the problem more directly. Producing a flask, he threw a copious amount of brandy over the nearest undead. An applied spark converted the corpse into a walking blaze.

Stryke was impressed. "Good thinking!" He dug out his own flask and drenched another of the creatures. Aflame, it collided with a fellow, igniting it too.

Haskeer looked resentful at his captain's approval of Dallog's initiative.

"Come on, Haskeer!" Stryke snapped. "What about yours?"

"My *brandy* ration?" His hand went to the flask at his belt, protectively.

"Haskeer!"

"All right, dammit." He took the flask and ripped out the stopper. Then he had an idea of his own. Snatching a scrap of clothing from a decapitated bloodsucker, he crammed it into the flask's neck. He used the flames from a burning corpse to light it.

Bringing his arm well back, he lobbed the flask at a group of three undead. It exploded in their midst, showering them with burning liquid. They staggered and fell, aflame. There were cheers from the orcs.

A further ten minutes of beheading and incineration put paid to the last of the creatures.

Stryke called out, *"Is anybody down?"*

"Here!" Coilla yelled back.

They ran into the graveyard. Wheam was sitting on the ground, Coilla bending over him.

"What happened?" Stryke said.

"He got bitten."

"Trust him," Haskeer muttered. "Stupid little bugger."

"I'm all right," Wheam told them.

Dallog knelt by him. "You don't look it."

"I'm... fine. Really. What... what were those things?"

"They were humans to start with," Stryke explained.

"Is that what... humans are... like?"

"No," Coilla replied. "They're vile, but not usually this disgusting. Well, not quite."

"So what —?"

"I think it's the magic," Stryke offered. "This land's steeped in it. Or it was until their sort came. Their greed and plunder let most of it bleed away. I reckon what's left went bad, got corrupted... I don't know; I'm no sorcerer."

Coilla took up the notion. "And when these humans died and were buried here the tainted magic brought them back like this?"

"Can you think of a better reason?"

"I don't know about that," Dallog said, examining Wheam's neck, "but I do know this wound needs binding."

"It needs more than that," Stryke replied.

"What do you mean?"

"We've run across vampyrs before. Not like these, but close enough. And they pass on the infection."

Coilla was nodding. "Stryke's right. If this isn't dealt with right now, Wheam's going to become like them."

"What?" Wheam squeaked.

"The bloodlust's a contagion, and it's in that wound. It has to be purified."

Dallog was rooting through his medical satchel. "How?"

"Not with some herb or salve, that's for sure."

"It needs the same thing that killed most of them," Stryke added. "Anybody got any brandy left?"

"I'm sure it'll be all right," Wheam protested feebly.

"Here." Coilla handed over her flask.

"Somebody get a flame going," Stryke said. "And hold on to him."

Wheam's puny resistance didn't amount to anything and they got him pinned. Dallog poured brandy on the wound, which had Wheam yelping. With ill-concealed delight, Haskeer applied the flame.

Wheam shrieked.

He carried on doing it for a good half minute while they let the brandy burn itself out.

"He's fainted," Dallog pronounced.

"Typical," Haskeer sneered.

"Think it worked?" Stryke wondered.

Dallog surveyed the damage. "Looks like it. But I suppose we'll know soon enough. I'll get him bound."

Stryke and Coilla stood. On every side, corpses smouldered and crackled.

"So much for no fires," she said.

8

A rough diamond lying among a fall of hailstones. A beetle moving unhurriedly across a table strewn with grapes. A wind-tossed lily petal caught up in a distant flock of doves. None are less real for being hard to see.

So it was in the limitless ocean of existence, where parallel worlds teemed in numbers beyond reckoning. There were anomalies, constructs that differed from the norm though superficially identical. They were rare to the point of improbability, but genuine enough.

One singularity of this kind was a radiant sphere created and maintained by the vigour of unimaginably potent magic. Within was a world whose entire resources and population were devoted to a single cause. This enterprise was carried out in secrecy, and its heart lay in their only city.

The city was as remarkable as the curious world fashioned to house it. Had an outsider been permitted to see it, not that any ever were, they would have been awed by its startling diversity. It embraced myriad architectural styles. Crystal spires and squat enclosures, soaring arches and faceless blocks. Grand amphitheatres standing adjacent to lofty tree houses; groups of round huts overshadowed by multi-turreted citadels. The city was made of stone, glass, timber, quartz, seashells, congealed mud, iron, brick, marble, ebony, canvas, steel and materials that resisted identification.

Many structures appeared incomprehensible, with no obvious practical or aesthetic function. Some melted into one another as though they had grown rather than been erected. A few appeared to disobey gravity, or continuously shifted, flowing into different shapes as they subtly remade themselves.

Highways and watercourses riddled the conglomeration. The twisting roads, elevated at some points, or burrowing into subterranean labyrinths, defied logic, and only a percentage of the canals and conduits contained water. What ran in others was viscous and of varying colours, and in certain stretches could be taken for quicksilver.

The whole bewildering muddle seemed hardly to qualify as a metropolis at all, yet it had an eccentric kind of organic coherence. Given enough time, a visitor, of which there were none, would realise that the city was best understood as the coming together of numerous cultures. A glimpse of its inhabitants would confirm it.

At the centre of the city there was a particularly imposing cluster of buildings. They were topped by a tower made of something that looked like polished ebony. It had no windows, or need of them; those inside saw infinitely more than mere glass could show.

The hub of the tower was a large chamber near its apex. Had a stranger entered they would have seen that the walls seemed to be covered in hundreds of framed works of art, all of the same size and uniformly rectangular. Closer inspection would reveal that they weren't paintings or sketches, and far from still life. They moved.

The frames were like apertures, through which a perplexing variety of constantly changing landscapes could be glimpsed: deserts, forests, oceans, cities, villages, rivers, fields, hamlets, cliff faces, towns, marshes, jungles, lakes and other, unrecognisable terrains, bizarre and alien.

One wall consisted of a single enormous aperture, its surface faintly rippling as though covered by an oily, transparent film. The scene it displayed was less easy to grasp than the others. It was entirely black, except for five pinpoints of golden light, clustered together and glowing like hot embers.

There were beings of many races present, and they were engrossed by it.

The highest ranking was human. Entering late maturity, Karrell Revers had silvering, close-cropped hair and beard, though he remained vigorous and straight-backed. Astuteness glinted in his jade eyes.

"That's it," he declared, pointing at the image. "We've found them."

"You're sure?" Pelli Madayar asked. She was a young female of the elf folk, dainty of form and with features so delicate she looked almost fragile. An appearance that belied both her stamina and the force of her will.

"You've not seen instrumentalities via the tracker before, Pelli," Revers replied. "Over the years, I have, though seldom. Believe me, we've found them."

"And they've been activated."

He nodded at the screen. "As you can see."

"Do we know who by?"

"Given where the artefacts are located, we can make an educated guess. I think they're with the one race not represented in the Gateway Corps."

"Orcs?"

"I'd bet on it."

"So you take this to be the set created by the sorcerer Arngrim."

"Almost certainly. We're sure they were fashioned there," he indicated the screen again, "in the region known locally as

Maras-Dantia, and that they passed through many hands before being seized by a band of renegade orcs."

"And then they disappeared."

"Several years ago, after we picked up their last flaring. Which indicated, of course, that they must have transported whoever possessed them to another habitation. Where that may have been, we have no idea. Tracking is an imprecise art, relying more than a little on luck. Wherever they were, the instrumentalities have lain dormant until now."

"So we don't know it's the set Arngrim made."

"Their provenance can be established. As you're aware, every assemblage of instrumentalities has a signature. Its own song. We can verify their origin once we've recovered them. That's not important. What is important is that a set has been activated, and the possible consequences of that are dire at the best of times. But to think they could be in the keeping of a race like the orcs—"

"We don't know that either. Perhaps they've passed to someone else."

"Someone capable of taking them from orcs? Unlikely. And I can't see the orcs trading them once they realised what they were capable of."

"Could they? See their potential, I mean. They don't have a reputation for being the brightest of races."

"But we can credit them with a certain base cunning. Which seems to have served them well enough to employ the instrumentalities. Though to fully direct the artefacts requires magical ability, and we should be grateful that's something orcs don't have."

"As do few of your race, Commander," she gently reminded him.

"You're not suggesting they're capable of mastering sorcery?"

"Who's to say what rogue intellect nature might have thrown up? Or perhaps they have help from someone who already has the necessary skills."

"So we have two alarming prospects. Instrumentalities in the hands of an ignorant race wedded to bloodletting, or somebody directing the orcs for purposes of their own. The ramifications of either are incalculable."

"What do we do?"

"We fulfil the remit the Corps was established for; the duty our forebears have carried out over the centuries. We do what we were all born to, Pelli. Whatever it takes."

"I understand."

"This needs dealing with at the highest level. As my second-in-command, I'm entrusting you personally with the task of recovering the artefacts."

She nodded.

Revers turned to face the rest of his team. Dwarfs, gnomes, brownies, centaurs, elves and representatives of half a dozen other races stared back at him. All were dressed in variants of the black garb he and Madayar wore, with a stylised field of stars motif on their chests.

"We have a crisis brewing," Revers told them. "Instrumentalities falling into unauthorised hands is such an uncommon event that, for some of you, this is the first time you would have experienced it. But you've been trained for such an eventuality, and I expect you to act in accordance with the highest standards of the Gateway Corps." He looked to the screen and its five luminous points of light. Everyone followed his gaze. "We take for granted the multiplicity of worlds. We don't know who first discovered their existence or the means to move between them. Some conjecture that it was an ancient, long-extinct race. Others among you credit your gods. We can speculate on that endlessly and never find an answer; any more than we will ever know the true origins of magic. But that doesn't matter. Our purpose is not to plumb the mystery but to bar irresponsible access to the portals." He scanned their faces and saw resolve there. "The Corps has never failed to recover known instrumentalities, or to punish those responsible for their misuse. This will be no exception. You all have your duties. Attend to them."

The crowd dispersed.

He returned his attention to Madayar. "We have to move quickly, before the artefacts are used again and we lose sight of them. Pick whoever you want for your squad and take any provisions you need."

"Do I have discretion in how I deal with this?"

"Act in any way you see fit. And I know it's asking a lot of you, Pelli, but bear in mind it's vital that the existence of the Corps remains secret."

"That won't be easy, particularly if we have to use force."

"Try persuasion if you can. Though I've little faith in that approach working with orcs. They're beyond the pale. Remember, you serve a higher moral purpose. If it's necessary to exterminate any who stand in your way, so be it. You'll have weaponry superior to anything you're likely to run into in Maras-Dantia."

"I hope it doesn't come to that. We elves like to think that few beings are beyond salvation. Surely even orcs are susceptible to reason?"

9

Stryke dragged his blade from the human's gizzard and let him drop. Spinning, he slashed the throat of another man-thing, unleashing a scarlet gush. Then he bowled into a third, thrashing at his sword with brutal, ringing blows.

To left and right, the Wolverines were joined in fierce hand-to-hand combat. Coilla and Haskeer dispatched two adversaries, she with a pair of daggers worked in harmony, he wielding a lacerating hatchet. Dallog impaled an opponent with the spar the band used to fly its standard. Underfoot, the withered sward was slick with blood.

It was dawn, and they fought in a makeshift campsite set in a hollow, screened from the trail by a thick copse. A covered wagon was parked, with over a score of horses tethered nearby. The same number of humans battled to defend it.

The conflict was intense but short-lived. With more than half of their strength downed, somebody on the human side yelled an order. They pulled back and fled.

"Let 'em go!" Stryke barked. "They're leaving us what we want."

Coilla glimpsed one of the retreating humans. It was a woman, and she had long, straw-blonde hair.

"See that?"

"What?" Haskeer said.

"Those humans riding off. One of them was a female. Young, barely adult."

"So?"

"I think I've seen her before. Though I'm damned if I can remember where."

"Humans all look the same to me."

"That's true." She shrugged. "Don't suppose it's important."

Stryke joined them. He was wiping the gore from his blade with a cloth. "Well, that was a lucky meeting. For us."

"Who do you think they were?" Coilla asked.

"Does it matter?"

"Notice how many of them were dressed alike? Could have been Unis."

"So humans are still divided amongst themselves. Surprise. Let's get on with it, shall we? That wagon should have drinking water and victuals. And now there's enough horses for everybody. If we move ourselves we can reach Quatt today."

For all that they were travelling south, and into supposedly milder climes, the terrain grew even more bleak. The trees were bereft of greenery, and a brook they passed ran yellow with filth.

"You sure we're on the right path?" Coilla asked.

Riding alongside, Stryke cast her a wry look. "For the tenth time, yes."

"Doesn't look much like the way I remember it, that's all."

"This place's had four more years of being broken by humans. That takes a toll on the land. And they've spoilt the magic. Those bloodsuckers were one upshot of that."

"At least Wheam seems to be on the mend." She turned and looked back down the line to where Wheam and Dallog were riding abreast. The youth wore a miserable expression, as usual, and his neck was bound, but some of his natural olive-grey colour was back.

"What's this?" Stryke said.

Coilla returned her attention to the road. A small group of figures was approaching. Some rode a rickety wagon, most were walking.

Haskeer galloped to the front of the line. "Trouble, Stryke?"

"I don't know. They don't seem too threatening."

"Could be a trap."

"*Stay alert!*" Stryke warned the column.

Coilla shaded her eyes and squinted at the newcomers. "They're elves."

"And a mangy looking lot," Haskeer added.

The party consisted of no more than a dozen. Those on foot trudged wearily. The wagon carried three or four old-timers, along with a couple of youngsters. All appeared fatigued and ill-nourished. They didn't react to the orcs in any noticeable way, or slow their somnolent plodding.

Leading them was a male. He was mature, although it was always hard to determine exactly how old an elf might be. His once fine clothes were shabby and he bore grime from too many days on the road.

When he reached the orcs he raised a painfully thin hand and his entourage ground to a halt.

"We have nothing," he declared by way of greeting.

"We've no need of anything from you," Stryke replied.

"Does that include our lives? It's all we have left." There was only fatalism in his voice.

"We don't harm those who show us no threat." Stryke eyed their sorry state. "You're a long way from home."

"What's brought a noble race like the elves down to this state?" Coilla said.

"I could ask the same of orcs."

STAN NICHOLLS

"We're doing all right," Haskeer informed him gruffly.

"Then you're rare among your kind," the elf returned. "No race prospers in this land anymore. Except one."

"You mean humans," Stryke said.

"Who else? They are in the ascendancy and the elder races are being pushed back to ever remoter enclaves. Soon, our kind will retreat into myth as far as humans are concerned."

Stryke could have told him that this was the humans' world by birthright, let alone conquest. Instead he asked, "Where are you headed?"

"Few havens remain, and all in distant parts. We decided on the far north."

"That's a bleak region to choose."

"It will be no more bitter than life here has become."

"You can't be all that's left of the elf nation, surely?" Coilla remarked.

"No. Our numbers are greatly decreased, but not to this extent. We are merely the remnants of one clan."

"And the rest of your race?"

"Those who aren't dead are enslaved or scattered. We seem destined to be a diaspora. If we survive at all."

"Why run?" Haskeer growled. "Stand up to 'em. Fight the human bastards."

"We don't possess the superior combat skills of orcs, or have as strong a taste for bloodshed. Magic was our only real weapon. But that's so depleted as to be near useless. It's come to one thing only for us: the hope that we may continue to exist."

"Is there any way we can aid you?" Stryke asked.

"You've spared our lives. That's aid enough in these troubled times. Now if you'll permit us to pass..."

Stryke brought out his water pouch and offered it to him. "You can probably use this. And we can spare a little in the way of food."

The elf hesitated for a moment, then took the pouch. He nodded his thanks. Then Stryke had a couple of the privates load some provisions on the wagon.

As the elves were about to depart, their leader paused. "Let me repay your benevolence with a word of caution, though you should know what I'm about to say well enough. Maras-Dantia holds nothing but misery and peril, even for orcs. It's become a wheel that breaks the hardiest spirit. You'd be well advised to find yourselves a fastness and try to weather the storm, as we are." Without waiting for an answer, he turned and left.

The Wolverines watched the little troupe make its way along the north-bound trail.

When they were out of earshot, Haskeer said, "What do you think of that?"

"I'll tell you what I think," Coilla replied. "Why won't you males *ever* ask for directions?"

Riding hard, they arrived at Quatt three hours later.

What was a particularly verdant district now looked as if it had been in the grip of an endless winter. In common with every other part of the land they'd seen, the terrain had an exhausted, washed-out quality.

They looked down on the wooded heart of the dwarfs' homeland from the crest of a hill.

"I feel a bit uneasy," Coilla admitted.

"Why?" Stryke said. "Think they won't welcome us?"

"We're *orcs*, Stryke; when is anybody ever pleased to see us? But it's not that so much. I'm more worried they might have moved on, like those elves. Or that Jup's dead."

"Or maybe the unfriendly ones have taken over down there," Haskeer put in.

Stryke stared at him. "Unfriendly?"

"The ones who sided with the humans for coin."

Coilla rolled her eyes. "Aah, not that again!"

"Dwarfs can't be trusted, you know that."

"Jup could," Stryke reminded him. "And his tribe didn't go over."

"I'm just—"

"You want to turn back?"

"No. I'm only saying—"

"*What?* What are you saying?"

"Fuck me, Stryke, I'm just saying what we all know. Dwarfs are treacherous. They're notorious for it."

"Keep that opinion to yourself. The band's got enough problems without your beef. Now get yourself back in line, Sergeant."

"We should be alert, that's all," Haskeer grumbled as he wheeled and spurred his horse.

Stryke caught Coilla's expression. "Was I too hard on him?"

"*Can* you be too hard on Haskeer? All right, maybe you were. A little."

"Well, it takes a lot to get through his thick skull. And I'd rather parley with Jup's folk than brawl with them."

"If Jup's still alive, do you reckon we'll be able to persuade him?"

"I don't know. He turned down the chance of leaving Maras-Dantia once before. We should be ready for a knock-back on this. But we're not going to find out sitting here. Come on." He gestured for the band to follow.

Quatt nestled in a great valley, wide enough that its far side was barely visible through the misty air. The trees surrounding its core were sorry things compared to the fecundity the band remembered. But the foliage was still abundant enough to make a dense barrier.

They followed a snaking, overhung path that filtered the dreary day's mean light even further. The odour of the forest was far from summery; its acrid smell of decay was more autumnal. There was no sound save the thud of their horses' hooves on mulch. They kept one hand on their sword hilts as they weaved their way to the interior.

Gloom gave over to watery daylight as they entered a sizeable clearing. At its centre was a large rock pool, fed by an underground spring, the sulphurous water gently bubbling. Garlands of withered flowers were heaped around it. Tracks branched off from the clearing in three different directions.

"Which way?" Coilla asked.

Stryke looked from one path to another. "Hold on, I've lost my bearings."

"Oh, good."

"Long time since I was last here. It all looks different."

"Should we send scouts out?"

"I'm not splitting the band. We'll find our way to the dwarfs together."

"Er, I think they've found us, Stryke."

Scores of stocky men poured into the clearing via the paths and through the undergrowth. They were armed with staffs and short-bladed swords, and outnumbered the Wolverines by at least four to one. Swiftly, they surrounded the orcs' column.

"*Steady!*" Stryke warned the band.

A burly dwarf stepped forward. "Who are you?" he demanded, scowling. "What are you doing in our forest?"

"We're here in peace," Stryke told him. "We mean you no hurt."

"Since when did orcs go anywhere in peace?"

"We do when we're seeking an ally."

"You've no allies here." The dwarf pointed to the rock pool. "This is a holy place. The presence of any but dwarfs offends our gods."

"Live underwater, do they, these gods of yours?" Haskeer piped up.

The dwarf gave him a murderous look, and his companions tensed.

"*Haskeer,*" Stryke hissed ominously.

"The gods dwell in all parts of the forest," the dwarf replied, swelling his barrel chest. "They are in the trees, and in the spirit of the woodland animals. They inhabit the very soil itself."

"Oh, right. Having a bath, are they?"

"*Haskeer!*" Stryke snapped. He turned to the dwarf. "Ignore my subordinate. He's...ignorant of your ways."

"Stupidity is no excuse for blasphemy."

Haskeer glared. "Who you calling—"

"*Shut up, Sergeant!*" Stryke bellowed. "Look," he told the dwarf, "if you'd just let me explain—"

"You can have your hearing. We're not unreasonable in Quatt. But give up your weapons first."

"That *is* unreasonable for an orc," Coilla said.

"She's right," Stryke agreed. "We don't do that."

"You want 'em, you take 'em," Haskeer added.

"If you won't disarm," the dwarf stated coldly, "then you're hostile. I'm giving you one last chance to throw down your blades."

Haskeer hawked noisily and spat, narrowly missing the dwarf's boots. "You can kiss my scaly arse, sawn-off."

Weapons raised, the dwarfs began advancing. The orcs drew their swords.

A figure elbowed through the crowd.

"Well fuck me slowly with a barbed pike."

"Only if you insist," Coilla said. She smiled. "Hello, Jup."

10

"So you have *control* of the instrumentalities?" Jup said.

"Some," Stryke replied. "Only because of this." He brought out the amulet.

"Can I see it?"

Stryke looped the chain over his head and handed it to him.

Jup examined it, absently tugging at his beard. "I've never come across anything quite like this script before."

"Nor me. But it's what got us here."

Jup gave the amulet back. "What about the influence the stars have? You know, the way they . . . What's the word? The way they captivated you, and Haskeer. Doesn't that worry you?"

"What's life without a few risks?"

"You can't brush it off, Stryke."

"No. Coilla's looking after one. I thought breaking them up might weaken their power."

"*You*, loosening your grip?" He smiled. "But no, it's a good idea."

They glanced to where she was standing, further along the row of oak benches.

The tables were set out in tiers in an even larger clearing than the one they first entered. It held a village of thatched huts, storage sheds and livestock pens. Fires had been lit in several shallow pits, to keep the unseasonable chill at bay and to roast meat.

Hospitality had been extended to the orcs once Jup insisted they were honoured guests. But many of the dwarfs appeared grudging. Now most sat apart, eyeing the Wolverines suspiciously.

Haskeer came and plonked himself down next to Stryke and Jup.

"And how are you, you old bastard?" Jup said.

"Hungry." He fidgeted. "And these seats are too small."

"They weren't made for a massive rear end like yours. Ah, how I've missed that scowl. You know, I can't get used to you all without your tattoos of rank. Looks odd. How'd you get rid of them?"

"A sawbones back in Ceragan," Stryke explained. "He used some kind of vitriol. Stung like fury, took an age to heal."

"Then itched like buggery for a month," Haskeer added. "Worth it though. Shows we're nobody's slaves." He stared at the struck-through crescents high on Jup's cheeks that indicated his one-time status as sergeant. "You should lose yours, too. Like me to cut 'em out for you?" He made to reach for his knife.

"Don't think I'll bother, thanks. They give me a certain distinction around here."

"Really?" Stryke said. "I'd have thought being in Jennesta's horde wasn't something to brag about."

"Not everybody saw her as the evil bitch we knew and hated. And that's something else I can't get my head around: her surviving that...vortex thing."

"Seems she did. If Serapheim's to be believed."

"Big if."

A dwarf arrived with tankards and deposited them on the bench without a word. Haskeer snatched one and gulped a long draught.

Stryke took a drink himself. "Strange to think," he reflected, lowering his tankard, "that if it hadn't been for Jennesta we'd never have known about Ceragan. I wouldn't have met Thirzarr and sired young."

"You have hatchlings?" Jup said.

"Two. Boys."

"Things *have* changed."

"And like I said, if Jennesta hadn't sent us after that first star—"

Haskeer slammed down his tankard. "We don't owe her a fucking *thing*. Whatever we got was our due."

Jup nodded. "Much as I hate to agree with latrine breath here, that's how I see it, too. It seems a fair exchange for all the grief she doled out. Talking of Ceragan..." He looked about the clearing. "I see some new faces, and the absence of others."

"The two are linked," Haskeer muttered darkly. He jabbed a thumb in the direction of Wheam and Dallog.

"Take no notice of him," Coilla said, arriving to claim a seat.

"When did I ever?"

She lifted a tankard. "Hmm. Potent stuff."

"We pride ourselves on our brew."

Coilla had another mouthful, then remarked in a lower tone, "Your folk take their gods a bit seriously, don't they?"

"Some do. More so since things really started to fall apart. Religious zeal's got even stronger in Maras-Dantia while you were away, and not just among humans."

"We met a bunch of elves on the way here. They reckoned humans are going to be the end of the elder races."

"I might have argued against that once. I'm not so sure they're wrong now fanatics have the whip hand."

Coilla snapped her fingers. "Fanatics. Of course. It was *her*!"

"Who?"

"The female I saw when we took those humans' horses."

"What about her?" Stryke said.

"I *thought* she looked familiar. It was Mercy Hobrow. That lunatic Kimball Hobrow's daughter. Grown up now, but still recognisable."

Jup expelled a low whistle. "You had a lucky escape then. She's as crazy as her old man, and she's carried on his work. Her group's a rallying point for Unis, and she's got an army of followers even bigger than her father's. They're a scourge in these parts."

"And we've given her another grudge against us," Stryke observed.

"You'd be well advised to steer clear of her in future."

"We don't intend being here that long. But talking of fathers and daughters, Jup, I meant to ask; last we saw of you, you were getting Sanara out of the palace in Illex. What happened to her?"

"Good question. Jennesta's army was in chaos, and these helped us get through." He pointed at his tattoos. "Then we were days crossing the ice fields. The woman was tough, I can tell you that. When we got down to the plains...well, I didn't lose her, exactly. But she went. Don't ask me how. She was there one minute, gone the next."

"Fucking magic-mongers," Haskeer grumbled. "Slippery as spilt guts."

"Anyway," Jup finished, "I gave up looking for her and made my way here. Haven't seen her since."

"Quite a family, eh?" Coilla said. "Serapheim and his brood."

Dwarfs were heading their way carrying wooden trenchers heaped with steaming meat.

Stryke nudged Haskeer. "Looks like your belly's about to stop rumbling."

"Sorry if it's less than a feast," Jup stated apologetically. "The forest doesn't bring the yield it once did, and game's scarce."

Wheam and Dallog wandered over.

"Mind if we join you?" Dallog asked.

"If you must," Haskeer grated.

Coilla shot him a hard look. "Course. Park yourselves."

Platters of spiced roast meat were set down on the table, along with baskets of warm bread. There were dishes of berries and nuts.

"You don't know how welcome this is after field rations," Stryke said.

"Hmmph," Wheam agreed, mouth full. "Food good."

"We're grateful," Coilla put in, "especially with hunting so poor." She jabbed Haskeer's ribs with her elbow. *"Aren't* we?"

He glared at her and dragged a sleeve across his mouth. "It's all right. Could be more of it."

"Is this usual dwarf fare?" Dallog intervened diplomatically.

"More or less," Jup replied. "Though we'd prefer a greater quantity." He aimed that at Haskeer, who stayed oblivious.

"Those of us from Ceragan have never seen dwarfs before," Dallog said, "so don't take my ignorance for a lack of courtesy."

"No offence taken. I remember how I felt when I first saw an orc."

"You didn't think we were as revolting as humans, did you?" Wheam piped up.

Jup smiled. "Nowhere near. Though the storytellers would have us believe you ate the flesh of your own kind, among other things."

"*I'm* a balladeer," Wheam declared proudly.

"I noticed the lute."

"That's putting it a bit grandly," Stryke said. *"Hoping to be* would give a better account."

"I can prove it," Wheam protested. "I could sing something."

"Oh gods," Haskeer groaned. He upended his empty tankard. "More drink."

"That we do have," Jup told him, beckoning a female dwarf carrying a laden tray.

She was fair of form, as far as the orcs could judge. Her skin was smooth as ceramic, and her long auburn hair was woven in plaits. She was hale, and though powerfully built she moved with graceful ease, for a dwarf.

Putting down the tray, she leaned over and kissed Jup. The clinch was lingering.

"Now that's what I *call* service," Coilla remarked.

The pair disentangled themselves.

"Sorry," Jup said. "This is Spurral."

"Somebody...special?" Stryke asked.

"She's my cohort." He saw they didn't grasp what he was saying. "My other half. Perpetual companion, mate, partner. *Spouse.*"

"You were right," Stryke said, "things really have changed."

Coilla smiled. "Good on you both."

Haskeer lowered his tankard. "Hell, I never thought you'd let yourself be tied down, Jup. Hard luck."

"You must be Coilla." Spurral smiled at her. "And you're Stryke."

"Good guess."

"Oh, I've heard a lot about you all." The smile faded. "And you just have to be Haskeer."

Haskeer bobbed his tankard at her and downed more ale.

"Spurral and me have known each other since we were kids," Jup explained. "When I got back here it just seemed right that we made it kind of official."

"So two proud dwarf families were joined," Spurral added. "Me being a Gorbulew and Jup a Pinchpot."

Haskeer choked on his beer. "You're right about that!" he spluttered.

"Pinchpot," Jup repeated through grated teeth. "*Pinchpot.*"

Haskeer rocked with mirth. "So you," he pointed at a stony-faced Spurral, "...you stopped being a...Gorbulew and... became a pis—"

"*Haskeer,*" Jup growled ominously.

"Talk about learning something new every day," Haskeer ploughed on, hugely amused and insensible to their sour expressions. "You never told us you were a...*Pinchpot.*"

"I wonder why," Spurral remarked dryly.

"That's enough, Haskeer," Stryke cautioned, a note of menace in his voice.

"Come *on.* I know getting hitched can kill your sense of humour, but—"

"We're guests here. Be mindful of it."

Haskeer sobered. "Seems to me there was no point in our coming."

"How's that again?" Jup said.

"Can't see you joining us, what with you having a mate and all. It was a wasted journey."

Jup and Spurral exchanged glances.

"Not necessarily," Jup said.

Coilla swept her arm to indicate the throng of dwarfs in the clearing. "I thought you stayed here because of them."

"Given the choice of spending your life with another race or your own, wouldn't *you*?"

"You could have been sent to the dwarfs' home world. Serapheim offered."

"I wouldn't have known anybody there either."

"So why the change of heart?"

"I never thought I'd say it, but I want to get away from here. The time's come."

"You can see this land's dying," Spurral said, "and our folk along with it. Did you get a close look at our tribe? Almost all are old, lame or infirm."

Jup shrugged. "We don't want to leave, but—"

"We?" Stryke said.

"There's no way I'm going without Spurral."

"That complicates things, Jup."

"Why should it? Unless you've got a problem with dwarfs in the band."

"You know it's not that. But we've no idea what we're going into, except it'll be dangerous."

"I can look after myself," Spurral protested. "Or is it taking females along that you don't like?"

"In case you hadn't noticed," Coilla told her, "I'm a female myself. What's important is being able to fight."

More than one pair of eyes flashed to Wheam.

"Spurral's a good fighter," Jup replied. "She's had to be."

"You're not going to shift on this, are you?" Stryke said.

"Nope. It's both or neither."

"I'm running this band just like I did in the old days, as a tight unit. Everybody in it takes orders."

"We've no gripes with that."

"Don't say you're going along with this, Stryke," Haskeer complained.

"I make decisions about the band, not you."

"Then don't make a bad one. We're carrying enough dead wood as it is, and—"

"Didn't Stryke just say you all obey orders?" Spurral interrupted. "Doesn't sound like it to me."

"Stay out of this."

"This is *about* me!"

"Call her off, Jup," Haskeer snarled.

"She can fight her own battles."

"Yeah," Spurral confirmed, squaring up to Haskeer. "Want to put your fists where your mouth is?"

"I don't hit females."

Coilla laughed. "Since when?"

"*That's enough*," Stryke decided. "Haskeer, shut your mouth. Jup, Spurral; back off. Everybody, sit down." They settled. "That's better. I'll think about Spurral, Jup. All right?"

"That's all we're asking for."

"So let it rest."

"Yes. This should be a celebration. More drinks." He reached for a jug and topped up their cups. "And we have a little pellucid if anybody's—"

"Oh, no. Not after the last time. Mission first, pleasure later."

Haskeer mumbled, "Shit."

"What about that song then?" Jup suggested. "Wheam?"

Coilla rolled her eyes. "Gods, must we?"

But Wheam had his lute in his hands. "This might be a little rough. I'm still polishing it." He began strumming.

> *"The Wolverines, that dauntless band,*
> *Fought their way across the land*
> *They beat a path through rain and mud*
> *And left their rivals in pools of blood*
>
> *They met rank fiends in battles dire*
> *And sent them to eternal fire*
> *No demons grim or human waves*
> *Could overcome the Wolverines' blades*
>
> *They came to where the dwarfs did dwell*
> *And saw that they had not fared well*
> *But still their welcome was quite fulsome*
> *And hospitality was truly awesome."*

"Shall I kill him or will you?" Spurral asked Jup.

"Here's the chorus," Wheam declared, upping the tempo of his discordant plucking.

> *"We are the Wolverines!*
> *Marching to foil evil schemes!*
> *Fleet of foot and strong of arm!*
> *We—"*

"Well, it's getting late," Stryke announced loudly.

Wheam came to a grating halt. "But I haven't—"

"Been a long day," Coilla added, stretching.

"Sure has," Jup agreed, "and a big day tomorrow."

Wheam's face dropped. "You never let me fin—"

"Turn in or I'll break that fucking string box over your head," Haskeer promised.

"Time we all hit the sack then," Dallog said, taking Wheam's arm.

"We set off in the morning," Stryke told them. "Early."

They dispersed to their various billets, with most of the privates making for a couple of long houses. Jup and Spurral led Stryke, Haskeer and Coilla to a pair of much smaller huts.

"Stryke," Jup said, "you and Haskeer are going to have to share this one." He pushed open the door.

Striding in, Haskeer cracked his head on the top of the door frame. He let out a stream of curses.

Spurral covered her mouth to stifle her glee.

"Don't forget everything's dwarf scale," Jup added.

"Thanks for reminding me," Haskeer retorted. He looked around the poky room and noticed the cots. "That goes for the beds too, does it? These are only fit for hatchlings."

"We'll sleep on the floor," Stryke told him. "And if you snore I'll kill you."

"We'll leave you to it," Jup said. "You'll let us know about Spurral, Stryke?"

"In the morning."

Coilla was taken to the adjoining hut.

Spurral ushered her in. "You get this one all to yourself. Though the bed's no bigger."

"I don't care. I could sleep on a rack of knives."

They left her stripping blankets and tossing them on the floor.

Coilla was so tired she didn't even bother taking off her boots. As soon as she stretched out, she was asleep.

There was only the black velvet of oblivion. Mindless, time-less. All embracing.

The first frail light of dawn seeped in through the cracks around the door and window shutters.

She stirred.

Instantly, she knew she wasn't alone. A figure loomed over her. She tried to move.

The cold edge of a steel blade pressed against her flesh.

And an unmistakably human voice whispered, "Don't make me cut your throat."

11

"If you're going to do it, get it over with," Coilla said, the blade tight against her throat.

"We don't want to hurt you."

"We?"

"I'm not alone."

Out of the corner of her eye she was aware of someone else skulking in the shadows.

"We're just trying to help you," the human added.

"You've a funny way of showing it." Coilla's fingers snaked towards her own knife.

"I didn't want you bawling the place down and bringing the others in here." He grabbed her hand, then wrenched her knife from its sheath and tossed it aside. "Or getting any bright ideas."

"Who *are* you?"

"Long story."

"Why would your kind help an orc?"

"Another long story."

"Not much of a talker, are you?"

"There's no time. This place's about to be attacked. But you might be able to do something about it if you can get your forces mustered."

"Why should I believe that?"

"We've seen what's massing out there. Take my word."

"A human's word?"

"How could warning you be a trap? Look, if I take this knife away are you going to behave?"

Coilla nodded.

He removed the blade and backed off.

She lay still. "At least let me see you."

The human fumbled for a moment before sparks were struck and a candle lit.

As far as Coilla could tell with humans, he seemed in his prime. He certainly looked fit. His mass of hair was blond, but he had none of the facial growth many of his race favoured.

He moved the candle. The circle of flickering light showed the other man's features. He was older, and had the build of someone used to sloth. There was grey in his thinning black hair and tightly trimmed beard. His pallid skin had a sheen of sweat, despite the early morning chill.

"You have names?" she said.

"I'm Jode Pepperdyne," the younger man replied. "This is my ... This is Micalor Standeven. You?"

She got up. "Coilla."

The older man spoke. "We're wasting time. A small army of religious fanatics are going to be here any minute." He was noticeably more nervous than his companion.

"Unis?" Coilla asked.

"Does it matter?" Pepperdyne said. "All you need know is that they're hell-bent on mayhem."

"We're well guarded."

"Really? We got in easily enough."

"I don't understand why you'd side with us against your own."

"They're nothing to do with us," Standeven insisted.

"Let's just say we have mutual interests," Pepperdyne offered.

"And we'll be mutually dead if you don't start mounting a defence *now*. Trust me."

"That's asking a lot."

"What have you got to lose? If we're lying, all you've done is put everybody on alert. If we're telling the truth, you've a chance to hold off the attack."

"But decide now," Standeven added. "Because if your answer's no we can try getting out of here ourselves."

"Will you do it, Coilla?" Pepperdyne said.

"I'll do it. But if this is a trick," she vowed, "you'll both pay."

He smiled his gratitude. "Do it quietly. We don't want to warn the raiders."

"Oh *really*? I never would have thought of that." She gave him a withering look, then headed for the door. "You two stick by me. Many here would bring you down soon as look at you."

She led them to the adjoining hut and barged straight in.

Haskeer still slept, snoring loudly. Stryke stood on the far side of the room, stropping a blade. He spun around.

Coilla held up her hands. *"Easy."*

He glared at the humans. "What the hell's this?"

"They're . . . friends. Or at least not hostile."

"What?"

"Listen, Stryke. There might be an attack coming."

"Says who?"

"They do." She jabbed a thumb at Pepperdyne and Standeven. "And I don't think we can risk ignoring them."

"But—"

"If they're right, there's no time to waste, and—Can't you stop that fucking *noise*?"

"Huh? Oh, yeah." He turned and gave his snoring sergeant a kick.

Haskeer leapt up, tangled in his blanket. "Uhh? Fuck! *Humans!*" He whipped out a knife.

"Calm down," Stryke told him. "We know."

"But what—?"

"There could be trouble."

"Trouble?" Haskeer was still negotiating wakefulness.

"Yes. According to them."

"According to *them*?" he replied, rubbing sleep from his eyes. "They're nothing but lousy—"

"We appreciate you don't know who we are," Pepperdyne said.

"We know *what* you are," Haskeer rumbled.

"And you've no reason to trust us. But brush us off and you'll have a crowd of lunatics down on you."

"Makes sense, Stryke," Coilla said. "We upset Mercy Hobrow and her Unis. If they tracked us here..."

Stryke looked from her to the humans. "What's your interest in this?"

"You don't have time for our life stories," Pepperdyne replied.

Several long seconds passed while Stryke studied their faces and thought things over. "All right, we'll sound the alarm." Haskeer started to object. Stryke waved him away. "Better prepared than caught unawares."

Haskeer gave a resigned sigh. "So what do we do with them?" He nodded at the two men.

"Lock 'em up somewhere."

Pepperdyne tensed. "Nobody locks us away. We're part of this."

"We can't have 'em running around armed," Haskeer objected.

"I don't carry a weapon," Standeven said. As proof, he held open his jerkin.

Haskeer was appalled. "No weapon? Humans *are* crazy."

"This one has a blade," Coilla said.

"And if anybody wants it," Pepperdyne came back defiantly, "they'll have to take it."

Coilla appreciated the sentiment. "We can respect that."

"But if this is some kind of ploy," Stryke promised, "being armed won't stop us taking it out of your hides. Now let's move."

They left the hut. Stryke ordered the humans to wait, with Coilla keeping an eye on them. Then he and Haskeer set off stealthily to rouse the others, creeping from door to door. In their wake, orcs and dwarfs emerged, bearing arms and treading softly.

Tousle-haired, Jup and Spurral made their way across the clearing to Stryke.

Spurral looked indignant. "What are *they* doing here?" she demanded, pointing at Coilla's charges.

"Warning us. They say. And before you ask, I haven't a clue who they are."

"You *believe* them?"

"Best not to take chances." He turned to Jup. "Can your people get into a defensive pattern?"

"In their sleep. What are we facing?"

"Don't know. Or if. But could be big."

"You've seen the state of our tribe. Not a lot of prime fighters."

"You've got us."

Jup nodded and moved off. Spurral glowered one last time at the pair of humans and went after him.

Haskeer arrived. "The band's ready, Stryke. How do we deploy?"

"We need to be mobile. We'll split into five units, headed by me, you, Coilla, Jup and Dallog."

"*Dallog?*"

"I'm not debating it. Get those squads sorted, and make sure you spread around the new recruits."

He left Haskeer to it and jogged to where Coilla stood with the humans.

"I'm splitting the band into groups," he told her. "You're leading one. There'll be a hideaway for non-combatants. These two can go there."

"Fine by me," Standeven responded eagerly.

Pepperdyne gave him a contemptuous look. "But not me."

"You've no say in it."

"I can fight, and you need every sword arm you can get."

"Your place is at my side!" Standeven retorted.

His tone had Stryke and Coilla exchanging curious glances.

Pepperdyne ignored his master's petulance. "I can be more use out here."

"Do as you please," Stryke decided. "We've no time for squabbles."

"You'd better stay with my unit," Coilla said. "Unless you want to be mistaken for an enemy."

Pepperdyne nodded. "Right."

"Haskeer's forming the groups," Stryke explained. "Get over there, and take him with you." He indicated Standeven. "He can cower with the old ones and sucklings." He thrust a finger in Pepperdyne's chest. "And *you*. Make a wrong move, or get in our way, and you're dead."

Practised at repelling intruders, the dwarfs were swift to take up positions. They occupied defensive trenches. Lookouts climbed tall trees. Archers were placed on the roofs of buildings. The five teams of orcs were stationed at strategic points across the clearing.

Those who couldn't fight, along with Standeven, took shelter in the sturdiest barn.

Wheam was assigned the job of guarding them. A meaningless role, given that if the enemy reached it, everything would already be lost.

The bout of furtive activity over, everyone settled in to wait. Nothing, not even birdsong, disturbed the early morning quiet.

Coilla's group sheltered behind a small cluster of bushes, ready to fire-fight where needed. Pepperdyne knelt beside her, his breeches moist with dew. Half a dozen privates under her command eyed him charily.

The minutes seemed unusually reluctant to pass.

"You'd better be right about this," she whispered, scanning the tree-line.

"I am."

"Sure? They're taking long enough showing themselves."

"They'll come." He twisted to face her. "Do you know what you're going to be up against?"

"We've tangled with Unis before."

"Lately?"

"Few years back."

"Word in these parts is that they're even more ruthless now."

"You're not from these parts then?"

He turned wary. "Not really."

"Then maybe you don't know about orcs."

"These fanatics are *savage*. They're a death cult."

She smiled. "So are we."

There was a shriek. Across the way, a dwarf plunged from the upper branches of a tree, his body peppered with arrows. Bolts winged through the greenery, slashing leaves and splintering bark; clearing the way for black-clad figures emerging from the forest.

Coilla snatched her sword. "Time to show what you're made of, pink skin."

Stryke's group was well away from Coilla's, and sharing one of the dwarfs' trenches. Jup's was stationed behind several hay wagons parked in the middle of the clearing. Dallog's had hidden themselves in and around an outlying barn. But it was Haskeer's group, concealed in undergrowth not far from the forest's edge, that took the first brunt.

The humans rolled in softly, like a wave on an ocean of pitch.

From their hiding places, defending archers loosed a hail of barbed shafts. A score of the raiders dropped. Then thirty or forty dwarfs broke cover and rushed forward to take issue, wielding short-bladed swords and staffs. That left Haskeer's troop with no option but to wade in.

The first few minutes of combat stretch time and overwhelm the senses. Movement, clamour and the stink of fear are all-pervasive. The only counter is bloodlust.

Haskeer plunged into the human deluge, cutting down two men in short order. The shield of a third took the full force of his broadsword. But its bearer was knocked off kilter. He yielded his guard and let in Haskeer's cleaving blade. Blood gushed and the man fell. Haskeer spun to face another.

The air was filled with the natter of quarrelling steel, bellowed curses and anguished screams. All around, Haskeer's unit fought to stem the tide of flesh, toiling like harvesters scything corn.

Though the dwarfs fought with passion, few races possessed the martial skills of orcs. So dwarfs were the first to fall.

One, his head split, collapsed across Haskeer's path. He stepped over the corpse to face its killer. Muscular, and of impressive girth, the human brandished a pair of axes that looked toy-like in his massive fists. And he moved with a swiftness that ignored his size.

Haskeer dropped, spurning a wild axe swing. Then dodged again when its partner came close to dismembering him. Lunging from all-fours, he scurried clear, turned and engaged for a second time. Slicing and ducking in equal measure, he searched for an opening. But the human handled his axes with practised agility, and appeared tireless. It was all Haskeer could do to keep clear.

Knowing that any one of the humans in the surrounding melee could elect to stab his back, he put on a spurt. Powering forward, he tried simply battering through. The human drove him off. Haskeer rallied and went in again. There was a moment of stasis, with fierce blows exchanged but no give on either side. Finally the man faltered and took a step in retreat. Haskeer upped the pace. He thrashed metal, his blade whipping a squall.

Then it was through, and cut deep. The man's arm was laid open crook to wrist.

Blood surged and he dropped an axe. Haskeer didn't loiter. A crisp flip of his blade had it homing in for another bite. He struck flesh again. The human cried out, an oblique wound reddening his chest. Grievous, but not fatal, though enough to let the other axe slip from his sweaty grasp. He staggered.

Haskeer rushed in, grabbed one of the axes and swung it solidly. The human's head bounced off into the melee. His body briefly stood, a crimson fountain, before buckling.

Nearby, Seafe was coming off second best in a scrap with a burly swordsman. Haskeer lobbed the axe. It struck the human square in his back. Arms flailing, he collapsed. Seafe gave his sergeant a thumbs-up and picked another foe.

Raiders were still coming out of the trees, and the struggle boiled on every side. Turning his sword on the next pallid human, Haskeer was beginning to think Quatt would be overrun.

A tight-knit group powered through the crowd. They travelled with purpose, hacking down any opposition. In minutes they reached Haskeer's team and joined the slaughter.

"Took your time!" Haskeer grumbled, batting at a human's probing spear.

"You're lucky we came!" Coilla retorted.

She whacked the sword from a Uni's hand and punctured his skull. His fellow took the edge of her blade across his belly. Coilla had enough wrath left over to run through the next human in line.

She stood panting as two more Unis approached warily.

Weighing up whether to spend her precious throwing knives on them, she noticed Pepperdyne.

The human moved among the enemy like a fish in limpid water. He was master of his blade and used it as a veteran would. Weaving and turning, he stayed clear of whistling steel with an almost contemptuous ease. When he struck, it was as quick as thought, and always to the true.

He killed two men in rapid succession. Neither so much as engaged him. As they fell he sought more flesh, wielding his sword with the skill of a surgeon. In seconds, his sinuous dance brought death to another black-clad human.

Haskeer saw it too. Then he tugged his blade from the spearman's guts and let him drop.

The attack was coming from all directions. There was no point on the clearing's boundary where there wasn't conflict. In places the line had broken and the defenders were falling back. Dwarfs were suffering casualties, and some lay dead, but so far, orc injuries were light. Stryke doubted that would last.

Using a sword and dagger combination, he reaped the flood of invaders. A twin thrust took down a pair as one. The swiftness of his blades caught three more in as many heartbeats. Still the enemy came.

Stryke found himself facing a studded mace. Its handler showed little finesse employing it, but his wild, two-handed swipes were no less dangerous for that. For a full minute Stryke managed nothing more than avoiding it. Then he got his opponent's measure. Holding back until the club was in full swing, he dived under the man's outstretched arms and pierced his torso. The Uni crumpled.

Stryke ran the back of a hand across his clammy brow and pushed on.

Despite all the resistance they met, humans were getting through to the settlement. Most stayed in groups, knots of belligerence fuelled by pious zeal, lashing out savagely at all in their reach. The defenders slowed them, but they were hard to stop.

Dallog's troupe, obeying orders by remaining at the barn, had seen no action. What happened next made up for that. A bunch of howling humans, twice their number, sped in to take issue. Half a dozen uneven duels broke out.

Standing to the fore, Dallog was set upon by a trio of enraged fanatics. Their frenzy and number worked to his benefit. Fury made for poor judgement, and fighting as a group had them getting in each other's way. He quickly profited. A scouring blow across the side of a Uni's head put him out of the picture.

The fallen man's companions were less easy to better. One jabbed at Dallog with a shortened spear, its tip wickedly barbed. The other contrived to circle him, for an attack from side or rear. They were working together. Lessening the odds had increased the threat, and the irony wasn't lost on Dallog.

Twisting away from the spear, he lashed out at the circling swordsman. Metal echoed as they pounded each other's broadswords. Deadlock ensued, and might have continued had not the spearman intervened. Losing patience, he rushed in, thrusting the weapon at Dallog, passion outwitting skill. His recklessness was a gift. Dallog spun, brought down his blade hard and knocked the spear from the Uni's hands. Without pause he followed through, delivering a fatal blow.

The swiftness of the kill threw the sword-bearer off his stroke. Before he recovered, Dallog got in close and nasty. He swiped, raking the Uni from armpit to waist. Then he put all he had into a high swing that buried his blade in the human's skull. The man plummeted, so much dead weight.

Dallog leaned on his gory sword, breathing heavily and hoping none of the grunts noticed his fatigue.

The Unis had torched the barn. Thick black smoke belched from its open doors. Flames scaled the wooden exterior and the roof steamed. A screaming human stumbled past, his clothes ablaze. Orcs and Unis fought without let. Havoc reigned.

Something caught Dallog's eye. Towering shapes were emerging from the tree-line. At first he couldn't make out what they were. As they entered the clearing he saw. Black-garbed horsemen, in their dozens.

"Second wave!" he bellowed. *"Second wave!"*

12

Riders were charging across the field of battle, trampling defenders and cutting them down.

In the middle of the clearing, by a couple of hay wagons, Jup's group was oblivious, absorbed as they were in vicious hand-to-hand fighting.

Spurral was at Jup's side. They were armed with the dwarfs' traditional weapons; he with a leaden-headed staff, she with a short, curved sword and knife. And they were working the weapons hard.

Jup dodged a blow and gave the head of his attacker a resounding crack. Flipping over his staff, he thrust the weighted end into the midriff of another. He used the staff with speed and seasoned grace. Spurral was no less skilful with her blades. Crowded by a pair of Unis, she expertly slashed the face of one and knifed his companion.

Eldo fought alongside them. Fending off the attentions of a brute with a club, the grunt took a hit that dented his helm and had him reeling. Spurral quickly deflected the clubman's follow-through and ripped his belly. A grateful if dazed Eldo nodded gratitude, and Spurral earned further respect from the grunts looking on.

After a seeming lifetime of grinding conflict there was a brief hiatus. But no respite.

Chuss, one of the new recruits, pointed. *"Look!"*

They saw the riders.

Then two horsemen broke through the forward defences and galloped their way.

"Take cover!" Jup bellowed, waving his group towards the wagons.

He made Chuss and fellow newbie Ignar shelter under one of them. The rest of the team clustered defensively. Jup and Spurral clambered to the top of the wagon nearest the approaching riders.

Seconds latter, the pair of horsemen arrived, brandishing cutlasses. Their mounts were steaming and foam-flecked.

One of the Unis made straight for Jup and Spurral. They battled to fend him off, but his mobility kept him frustratingly beyond reach. His companion, meanwhile, was leaning and slashing at the knot of orcs. Trying to avoid his horse's thrashing hooves, they jabbed and swiped at him.

The skirmish ground on, with neither side gaining the advantage. Then seasoned hand Gleadeg had an idea. He dug out a slingshot, quickly primed it and commenced swinging. The unleashed shot peppered the rider's face and chest. He cried out, lost his balance and crashed to the ground. His horse bolted. The orcs rushed in and pounded out his life.

Jup made to follow Gleadeg's example and use his own sling on the remaining horseman. But as he reached for it a keen hissing filled the air. A swarm of arrows thudded into the horseman, hurling him from his saddle.

When Jup and the others looked for their source, they saw a dozen or more dwarf archers on the longhouses' roofs. The Wolverines waved their thanks. They were ignored. The dwarfs were busy picking off more riders.

That wasn't the end of the Unis. They were still worming their way into the clearing, though there were fewer of them. Jup and his comrades took up their swords again.

Those near the perimeter had more than a couple of horsemen to contend with. Their burden was thinning the stream of incoming riders. Haskeer and Coilla's groups had faced a virtual cavalry charge. Dead and dying humans, dwarfs and horses were scattered across the forward combat zone. But the fighting went on.

Seizing a discarded lance, Haskeer impaled a charging Uni. The man was propelled from his horse, the spear lodged in his chest. Haskeer made do with his dependable blade to challenge the next interloper.

Coilla had spent her knives freely. Now there were just two left. She lobbed one at a rampaging horseman. It was aimed at his chest. He turned and the blade struck above his armpit, but the force was enough to spin him in his saddle. He lost control. The reins whipped free. A couple of orcs grabbed them and tugged hard, bringing down horse and rider. Spears and hatchets sealed his fate.

Pepperdyne battled on. He showed no loss of stamina, or lessening skill. His sword was a blur, slashing throats, puncturing lungs, severing limbs. He outfought or outwitted any who faced him.

For her part, Coilla was eyeing another rider. He was laying about a group of dwarfs with an axe. As she watched, he cracked open someone's skull, dropping him like a stone. Drawing her last knife, she took aim, reckoning on a clean kill this time.

She missed. The knife clipped the neck of the Uni's horse. Startled, the wounded animal bucked, throwing its rider. He fell heavily, but found his feet at once, buoyed with rage. Spotting Coilla, he battered his way towards her. She was bracing herself to meet him when a swinging blade came within a hair's-breadth of hacking her flesh. Unnoticed, another Uni had emerged from the scrum to challenge her.

Coilla spun to the new foe and their swords collided with a strident impact. They fell into a frenzied bout of swordplay. He was powerfully built, and what he lacked in finesse he made up for with might. They didn't so much fence as hammer at each other, and Coilla parried a series of jarring blows.

Then the human got lucky. She was slow in dodging a wild swipe. His blade skinned the knuckles of her sword hand, dashing the weapon from her grasp. It bounced beyond reach. Backing off, Coilla went for her dagger, the only weapon she had left. As she fumbled for it, the unhorsed Uni appeared.

The pair of glowering humans closed in on her. One had a broadsword, the other an axe. No way was her dagger a match for their reach. She could only twist and duck to avoid their aggression. But there was a limit to how long she could evade them. Rapidly, she lost ground. The humans came on for the kill.

"Coilla!"

Suddenly Pepperdyne was there. He tossed her a sword. Then he took on the second Uni, leaving the axeman to her.

She piled into him, intent on a reckoning. Bobbing to elude a swing from his axe, she went in fast and low, blade level. He swerved and half turned, hoping to sidestep her attack. Coilla's sword connected, but it glanced, skimming the side of his waist. Far from a fatal wound, it was still a painful enough distraction. Sufficient for Coilla to spin and strike again.

This time, the blow was true. She buried a third of her blade in the Uni's midriff. Jerking the sword free, she arced it and swept down hard to brain him. The man sprawled, lifeless.

Breathing hard, Coilla looked to Pepperdyne. He had bettered his own opponent, and was stooping to deliver the killing stroke. As he rose from slashing the Uni's throat, she caught his eye. She nodded her thanks, puzzled that he should side with her against one of his own kind.

"Look at that!"

Haskeer was pointing to a rider near the tree-line. The figure was unmistakably female. Her long blond hair flowed free, and she wore a metal breastplate that glinted in the feeble sunlight. She was mounted on a pure white horse that reared as, sword held high, she rallied her remaining followers.

"Mercy Hobrow," Coilla spat.

"You were right," Haskeer conceded.

"The bitch. Why don't you ever have a bow when you need one?"

As they watched, the woman wheeled her mount and headed into the trees.

The defenders at the vanguard, by the defensive trench, saw Hobrow too. Her supporters were retreating in her wake, the stragglers chased by angry dwarfs seeing them off with arrows and spears. All across the village clearing the last of the Unis were pulling back.

"More a last gasp than a second wave," Stryke reckoned, looking on.

Breggin nodded.

"Not much more we can do here. Round up the unit."

The private grunted and went off.

Stryke surveyed the carnage around him. The bodies of dozens of dwarfs were scattered about, and many more humans. They were outnumbered by the wounded, walking and prone, though he saw no orcs in the latter category. Or humans in either.

He made for the cluster of huts, his crew in tow.

The rest of the Wolverines were already gathering there.

"Anybody hurt?" Stryke called out.

"A few," Dallog replied. "Nothing too serious."

"Coilla? You all right?"

"This?" She waved her bandaged hand dismissively. "Just a sting."

"She ain't the only one stinging," Haskeer butted in.

"Meaning?" Stryke asked.

"Wheam."

Stryke sighed. "What about him?"

"Caught an arrow in his arse." He jabbed a thumb.

A small group was arriving. Several grunts carried Wheam, face-down on a plank, a bolt protruding from his rear. Standeven followed sullenly.

Haskeer was gleeful. "It gets better," he went on. "The arrow was one of our own."

Wheam's makeshift stretcher was brusquely dumped on the ground. He groaned loudly.

"Get him sorted," Stryke ordered.

Dallog knelt and began rummaging in his medical bag.

To one side, Coilla got Pepperdyne alone.

"Thanks," she said.

He nodded.

"You fight well."

The human smiled tightly.

"Where'd you pick up the skill?" she persisted.

He gave a cursory shrug. "Here and there."

"You're talking me to death again."

This time his fleeting smile had a speck of warmth in it. "It's a long story."

"I want to hear it."

"*Pepperdyne!*" Standeven was elbowing their way.

Pepperdyne's expression went back to pokerfaced.

"Your place is with me," the older man asserted.

"I know."

To Coilla, Pepperdyne's manner seemed almost subservient. "What is it with you two?" she asked.

"*Coilla!*" Stryke beckoned her over.

She gave the pair of humans a last, hard look and left them to it.

Stryke was with Jup and Spurral, and they were obviously troubled.

"What's up?" Coilla said.

"Our people have paid a high price for this," Spurral replied, indicating the detritus of battle.

"But they did well. Specially as you've so few veterans."

"We've even less now," Jup came back gloomily.

"There are casualties in a fight," Stryke told him. "You know that."

"The Wolverines haven't come out of this nearly so badly."

"We're born to combat, and we've got the skills. If we'd had losses we'd accept 'em."

"Most dwarfs don't have the orcs' attitude to these things."

"So I see," Coilla said, nodding.

They followed her gaze to a group of villagers standing in the clearing. They were looking the Wolverines' way and whispering amongst themselves. Others were drifting over to swell their ranks.

"This could get nasty," Stryke judged. "Jup, what do you think?"

"They're angry. It'd be as well to tread lightly 'til this blows over."

"Coilla?"

"I'm thinking of that old saying. You know, the one that goes, Trust in the gods, but tie up your horse."

Stryke eyed the growing crowd. "I'll go along with that. We'll do nothing to goad them. But we stay alert." He turned to Dallog. "Get Wheam on his feet."

"I'm not sure if he's—"

"He'll live. Just do it."

Dallog shrugged and beckoned a couple of grunts. "Give me a hand here," he instructed. "Hold him. *Tight.*"

He bent to his patient. Wheam began whimpering. Dallog swiftly plucked out the arrow, drawing a yell from the newbie. Then the corporal produced a flask of raw alcohol and sprinkled it liberally over the wound. Wheam howled. Dressing hastily applied, the grunts tersely hauled him to his feet, raising more yelps. Wheam was ashen. His grimace made him look like he'd sucked a bushel of lemons.

Giving off a disgruntled mutter, the throng of dwarfs had started to move towards the orcs. A number of them nursed wounds or hobbled. Many had their weapons drawn.

"To me!" Stryke ordered.

His band fell in beside him.

Out in front of the mob was a familiar face; the dwarf who harangued them in the glade when they first arrived in Quatt.

He marched up to the Wolverines, chest puffed, and holding aloft a short spear.

"Have you any idea what mayhem you've caused here?" he shouted.

"That was down to the Unis," Stryke replied evenly.

"And look how many of our people paid for it!"

"The orcs fought at our side, Krake," Jup reminded him. "We wouldn't have won otherwise."

"We wouldn't have had to fight at all if it weren't for them!"

There was a murmur of agreement from the crowd.

"That's not fair," Jup returned. "We should count ourselves lucky they stood with us."

"Trust you to take their part. All you've done is bring us trouble."

"Seems to me," Stryke said, "it was time you stood up to those humans."

"You think we *haven't*?" Krake was red faced. "What we don't do is go round provoking 'em!"

Again the mob backed him.

"You can't blame the orcs for that," Jup reckoned. "You know how crazy those Unis are. If it hadn't been the Wolverines it would have been something else."

"Backing outsiders again," the ringleader spat. "You're too fond of these ... *freaks*."

"Who you calling a freak?" Haskeer demanded indignantly.

Krake glared at him. "If the cap fits."

"I wouldn't push it with our sergeant," Coilla advised.

"Let's just be calm," Jup appealed.

"Traitor!" Krake seethed.

"Don't you call my Jup a traitor," Spurral waded in.

"Wotcha mean *freak*?" Haskeer repeated.

"It's what I'm looking at," Krake told him. He waved his spear in Haskeer's face.

The crowd was cheering him on.

"I wouldn't do that," Coilla warned.

"I don't take advice from grotesques," Krake informed her, "least of all a female." He laughed derisively. Most of the crowd joined in.

Haskeer snatched his spear, upended it deftly and plunged it into the dwarf's foot.

There was a crimson geyser. Krake shrieked. He hobbled a couple of steps before falling into the arms of his fellows. The crowd let out a collective gasp.

"Oh, great," Jup groaned.

The enraged mob surged forward, weapons raised, and the orcs primed themselves to meet them.

"I don't want you fighting our people, Stryke!" Spurral pleaded.

"No, we don't need this," Jup added, one eye on his advancing countrymen.

"Pull back, Wolverines!" Stryke barked. *"All* of you!"

The band withdrew. Soon they were clustering in front of a large wooden hut.

"In here!" Stryke bellowed, kicking open the door.

Everyone piled through. Furniture was dragged over to barricade the entrance, and the lone window was blocked. Outside, the roar of the mob grew louder.

Coilla glowered at Haskeer. "So much for not goading them!"

"The little shit asked for it. He was lucky I didn't—What are *they* doing here?" He thrust a finger at Pepperdyne and Standeven.

"They warned us, remember?"

"So what?"

"So there's not much we can do about it now, is there?"

"I could," Haskeer replied menacingly.

Stryke stepped between them. "You going to disobey another order?"

"I don't remember one about them."

"There is now: *leave it.* I'm no happier with humans around than you are, but we've more pressing worries."

A grunt jogged from the back of the building. "That's the only door, chief. No other way out."

Stryke looked up to the distant rafters. "We couldn't reach the roof either."

As soon as he said it, they heard the sound of movement overhead.

"But they can," Coilla said.

There was a battering at the door. It shook in its hinges. Several grunts rushed forward and threw their weight against the barricade.

"Can't fight, can't run," Haskeer grumbled. "What do we do, Stryke?"

"We'll try smashing our way through that back wall and—"

"Can you smell something?" Spurral exclaimed.

The hammering had stopped.

"*Shit.*" Coilla pointed towards the door. Thick black smoke was seeping through the cracks. "They've torched the place."

Smoke was coming in through some of the wall planks too, and it began to billow up above, over the rafters.

"They want us so badly they'd burn one of their own buildings?" Stryke said.

"They're pretty pissed off," Jup confirmed.

"*Now* what?" Haskeer wanted to know.

Stryke held out a hand. "Coilla, the star. You've got it?"

"Course. I check the damn thing every ten breaths." She dug it out and passed it to him.

He moved to a crude table and placed the instrumentality on it. Then he added the others from his belt pouch. He consulted the amulet about his neck then, brow taut with concentration, began slotting the stars together.

The smoke grew denser. Coughing broke out and eyes were stinging. Dallog was ripping up portions of cloth, dunking them in a water butt he'd found and passing them out to the grunts to cover their mouths with.

The ceiling was on fire. Sparks drifted and embers fell. The stink was acrid.

Still Stryke fiddled with the stars.

Everyone had gathered round him now, watching intently. Only Pepperdyne and Standeven, silent and forgotten, stood further back.

Stryke had just the final piece to fit in.

"I don't like this bit," Wheam snivelled.

"Oh, *shut up,*" Haskeer chided.

Stryke began easing the last star into place.

"Hold tight, everybody!" Coilla yelled.

Pepperdyne grabbed Standeven's wrist, dragging him closer to the scrum.

There was an implosion of non-light.

And the bottom fell out of the world.

13

Only tender sounds disturbed the calm. A tinkling brook flowed down a mild rocky incline to join a lazy river. The distant baas of sheep mingled with the soothing drone of honeybees.

Green fields and softly undulating meadows extended from the banks of the river. Trees in full blossom dotted the landscape. Gentle hillocks marked the horizon, crowned with leafy copses. High above, languid birds flapped across a perfectly blue sky.

The day was still and warm. All was bucolic tranquillity.

There was a subtle change in the quality of the air. At a point just above the ground it wavered, like heat over stone on a summer afternoon. Soon, a spot of dull milky radiance appeared, and grew. It became a vortex, spinning frantically, and coloured pinpoints swirled in the mix. The whirlpool birthed a breeze, which swiftly built to a wind. Then a gale. Grass bowed under its force, and plants and trees.

It climaxed in a blinding white flash that rivalled the noon-time sun.

The gaping maw of the churning radiance spewed out its load. A mass of shapes tumbled on to the sward.

Instantly, the wind vanished and the vortex snapped out of existence.

A sulphurous odour hung in the air.

Thirty and more figures were strewn along the riverbank. For some minutes none of them moved. Slowly, they began to rouse. A few groaned. Several vomited.

Stryke and Coilla were among the first to get to their feet.

"Gods, it's no easier the second time, is it?" Coilla said, shaking her muzzy head. She took in the scene. "You brought us home? To Ceragan?"

"No. Though it looks a lot like it. I set the stars for the place Serapheim told us about."

"This is supposed to be a land oppressed, is it? And there are orcs here?"

He scanned the landscape. "Somewhere."

"If we've wound up where we're supposed to."

"That we'll find out." Stryke realised he was still clutching the assemblage of stars. He plucked one free and offered it to her. It was green, with five spikes. "Are you still willing to—?"

"Sure." She took it. "It's not the same one. The one I had was blue and it only had four—"

"Does it matter?" He was pulling the others apart and putting them in his pouch.

"No, course not. I'm being stupid. Still dazed from getting here. Wherever *here* is."

Jup and Spurral joined them. They were pale, and looked mildly shocked.

"That's a hell of a way to travel," Jup said.

"Where *are* we?" Spurral asked.

"Don't know," Stryke told her. "But it's where our mission is."

Haskeer had been haranguing the band. Now he strode over.

"Everybody all right?" Stryke wanted to know.

"More or less. No thanks to his lot." He glowered at Jup.

"My people were out of order," Jup conceded. "But they felt they had cause."

"*Cause?* That's one word for it."

"What are you saying?"

"You dwarfs know which way the wind blows."

"Meaning?"

"What happened back there, turning on us, you're well known for that."

"Oh, that old song again."

"And it's got a name." Haskeer leaned and put his face close to Jup's. "*Treachery.*"

Jup made an effort to keep his temper in check. "Some of my folk...*some*...escaped the poverty we've been pushed into by working as soldiers of fortune. You could say I did myself, when I joined Jennesta's horde. The same army you served in."

"You had a choice. We didn't. *Pisspot.*" He drove his forefinger hard into the dwarf's chest.

"You want to settle this?" Jup flared, balling his fists.

"Jup, please!" Spurral begged. "This is no time to—"

"Whenever you're ready," Haskeer growled. He raised his own ham-like knuckles.

Stryke barged in and flung them apart. "*Cut it out!*" he roared. "We're a disciplined band, not a rabble!"

"He started it," Jup mumbled.

"That's *enough*! I won't have disorder, and I'll back that with a whipping if I have to!"

Unable to meet his gaze, Haskeer and Jup resumed glaring at each other.

"Just like old times, eh?" Coilla observed, breaking the impasse. "Your memory's short, Haskeer. When did Jup ever let us down? And Spurral fought righteously today."

"Well, that's fine, ain't it?" Haskeer replied with a hint of mockery. "And now you've got another female to play with."

"Yeah, we can press flowers together."

Spurral stifled a grin.

"Waifs and strays," Haskeer muttered disgustedly. "Bloody circus."

"*Haskeer,*" Stryke intoned menacingly.

"All right, all right. But what about them?" He pointed along the riverbank, to Pepperdyne and Standeven. "If they're not deadweight then I don't know —"

"The younger one helped me out of a tight fix," Coilla reminded him.

"Ask yourself why," Haskeer came back. "What're they after?"

"You're right," Stryke agreed. "For once. I want some answers from those two before we move on."

"About time." Haskeer started to move.

"Not you, Sergeant. You posted guards? Sent out scouts? No. Do it. *Now.*"

Haskeer departed, grumbling.

"Is it always like this in the band?" Spurral asked.

"Just about," Coilla replied.

"Particularly when Haskeer's got a wasp up his backside about something," Jup added.

"I don't want to tackle those two mob-handed and make this look like a grilling," Stryke decided. "They're bound to clam up."

"We could beat it out of 'em," Jup suggested, half seriously.

"I will if I have to. But they get a chance to talk first. We owe them that much for the warning, and for aiding Coilla. So help out with the band, Jup. And stay away from Haskeer. Hear me?"

Jup nodded and left. Spurral went with him.

"What about me?" Coilla said.

"We'll see the humans together. You get on with them."

"*Whoa.* I don't count humans as friends."

He turned without answering and headed along the riverbank. She followed.

The band was recovering. Those who didn't have a chance

earlier were cleaning the gore from their blades. Others were having wounds tended. Haskeer was working off his temper by barking orders.

They found the two men by the water's edge. Pepperdyne stood looking down at Standeven, who sat on the grass, clutching his knees to his chest. He was sweaty and trembling.

"What's the matter with him?" Stryke said.

"You might have noticed that getting here was quite a ride," Pepperdyne replied.

"You seem all right."

He shrugged. "Where the hell are we?"

"We're asking the questions. Who are you?"

"Like I said. I'm Jode Pepperdyne and—"

"I mean *what* are you."

"Merchants," Standeven said, a little too quickly. He glanced up at them and shuddered. "That was hellish. I never believed them. I never thought it was true."

"What you talking about?"

"Those...objects that got us here."

"So you knew about them? Before you came to us, I mean."

The pair of humans exchanged the briefest of glances.

It was Pepperdyne who answered. "There've been rumours about instrumentalities for as long as I can remember."

"We knew no such stories," Stryke said. "Not until recently."

"You hear all sorts of tales in our business. Including things outsiders aren't privy to."

"You say you're merchants."

"Yes," Standeven replied. "That is, I am. He's my aide."

"He fights pretty well for a merchant's lackey," Coilla remarked.

"His duties include guarding me. You attract the attention of brigands in our line of work."

She addressed Pepperdyne directly. "You didn't pick up your skills from traders."

"I've been around," he told her.

"Military service?"

"Some."

"You Manis?" Stryke wanted to know.

Standeven looked surprised. "What?"

"You tipped us off about them Unis."

"No, we're not. Not all humans support religious factions. Besides, we're not from Centrasia. Things are different in our part of the world."

Coilla bridled. "It's called *Maras-Dantia*. Centrasia's the name foisted on us by you outsiders."

Pepperdyne spoke for his flustered master. "Sorry," he offered.

"I don't get it," Stryke said, frowning. "You're not Manis, yet you helped us against other humans. Why?"

"You're after something, aren't you?" Coilla added.

"Yes," Pepperdyne admitted.

Standeven looked shocked, and opened his mouth to speak.

Pepperdyne got in first. "We need your help."

Stryke stared hard at him. "Explain."

"We didn't warn you because those Unis were our enemies. We warned you because of someone who is. Your enemy and ours."

"That's clear as mud."

"The sorcerer queen," Pepperdyne said. "Jennesta."

A cold chill took hold of Stryke's spine, and he knew Coilla felt the same way. "What the hell are you talking about?"

"She owes us. And we heard she's in debt to you too, in a manner of speaking."

"What do you know about Jennesta? Be plain, or this ends here and now. The hard way." Stryke's expression left no doubt as to what he meant.

"My employer here lost a valuable consignment. It turned out to be her doing."

"What was it?"

"Gems. Along with not a few good men. Including some of my master's kin."

"This happened where?"

"On the edge of the wastelands. That's what we call it anyway. The wilderness separating the wider world from Cen—... from Maras-Dantia."

"So you went to Maras-Dantia yourselves."

"To seek recompense, yes."

Coilla was sceptical. "Just the two of you? And only one with the guts for a fight?" She glanced at Standeven.

"We weren't alone. We had a group of fighters with us. But when we got here... *there*, rather, we found the place in chaos. Unis ambushed us and most of our men were killed. Some of us were caught and held for a while. That's how we knew about the attack, and where we learnt your story."

"The Unis told you about us?"

"Yes. Didn't you know the Wolverines are a legend in those parts? Anyway, we escaped and—"

"How?" Stryke said.

Pepperdyne shrugged glibly. "Nothing very heroic. They were more interested in attacking you and the dwarfs. We were lightly guarded."

"And you thought that by helping us..."

"We hoped you'd aid us in exacting revenge on Jennesta."

"Jennesta's thought dead. Didn't the Unis tell you that?"

"They said she hadn't been seen for quite a while. That's not the same, is it? Unless you know different."

Stryke and Coilla stayed tight-lipped.

"So you reckoned we'd be so grateful that we'd join your little mission," Stryke summed up.

"Something like that."

"And if gratitude wasn't enough?"

"A reward, maybe. If the gems were recovered, my master would be willing to share them with you."

"We kill what we eat and take what we need. We've no use for riches."

"Where does that leave us?" Standeven asked uneasily.

"Where you're not wanted."

"What do you intend doing?" Pepperdyne said.

"I'll think on it," Stryke replied. "Stay out of the band's way. I'll deal with you later."

He turned on his heel and strode away, Coilla in tow.

When they were out of earshot, she remarked wryly, "So, how does it feel to be a legend?"

"Did you believe any of that?"

"I don't know. Maybe."

"Sounded like horse shit to me."

"Notice how the servant had more to say than the master? That's the most I've ever heard him say."

"Perhaps he's the better liar. And I think it was a slip when they said they knew about the stars. We didn't ourselves until a few years ago."

"There might be no mystery in that. We lived closed-off lives when we were in the horde. A lot was kept from us."

"That didn't stop us picking up hearsay. I don't buy it. And why would Jennesta hijack shipments of jewels? She had whatever she wanted nearer to home."

"I don't know; I wouldn't put anything past her. But, Stryke... I owe Pepperdyne. I might not be here if he hadn't—"

"I know. And they did warn us about the attack, whatever their motive. That's why I didn't just have their throats cut and done with it."

"Would you?"

"If I thought they were set on betrayal, sure I would."

"But they *could* be telling the truth. What do we do about them?"

"Dump 'em as soon as we can."

They came to where Dallog had planted the band's standard.

It fluttered feebly in the light wind. The corporal was busying himself with the wounded, though he still seemed queasy after the transference.

Wheam looked a lot worse. He lay on his side, presumably to avoid putting weight on his earlier injury. Propped on one elbow, he stared into a wooden bowl he'd been filling.

Dallog rose when he saw Stryke and Coilla.

He indicated the landscape with a sweep of his hand and said, "You know, this could be Ceragan."

"We've done that," Coilla informed him.

Pepperdyne and Standeven watched Coilla and Stryke go.

When they were far enough away, Standeven's expression hardened. "What were you hoping to achieve with that bullshit you just fed them?"

"Only saving our lives, that's all. And giving them a reason for letting us stick around."

"But shipments of gems? And this Jennesta woman, who we've only heard about in tall tales? You're digging us in deeper here."

"They can't disprove any of it."

"The thing about lies is that you have to build other lies to support them. Believe me, I know."

"As you're such an expert on the subject it shouldn't be too hard for you to keep up, should it?"

"Tall tales need to be thought through. They have to be plausible. When we overheard those Unis planning the attack, when we hid there listening, we should have formulated a plan. A watertight lie."

"We didn't have the time; we had to grab the opportunity. We knew these orcs were rumoured to have the instrumentalities. Now we're sure."

"Oh, yes, we're sure now," Standeven replied, the trauma of the crossing etched on his face. "But what good does it do us?"

"Do you want those artefacts or not?"

"Do I need them now?"

Pepperdyne gave an exasperated sigh. "You've been slavering at the prospect of getting your hands on them! If you've bent my ears once about their value, you've done it a hundred times."

"Watch your tongue!" Standeven retorted, haughtily puffing himself up. "Remember who's master here."

"Or you'll do what? Circumstances have changed. It's about survival now."

Standeven seethed, but didn't push the issue.

"I'll tell you why you need the instrumentalities," Pepperdyne said. "Kantor Hammrik. He'll never give up until he's found you, and they're the only thing you can barter with."

"How could he find us here?"

"I intend getting back. Don't you? And it's my neck as well as yours."

"I still don't think—"

"I can't fight our way out of this like I did with Hammrik's escort. It'd be insane to square up to an orc warband. We have to use stealth, and bide our time. Or do you have a better idea?"

If Standeven had an answer there was no chance to give it. A clamour broke out further along the riverbank, where most of the band was concentrated. Two of the scouts were back, and they had someone with them.

"Let's see what's happening," Pepperdyne said.

Standeven held out a hand. Pepperdyne hoisted him to his feet.

As they approached, they saw that the scouts had brought back another orc. He looked mature, perhaps old, as far as the humans could tell. His garb consisted of a sleeveless lambskin jerkin, baggy cloth trews and stout leather ankle boots. He was nearly as tall as the wooden crook he carried, which he used to help him walk.

They took him to Stryke. The prisoner's anxious eyes darted from face to face as the band gathered round.

"We're not going to hurt you," Stryke assured him. "Understand?"

The shepherd nodded.

"What's your name?"

"Yelbra." He spoke hesitantly.

"Are you alone out here?"

He nodded again.

"We didn't see anybody else," one of the scouts confirmed.

"Where's the nearest town, Yelbra?" Stryke asked.

The shepherd ignored him. He was staring at Jup and Spurral. "What are . . . *they*?" he exclaimed, pointing at them.

"You've not seen dwarfs before?"

He shook his head, much more vigorously than he'd nodded.

"They're with us. Don't worry about them, they won't harm you. The nearest town?"

"You don't know?" he said, his confusion mounting.

"We wouldn't have asked otherwise," Haskeer rumbled.

"It's—" His attention had shifted again, and his eyes widened. He let out something between a gasp and a groan.

The cause of his alarm was Standeven and Pepperdyne, who were pushing their way through the crowd.

Visibly shaking, Yelbra sank to his arthritic knees and uttered, "*Masters*." His manner was one of complete obeisance.

"What the *fuck's* going on?" Haskeer wanted to know.

The shepherd gazed up at him with something close to terror distorting his features. "*Get down*," he hissed. "Show respect!"

"To *them*?" Haskeer sneered. "*Humans*? They can kiss my scaly arse!"

Yelbra seemed profoundly shocked. His mouth hung open and all trace of colour left his face.

"Since when did orcs prostrate themselves in front of humans?" Coilla said.

The shepherd looked as though the question made no sense to him.

"Serapheim said humans had the upper hand here," Stryke reflected. "Seems he was right. Get up," he told Yelbra.

He stayed where he was, eyes fixed on Pepperdyne and Standeven.

Stryke nodded at the scouts. They heaved the shepherd to a standing position. He clutched his crook as if it was all that kept him upright.

"I'm asking the questions," Stryke reminded him in a harsher tone, "not them. What's the name of this land?"

Still he remained under the spell of the humans, staring their way and trembling. He said nothing.

Stryke beckoned Pepperdyne. "Here."

The human hesitated for a second, then came forward.

"You ask him," Stryke said.

"Me?"

"He's more in thrall of you two than us. Do it."

A little awkwardly, Pepperdyne cleared his throat. "Er, Yelbra. What's this land called?"

Even with his head bent to avoid Pepperdyne's gaze, it was apparent he was taken aback at them not knowing. "If it pleases you, master; Acurial."

"It does please me. But I'm not your master. Do you hear me?"

The shepherd shot him a glance suffused with bewilderment, and a hint of what might have been pity for someone self-evidently insane. "Yes, mas—Yes, I hear you."

"Good. What's the name of the nearest settlement?"

"Taress."

147

"And there are orcs there?"

"Of course. Many."

"Where is it? How far?"

"Due south. On foot, it can be reached by sundown."

"Thank you, Yelbra." Pepperdyne looked to Stryke, and was about to step back when the shepherd spoke again.

"Begging your pardon, my...You pardon, but I'm at a loss to understand why you don't know these things. Is it a test?"

"No. We're...from a far country."

"It must be *very* far from here."

"More than you can guess," Stryke put in. He waved Pepperdyne away. "I meant what I said, Yelbra; we won't harm you. But I want your word that you'll tell nobody about seeing us. Or do you need to hear that from him, too?" He jabbed a thumb Pepperdyne's way.

"No one would believe me if I told this story. Anyway, I see few others out here. Tending sheep is a solitary business."

"What kind of job is that for an orc?" Haskeer said with contempt.

Once more the question seemed irrelevant to the shepherd. In any event something else had caught his eye. "You bear arms," he whispered, as though noticing for the first time. There was wonder and fear in his voice.

"That's unusual in these parts?" Coilla asked.

"You are indeed from a distant land. It's forbidden by law."

"We've spent enough time here," Stryke decided, turning away from Yelbra.

Clear of the others he went into a huddle with his officers.

"We'll get ourselves over to this Taress," he told them. "And it looks like we'd do well to conceal our weapons."

"Are we all going?" Coilla said. "What about a base camp?"

"Not this time. If we have to use the stars again in a hurry I want us all together."

Jup glanced over at the humans. "How do we deal with them?"

"They'd better come along. From what we've just seen they might be the only way anyone's going to talk to us."

"I don't like it," Haskeer grumbled.

"Me neither. But we can be rid of them as soon as they stop being an asset. Now get the band organised for a march."

As they scattered to their duties, the shepherd called out to them.

"What about me? I've my animals to tend to."

"You can go," Stryke shouted back.

"Yeah," Coilla added. "Get the flock out of here."

14

In sharp contrast to the ruined land of Maras-Dantia, Acurial was fair.

Its jade-coloured fields and lush pastures washed against the rims of dense forests. The streams ran crystal clear. An abundance of wildlife roamed the woods, and smaller creatures burrowed in the undergrowth. Birds of many hues wheeled in the cloudless skies.

The river flowed southward, so the Wolverines marched beside it for several hours. When it curved to the west, they found a trail running in the direction they sought, and took that. They met no other travellers.

As the day lengthened the earlier warmth began to abate.

Stryke was at the head of the column, with Jup at his side.

The dwarf looked back at the band. "They're starting to flag a bit. Can we spare time for a break? They haven't eaten properly since yesterday, and that was a world away."

Stryke nodded. "But we'll keep it short, and no fires. And we eat the rations we're carrying; I don't want anybody off hunting."

The band left the trail and made for a stand of trees. Lookouts were posted, and hardtack and water was distributed.

When everyone had eaten their fill, Stryke allowed them a brief rest. Perched on fallen tree trunks, some of the band reflected on how Acurial differed from the world they recently left.

"Compared to this place," Jup was saying, "Maras-Dantia's completely bust. Failing harvests, barren livestock, fouled rivers; you know the score."

"Yet there are humans in Acurial too," Coilla replied, "and they don't seem to have screwed things up here."

More than one pair of stern eyes turned to Standeven and Pepperdyne.

"So far," Jup amended. "We don't know how long they've been here. It took them a generation or more to devastate Maras-Dantia, and maybe longer before the magic started to bleed away."

"I wonder if magic works in this world," Coilla mused.

"That hadn't occurred to me. But...why shouldn't it? Unless Maras-Dantia was special in some way, maybe all worlds have magic. Or at least the energy to make it work."

"Find out," Stryke suggested. "Your skill could be useful to us."

"All right." Jup got to his feet and surveyed the area. "I'll try over there."

As everyone watched, he set off for a gully thirty or forty paces away. A small stream trickled along it, and it was shaded by a couple of mature trees. Jup took out a knife and squatted by the stream. He gouged a hole in the earth, and when he judged it deep enough, wormed his hand into it.

"What's he doing?" Wheam asked.

"Magic shows itself in different ways for different races," Stryke explained. "With dwarfs, it's farsight."

Wheam was puzzled. "Farsight?"

"Being able to sense things beyond what can be picked up with eyes or ears."

"Which is handy for tracking," Coilla added.

"There's energy in the earth that governs the magic," Stryke said. "It's most powerful near water. I don't know why. But dwarfs with farsight can feel the energy's strength, and how it flows."

"How does magic show itself with orcs?" Pepperdyne said.

"It doesn't. We've no command of magic, and neither do humans."

"So if this world has only orcs and humans, nobody practises magic?"

"Right." Stryke didn't mention the likes of Serapheim, who was an exception among humans anyway. Or the possibility that Jennesta was in this world. He saw no reason to tell Pepperdyne and his master any more than he had to.

Jup came back, slapping the dirt from his hands. "I was right. There's energy here, and it's strong. Pure. I'd say there's a big concentration of it not far away, and the flow's southward."

"Taress?" Stryke wondered.

"Suppose it must be."

"We should be moving then."

Wheam popped up. Somehow his beloved lute had survived intact, and he brandished it. "Time for a song before we go? To put a spring in our step?" He saw their expressions. "A tune then? A rousing air to send us on our—"

"If you do," Haskeer told him, "I'll kill you."

"*On your feet, Wolverines!*" Stryke barked. "*We're marching!*"

The old shepherd was right about them arriving at sundown.

Standing on the crest of a steep hill, the band looked down at the settlement. They were surprised at how big it was. The fringes of the city consisted of acres of dwellings, shot through with alleys, lanes and crooked streets. Nearer the centre there were taller structures, with a dotting of towers and spires, and what could have been fortifications. Although it was dusk, few lights were visible.

Weapons concealed, they began their descent.

They arrived at the outskirts without seeing anyone, and came to a wide cobbled road leading into the city. Halfway along its length stood the first houses. They looked shabby, and there was no sign of the inhabitants.

"Orcs live here?" Coilla said.

"It looks as though nobody lives here," Stryke replied.

They entered the maze of streets. Every door was closed, all windows were shuttered. There were no lights.

"Where is everybody?" Spurral wondered.

Jup pointed. "Here's somebody."

On the opposite side of the road, a lone figure was sprinting in their direction.

"Get out of sight, all of you," Stryke ordered.

The band quickly retreated into the shadowy mouth of an adjacent alley.

As the running figure drew level, Stryke saw that it was a young orc, wrapped in a grey cloak.

"What's going on?" he shouted over to him.

The orc slowed and looked Stryke's way. He was obviously puzzled. "What do you mean?"

"Where is everybody?"

"Don't you know what hour it is?"

"What's that got to do with—"

"It's almost *dark*! Get off the streets! They'll be here soon!"

"Who?"

The orc didn't answer. He ran on and disappeared round a corner.

Coilla emerged from the alley. "What the hell was that all about?"

"Perhaps we found the only crazy orc in town," Jup ventured.

"What now?" Haskeer wanted to know.

"We push on," Stryke decided, "and keep alert."

They moved deeper into the silent, deserted metropolis. In street after street it was the same story; bolted doors, barred windows and unlit dwellings. They didn't encounter so much as a stray dog or prowling cat.

At length they came to a public square, bordered by houses on all sides and fed by a street at each corner. In its centre was a large patch of muddy grass, and in the middle of that was a tall wooden structure.

"Do you see what that is?" Coilla said.

Stryke blinked in the gloom. "No, what?"

"It's a gallows."

"So they go in for public executions here."

"Yeah, but of who?"

"Stryke," Haskeer said, looking restless, "what's our aim? Where we heading?"

"I don't know. I didn't expect a ghost town."

"Great. So we've gone into this half-arsed."

"Think you could have done better?"

"I'd at least have a plan."

"Gods protect us from any plan of yours."

"I wouldn't have us wandering like tits in a trance."

"Hold your tongue, Sergeant. Unless you want me to take that helmet and shove it up—"

Coilla put a finger to her lips. *"Sssshh!"*

"Stay out of this, Corporal."

"No! I mean *listen*."

Everyone froze.

Although a way off, the sound was unmistakable, and it was swiftly growing louder.

"Marching," Jup whispered.

"Where's it coming from?" Stryke said.

"Can't tell."

The sound was swelling, and close to hand.

"Take cover!" Stryke ordered.

The band began to move

None of them got more than ten paces before a group of humans entered the square at the next turning. They were about forty in number, and wore uniforms that in the half light could have been black or dark blue. All were heavily armed, and perhaps a third of them held shaded lanterns

At their head was the unit's commander, and it was he who bellowed, *"Halt!"*

His troop spread out to either side of him as they advanced, so that they approached almost in a line.

The Wolverines stopped in their tracks and looked to Stryke.

He knew they might have made a run for it, but he didn't want to risk scattering the band. In any event, running wasn't their way. He signalled for them to stay put.

He caught a glance from Coilla and mouthed, "Maybe we can bluff our way out of this."

She raised a sceptical eyebrow.

The human commander was short and thickset. He had a bushy black moustache that perched beneath his nostrils and didn't reach either end of his sneer. His raven hair was longish and slicked back.

When the line of humans were close enough to spit at, he barked an order and they halted. The commander himself continued walking, and two subordinates dogged him, one on each side, a pace or two to his rear. There was a practised air to the manoeuvre, an exhibition of military precision that was almost comical.

The trio stopped when they came to Stryke, Haskeer and Coilla, who were foremost.

"What the hell do you think you're doing?" the commander thundered.

"Just taking the air," Stryke replied, feigning innocence.

"*Just . . . taking . . . the . . . air,*" the human repeated, his tone pure mockery. "And the curfew be damned, is that it?"

"Didn't know there was one."

The commander's face reddened. "Are you trying to—" He checked himself and stared past Stryke at Jup and Spurral. "What are *they*?"

"Not again," Jup sighed under his breath.

Shoving forward for a better look, the commander caught sight of Pepperdyne and Standeven at the back of the crowd. His confusion doubled. "Are you these creatures' prisoners?"

"No," Pepperdyne told him, "we're together."

"*Together?* You're fraternising with the natives?"

"What'd you mean, natives?" Haskeer objected.

"We've got a troupe of jesters here," the commander declared, loud enough for his men to hear. "A company of fools. But we'll see who has the last laugh."

"Doubt it'll be you," Coilla said.

He turned to her. "What did you say?"

"Won't be you laughing."

"Is that so?"

"Sure. You need a heartbeat for that."

"Which I have."

"Not for long."

"Are you *threatening* me?" He seemed to find the notion amusing.

"Call it . . . a prediction."

"Well, here's a prediction of mine. You freaks are about to pay the price for disrespecting your betters."

Coilla smiled. "Bring it on."

He clutched a pair of studded leather gloves. Seething with fury, he cracked her savagely across the face with them.

The band tensed.

Coilla lifted a hand to her cheek. Blood was trickling from the corner of her mouth. She spat it out, narrowly missing the commander's shiny boots. Staring into his eyes, she announced evenly, "He's mine."

The commander laughed. "Oh, really. And since when did your kind have the guts to stand up to a superior?"

"How about since now?" she informed him pleasantly.

Quick as thought she delivered a mighty kick to his crotch. He let out an agonised yelp and doubled. She sprang forward and grabbed him by the ears. Pulling his head down, she pounded his face against her upraised knee a couple of times. There was a satisfying crunch of cartilage.

As she let him drop, Stryke and Haskeer whipped out their blades. Haskeer rammed his sword deep into the chest of one lieutenant. Stryke buried twin daggers into the flanks of the other.

It all happened so fast that the rest of the humans were too stupefied to act. Many wore expressions of shocked disbelief.

Then someone yelled, *"Terrorists!"* and mayhem broke out.

Weapons drawn, the mob of Wolverines and the line of humans rushed at each other. In the middle of the square they melded, then spiralled into a score of fights.

Though outnumbered, the more so as Standeven and Wheam effectively counted as non-combatants, the orcs made up the deficiency by battling with their habitual ferocity. And at first, they had another edge: the humans seemed stunned that orcs would fight at all.

There was a terrible harmony in the way the warband worked together. They hacked, cleaved, slashed and battered their way through obstructing flesh. If there was finesse, Pepperdyne was its only practitioner.

In this, his fighting style was nearer the humans. Where orcs pummelled, he engaged. Though whether employing savagery or swordsmanship the upshot was the same. Soon the cobblestones ran red and slippery. Of the human company's original number, only a third were still on their feet. The Wolverines had taken minor wounds, but no fatalities.

"We've got 'em licked!" Haskeer bragged.

"Don't crow too soon," Stryke told him. "Look."

More uniformed men were running into the square from the streets on its far side. There were at least twice as many as in the unit the orcs were fighting.

Haskeer was contemptuous. "Since when did we worry about odds?"

"They could be the van of a lot more."

"So what do we do?"

"Kill 'em," Stryke hissed.

"Why didn't you just say that in the first place?" He turned and swiped at an encroaching human, cleaving his ribs.

Fighting alongside Jup and Spurral, Coilla spotted the newcomers too. "They've got back-up!" she yelled.

Jup shattered a skull with his staff. "I see 'em. Never a dull moment with this band." He spun to break a foe's arm, before toppling him into Spurral's path, who deftly finished the job with twin knife thrusts.

Coilla admired their teamwork.

"Maybe we shouldn't have taken on this lot," Spurral said.

"And missed a scrap?" Coilla replied. "We don't think like that."

But she could see that the humans were taking heart from the reinforcements and fighting harder.

And then a fresh element was added.

As though obeying an unheard signal, the humans fighting the orcs began to disengage and pull back. They left their dead and dying where they fell.

Jup punched air. "They're retreating!"

"I wouldn't count on it," Coilla said.

As the humans hastily withdrew they moved aside, giving a clear view of the new contingent. At their head stood three figures dressed differently to all the others. They wore what appeared to be robes, and they were hooded.

Where there had been the cacophony of battle, there was now a deathly silence. The Wolverines held their ground, looking on.

"Are they priests or what?" Haskeer wondered.

Stryke shrugged.

"Whatever the fuck they are, what are we waiting for?"

"Steady. Something's going on."

The three hooded figures pulled objects from their robes. It was difficult to tell what they were from a distance, but they resembled small metal tridents the size of long daggers.

"What the hell they doing?" Haskeer said.

"Don't know. But I don't like it."

The trio raised the tridents and pointed them in the orcs' direction.

Stryke bellowed, *"Everybody down!"*

There was a blinding flash of light. The tridents spewed intense shafts of red, green and yellow iridescence.

The band hit the ground a split second before the crackling beams of energy streaked above their heads. Two struck buildings behind the prone warband, demolishing a heavy door and punching a hole in a wall. Bricks and mortar rained down. The third bolt impacted the corner of the gallows, instantly igniting it.

A second volley had Wolverines rolling in the dirt to avoid the searing beams. The shafts raked the ground like small lightning strikes, dislodging cobblestones and throwing up sparks.

Stryke lifted his head and looked around. He saw Hystykk and Jad stretched out nearby. Both had bows. Hugging the ground, he slithered over to them.

"Bring those bastards down!" he ordered.

Awkwardly, the grunts wriggled the bows from their backs. They quickly nocked arrows and took aim at the robed figures.

An arrow zinged into the chest of one of the trident bearers. He staggered and fell.

"Eh?" Hystykk muttered.

He hadn't loosed his arrow. Neither had Jad.

Arrows peppered the other two robed figures. One unleashed a glaring energy bolt as he fell. It lanced straight up, illuminating the sky. Then died.

There was a roar.

Another mob swept into the square. They outnumbered the humans, and rushed to attack them.

Stryke clambered to his feet.

Coilla ran to him. "They're orcs!"

"What the *fuck's* going on?" Haskeer exclaimed.

Stryke shook his head. "Pull back the band. Get 'em into a defensive pattern."

Obeying yelled orders, the Wolverines quickly came together.

Ahead, a bloody melee raged. A group of five or six orcs peeled off from it and raced their way.

The one leading them shouted, "Who's in charge?"

"Me," Stryke told him.

"Come with us." He saw the humans and dwarfs. "Prisoners?"

"No, we're together."

The orc was taken aback. "You're kidding."

"They're with us," Stryke repeated.

"We can't take humans," one of the other orcs protested. He glared in turn at Standeven and Pepperdyne, and at the dwarfs.

"We'll sort this out later," the leader decided. "Let's move!"

"Where?" Stryke asked.

"More of them are on the way. Stay and you'll die."

"Who *are* you?"

"Come on!" He began to move off.

Stryke hesitated for a second, then signalled the band to follow.

As they ran into the darkened streets, Coilla said, "Stryke, those humans used magic!"

15

If the structures rulers occupy reflect their regard for the ruled, then the fortress that stood at Taress' heart spoke volumes.

Its entryways were heavily guarded and its gates were locked. Archers walked its ramparts. Lookouts were positioned on its towers, and a garrison was permanently stationed within its grim, impenetrable walls.

It was a measure of the castle's reputation, or more accurately the nature of its inhabitants, that few entered willingly.

An entire level at one of its highest points was the exclusive province of a single individual. Given his status, it would be reasonable to assume that the chambers were well appointed, if not actually luxurious. But they were sparse. Furnishings were minimal, there was little in the way of embellishment and nothing of comfort. In this, the apartment reflected the disposition of someone who had given his life to military service. To the subjugated, Kapple Hacher was commonly known as Iron Hand.

Yet his appearance and manner were at odds with the epithet. He was of advancing years; not yet old, but in the later stages of maturity. His close-cropped hair was silver, and those who didn't know him assumed that was the reason he was beardless. But he displayed no trace of vanity. He had the physique of a much younger man, for all that his face was lined and the backs of his hands were liver-spotted. His bearing was javelin straight, and he wore his immaculate uniform as though born in it. Overall, the impression was of a somewhat meticulous, kindly uncle. At least, that was the impression he gave to other humans.

For someone in such a position of authority he seemed to wear his responsibilities lightly. And the power he exercised was great. Hacher was both governor of what its conquerors regarded as a province, and commander of an occupying army. In the latter capacity he held the rank of general.

He was dining. As was his custom, he ate alone. He fed sparingly, and the fare was plain; fowl, bread and fruit. Wine was something he rarely drank, and when he did, it was watered. Which made him doubly unpopular with his poison tasters.

He was served by a pair of ageing orc females. They placed the food, such as it was, on a well-scrubbed table that constituted the main item of furniture, and performed their duties in silence. For all the attention Hacher paid to them, they could have been invisible.

There was a knock at the door.

"Come!" Hacher responded crisply.

Two humans entered, one in a dark blue military uniform, the other in a brown robe with the cowl down. Both men were half the general's age.

"Begging your pardon, sir," the uniformed aide said, "but we have news of—"

Hacher raised a hand to pause him, then dismissed the servants with a nod. They went out with heads bowed, the visitors looking on disdainfully.

"You were saying, Frynt?" Hacher laid down the knife he was eating with.

"There's been another disturbance. And during curfew."

"Casualties?"

"We're still counting, but significant."

"Including three members of the Order," the robed one added, shooting Frynt a hard look.

"That's unfortunate, Grentor," Hacher commiserated. "The state recognises their noble sacrifice, and they'll be honoured for it."

"Tributes are all very well. We would prefer adequate protection from the military. We have a right to expect that much."

"Given your brothers' magical expertise, I would have thought they were quite capable of defending themselves."

"I do hope you're not implying any criticism of my order's competence, General."

"Far from it. I'm the first to acknowledge that their contribution is invaluable."

Frynt glared at Grentor. "They *were* afforded protection. The number of casualties we took confirms that."

"Yet my brothers accompanying the patrol were slain."

"You lost three. Our fatalities were much higher."

"What of the losses we inflicted on them, Frynt?" Hacher intervened to ask.

"We killed a few, sir, and took half a dozen prisoners."

"You see, Grentor? The balance wasn't entirely in their favour."

"And that's supposed to be some kind of consolation, is it? What are the lives of those beasts compared to men's?"

"Every rebel we eliminate is one less. A step nearer purging Acurial of this... difficulty."

"But it's a situation that shouldn't have arisen at all!"

"Let's keep things in perspective. The vast majority of orcs are placid, you know that. How much resistance did they put up when we conquered this land? The present trouble is being caused by a small minority. A bunch of throwbacks, no more."

"And if these *throwbacks* should gain a hold on the rest of the populace? Fevers have a way of growing into a pestilence, General."

"This is one contagion they won't fall prey to. It's not in their nature."

"They have a rallying point; this Sylandya, their so-called Primary. She should never have been allowed to slip through our fingers."

"No one's rallying to her. She could be dead for all we know. You're aggrieved at the loss of your brothers, Grentor. I understand that. But it's vital that our military and magical forces work in harmony."

"So what do you propose doing?"

"More of a presence on the streets, a further drive to recruit informers, stricter punishments for those fraternising with the dissidents. And increased surveillance. The Order can be of great assistance in that respect, Grentor. If this nut requires a sledgehammer to crack, so be it. As for Sylandya, we'll step up efforts to find her or confirm her fate."

"Your words are reassuring, General."

"I'm glad you approve."

"Approval depends on outcomes, not intentions. The Order will judge your measures on their results."

"Naturally." Hacher rose. "Now if you'll excuse me, Brother Grentor, you'll appreciate that I have a great deal to discuss with my aide."

Grentor glanced at Frynt. There was no warmth in either's gaze. "Of course." He gave an almost imperceptible nod, turned and left.

Frynt closed the door behind him and let out a weary sigh.

"I know," Hacher sympathised, a faint smile playing on his lips. "Our sorcerer confederates can be a trial at times."

"Anyone would think they bore the brunt of these disturbances rather than us."

"Quite. But I meant what I said about better cooperation between the services. We need everybody working together to be rid of incidents like tonight's."

"Yes, sir. Talking of which, do you have any special instructions concerning this new batch of prisoners?"

"You know my philosophy, Frynt. We must leave the world a better place than we found it. Execute them. After extracting whatever intelligence they possess under torture, of course."

"Sir. And you'll be issuing fresh orders pertinent to the tightening up of security?"

"I will." He massaged the bridge of his nose with thumb and forefinger. "In the morning."

"I think you might have impressed Grentor with these new measures," the aide ventured. "You don't normally concede so willingly to his demands, if I may say so, sir."

"It wasn't entirely to placate Grentor and the Order."

"Sir?"

"It's a bad time for all of this to flare up again." His tone had grown sober. "Keep it to yourself, but I've been informed to expect a visit from a higher authority."

"Is that a problem, sir?"

"When it comes to this particular superior, that would be putting it lightly." He suddenly appeared weary. "Leave me now, Frynt. I need to rest."

"Certainly, sir."

The aide quietly removed himself.

On the far side of the room there was a pair of doors. The evening being warm, they were wide open. Hacher walked out onto the balcony.

He was renowned for his unruffled nature. But even he felt a pang of dread as he looked down at the darkened city.

The gloomy streets the Wolverines were taken through looped and twisted so much that they soon lost their bearings.

Eventually they were led along a narrow alley to a darkened house that appeared no different to hundreds of others they'd passed. The orc guiding them rapped a signal on the door with the hilt of his sword. Everyone was quickly ushered in. The door guard's eyes widened when he saw the humans and dwarfs, but he said nothing.

The house looked abandoned. There was no furniture and the bare floors were carpeted with dust. The large group was kept moving until its head reached a small back room. A pile of rotting wooden planks lay on the floor. Swept aside, a trapdoor was revealed. Stryke hesitated for a moment, then stepped onto the ladder. The band filed down after him.

They found themselves in an extensive cellar. A large number of orcs were present, and their expressions were uniformly wary.

The orc who brought the Wolverines there was the last one down. In the light thrown by brands and lanterns they got their first clear look at him. He was around four and twenty summers old, and fairly tall, almost rangy, by the standards of his race. His features were strong and his bearing upright. Self-evidently he was robust, and a female might well have seen him as fetching. From the way those present regarded him, it was also plain that he had authority.

"We should take your weapons," he said.

"You'd have to prise them from our corpses," Stryke told him.

"I hoped you'd say that."

"Why?"

"It's further proof you're like us. Special."

"Special?"

"You *fight*. That's why you're here."

"What's so unusual about—"

"But there's a way you're not like us." He pointed at Standeven, Pepperdyne and the dwarfs, who had been herded together in a corner. "Why are you mixing with *humans*?" He all but spat the word. "And whatever they are," he added, indicating Jup and Spurral.

Stryke had no choice but to elaborate on the story he told when they first arrived, and hoped these orcs were as parochial as the shepherd. "We're not from these parts."

"What?"

"We're travellers."

"Where have you travelled from?"

Stryke took his gamble. "The world's a big place. You know there's a lot more to it than Taress."

"In what part of the world do orcs consort with humans and..."

"They're called dwarfs," Stryke supplied.

"Where do orcs, humans and these dwarfs live together?"

Stryke had hoped to keep things vague. He was forced to take another stab in the dark. "The north. Far north."

A murmur went up from the onlookers.

"The wilderness?" the leader said. He seemed impressed, possibly awed. Or perhaps disbelieving. It was hard to say.

Stryke nodded.

"We know little of those climes. Things must be very different there."

Stryke barely believed his luck. It took an effort not to let out a sigh of relief. "Very."

"But you fight like a disciplined unit, the way we do. We saw it. If humans and these others are in league with orcs, *who* do you fight?"

Yet again, Stryke had to think on his feet. "Humans."

"Then how —"

"Some humans, like our comrades here, condemn what their kind have done to our race, and make common cause with us. And the dwarf folk have always sided with us."

"I've never heard of such a thing. Here, humans treat us like cattle."

"As you said, you know little of northern climes. Our ways are unlike Taress'."

"If what you say is true," the leader replied thoughtfully, "I can see benefits in having human allies. Assuming they can be trusted."

"Some can." Stryke knew that could be the biggest lie of all.

"What I don't understand is how you came to be fighters at all."

"Where we come from, all orcs fight."

There was another, even louder murmur from the onlookers. *"All?"*

"Why be surprised?" Stryke said. *"You* fight."

"I said we were special. Different. The norm in Acurial is that most orcs aren't warlike."

"It's the other way round with us." He made an effort not to look Wheam's way. "But how did you come to this?"

"Who knows? Too soft a life for too long, maybe, before the invaders arrived. Some of us, a few, have a taste for blood. The citizens think of us as freaks because of it. We see ourselves as patriots." He gave Stryke a hard look. "So why did your group come south?"

That almost wrong-footed Stryke. He said the first thing that came into his head. "To recruit fighters."

"You thought it'd be the same here as in your land? That all orcs fought?"

"We hoped."

"You must have felt let down."

"We just arrived. We're still finding out how things are."

"There's no cheer in what you're saying. If you come from a land where all orcs fight, yet you still can't overcome the oppressors... You haven't beaten them, have you?"

"No."

"Then what chance have we, with hardly any willing to take up arms?"

"There are far fewer orcs in the north lands."

The leader sighed. "That's our problem, too. Not enough of us."

"Who *are* you?" Stryke asked.

"I'm Brelan." He beckoned to someone standing in a shadowy part of the cellar. "And this is Chillder."

A female orc strode into the light. Her resemblance to Brelan was remarkable. Except for obvious gender differences, they were identical.

"Never seen twins before?" she asked of Stryke, who was staring intently.

"Rarely."

"And how are they thought of in your land?"

"As lucky," he answered truthfully.

"Then that's another difference. Here we're seen as bringers of ill fortune."

"Let's hope it's to your enemies."

Chillder allowed herself a fleeting smile. "We know you're Stryke. But who...?" She waved a hand at the rest of the Wolverines.

"This is Haskeer, Coilla and Dallog," he replied, "my seconds-in-command." He didn't think they were ready to accept the idea of Jup being an officer. Jabbing a thumb at the grunts, he added pointedly, "The rest you'll get to know later, given a chance."

"Perhaps," she returned, her expression inscrutable.

Stryke scanned the watchful faces surrounding them. "So this is the resistance?"

"Some of it."

"And you lead them?"

"Along with my brother."

"We're outsiders," Coilla said. "Tell us what happened here."

"It must have been the same as happened to you," Chillder replied. "We had a good life for a long time. Maybe too good, like Brelan said. Then Peczan invaded."

"Peczan?"

She eyed Coilla suspiciously. "The human's empire."

"Oh, *right*. We tend to think of them as just...filthy, brutal humans." It sounded lame, even to her.

Chillder let it pass. "When the invaders came, opposition was weak. They overran us between new moon and full."

"Didn't anybody organise a proper defence?"

"Sylandya tried. Our Primary." She saw Coilla's quizzical look. "Acurial's leader. She was the only one in power who really strived to mount a defence."

"What happened to her?"

Chillder paused before answering, "No one really knows. But the upshot is that Taress is under the heel of foreign occupiers. We're a province of Peczan now. They *reckon*." There was real venom in her voice. "And life gets harsher by the day under Iron Hand."

"Who?"

"His name's Kapple Hacher. Calls himself our governor."

"And the humans use magic?"

"Too right! Don't say *that's* different in the north too?"

"Er...no, course not. Just wondered."

"It works the same as in your parts, I guess. Magic's in the hands of an elite among the humans, the Order of the Helix. Most just call them the Order."

Coilla nodded knowingly.

"Don't know how it was with you," Chillder went on, "but magic was the ploy they used to invade here in the south. Peczan said we had weapons of magical destruction and posed a threat to them. What a joke."

"Did you?"

"I wish. If we did, *and* had the ability to use 'em, things might have been different."

"We want to help fight the humans," Stryke said.

"We always need recruits," Brelan told him. "But...We need to confer." As he was turning away he noticed the tattoos on Jup's cheeks. "What's that on his face?"

"I can speak for myself," Jup informed him.

"So what are those markings?"

"A sign of enslavement."

Chillder scrutinised the faces of several Wolverines and saw their fading scars. "You all had them," she said.

Stryke nodded. He assumed the twins took it for granted that humans were responsible.

Chillder and Brelan exchanged glances, then walked away. When they reached the farthest end of the cellar they were joined by several others. A hushed conversation ensued.

The Wolverines waited, several score pairs of distrustful eyes on them.

"That was some fine bullshit you fed them, Stryke," Coilla whispered.

"I don't know. I'm not sure I'd have believed it."

"The bit about coming from the north seemed to go down well."

"Pure luck."

"What do you think they'll do?" Haskeer asked.

Stryke shrugged. "Could go either way."

Wheam sidled up. "Are we gonna fight 'em?"

"That's rich coming from you," Haskeer sneered. "I'd have thought you'd be right at home here with so many cowards around."

Wheam was about to mouth a retort when Dallog motioned him to silence.

The twins were coming back, at the head of a small delegation.

"Well?" Stryke demanded.

"We said we could use recruits," Brelan told him. "But if you really want to be part of this, you'll have to prove yourselves."

"You want to set a task, that's all right by us."

"Let's call it a test. We lost some good orcs tonight helping you out. Nothing can be done about them. But seven of our group were captured, and they face certain death because of you."

"I could argue with that."

"Don't bother." He looked to the humans, and pointed at Pepperdyne. "The younger one looks the fittest."

"For what?" Stryke said.

"He could be useful on your mission, being one of *them*. Like a key, you know?"

"What is this mission?"

"You're to free our captured comrades. You and your three officers, this human and ten of your band. You can pick which ones."

"I'd need the full strength to pull off something like that."

"No. The other human, the dwarfs and the rest of your unit stay here. And if you fail, they die."

16

Dawn had yet to break, and the air was chill.

The compound was a bleak collection of slab-like buildings on the outskirts of Taress. It was surrounded by a high timber wall, and there were several lookout towers. Guards patrolled inside the perimeter, and a small contingent defended the only set of gates.

In a copse on the side of a nearby hill a number of figures were stretched out on the ground, surveying the scene. Stryke, Coilla, Haskeer and Dallog were there, along with Pepperdyne, ten Wolverine privates and two resistance members. Pepperdyne was wearing a dark blue military uniform.

"They use this place solely for interrogation and executions," one of the resistance orcs explained. "Prisoners are kept in the biggest block, over there." He pointed. "The smaller ones are the torture and death chambers."

"Where will your comrades be?" Stryke asked.

"Could be anywhere."

"Great," Coilla said.

The orc pointed again. "See those two buildings? With the thatched roofs? That's the officers' mess and the barracks."

"They're your remit, Dallog," Stryke said.

The corporal nodded, and in turn looked to Nep, Zoda, Gant and Reafdaw, who all had bows strapped to their backs. "Think you can manage 'em?" The quartet gave the thumbs up. "Those *and* the towers are asking a lot, Stryke," Dallog reckoned.

"This whole mission's asking a lot." He directed that at the resistance members.

"Curfew's going to end soon," one of them said, "so your timing's gotta be spot on."

"We kind of knew that," Coilla replied dryly.

"Least you'll have the element of surprise. They won't be expecting something so bold."

"You mean you've never tried anything like this before?"

He shook his head. "Nobody has."

"This just gets better."

"Can we count on you two for help?" Stryke wanted to know.

"We're only here to observe and report back. But we'll be waiting with transport if you get out again."

Stryke bit off a response and turned to Pepperdyne. "You all right with this?"

"Do we have a choice?" He wriggled a couple of fingers into the buttoned-up collar of his uniform and tried stretching it. "Damn thing's too tight," he complained.

"Fidgeting won't make it any bigger," Coilla said.

"This concerns me more." He pointed at a small, dark red stain on the breast.

"Guess that was from the last owner. You'll have to hope nobody notices."

Pepperdyne stared at the compound. "What if they want a password or something?"

"It's a risk we'll have to take," Stryke told him.

"That's an officer's uniform," one of the resistance members explained. "High ranking. It should be enough to get you in."

"What worries me," Haskeer said, "is there'll only be three of us." He glanced at Pepperdyne. "And one a human at that."

"Any more would be too suspicious," the resistance member pointed out.

Stryke sighed. "All right, let's do this." To Coilla he added, "Be ready to shift, and fast."

Keeping low, he moved away. Haskeer and Pepperdyne followed.

At the foot of the hill, and out of sight of the compound, they came to an open wagon. They clambered on to it.

"Time to bind you," Pepperdyne said, taking up a coil of rope.

"I'm not happy about this," Haskeer grumbled ominously.

"Bit late for that," Stryke commented. "Here, do me first." He turned his back.

The human bound his wrists. Then Haskeer reluctantly allowed himself to be tied.

"I've made the knots loose," Pepperdyne assured them. "One good tug and you'll be free. Now sit down."

He climbed into the driver's seat and flicked the reins over the pair of horses.

They bumped around the base of the hill and joined the road. A moment later the compound came into view.

As Pepperdyne steered the wagon on to the slip road, the trio of guards lounging by the gates straightened up. Recognising his rank, but not him, they hesitated for a second before offering salutes. Then the most senior of them came forward.

"Can I help you, sir?"

"Two prisoners," Pepperdyne replied crisply.

The guard glanced at Stryke and Haskeer. "We've had no orders to expect prisoners."

"What did you say?"

"I said we've had no—"

"I was referring to the way you addressed me, Sergeant! Is that how you talk to all superior officers?"

"No, I...*Sir*! No, sir!"

"Better. There's far too much sloppiness in the ranks. Some might accept it, *I* don't. Now, you were saying?"

"Begging your pardon, sir. But we've had no notice that prisoners are due, sir."

"Well, I had orders to bring them here."

The sergeant looked uncomfortable. "Sir, our instructions are plain. I'd need to check this with the camp commander, sir."

"So you're questioning my authority."

"*No* sir. I only—"

"You're saying you don't trust the word of a superior officer. You're adding insolence to insubordination. Perhaps you'd like to see my orders, is that it? *Is* it? Here." He reached into his tunic pocket. "I'm sure General Hacher would be more than happy to have a *sergeant* inspect the directive he issued to me personally."

The sergeant blanched. "General...Hacher, sir?"

"Don't let that stop you. I'm sure you can explain your actions to him when he has you flogged, *Private*."

"I didn't mean...that is, I...Go right in, sir!" He turned to his two companions. "Open up and let the officer through! *Move yourselves!*"

The gates were hastily parted and the wagon rolled in.

Inside, there were two more guards. Much further away, in the compound proper, other soldiers could be seen going about their duties.

To Stryke and Haskeer, Pepperdyne whispered, *"Be ready."*

He brought the wagon to a halt, then glanced at the nearest watchtower. The lookout was paying them no attention. One of the guards approached, and Pepperdyne jumped down to meet him.

"What can I do for you, sir?" the guard asked.

"Take a nap."

"Eh?"

Pepperdyne gave him a hefty crack to the jaw. The man went down like a felled tree.

Stryke and Haskeer shed their bonds and leapt from the wagon. They pulled out concealed blades, and Haskeer grabbed the sword of the unconscious guard.

The other guard stopped gaping and dashed for a wall-mounted alarm bell. Stryke lobbed his knife and hit him squarely between the shoulder-blades. The man fell headlong.

They hauled up the first guard and brought him round with a couple of slaps.

A blade was put to his throat.

"The ones outside," Stryke said. "Get them in here."

"Go to hell."

"You first. Now *do it.*"

Pepperdyne looked to the watchtower. Still the lookout hadn't noticed what was happening. He felt sure their luck wouldn't hold much longer. "*Stryke*, get a move on!"

Stryke raised the blade and held the tip a hair's-breadth from the guard's eye. "Let's try this another way."

"All right, all right! I'll do it!"

They shoved him towards the gates.

"Any tricks and you're dead," Stryke promised.

He and Haskeer moved aside, leaving Pepperdyne with a dagger to the guard's back.

"What do I say?" the man asked.

"Just get their attention. I'll do the talking."

Trembling, the guard rapped on the gate a couple of times. A few seconds later it was opened a crack.

"What is it?" They recognised the sergeant's voice.

"We need a hand in here."

"Why?"

Pepperdyne put a little more pressure on the blade and took over. "Sergeant, the axle's broken on the wagon. We need help shifting it."

"*Sir!*"

The sergeant and one of the other guards sidled in.

Stryke and Haskeer leapt on them. A flurry of blows and kicks put them down.

They used the rope to tie them, and the guard Pepperdyne held. Securely trussed, they were dragged into a small gatehouse, along with the dead sentry.

"This is taking too long," Haskeer complained.

As if on cue an arrow zinged towards the nearest watchtower. It struck the lookout and he dropped from sight.

"It's started," Stryke said.

Haskeer scowled. "We're not ready. There's still one of 'em outside."

Another arrow soared overhead, winging its way to the second tower.

"I'll take care of it," Pepperdyne told them.

He slipped out of the gates. Seeing him, the remaining guard snapped to attention.

"We need you too," Pepperdyne said.

The guard hesitated. "Sir, I—"

"What?"

"Standing order, sir. This post is never to be left unmanned."

"But... Oh, to hell with it." He booted the guard's solar-plexus. The man doubled and Pepperdyne dragged him through the gates.

While they were dealing with him, flaming arrows cut across the sky towards the thatched buildings.

"Get those gates opened wide!" Stryke ordered.

When they had, they saw Coilla and the other Wolverines tearing down the hill.

"Here they come," Haskeer said.

"And here comes somebody else," Stryke added.

A group of soldiers were running their way across the compound. Others were moving in another direction, towards rising black smoke.

"Onto the wagon!" Stryke yelled.

They jumped aboard, and this time Stryke took the reins. He urged the horses and drove straight at the approaching soldiers. Pepperdyne and Haskeer stood in the back, hanging on with one hand, outstretched swords in the other.

The wagon picked up speed. Stryke kept on course, and the advancing troops went from distant figures to clearly defined individuals. Several were shouting, but their words were impossible to hear.

Then the wagon was on them. Soldiers scattered, and there were yells and curses. Most leapt clear. Several avoided the wagon but fell prey to Haskeer and Pepperdyne's blades. One managed to loose an arrow. It flew hopelessly wide.

Stryke got his bearings and swerved. The wagon turned so sharply that on one side its wheels briefly left the ground. The jolt when they came down again all but dislodged everyone on board.

They glimpsed the thatched buildings in flames. Men were dashing in all directions. Buckets of water were being chained.

The wagon turned again and headed for the prisoners' block.

Coilla's team got to the main gates. There were just six Wolverines with her. Dallog and his archers were bringing up the rear and had yet to arrive.

There was no chance for Coilla's group to properly collect themselves. Eight or nine of the troops Stryke ploughed through had kept on to the gates. They reached them at almost the same time as the Wolverines.

Coilla took on the first of the troopers. He was an officer, and spitting mad. She liked angry opponents; it clouded their judgement.

He attacked in a frenzy, slashing wildly with his sword and bellowing incoherently. It took no great skill on her part to dodge his blows. Getting past his blade's lacerating passes was a bit harder. And she was all too aware that there was no time for delay.

She grew furious in her response. Flaying the man's blade, she laid siege to his defences, such as they were. Having bludgeoned her way past his guard, she bored steel into his chest.

Coilla looked about, ready to engage another foe. There was no need. The group was putting down the last of the humans without her help.

Seafe joined her. "Not much of a scrap, was it?" He looked disappointed.

"I think they're not used to orcs standing up to them. But it won't take long to soak in."

"*Corporal!*" one of the privates shouted.

It heralded the arrival of Dallog and his four archers.

He surveyed the corpses. "You've made a good start then."

"There's going to be more than just these. Now let's get organised. You and you." She nodded at two grunts. "Stay here and guard our exit. The rest, follow me."

They hastened into the compound.

The wagon Stryke was driving arrived at the prison block. An imposing building, it was tall and windowless, save for a series of niches, like arrow slits, way up near the roof. They saw only one entrance; a pair of solid double doors, set smack in the middle of the facade.

As Stryke slowed down, one of the doors opened a fraction. Just enough to show a pale human face gazing out from the ill-lit interior. Ponderously, the door began to close again.

Pepperdyne vaulted from the still moving wagon and ran towards it.

"*Hold!*" he shouted.

The muscular doorkeeper froze. Pepperdyne saw that he held a length of thick chain suspended from a point somewhere overhead. It obviously worked a mechanism of pulleys and weights that operated the heavy door.

"Let me in!" Pepperdyne demanded.

The doorkeeper stared at Pepperdyne. Then his gaze flicked over his shoulder to Stryke and Haskeer pulling up in the wagon. "I can't do that, sir."

"This is an order!" Pepperdyne thundered.

Ignoring him, the man resumed hauling the chain. The door started to move again.

Pepperdyne tried to stop him. He put his shoulder to it, pushing with all his strength. The door inched closer to the frame.

Haskeer ran over and added his muscle. Straining, they halted the door's progress, but couldn't reverse it. The doorkeeper continued tugging mightily on the chain, face contorted with effort. For a few seconds, there was stalemate.

Then Stryke joined them. Drawing his sword, he stooped and thrust it through the gap in the door. The tip penetrated the doorkeeper's thigh. He cried out, but stubbornly hung on. Stryke jabbed at him repeatedly, staining the man's breeches crimson. Trying to squirm away from the blade and maintain his hold on the chain at the same time proved too much. He let go and fell. The tautness went out of the chain and it shot up, jangling. Released, the door suddenly gave under Haskeer and Pepperdyne's weight. They practically fell in.

On his knees, the gatekeeper was scrabbling for his own sword. Stryke cut him down.

Stepping over his body, they took in their surroundings.

They were in a chamber just about large enough to accommodate their wagon. Its ceiling was as high as the building itself, and near the top was one of the slit windows they saw from outside, presumably for ventilation. Apart from a couple of wall-mounted brands providing the only real light, the walls were plain and unadorned.

On the other side of the chamber was another, much smaller door. Hanging beside it was a bunch of keys on a metal ring the size of a female orc's anklet. The door was locked, unsurprisingly, and they went through the keys until they found a fit.

Entering cautiously, they found themselves in the core of the building. It was long, quite narrow, and simply laid out. There was a central aisle, with cages on either side. Not cells, as they might have expected, but what were essentially pens, fashioned from metal bars. They were too low for the occupants to stand, and their floors were covered in grubby straw. Each cage contained a despondent-looking orc, and the place stank.

"Kept like animals," Haskeer growled.

"Why're you looking at me?" Pepperdyne said.

"Why do you think?"

"I didn't do this."

"Your kind did."

"*Shut up,*" Stryke hissed, "the pair of you. We're not out of this yet."

The prisoners had begun to notice what was happening and were growing noisily restive. At the far end of the aisle a door opened and a man in uniform entered. He didn't notice the intruders. His attention was on quietening the prisoners, and he went about it with something that looked like a javelin. Shoving the pole between the bars, he jabbed at them with its barbed point.

"I've had enough of this shit," Haskeer declared. He headed down the walkway at a run.

"Leave him to it," Stryke said, clutching Pepperdyne's sleeve.

Haskeer was halfway along the aisle and gathering speed before the human noticed him. For a second he just stared, bemused. Then he started withdrawing the pole from a cage, working frantically, hand over hand. He almost had it clear when Haskeer smashed into him.

The human was knocked backwards, losing his hold on the pole. He should have fallen, but Haskeer seized him by the shoulders in a steely grip. The man cried out. Haskeer propelled him to one side, savagely driving his head into the bars of a cage, the impact raising an almost melodic chime. He kept on pounding him against the cage until his skull was a bloody pulp. At length he let go, and the human dropped lifeless to the floor.

The caged orcs, who had been clamouring throughout, fell silent.

Stryke and Pepperdyne caught up. Stryke moved past Haskeer and made for the door the dead human had come out of. He booted it open. It was an empty guardroom.

He still had the bunch of keys. Walking back to the centre of the aisle, he held them up for the prisoners to see. "We're here for the Resistance members captured last night!" he told them. "We'll sort out who's who later! But remember: it's not over when we unlock these cages! If you want to leave this camp alive, be ready to fight! You'll have to scavenge weapons or improvise!" Glancing Pepperdyne's way, he added, "And this human's with us!" He tossed the keys to Haskeer and said, "Let 'em out."

Outside, there was chaos. The barracks and officers' quarters were burning fiercely. Oily black smoke all but obscured the rising sun and the smell of charred timber perfumed the air. Most of the soldiers were fighting the fires; others milled in confusion. The Wolverine archers added to the turmoil by picking off random targets. For good measure they unleashed a few more flaming arrows at anything that might burn. A guards' hut was ablaze, and the wooden supports of a bulbous water tower.

Coilla and Dallog's group arrived at the two buildings given over to torture and execution. They had no idea which was which. Not wanting to split their forces, they went for the first they came to. Like the prison block, it was a featureless structure with no windows and a single entrance. But they didn't have Stryke's good fortune. The door was firmly closed.

"What now?" Dallog asked.

"When in doubt," Coilla replied, "blag your way through."

A couple of the Wolverines toted two-handed axes. She ordered them to take down the door. As they hammered at it, the archers stood by with taut bows. The door proved as solid as it looked, and it needed repeated blows before the wood began to splinter and groan. Finally it gave.

They expected defenders to be waiting. There was no one to be seen. Kicking aside the jagged remains of the door, Coilla led the way into the building.

There was a wide flight of stone steps that went down to a short corridor, with a further door at its end. It was also locked, but nowhere near as robust as they one they just broke down. After a couple of strokes from an axe it sprang open.

Now they were in the heart of the building, and its function was immediately obvious. On one side stood a chest-high platform running the length of the room, with steps at each end. Above that was a sturdy beam of equal span, from which six ropes were suspended, each ending in a noose. Beneath each noose was a trapdoor. On the other side of the room there were tiers of benches for observers. The place seemed deserted.

"There's no doubt what they do here," Dallog remarked grimly.

Coilla nodded. "Let's get out. There's nothing—"

"*Corporal*," Reafdaw whispered. He bobbed his head towards the dark hollow under the platform.

Everybody caught his meaning and listened. A second later there was the faintest of noises. Coilla silently gestured to the two orcs nearest the platform.

Moving fast, they stooped and darted into the hollow. There was the sound of a scuffle and the smack of fists on flesh. Then they emerged dragging a human between them. His face was bloodied and his terror apparent.

"Just him under there," one of the grunts reported.

"So what are you?" Coilla wondered.

"Bet he's an executioner," Dallog offered.

Reafdaw slipped out a dagger. "Shall we kill him?"

The man turned chalk white. He started to plead.

"*Shut up*," Coilla said. "Hold on for a minute, Reafdaw." She moved her face closer to the quaking human's. "You've one chance to save your neck. Can you get us into the torture block?"

His panicky gaze darted from her to Reafdaw to Dallog, then back again. He didn't speak.

"All right," Coilla said, turning away, "cut his throat."

"*No!*" the human begged. "I can do it! I'll get you in!"

"Then get going." She shoved him towards the door.

The human resisted. "Not that way."

"Why not?"

"I couldn't get you through the main entrance. It'll be secured because of . . . whatever's going on outside."

"No point keeping you alive then."

"No, wait! There's another way. Under there." He pointed to the space below the scaffolds. "It's where I was going when you caught me."

Coilla gave him a chilling look. "If this is a trick . . ."

"It's *not*. I'll show you."

They kept close to him as he moved underneath the platform. After hunching for about ten paces they came to an area where it was possible to stand. Overhead were the trapdoors.

The human carried on to the wall. "Here," he said.

At first, Coilla couldn't see what he meant. She reached out to touch the wall with her fingertips, and felt a ridge. Then she realised it was a doorframe, hidden in shadow. She pushed. There was light.

They were looking along a tunnel. It was softly lit by fat candles set in recesses.

"Straight from torture to death, eh?" Dallog said.

"And to tidily remove the...deceased," the human told him.

"Tidily," Coilla repeated, a note of menace in her voice. She gave him a hard shove. "Keep moving!"

The tunnel ended at a series of metal rungs that climbed to a trapdoor.

"How many are up there?" Coilla whispered.

"I don't know," the human replied. "I really don't."

Coilla looked back at the rest of her group, crowding the narrow tunnel. She didn't like the fact that they could only go up the rungs one at a time. It seemed perfect for an ambush. "No lingering," she told them. "We get up there fast. And be ready for anything." To the human she said, "You first."

He climbed the rungs and lifted the trap. Coilla went next, with Dallog right behind her.

They emerged in a building of roughly the same dimensions as the one they just left. But it was laid out differently. Ahead of them, hugging the left-hand side, was a paved walkway. The space to the right was divided into sections by floor to ceiling brick partitions, nine or ten paces apart, forming a succession of cubicles. It remind Coilla of a stable.

The rest of the orcs were beginning to surface from the tunnel, and Dallog was hauling up the slower ones by their scruffs. Coilla turned her head to check the bottleneck. That fleeting distraction was all their captive needed.

He bolted. Running along the gangway, he started shouting. Most of it was gabble, but the note of alarm was unmistakable.

"Shit!" Coilla cursed.

Before she could act, Dallog shot past her. He moved at a surprising clip given his age, and caught the human with apparent ease. There was a brief, futile struggle. Then Dallog seized the man's head and twisted it sharply. There was an audible crack as his neck broke. Man became corpse in the blink of an eye, and dropped.

But his shouted warning had a result. Up ahead, several figures came out of cubicles. They headed towards the orcs, weapons drawn.

"*Down!*" Coilla yelled.

It took Dallog a second to realise she meant him. He hit the deck. A small swarm of arrows soared over his head. They thudded into the first two humans, flattening them. The third and final man dashed for shelter as Wolverine archers loosed another volley. He almost made it.

"Nice move," Coilla told Dallog as he got to his feet. "Search the place," she ordered the rest of the group.

Moments later she was called to one of the cubicles.

A manacled orc was suspended on the wall. He was unconscious and bloodied.

Nearby stood a brazier steeped with glowing coals. Cruellooking irons were heating in it. Other tools of the torturer's trade were laid out on a gore-splattered bench.

"There's another one a few cubicles along," a grunt told her. "He's in a similar state."

"Get them down. Have Dallog look at their wounds."

A commotion arose along the walkway. She went out and saw several of her crew with a captive. They frogmarched him towards her.

"Look what we found," one of them said.

The man was big and powerfully built. He wore the traditional black leather garb of an inquisitor, complete with integral skullcap and eye mask. His chest was bare and sheened with sweat from his labours.

"Your work?" Coilla nodded at the prisoner being taken down.

"And proud of it." His manner was contemptuous, and he showed little of the fear their last captive displayed. "Besides," he added haughtily, "your kind don't feel pain the way your superiors do."

"If you say so." She swiftly snatched an iron from the fire and drove it into his chest.

He howled. The smell of scorching flesh perfumed the air. Coilla contemplated doing it again, thought better of it and tossed aside the iron. Instead she raised her sword and cut off his shrieks with a clean thrust between the ribs.

"I reckon that's enough to hurt anybody," she told his lifeless body. "Improvise a couple of stretchers," she ordered, "we're getting out of here."

They smashed the legs off two benches and used the tops to transport the tortured orcs. Then they found the main entrance and left that way.

Out in the compound, confusion still reigned.

Somebody shouted, *"Look!"*

Stryke, Haskeer and Pepperdyne were running their way. They had a large number of freed prisoners in tow.

"All right?" Stryke asked.

Coilla nodded. "Yeah. They've made suffering and death a fine art here." She couldn't help eyeing Pepperdyne. He said nothing.

"At least we can get this bunch out," Stryke replied.

There was a thunderous crash. The burning supports of the water tower had given way. Shattering as it hit the ground, the huge wooden container disgorged its contents. Several hundred gallons of water swept across the compound, knocking nearby soldiers off their feet.

"That should keep 'em busy," Haskeer reckoned.

"Time to leave," Stryke said.

They ran to the main gates and were joined by the pair of Wolverines they left as back-up. Almost as soon as they got out to the road, a couple of large covered wagons drew up. They were driven by the two resistance members who guided the Wolverines to the camp. The injured were put on board, then everyone else crammed in at the double.

It was still early, and there wasn't much in the way of people or traffic on the streets. In any event the journey wasn't too long. Instead of driving into the city proper, the wagons skirted it and made for a rural area. Soon, they came to a collection of seemingly abandoned farm buildings. The gateway was guarded by a contingent of orcs who waved the wagons through. They pulled up in a spacious yard.

Stryke got out. The place was full of resistance members. Brelan was foremost. Chillder hovered in the background.

"You asked for seven," Stryke said, jabbing a thumb at the disembarking passengers, "I've brought you thirty."

"I'm impressed," Brelan admitted.

"And here's something else for you," Stryke added. He balled his fist and delivered a heavy punch to Brelan's jaw, flooring him. "That's for putting my band in danger."

On all sides, resistance members went for their weapons. A number moved forward.

Brelan raised a hand and stopped them. "Right," he said, spitting a mouthful of blood. "I think we can work together."

17

"What I still find hard to take in," Brelan said, spearing a chunk of meat with his dagger, "is the idea of humans taking the side of orcs."

"The way I see it," Pepperdyne replied, "it's not about humans and orcs. It's about right and wrong."

"And is that how your companion sees it too?" Chillder asked, staring at Standeven. "He doesn't say much."

"Er...I..." Standeven jabbed a finger at Pepperdyne. "What he said."

"He's a deep thinker," Pepperdyne explained. "Not much of a way with words."

"Is he as good a fighter as I've heard you are?"

"You'd be...surprised at his talents, Chillder."

Servers arrived to replenish their cups with wine, and conversation dwindled.

It was evening. Brelan and Chillder had invited Stryke and his officers to join them for a meal. The humans had been included, along with Jup and Spurral, though Stryke wasn't alone in thinking it was with some understandable reluctance on the twins' part. The rest of the Wolverines were taking their food elsewhere in the dilapidated farmhouse.

It was Stryke who broke the silence. "So what's the plan?"

"Plan?" Brelan said.

"How are you going to stoke your rebellion?"

Brelan smiled. It was more cynical than amused. "Rebellions need popular backing. Unlike your far northern lands, the orcs here have no taste for rising up. As I said, we of the resistance are different; we're prepared to fight the invaders. But we're no more than a thorn in their side. Though what you did today—"

"You could do every day," Coilla assured him. "Our numbers are small too, if you hadn't noticed. Resolve counts more than numbers."

"Along with training and experience," Stryke said.

"Not that you couldn't do with a much bigger force," Dallog added.

"I'd give my sword arm for another thousand warriors," Brelan agreed. "But warfare's not in the nature of orcs. At least, not in this part of the world."

Haskeer had been stuffing his mouth with fowl. He dragged a sleeve across his greasy chin. "Yeah, why *are* they so gutless in these parts?"

Stryke shot him a look. "Sorry. My sergeant's not used to civil company."

Haskeer shrugged and tore a large chunk from a loaf of bread.

"Orcs tend to be blunt in their opinions," Chillder replied. "It seems we *are* like our northern brethren in that way, and long may it last. But he's right. Our race's weakness shames us."

"And we find it puzzling," Stryke remarked. "That orcs should shy from a fight...well, that's something we don't understand."

"I think we've become too civilised. It seems you of the northern wastes aren't as soft in your ways. Life here has been too easy for too long, and it's buried our natural passions."

"But underneath the fire's still there. You're proof of that."

"You're the proof," Brelan said. "We differ a little from Acurial's citizenry; you could almost be from another world."

Stryke smiled stiffly. "I wouldn't say that."

"I would. You're unlike any orcs I've ever known. I mean, you even have ranks, like the humans. How did that come about?"

Stryke felt as though he was about to start walking on eggs again. He could hardly say it was imposed on them as members of a horde headed by an insane sorceress. "We got organised, created a clear line of command so we could better fight the enemy. It's something you should think about doing yourselves."

"It's so like the way humans do it, and what with those tattoos you all had, I thought you might have been press-ganged by them."

"Is that something they do here?" Coilla asked.

"No. They've tried, mind you. But they find orcs poor material for fighting. We've been such an unwarlike race there isn't even a tradition of weapon-making. We have to forge our own, or steal them from the occupiers."

"Things do seem in a bad way here," Stryke reflected.

Chillder nodded. "They are. But what your band managed in one day gives us hope. If you'd help us organise and train, we could do some real damage to the occupiers, not just harass them."

"Now you're talking," Haskeer said. He gulped his wine. Some of it dribbled down the front of his jerkin.

"We can help," Stryke confirmed.

Chillder looked to the dwarfs. "Jup, are your folk as warlike as these orcs of the north?"

"We hold our own."

"As well as any in the band," Stryke told her.

"And how do you see us faring against the humans here, Jup?" Brelan asked.

"I'd imagine their greater numbers would be a problem."

"They aren't that great. Granted there's more than the

resistance. A lot more. But not as many as you might think to cow a nation."

"How so?"

"Isn't it obvious? With a population this meek, they don't *need* vast regiments to keep us down. That's why we were such a tempting prize. It's not force of arms that holds the balance, it's damn magic."

"And with orcs lacking that ability, it's not likely to change."

"Yet it was the lie that we could control magic that led to the invasion."

"How is it with dwarfs?" Chilider said.

Spurral had been picking at her food. She looked up. "What do you mean?"

"We know some humans can master sorcery. Is it the same with dwarfs?"

"We may look a little like them, but we don't share that particular gift. Our troubles would have been over long before now if we did."

"Pity." Chilider turned her gaze to Pepperdyne and Standeven.

"It's no good looking at us," Pepperdyne said, raising his hands in denial. "Magic's practised by an elite we've never been acquainted with."

"You can't help us turn sorcery against them then," Childer sighed.

"Forget magic; it's not likely to be part of the orcs' armoury," Stryke reckoned. "But cold steel can match it."

"How?" Brelan wanted to know.

"A dead wizard casts no spells. Humans are flesh, and they bleed. Concentrate on that."

"It's easier said," Chilider reminded him. "What can we do to bring it about?"

"What you've *been* doing, only better. We've fought humans and we've fought magic. Both can be overcome. We'll share our skills with you, show you how to make the best of what you've got."

"I had an idea about that," Coilla ventured.

"Go on," Brelan said.

"I noticed that you have a number of females in your ranks. But as far as I can see they're menials. Do any of them fight?"

It wasn't Brelan who replied, but his sister. "Ah. You've touched on a sore point, Coilla. Of the resistance females, it's just me who takes on the enemy in battle. And that's only because my brother wouldn't dare deny me."

"That's not really true," Brelan protested. He saw how his twin was looking at him. "Well, all right, it is. But as a general rule we don't let the females fight."

"Why?" Coilla demanded.

"I'll say it again: we are few. We've a duty to protect the child-bearers."

"Have you asked *them* what they think? Look, Brelan, you're an orc, but the way orcs are in Acurial isn't...natural. You need to understand that females of our race are as ferocious as the males. Or could be. They're an asset you're wasting."

"That's never been our way."

"Then change it. You're fighting for freedom for all. All should fight."

Chillder backed that with, "Hear, hear."

Brelan was silent for a moment, and seemed to be mulling over Coilla's words. Then he said, "They couldn't fight alongside the males. Their lack of skill would endanger them."

Coilla nodded. "That's what I thought. So why not let me put together an all-female band? Not to fetch and carry for you males, but to fight in their own right."

Chillder smiled. "It gets my vote."

"I hope you'd be a part of it; and you, Spurral."

"Why not?" Brelan conceded. "If it helps the cause—"

"Good. There must be twenty or thirty females here who could form a warband."

"You should ask Wheam to join," Haskeer muttered.

"What did he say?" Brelan asked.

"Ignore him," Coilla said, aiming a glare at Haskeer.

"All right then, we'll make a start in the morning," Chillder promised.

Things wound down after that. One by one, the diners drifted from the table to find somewhere to sleep. Stryke and Coilla felt need of air, and slipped out of the farmhouse. They propped themselves against a fence rail, well away from the patrolling guards.

"You look troubled," she said.

"I don't like lying to these orcs. About who we are, where we're from, why we're here..."

"You think they'd find the truth more to their taste?"

"Hell, no. They'd probably burn us at the stake."

"So you're doing the right thing. Just like Spurral did back there, denying dwarfs had any magical powers. They're not ready for the truth, however let down Chillder seemed."

"Maybe."

"Everything's on its head here. I mean, now we know why the humans haven't despoiled this place the way they did Maras-Dantia. They understand that the magic depends on the land staying hearty."

"They'll find another way of fucking things up."

"That's for sure." She turned to look at him. "I thought you might have been ticked off with me."

"Why should I be?"

"This idea of a female warband. I should have asked you first. But just in the short time we've been here I've got crabby about the bullshit. You know, they call themselves civilised, but don't seem so damned civilised when it comes to females doing their bit."

"Don't be too hard on them. They've lost touch with their roots, with what it means to be an orc. And no, I don't mind. Whatever gives the humans a kick in the arse is fine by me."

"*Good*. I even thought of a name for the band. We're the Wolverines; I thought they could be the Vixens."

He smiled. "Sounds fitting."

"But we're dodging the main issue."

"Which is?"

"Jennesta. There's no sign of her. And she's why we're here, isn't she?"

"Part of it."

"You saying we wouldn't be here if it wasn't for the chance to settle with her once and for all?"

"No. But we've barely seen Taress yet. Jennesta's not likely to be strolling around unprotected."

"Getting even with her is why most of the band signed on for this mission. You shouldn't forget that."

"I won't."

"And it's all about a grudge for Pepperdyne and Standeven, too. They say."

"That's another bucket of worms."

"We're getting in deep here, Stryke. In more than one way."

He raised a finger to his lips and nodded towards the farmhouse.

Brelan was heading their way.

"There you are," he said.

"I'm glad to have you without the others around," Stryke told him. "About that punch I threw at you—"

Brelan rubbed his chin, as though still stinging from the blow. "I got the message. But that's done. I'm not here to go over it. We've had news."

"What is it?"

"Seems an emissary of some kind's about to arrive from Peczan."

"So?"

"The word is this isn't some lowly bureaucrat. They're high up. Important. And it's causing quite a stir among the governor's staff and the garrison."

"How do you know this?"

"Not all orcs want to fight, but some of them are happy to pass on intelligence. This came down the line from servants in Hacher's headquarters."

"So if we could get at whoever it is—"

"Perhaps. Or stage something that makes Hacher look inept in their eyes. Either way, with your help, we might be able to strike a blow."

"And you've no idea who this envoy is, or how much power they wield?"

"None. Except that as far as Hacher's concerned, their coming doesn't bode well."

"Yes," Coilla said, "but for who?"

18

The orcs of Acurial, and especially of Taress, were accustomed to having the military hammer on their doors at dawn. Usually it was a prelude to being locked up, tortured or summarily executed. Or perhaps to be forced to witness the execution of others. Sometimes it was part of a collective punishment for a real or imagined defiance of the occupiers' will; the citizenry made to watch as their homes burned, their cattle were slaughtered and their fields sown with salt.

It was much rarer for them to be turfed from their beds to line the streets. To be issued with pennants bearing the colours of their conquerors' nation and compelled to acclaim a visiting dignitary.

Most singular of all was to have the object of their ersatz approval gallop past at speed in a black carriage with its windows shuttered against curious eyes.

The carriage, accompanied by an entourage of similarly impenetrable vehicles and an honour guard of hard-faced elite troopers, made its way to the fortress at the centre of the city. As soon as it entered, the gates were hastily secured.

Near the castle's apex, in Kapple Hacher's eyrie, the governor awaited his guest.

As ever, he was outwardly calm. The sorcerer Grentor, who stood at his side, was less so.

"Tell me, Governor," Grentor said, toying nervously with a string of worry beads, "have you met our guest before?"

"I have. In Peczan."

"And your impression?"

"I think...profound would be an appropriate word. And you, Brother? Have you been in the presence?"

"No. Although our visitor is technically the head of our Order, I've never had that pleasure."

"Pleasure is a word you might wish to reconsider."

"How so?"

There was a knock at the door.

"Come!" Hacher called.

His aide, Frynt, entered. "They're here, sir." He was breathless.

"You seem flustered," Hacher said. "I take it you've had sight of our guest."

"Yes, sir. The party's on its way up."

"All right. Leave us. No, use the other door."

The aide went out, looking relieved to be going.

Grentor wore a perplexed expression.

"A word of advice, High Cleric," Hacher told him. "You'll find that the emissary is...let's say strong willed, and does not easily tolerate dissent. This is a person of enormous power and influence. It's as well to keep that in mind."

Grentor would have replied, had not the double doors leading into Hacher's chambers not flown open with a crash.

Two figures walked in. They were human. At least, nominally so. Both were males, and impressively muscular. They were dressed for combat, in black leather trews, jerkins and steel-tipped boots, and they carried scimitars.

Beyond these superficialities, they were wrong. Their eyes

were wrong. They had a fixed, glazed quality that seemed devoid of any spark of humanity. Their faces were wrong. The skin appeared overly taut and expressionless, and it had an unhealthy yellowish tinge. The way they moved was wrong. They progressed inflexibly, as though their spines were too rigid, and there was a slight tendency to shuffle.

The pair inspected the room, looking behind drapes and opening doors. They said nothing. Seemingly satisfied that no assassins lay in wait, they shambled to Hacher and the priest. One extended a beefy, parchment-coloured hand.

"I hope you've no intention of searching *me*?" Hacher complained indignantly.

"*We'll let it pass this time.*"

As they turned to the source of the voice, a female swept into the room. Even Hacher, who had seen her before, was taken aback by her appearance. For Grentor, it was a new and startling experience.

There was something perplexing, not to say downright disturbing, about the way she looked. The structure of her face was strangely off beam. It was just a little too flat and wide, especially across the temples, and her chin narrowed almost to a point. Her skin was curious. There was a light silvery green patina to it, as though stippled with tiny fish scales. Her nose was slightly convex, and her shapely mouth seemed overly broad. She had ink-black hair that fell to her waist.

What held Hacher and Grentor were her eyes. They were dark and undoubtedly mesmeric. But they had a deeper, more unsettling feature. Like portals, they allowed a glimpse into a realm of shadowy matter; infinite, merciless, chaotic.

Ignoring any rational definition of the word, she was beautiful. Beautiful in the way of a carnivorous plant, a wolf spider or ravening shark. Nightmarish yet alluring. Unwholesome.

She snapped her fingers. The sound was loud and brittle. In

the silence that had settled on the room, it was almost shocking. The two dead-eyed bodyguards responded to it as surely as a spoken command. Turning as one, they strode out, Hacher and Grentor staring after them.

Hacher collected himself first, and greeted their guest. "My Lady Jennesta." He bobbed his head respectfully.

"Hacher."

"May I introduce Brother Grentor, High Cleric of the Order of—"

"Yes, yes." She waved away the rest of his sentence with a lazy motion of her hand. "I'm aware of who he is."

Grentor was halfway through a low bow. He straightened, looking uncomfortable.

"Please, ma'am," Hacher said, gesturing to the best chair in the room, "be seated."

She regarded it with the disdain of someone expecting to be offered a throne. But she suffered the indignity, the silk of her emerald gown giving a gentle swish as she sat.

"Those bodyguards..." Hacher began, his gaze flashing to the door in anticipation of them returning any second.

"A fitting way to employ miscreants, don't you think, Governor?" Jennesta smiled.

Her teeth were small and white and quite sharp.

"Miscreants?"

"Enemies of the state. Dissenters. Those who would challenge our authority."

Hacher felt sure she meant *her* authority, but kept that to himself. "One of them... I thought I recognised—"

"You probably did. Disloyalty has no respect for position. The blight can even infect those quite high up in the administration."

Hacher had no doubt that was a not very veiled warning directed at him.

"How better to punish traitors than having them serve the state they sought to undermine?" Jennesta went on. "Dead yet undead; an exquisite fate." Her relish was palpable. "But I'm not here to discuss my pets. There are concerns, Hacher."

"Ma'am?"

"You know my meaning well enough. The situation here is displeasing."

"It's true we've had our problems. But there are stirrings in all the provinces from time to time. We have things under control."

"Really? And what happened yesterday, was that an instance of how in control you are?"

"Ah, you heard about that."

"I hear about everything, Governor. Have no doubts on that score."

"We have a small seditious element. They got lucky."

"They had a *human* with them." She glared balefully. "Is treachery rife here, too?"

"It was some kind of fluke. Such a thing has never been known."

"Until now. How many more humans can we expect to side with the beasts?"

"The event was serious; I'm not denying that, ma'am. But it would be a mistake to take one incident and —"

"But it isn't just one. You have the makings of a rebellion here."

"I wouldn't go that far."

"Of course you wouldn't. You're complacent. What measures have you taken against the military who allowed the raid to succeed?"

"Reprimands have been issued and —"

"Have all those responsible executed."

"Our own people?"

"To think they call you Iron Hand." She laughed derisively. "You're soft, Hacher. That's why the governance of this region is so dismal. Discipline will be imposed, and you'll start by signing death warrants as I dictate."

"I protest at this blatant—"

"And if you don't want to see a warrant bearing *your* name nailed to the castle gate, they'll be some changes of attitude in this administration."

In deference to her superior position, Hacher suffered the threat in silence.

Jennesta turned her attention to Grentor. "There's no call for you to feel smug about this."

"I can assure you, ma'am—"

"The Order has done as badly in Acurial as the military," she ploughed on. "The martial and magical wings are expected to cooperate and support each other. That obviously isn't happening."

"I beg to differ. We've never faced this kind of situation before."

"But it's just a handful of rebels, according to the Governor." Her words dripped sarcasm. "Oh, and a lone human who's made cause with them. But that's too much for you, even with the sorcery you have."

"With respect, members of the Order have lost their lives fighting these rebels," Grentor informed her gravely.

"Then they deserved to, and good riddance. Any who aren't up to the task have no place in any Order I lead."

"That's a little harsh, if I may say so. As you know, ma'am, magic can be an imprecise art."

"Fool. It's only as crude as those practising it." Jennesta deftly unwound the silken scarf she wore, and bunched it. "Here, catch." She lobbed it at the priest as though it were a child's ball.

By reflex, he made to catch it. The ball sailed over his outstretched hand. It unravelled and became a streamer. Then it grew indistinct, and seemed to alter in form as it fluttered against his upper body.

Grentor gave an audible intake of breath. The scarf was wrapped around his neck. Only it was no longer a scarf. What had been embroidered silk was now a three-headed brimstone-coloured viper with a black zigzag stripe running the length of its scaly body. It constricted, choking off the priest's air. Forked tongues whipped from each of its hissing heads. Wickedly sharp fangs sought his flesh.

Despite knowing it had to be a glamour, Grentor began to panic. He tried to cry out, but only managed a croak. His face turned ashen. The snake squeezed tighter.

Hacher had looked on in horror. Now he moved in the priest's direction.

Jennesta made a casual hand gesture.

The viper disappeared. Grentor let out a sigh of relief. He staggered a few steps to the room's large oak table and leaned against it, palms pressed on its surface, head down. He was panting.

The scarf was in Jennesta's hand. She put it back on, heedless of the little drama playing out in front of her. "There's no excuse," she said. "The magic flows strong through this land, pure and powerful. Unlike some places I've been."

If Hacher and Grentor wondered what she meant, they were too awed or too discomfited to comment.

"Heed me, priest," Jennesta continued. "Things will improve. Because High Clerics can find themselves demoted to humble brothers. And worse."

Grentor nodded, still dazed. He rubbed at his neck, and there was fear in his eyes.

A silence descended. It didn't seem to bother Jennesta, but Hacher found it awkward. For want of anything better to say, and incongruous as it sounded, he heard himself mouthing,

"You must think me a poor host, my Lady. Can I offer you refreshments?"

She fixed him with a stare he had difficulty holding. "The refreshments I take are of a special order, and something I enjoy privately. But that does remind me..." She looked to the doors and, as if bending to her will, they opened.

Her pair of mindless bodyguards hobbled in. One had an ornately carved wooden box under his arm. This was presented to Jennesta. When she opened it, the minders' usual sluggish manner became something like excited. They licked their cracked lips with black, mottled tongues, and began to drool.

Jennesta fished something out of the box. It was russet in colour, and looked like a chunk of desiccated meat, or perhaps a greatly engorged worm. She dangled it at arm's length. In what appeared to be a well practised movement, the bodyguards sank to their knees, as though begging. She tossed the morsel.

There was a brief scuffle. Then one of the minders was stuffing the meat into his mouth and crunching it with pleasure. His companion was aggrieved, but brightened when she threw him a titbit of his own. They sprawled on the floor, chewing earnestly, brown juice running down their chins.

Jennesta noticed Hacher staring at the open box. "They require sustenance," she explained. "I also find it convenient to neuter my subordinates. So in a spirit of waste not, want not..."

Hacher gaped at her. "You mean..."

"Privy parts are very nutritious. I can attest to that myself." She continued feeding them like dogs.

Grentor's complexion went grey. He put a hand over his mouth and turned his head.

Hacher steadied himself with a deep breath. "What do you want us to do about the situation here, my lady?" he asked.

"I know orcs of old. However placid this Acurial variety

may seem, I know what they're capable of. Particularly when exposed to a malignant influence from elsewhere, as I've reason to believe is happening." Jennesta flung another piece of meat. "What Taress needs," she said, as her minions bit noisily into their treat, "is a reign of terror."

19

The sun rose blood red. A run of fine days looked threatened by drab clouds and chill breezes.

The weather was of no concern to a group concealed among the trees on the peak of a hill overlooking Taress. They were a motley collection of beings that would have dismayed both humans and orcs had they been seen. Which was why they employed means both practical and magical to make sure they weren't.

One of their number required solitude for the task she had to perform. At a distance from the others, she knelt by the edge of a pool. She had sprinkled certain herbs and compounds over its still waters while reciting the necessary incantation. The pool had bubbled and seethed, and took on the quality of a finely polished mirror.

Now Pelli Madayar of the elfin race looked down at the image of the human Karrell Revers. Through the power of sorcery she and the principal of the Gateway Corps conversed across dimensions.

"I think I made a mistake," she confessed. "I should have approached the Wolverines in Maras-Dantia."

"Why didn't you?" Revers asked.

"There was little opportunity. The land was in such turmoil. I was afraid that if we revealed ourselves to them it would have been seen as hostile."

"If that was your best judgement you acted wisely."

"But *because* things in Maras-Dantia were so chaotic it might have been a better place to approach the warband, and do battle with them if necessary. Here, the potential for harming innocents is greater."

"That you want to retrieve the instrumentalities by peaceful means does you credit, Pelli. But bear in mind that retrieve them you must, by whatever means."

"Let me try it my way."

"I'm content with that. But should you meet opposition you have what it takes to overcome it."

"This is a much more regulated, oppressed world than Maras-Dantia. There are only two races, orcs and humans; and the orcs are cruelly subjugated. Our freedom of movement is greatly restricted. We wouldn't last a moment here without being spotted."

"Then use the art to cloak yourselves."

"We will if necessary. But you know how draining that can be."

"I trust your discretion. And Pelli... I appreciate that you feel some sympathy for downtrodden orcs, and that's praiseworthy. But you must put that out of your mind. These creatures have a potential for savagery unmatched by virtually any other race. Be sure your compassion isn't misplaced."

"I understand."

"This is all the more important because of something that's just come to our attention."

"Sir?"

"Our seers have picked up an anomaly in your sector."

"Another set of instrumentalities?"

"We're not sure. But it's certainly a source of great magical power, and not far from your present location. It could be an individual, or a group. We can't tell at this stage."

"Another player?"

"Perhaps. Whatever it is, you need to be doubly cautious."

"We will."

"What are your plans?"

"At the moment the group's recovering from the transference. We'll begin our surveillance shortly. As soon as an opportunity arises to confront the warband, we'll take it."

"Good. Meantime, let's hope the Wolverines don't do anything that might lead to the instrumentalities falling into even more malign hands."

"So we're agreed," Stryke whispered. "If either of us falls, the other takes the stars. If we both go down, it's Dallog's job."

"And if he's not around?" Coilla wondered.

"One of the grunts."

"Anybody but Haskeer, eh?"

"I'd trust Haskeer with my life. The stars are something else."

"If he ever finds out we were plotting behind his back—"

"We're not *plotting*, just protecting something precious."

"All right. But it's a pity we couldn't just hide the damn things somewhere."

"Where?"

"Like I said, it's a pity we can't. Now can we concentrate on what we're supposed to be doing?"

They were in the centre of Taress. Although it was early, the streets bustled. Carts loaded with provisions vied with traders leading strings of mules. Costermongers hawked their trays of wares, and roadside stalls dispensed meat, flour and wine.

The vast majority of those abroad were orcs. But human patrols were much in evidence, and pairs of soldiers could be seen on many street corners, eyeing the crowds. Occasionally, troopers on horseback ploughed the throng.

Despite all the activity there was surprisingly little in the way of idle chatter or raised voices. The citizenry's mood seemed sombre. Up above, the sky was growing slate coloured, and the day was already uncomfortably muggy.

Stryke and Coilla kept their heads down and tried to look as though they were going about their business like everybody else. They dressed soberly in work clothes supplied by the resistance, and their weapons were well concealed.

Following directions they'd been given, they skirted the central, most populous part of the city. Across squares and through alleys, their pace even and expressions bland, they finally reached their destination. It was a quarter largely given over to storehouses and stockyards. But there was one, down-at-heel, tavern.

Brelan and Chillder were waiting for them, seated at one of the empty wooden tables scattered outside.

"We thought you weren't coming," Chillder gently teased.

"Are we running to plan?" Stryke asked as he sidled between table and bench to sit.

"More or less," Brelan replied. "Though we'll be tight if there are foul-ups."

"We'll have to be sure there aren't," Coilla said. She had perched herself on the end of the table, one booted foot on the seat. "Which there won't be if everybody follows orders."

"Our side will."

"No worries then."

"Everything all right with Jup and Spurral, and the humans?" Stryke said.

"They're back at HQ helping with training, as we agreed," Chillder told him. "You do understand, don't you, Stryke, that we couldn't let them take part in this operation? If anybody saw them—"

"I understand." He did, but also smelt an undercurrent of prejudice. Though it wasn't hard to see why, at least as far as the humans were concerned.

"Heads up." Coilla nodded.

Haskeer and a quartet of non-ranking orcs were heading their way; and from another direction, Dallog with three more.

"Good place to meet," Haskeer announced on arrival. "How about a drink?"

"*No*," Stryke said. "We need clear heads for this."

Brelan got up. "The others will be in position by now. We should be moving."

"Does everybody understand their part?" Coilla asked.

"Yeah, yeah," Haskeer came back impatiently. "Let's get on with it."

They formed three groups. The first consisted of Stryke, Coilla, Chillder and two privates. Haskeer, Brelan and another pair of grunts made up the second. That left Dallog and the three remaining grunts as the third. The groups were mixed in such a way that each had at least one resistance member who knew the territory.

Without further word, the three groups moved off on their respective missions. Haskeer's and Dallog's went toward the city centre; Stryke's headed deeper into the warehouse district.

The streets were lined with substantial, faceless buildings here, and the roads were wider than in the residential quarters, to allow for heavier wagon traffic. There were few signs of life.

"Your plan's good, Coilla," Stryke said.

"But?"

"There are risks."

"We know that."

"Not so much to us. There's going to be a lot of non-combatants in the path of—"

"We've been through this. Look at these streets. Tall buildings with hardly any breaks between. A perfect funnel."

"It's not these streets I'm thinking about."

"The other teams are going to channel the flow. Besides, the resistance will do their best to make sure the citizens are away from harm."

"The humans will do that for us," Chillder reminded them, "because of what's happening today. That's the beauty of it." She pointed. "This is the place."

Ahead, the road ended at chest-high wooden fencing. In its centre was a wide bar gate. Beyond the fence was rougher land, littered with outbuildings. Set well back was a large enclosure made of stout timber rails.

Even from a distance they could hear and smell what was housed there.

"Sure about guards, Chillder?" Stryke said.

"There'll be just a few. They don't think of this as a target."

"And the guards are human?"

"Always. Orcs aren't trusted with arms. They get the menial jobs."

Checking that no one was about, they approached the gate. It was simply secured with an iron bolt, and a length of chain looped over the gatepost. They undid it and slipped inside, leaving one of the grunts to stand watch.

There was churned, hardened mud underfoot, and not a blade of grass. Off to their right stood the largest building on site.

"Slaughterhouse," Chillder mouthed.

As she said it, a door opened that they hadn't noticed before. A figure was outlined by a light burning inside. Then there was shouting, unmistakably human, and a group of men came out. There were four of them, matching Stryke's crew in number, and they carried weapons.

Striding forward, the thickset, shaven-headed individual leading them yelled, *"What're you doing here?"*

Stryke's team halted, but none of them replied.

"You better have a damn good reason for trespassing!" shaven-head growled.

The men fanned out in front of the orcs, weapons at the ready.

"Well?" the leader demanded, irate at the silence.

"They're too stupid to answer," one of his sneering companions offered.

"If it's jobs you're after," the leader said, "you're out of luck. We've got all of your kind we need. Now *get out*."

Stryke slowly folded his arms. No one spoke.

Shaven-head took a step nearer, and adopted a mock reasonable tone. "Look, we don't want trouble."

"We do," Coilla said. "We're orcs."

Her hand darted into the loose-fitting sleeve of her shirt. Yanking a knife from her arm sheath, she flung it at him. The impact of blade against flesh knocked the human off his feet.

Stryke and the others weren't idling. Quickly drawing hidden weapons, they laid into the rest of the humans. The deed was short and brutal. Stryke and the grunt took down their opponents with two blows each. Chillder earned credit by needing only one.

"Now we *move*," Stryke told them.

Leaving the bodies where they fell, they ran towards the enclosure, keeping an eye out for other humans.

The pen was a lot bigger than Stryke expected. Standing on one of the fence bars, he gazed out over an ocean of brown backs and jutting horns.

"Nearly a thousand head," Chillder informed him. "Somewhere the size of Taress gets through a lot of meat every day."

"Well, it should do the trick." He pointed at the grunt. "Stay by this gate. When you see our signal, do your job and get clear. Coilla, Chillder; let's go."

They jogged around the corral to its far end. From the folds of their peasant garb they produced flints, bottles of oil and three club-like torches with tarred heads. Stryke held one out. Chillder soaked it with oil, and Coilla brought the spark. It spluttered into yellow flame.

Stryke scrambled on to the enclosure's fence. The nearest cattle immediately grew alarmed. They mooed wretchedly and tried to back away from the flame. Holding the torch above his head, he waved it from side to side.

The two grunts he'd stationed saw the signal. They unlatched the gates, then ran for higher, safer ground.

Stryke shared the flame by touching his brand to Coilla and Chillder's. Mounting the fence, they goaded with fire and hollering.

At first, the spooked animals milled anxiously, and without accord. But herd instinct quickly took over. The cattle by the gate found it was open and began to spill out. With a vent for the mounting pressure, an exodus was triggered. The livestock poured from the corral and took the only available route. Charging across the mud-covered yard, driven by panic, they channelled into the path that led to the road. By the time they reached it, flight had turned into a stampede.

They thundered along the road, jamming its width, cows scraping their hides against the walls on either side. The rumble of pounding hooves shook buildings as they passed.

Curving, the road took them towards the city's core. The cows met the bend at speed, striking sparks from the cobblestones as they swerved. A mature tree grew by the roadside. The living flood uprooted it. Carried along by the surge, it briefly stood erect, like the standard of some maddened bovine army.

The road narrowed, increasing the herd's terror. And as they approached more populous quarters, the streets were no longer empty. Orcs scattered, racing to sanctuary through open doors, or leaping to cling precariously from window frames. Some abandoned carts in the stampede's path. It made kindling of them.

But the streets had become a lot less crowded. Mostly due to what was about to happen in the city centre, partly because of discreet warnings from the resistance.

The rebels had been busy in other, more tangible ways. Aided by Haskeer and other Wolverines, they hijacked wagons and used them to block off certain streets. For good measure, and added chaos, they set fire to the roadblocks. The upshot was to direct the cattle along a particular path.

Most of the citizenry, and the occupying troops, were gathered in another part of the city. During the night, six Peczan ships had entered Acurial's waters. Hugging the coast, the flotilla nosed its way to an inlet and joined the land's principal river. They arrived at Taress' port with the dawn.

Close on fifteen hundred troops disembarked, reinforcements for Peczan's intended crackdown. Forming ranks on the quayside, they set off accompanied by the drums and pipes of a military band, and with pennants flying. The orc population, bar essential workers, were again dragooned into acting out a welcome. They crowded the sidewalks, but were kept behind wooden barriers in case affection for their glorious liberators got out of hand.

The conquering forces marched eastward, towards the centre of the capital.

The stampede moved in a westerly direction, heading for the capital's centre.

Increasingly frantic, the cattle downed more trees, destroyed kerbside food stalls and snatched away traders' awnings. The torrent wrecked discarded wagons and carried off riderless horses. Under the shock of countless pummelling hooves, cracks appeared on the road's surface.

The pipes and drums kept up a jaunty martial rhythm. Strutting proudly, the troopers passed browbeaten crowds cheering by rote. A cavalry division trotted alongside them, lances raised. Supply wagons and the buggies of officers' wives bobbed along in the multitude.

Even above the listless cries of the spectators, and their own marching, the soldiers became aware of a sound. More than a sound; a vibration. A tremor.

The buildings in this densely populated quarter were tall by Taress standards, and gave the impression of a shallow canyon. There was a sharp bend in the road ahead. The gorge of wood and stone turned, off to parts unseen.

On the corner directly in the marchers' path stood a house. It was three storeys high and extended nearer to the road than any of its neighbours. As they watched, it began to tremble. Dust and plaster fell, and as the building shook more violently, chunks of facing dislodged.

The marchers slowed. Behind their barriers, the orc spectators quietened. Now the mysterious, rhythmic sound could be heard more plainly, and felt through the soles of the troops' boots. Further scraps of stonework dropped from the quivering building. The marchers all but came to a halt.

A lone cow appeared. It loped along, but moved erratically, as though drunk. There was some ragged laughter from the crowd, and even from the column of soldiers.

Then a thousand head of enraged cattle rounded the corner.

It was a leathery deluge, with horses, ruined wagons and general detritus sucked in. The animals were steaming from their frenetic rush. Those in the vanguard foamed at the mouth and tossed their spiky-horned heads from side to side. If they were aware of the obstruction they approached, it made no difference. They kept on coming.

At first, the rear of the procession had no idea what was happening at the front, and continued marching. But the troops at its head had not only stopped; they were retreating into their advancing comrades.

As the stampede drew closer, what had been an orderly progression turned into milling anarchy. There was chaos, and a mounting sense of panic. Numbers of men tried scaling the barriers designed not to be scaled. A handful of cavalry officers, leaping from their saddles, actually managed it. But it proved no salvation for the majority.

The spectators, who had fallen silent, spontaneously resumed cheering, and what before had been half-hearted now took on a new vibrancy.

Some of the troops had the presence of mind to loose arrows at the cattle. It was a resourceful, if futile, gesture. A couple of the lead steers were hit and went down headlong. The animals behind piled into them, causing knots of squirming, kicking bedlam. But it didn't slow the stampede's pace. If anything, it increased the cattle's alarm. They either streamed around the stricken or simply ran over them. The column of troopers had compressed, and unable to back up further with any speed, made a stand, as though about to repel an enemy offensive.

The wave swept in. Men and beasts clashed in a shattering of bone and rending of flesh. Packed as the human ranks were, the cattle penetrated deep, and pressure at their backs kept them moving forward. The effect was similar to striking a block of butter sidelong with a mallet.

Scenes of mayhem were played out. A cow momentarily rose from the scrum, impaled on a trooper's spear. Another, running into a wagon at speed, was sent flying and smashed against the barrier. Soldiers attacked the cattle with swords, and only incensed the greater herd. Men were trampled.

The cavalry fared a little better, though many had their horses caught in an unstoppable tide that carried them off, the riders helpless. There were sorcerers amongst the shambles of the column. The flash and crackle of magical energy bolts erupted, and the smell of charred meat drifted across the crowd. Havoc spread.

The sullen sky birthed a clap of thunder. Fat raindrops started to fall.

The devastation played out in the shadow of the fortress. On a lofty balcony jutting from its bleak facade, Jennesta observed the scene. Her black cloak billowed in the wind, making her look like some oversized bird of prey, about to swoop. Her expression was unreadable. But she gripped the rail so tightly her knuckles were bloodless.

Not far away, on the rooftop of a lower and humbler building, other eyes took in the carnage.

"This is better than I hoped," Brelan said.

"We aim to please," Coilla told him.

Chillder turned to Stryke. "Your band's proved itself today."

"I thought we'd already done that."

"More so, then. And now we think the time's come for you to meet somebody."

"Who?"

"The most important orc in the country."

20

The occupiers' retaliation was swift and brutal.

Homes were raided. Alleged sympathisers were dragged off for interrogation. Certain taverns, thought to be gathering places for dissidents, were closed down or put to the torch. There were arbitrary arrests and roadside executions. On the streets, there was an even greater military presence.

All of which made travel awkward and dangerous. But after more than an hour of dodging patrols and taking circuitous routes, the small group led by Brelan and Chillder reached their goal.

"Looks a shit place," Haskeer reckoned.

"I knew we shouldn't have brought him," Coilla sighed.

"Knock it off," Stryke told them. He turned to Chillder, and said in an undertone, "It does seem mean for somebody as important as you say."

"Never judge a tome by its binding. Come on."

The tiny house was situated in a narrow, filth-strewn alley. All the dwellings appeared shabby and tumbledown, but none were as unprepossessing as their goal. The windows were boarded and its timbers were rotting. It was hard to believe the place was occupied.

Brelan tapped a signal on the door. A cunningly concealed spy-hole flipped aside. After a few seconds, bolts were drawn and the door opened.

"Inside," Chillder prompted. "Don't linger."

A pair of stony-faced guards looked them over as they entered. The unlit interior was gloomy, and there was a pungent smell of decay.

The house was narrow but deep, and bigger than it seemed from outside. A long passageway stretched ahead of them, disappearing into shadow. On their left was a staircase. The twins motioned for them to climb it, and they ascended the creaking treads. On the first landing, they stopped at a door. Brelan rapped on it, and without waiting for an answer, pushed it open.

The cloyingly sweet aroma of incense wafted out, partly disguising the mouldy niff. Inside, the room was candle-lit, and the first impression was of clutter. Most of which, on closer observation, proved due to books. They lined the walls and stood in uneven piles on the bare floor. Books of all sizes, bound in leather, vellum and plain boards. Most looked old, and not a few were greatly worn and crumbling. Some lay open. There was little in the way of furnishings beyond a crude table, covered in books, and a couple of chairs that had seen better days.

A female orc sat in one of them. She was mature, beyond breeding age but not yet old. Her dress was simple, consisting of a plain grey robe and slippers, and she wore no jewellery or other adornments. Yet there was something in her bearing that made the dilapidated chair seem like a throne.

"This is Primary Sylandya, true ruler of Acurial," Chillder announced. To the female she said, "These are the warriors we told you about. Stryke, Haskeer and Coilla. They've been of great help to the resistance."

The female gave the trio a faint nod.

"I don't know how we're supposed to greet you," Stryke told her. "We're not keen on rulers. Most we've met didn't deserve bowing and scraping."

"Yeah," Haskeer agreed, "we don't kiss arse."

She smiled. "Orcs who speak their mind. Refreshing."

"We mean no disrespect," Stryke assured her.

"Don't go spoiling it. I value honesty. It was so rare in politics."

"You need more than talk to fix the problems you've got," Coilla reckoned.

"Sylandya's aware of that," Brelan said. "She's head of our resistance group."

"And our mother, as it happens," Chillder added.

Stryke nodded. "Should have guessed."

"Family likeness?" Brelan asked.

"Same spunk."

"I'll take that as praise."

"You've come down in the world," Haskeer judged, "to end up in this shithouse."

"I *knew* we shouldn't have brought him," Coilla muttered.

Sylandya raised a mollifying hand. "I said I favour plain speaking. Yes, I'm reduced. As are all orcs under the invaders' yoke. The least I can do is endure it with them."

"More than endure," Stryke said. "Overcome."

"You think we're not *trying*?"

"Too few of you are. You like straight talk, so I'll put it bluntly. Somehow, the orcs here have grown placid. Meek."

"Cowards, more like," Haskeer remarked.

"Like hell they are," Brelan thundered. He took a step in Haskeer's direction.

Sylandya checked him with a wave. "We can't deny it, son. They may not be craven, but their fighting spirit's been lost." She looked to Stryke. "Though that hasn't happened with every orc, it seems."

"Your own offspring prove it," Stryke replied, "and those who volunteered for the resistance."

"A pitiful few. There was a time, long ago, when our kind would never have allowed themselves to be subjugated. We were a fearsome warrior race, beholden to none. The way you still are, you orcs from the north. Or wherever you come from," she added pointedly.

"Maybe our remoteness shielded us from the changes in regions where life's softer," Stryke suggested, hoping to turn aside her suspicions.

"Perhaps. Though it seems strange that martial fortitude should be almost bred out everywhere but your homeland."

"We can talk forever about why," Coilla intervened. "What matters is how we get these orcs fighting."

"I think the humans could help with that."

"What do you mean?"

"They lied about us, and made war on us with words. The citizens of Acurial did nothing. They dreamed up excuses to invade us. We did nothing. They took our land and wealth. Still we did nothing. They treated us like cattle, humiliated us, and killed us at will. Except for the few, we suffered and did nothing. They impose ever harsher rule, and most of us do no more than shoulder the burden. But the time must come when the bough breaks under the weight of oppression. Then the spirit will reawaken."

Haskeer snorted. "I wouldn't hold your breath."

"I believe that, deep down, our race still has its fire. Given a push, it could flare again."

"What would it take?" Stryke asked.

"Two things," Sylandya replied. "First, we need to harass the humans, to hit them as often and as hard as we can. Your band can help greatly with this."

"They won't take it lying down. There'll be reprisals."

"We're counting on it." She held his gaze. "I know that sounds harsh. But it's no more than the harm humans will do us in the long run. If it lights the kindling of revolt, it's worth it."

"You said two things."

"At the critical point I'll call on the citizenry to rise up, and do my best to lead them."

"And they'll heed you?"

"I'm hoping they'll heed Grilan-Zeat."

"Who?"

"Not who, *what*," Chillder said.

"Look about you." Sylandya indicated the profusion of books littering the room.

"Books," Haskeer muttered contemptuously. "Never read one." It was a proud declaration.

Coilla gave him a sceptical glance. "You can *read*?"

"I've filled the many hours of my internal exile with these tomes," Sylandya went on, "looking for some clue from our past that might hold the key to our present. I may have found it in Grilan-Zeat."

"You'll have to explain," Stryke said.

"We have a history, for all the invaders have done to wipe it out. Had they not been rescued by patriots, these books would have been burned. We pored over their pages for anything that could aid us in our plight. It was ironic that we should find it in something as celebrated as the story of Grilan and Zeat." She eyed him astutely. "A story I would have expected you to know."

"We're cut off from things in the north. Remind us."

"A century and more ago, Acurial faced a crisis. Our leadership was still drawn from the clan chieftains in those days. It was hereditary, and two lines laid claim. Grilan was one contender, Zeat the other. The land was divided. Civil war threatened."

"Between orcs who don't fight?"

"But they very nearly did. Passions were inflamed. It was the last time we came so close to warfare."

"What stopped it?"

"A portent. A light appeared in the sky, and grew to fill it. As priests had been petitioning the gods to resolve the deadlock, many chose to see it as a sign. Not least Grilan and Zeat, who made peace and agreed to rule in harness. Well, as it turned out. They laid the foundation of our modern state. Before the comet faded from view it had already been named after them."

"What's this got to do with now?" Coilla wanted to know.

"As we dug deeper into the chronicles we unearthed a curious fact. The comet had come before. It appeared more than a century prior to the days of Grilan and Zeat. And over a century before *that*. In all, we found records of four visitations, and mention of even earlier ones. We don't know if great events attended those past visits, as with Grilan and Zeat. But one thing we do know. The time between each arrival was exactly the same. It returns at precise intervals, and if it sticks to this pattern, it's due back. Soon."

"Let's get this straight," Stryke said. "A comet stopped your ancestors taking up arms. Now you're hoping it'll come again and do the opposite."

"And be seen as an augury," Coilla added.

"There's a prophecy to do with the comet," Brelan told them. "It's said to arrive in times of most need, to light the way to salvation."

"Oh, *please*. Prophecies are as common as horse shit, and less useful."

"Maybe. But it's what the citizenry believes that's important."

"The prophecy said something else," Chillder explained. "It spoke of the comet being escorted by a bodyguard of warriors. A band of hero liberators."

Stryke stared at her. "You can't mean—"

"If the helm fits."

"*Bullshit*. That's laying too much on us."

Haskeer gave a low whistle. "Fuck me, we're heroes."

"We shouldn't have brought him," Coilla repeated.

"Old prophecies are one thing," Stryke declared, "but don't drag us into your fancies. We're fighters, yes, but we're just ordinary."

"Hardly," Sylandya replied. "You came here at our time of crisis, didn't you? You're helping our cause, aren't you? And you have a taste for combat our own folk have lost. Whether you believe it or not, it gives us heart. The gods know we've little else to sustain us."

Stryke was about to rebuff her. Then he looked at their faces and checked himself. Instead he said, "When's this comet due?"

"We don't know exactly, not to the hour. But if it's true to form it should start to be seen around the time of the waning moon."

"That's...when?"

"In thirteen days," Brelan said.

"And you want to stir up a rebellion by then."

"We have to," Sylandya declared. "Unless you have qualms about going against the humans."

That puzzled Stryke. "Why should we?"

"I've heard you consort with them."

"Ah. You mean Pepperdyne and Standeven. I'll vouch for them."

"You'd stand by humans?"

"These...yes."

"I wonder if they'd stand by you."

"They already have. One of them, anyway."

"Run with humans and you invite trouble."

"They're different," Coilla interjected. "They're not like the ones here. They've sympathy for the orcs' plight."

"Sympathetic humans. I've seen many strange things in my life. I never thought to hear of that."

"You'll have to take our word," Stryke said, hoping Haskeer would keep his mouth shut.

"Part of me would like to meet these singular humans. But I have no taste for that just yet. I'd feel too much like a lamb seeking the company of a wolf. I would like to have met your other companions though, the..."

"The dwarfs, Mother," Brelan supplied.

"But it wouldn't have been wise to bring them here. Some other time, perhaps." Her eyes were on Stryke, and they were sharp. "Compassionate humans and an unknown race of little creatures. So many riddles surround you." She eased, and managed a slight smile. "But I don't care, as long as you help us."

"The two humans could be useful to us," Brelan said. "And the gods know we need all the allies we can get. Particularly with the arrival of this new Emissary."

"Have you learnt any more about them?" Stryke asked.

"What we're hearing doesn't bode well. It seems we're up against a ruthlessness that makes even Hacher's governance seem kindly."

"You can tell that already? The Emissary's only been here a couple of days."

"But long enough for acts of cruelty and a vicious purge at the humans' headquarters. That's what our spies tell us, anyway. And what we did yesterday can't have gone well for Hacher. So score one for our side."

"Can we get to this Emissary?" Coilla wondered. "Their assassination would land a heavy blow."

"Doubt it. They're bound to be well guarded, and by all accounts we'd be up against a fearsome target. They say there's something very strange about her."

Stryke and Coilla exchanged glances.

"Her?" Stryke said.

"Didn't I say? They've sent us a sorceress."

21

"No, no, *no!*" Dallog snatched the staff from Wheam and held it correctly. "Like *this*." He thrust it back. "Try again."

Wheam fumbled with it, and Dallog had to show him one more time. "That's right. Now there's your opponent." He pointed at a straw-filled dummy hanging from a beam. Its painted features depicted an orc's idea of a human face.

Wheam dithered.

"Don't just stand there," Dallog told him. "Attack!"

The youth gingerly approached the mannequin and swung at it feebly.

"You're going at it like a hatchling. This creature's going to kill you if you don't kill it first. Put some back into it!"

Wheam had another go. He summoned a bit more energy, but was no better coordinated. Taking a clumsy swipe with the staff, he missed the dummy and struck a wall-mounted oil lamp, shattering it.

"All right," Dallog said, "take a breather."

Wheam dropped the staff and slumped to the floor. He propped himself against the wall, chin on raised knees. "I'm useless," he sighed.

"Not true."

"So you say."

"You're unskilled, that's all."

"It's not just that. I'm..." He looked around to see if anybody was in earshot, and whispered, *"I'm afraid."*

"Good."

"What?"

"Nothing wrong with fear. Show me an orc who goes into battle without it and I'll show you a fool."

"I don't understand."

"Fear is a warrior's ally. It's a spur, a dagger to the back. Courage isn't being without fear. It's *overcoming* fear. If you're wise you'll make it your friend, and turn it on your enemy. Understanding that is what makes our race so skilled at warfare."

"Then why don't the orcs here see it that way?"

"Somehow, I don't why, they've gone wrong."

"Have they? They live in peace. They're not bent on death and destruction the way we are. Maybe I should have been born in Acurial."

"I'll pretend I didn't hear that. Look where their ways have landed them. You should be proud of your heritage."

"You sound like my sire. He was always telling me what I should be, and saying I was a coward."

"It's hard trying to follow in the footsteps of a great orc like your father. But he was wrong to call you a coward."

"You must be the only one around here who believes that. Everybody hates me."

"No they don't."

"They hate me because of who I am. And those Wolverines who died... it was my fault."

"It *wasn't*. Get that through your head. I know what it's like being an outsider too, and trying to fill somebody else's boots. But if you want the band's respect, don't throw away your birthright. Honour it."

"That's easy said."

"You can start by working on your training. *Really* working."

Wheam stared at the discarded staff. "I'm not very good at this."

Dallog stooped, took hold of the staff and held it out to him. Wheam grasped it and allowed himself to be pulled to his feet.

"Look at your foe," Dallog said, nodding at the swaying dummy. "It's everything you feel bitter about. Everything you hate and fear. It's all the bile you've stored up about this warband, about yourself, about...*your father.*"

Wheam let out a piercing yell and rushed at the dummy. He set about beating it, swinging the staff wide and hard, delivering great clouts. After three or four blows straw started to spill from the dummy's split torso. Wheam carried on thrashing it.

"Good!" Dallog exclaimed. *"Good!"*

The farmhouse door opened. Stryke and Coilla came in.

As they passed, Coilla called out, "Good job, Wheam!"

The youth beamed and continued the battering.

"He could be of some use yet," she said.

"If we ever have to fight dummies," Stryke replied.

They made their way to a large room at the back of the house that had been set aside as a refectory. Hardly any of the benches were occupied. They picked one farthest away from anybody else.

There was a water butt at the end of their table. Coilla ladled herself a cup, then took a swig. "I still can't get over it."

"Jennesta? It should be no surprise; Serapheim said she was here. It's why we came."

"Knowing she's close makes it sort of more real. Back in Maras-Dantia we spent a lot of time trying to get as far away from her as we could. It seems strange doing the opposite."

"I'd like to get near enough to slit her throat."

"Who wouldn't? It'd certainly help bring on the rebellion Sylandya wants."

"But an attack on Jennesta's going to be a suicide mission."

"Is it? The resistance has spies in the fortress. Maybe they could get us in."

"It's a thought. I'll talk to Brelan and Chillder. Though their minds are going to be on other things. Like trying to incite an uprising in thirteen...no, twelve days."

"Surely they'd see how taking out Jennesta would aid that."

"They might see the benefit; I don't think they'd be keen to allot their stretched forces to it."

"They wouldn't have to. If we can get help from the inside it'd take just a couple of us to do the job. I'm thinking stealth rather than storming the place."

"You're counting on Jennesta being that easy to overcome. Blades against sorcery; it'd be a close call."

"I'm willing to try. See if the twins can get us a plan of the fortress. That'd be a start."

"I'll ask."

She raised the cup again and drained it. "Talking of plans, what chance do you think they have with this comet thing?"

"It turns on a lot of maybes. But it's all they've got."

She smiled. "I nearly put my foot in it when they were talking about the waning moon. I didn't even know this world *had* a moon."

"Me neither."

"There's so much we don't know. I keep thinking I'm going to give us away. Though I wonder how bad that would be."

"If they knew where we were really from? It's too big a risk. Orcs are different here. We don't know how they'd take it."

"They're different all right, and not just in being so timid about fighting. I mean, a *state*? Cities? It's not what orcs do. If I thought we had no way of getting home again—"

"The star's still safe?"

"Don't look so anxious. Course it is." She slapped the pouch at her waist. "Stop worrying about it."

The farmhouse door slammed loudly. They turned to see Haskeer swaggering in. Pausing only to throw a disparaging remark at Wheam and Dallog, he joined them at the table.

"How's my fellow heroes this morning?" he said.

"Oh, shut up about that," Coilla chided.

"That's not showing much respect for the prophecy."

"Only idiots believe in prophecies."

He ignored the insult and looked about the room. "Anything to drink?"

"Not the kind you want," Stryke told him, nodding at the water barrel.

Haskeer pulled a face. "No alcohol, no crystal, no action. Where's the fun? I thought we were getting a revolution started."

"There'll be fighting enough, and soon."

"Good. I'm keen for a bit of mayhem."

"We all are. How are the new recruits shaping up?"

"All right." He shot Wheam a scornful glance. "Mostly."

"I need to count on them. They have to work as part of the band and—"

"Don't sweat it, Stryke. They're knuckling down."

"I'll hold you to account on that."

Haskeer would have come back, had Jup and Spurral not arrived. He greeted them with, "Ah, the pisspots."

"How'd you like that water butt shoved up *your* butt?" Spurral asked.

"Ooohhh!" Haskeer lifted his hands in feigned dread. "Call her off, Jup!"

"I'd prefer to help her. Only I'd use your head. It'd improve your looks."

"I'd like to see you try, you little tick."

"Whenever you're ready."

They both stood up, glaring at each other.

"*Shut it!*" Stryke snapped. "Sit down, the pair of you! We don't need this shit. Save it for the enemy."

"I'll be lucky to see 'em," Jup complained, sinking back into his seat. "Spurral and me are going stir crazy stuck in this place."

"I know it's tough," Stryke said, "but we can't afford letting you be seen."

"So why the hell are we here? What's the point if we can't come out of hiding?"

"You'll have your part. Things are due to hot up over the next twelve days. You two on the streets is going to be the least Taress has to deal with."

"I don't know whether to be flattered by that," Spurral remarked. She looked to Coilla. "We should be moving."

"You're right. Come on."

"Late for your sewing circle?" Haskeer teased.

"Yeah. Want to join us?"

Coilla and Spurral made for a door at the far end of the make-shift mess room.

They stepped out to a plot of land surrounded by a low dry-stone wall. A group of around twenty females were waiting for them. They were dressed for combat, and armed. Childer stood at their head.

"Good turnout," Coilla said.

"And champing at the bit," Childer told her.

Coilla faced them, and raised her voice so all could hear. "You've been told the plan. Things are going to turn pretty lively in the days ahead, and we have to get combat ready fast. That means working together as a unit. The best way is to have the sort of set-up my warband has. A military structure, like the humans. I'm the most experienced, so I'm leading this group. If anybody objects to that, spit it out now." Nobody spoke. "All right. Childer here is second-in-command. We'll be picking other officers if we need them." She indicated the dwarf with a jab of her thumb. "For those who haven't met her, this is Spurral. She's of a race you don't know, and you might see her as...different. But she's a good fighter and loyal to the orc cause. You can trust her." Coilla couldn't tell what they thought about that. She carried on. "We're hoping our first mission's soon. Very soon. So we'll be pushing you hard to get in shape. The resistance needs all the swords it can get, but the males in these parts don't seem to value what we have to offer. Let's show 'em what we can do, Vixens!"

They cheered, and there were catcalls. They waved blades in the air.

"That went down well," Spurral whispered to Coilla.

"I don't think I've had that much to say since...well, I don't know when. But we have to—" Something caught her eye.

Just beyond the stone wall stood a row of stables. One had an open door. A figure was outlined there for a second, then disappeared.

"What is it?" Chillder asked, following her gaze.

Coilla shook her head. "Nothing."

Standeven drew back from the door and retreated into the gloomy stable. "Look at them," he said, his fury barely in check. "They've even got the females involved now."

"What's the problem?" Pepperdyne answered. "They're just practising."

"I should have known you'd take their part."

"In what? They're only training."

"They're getting ready for more trouble."

"It's what they *do*. They're a warrior race."

"These creatures are fighting against our side. Doesn't that worry you?"

"Our side?"

"Our race, then. Our *kind*."

"They're fighting oppression. They want their freedom back."

"They're provoking the wrath of the rulers of this place, and we're in the middle."

"What you call the rulers are usurpers. This isn't their land. They took it."

"Trust you to see it that way."

"It's hard not to, given my people's history."

"That's no excuse for going native now."

"You've a short memory. It wasn't me who crossed Hammrik. We're in this situation because of you."

Standeven's complexion turned a deeper scarlet. "There was a time when you wouldn't *dare* speak to me that way!"

"That time's over. It's not about master and slave now. It's about survival."

"And you think you'll ensure that by throwing in your lot with these creatures?"

"They've grounds for discontent. It's a just cause."

"I wonder how interested they'd be in you as an ally if they knew what I know about you."

"No idea. Maybe they look at these things differently. Why don't you try telling them?"

Standeven said nothing.

"Your threats don't wash here," Pepperdyne told him. "You need me to get through this and you know it. That's what sticks in your craw, isn't it, *master*?"

Outside, the Vixens had paired off to rehearse swordplay. The clatter of blades filled the air.

"I want to get out of this place," Standeven said, more subdued. "Preferably in one piece."

"So do I. But it's not in our hands."

"Well, it should be. It's only the instrumentalities that stand between us and going home."

"Knowing how to use them might help. And taking them away from Stryke would need a damn sight more than luck."

"Not that he has all of them."

"What do you mean?"

"The female, Coilla; she's carrying one."

"How do you know that?"

"There's a lot to be said for keeping low and using your ears."

"It's called snooping."

"I happened to overhear," Standeven came back huffily. "Seems Stryke wanted to split up the artefacts for some reason. Though we can only wonder why."

Pepperdyne shrugged. "Probably to stop somebody like you getting hold of them."

"I got the impression it was something more than that."

"None of this matters. We're not going to get the instrumentalities away from the orcs. Even if we could, we'd need that amulet Stryke has as well, *and* to make sense of it."

"But we have to have them. If we do get back to our world we'd never be safe from Hammrik. They're the only thing we could barter with."

"Sell to the highest bidder, more like. I know how you operate."

"Buy off Hammrik with them, or sell them for enough to get us far away from him; either way they're our warranty."

"*Our?*"

"I'd not be ungrateful to a loyal servant who stuck with me through this mess."

"As I said, it'd take a miracle to get hold of them here. We'd have to try for it once we got home. If we ever do."

"So we'll have to stay on the Wolverines' good side, if they have such a thing, in the hope they'll take us back. I'm not as sure of that as you seem to be."

"What's the alternative?"

Standeven looked him in the eye, and there was a chill in his gaze. "Perhaps there are such things as miracles."

22

"Well, here we go," Coilla said, adding a hatchet to her other concealed weapons. She wrapped a shawl about her shoulders.

"Think this is going to work?" Pepperdyne asked.

"A human and a bunch of orc females? We can't fail to get in."

"Never did get the stain completely out of this." He licked his fingers and rubbed at the front of his stolen uniform tunic.

"Stop fussing, it's all right."

"We've pulled this trick once before. Are they going to fall for it again?"

"I'm counting on them thinking we wouldn't try it twice."

"And if you're wrong?"

"Then they'll find they've got more than feeble menials to deal with."

His expression turned sombre. "You're trusting me with a lot, you know."

"You've shown yourself as upright before. You going to change now?"

"I'm one of their kind, when all's said and done. The enemy."

"Don't sweat it. If I think you're up to anything, I'll kill you." She smiled pleasantly.

"Let's move," he said.

The Vixens occupied two open wagons. Coilla and Pepperdyne climbed aboard the first, he taking the driver's seat. Spurral sat at the back, near the centre, wedged between a pair of females, a generous headscarf hiding her features. Like all the Vixens, she wore drab workers' clothing. Brelan drove the second wagon.

For a settlement founded by orcs, Taress was arranged along surprisingly organised lines, at least at its heart. Most of what a city needed to function—the storage and distribution of supplies, the provision of drinking water, the housing of livestock and so on—had its own quarter. Since the invasion, the humans had added another, to direct the running of their colony. It was to this sector that the wagons headed.

Orc labourers were still repairing damage caused by the stampede. Under the cold watchfulness of human overseers, trees were being hauled away and walls rebuilt. Gangs of workers shovelled debris into fleets of drays.

The Vixens' journey was short, but not without risks. There were roadblocks to negotiate. The first, at the main thoroughfare leading into the administrative sector, was the most formidable. A guard-post stood on one side, and the road was sealed with a timber blockade. Sentries were out in strength.

The pair of wagons joined a queue of vehicles waiting to be let in. A couple were orc merchants' carts. There were several carriages bearing humans with an officious look; and a gig occupied by a woman who could have been an officer's wife, riding next to a beefy driver. The line was made up with a handful of men on horseback, mostly uniformed.

"They seem to be waving the humans through quicker," Pepperdyne whispered.

"*Course* they are," Coilla replied. "What'd you expect? But don't count on it being the same for us."

They finally reached the head of the queue. A sergeant stepped forward, saw Pepperdyne's rank insignia and saluted.

If he noticed the ominous stain on the phoney officer's jacket, he gave no sign.

He held out a calloused hand. "Your papers, sir?"

Pepperdyne gave him a folded sheet of parchment.

The sergeant studied it, paying particular attention to the seal. He nodded at the wagons' passengers. "Who are they?"

"Clean-up detail," Pepperdyne said.

"For where, sir?"

"Bureau of Tallies."

The sergeant moved along the side of the wagon and looked in. All the females kept their heads bowed submissively. Several held wooden pails on their laps. Brooms, scrubbing brushes and other tools were laid on the deck. He walked to the second wagon and gave that a cursory once-over too. Then he sauntered back to Pepperdyne.

Coilla eyed the sergeant's jugular and fingered a concealed knife, just in case. He caught her look, read it as simple impertinence and glared at her. She dropped her gaze and tried for passive.

"Need any help keeping 'em in order, sir?" the sergeant asked Pepperdyne. "I could spare a couple of troopers to go with you."

"To mind these bitches? Waste of manpower. This lot are meek as cows."

The sergeant glanced at the orcs and grinned. "Take your point." He handed back the parchment, then waved them on.

A safe distance later, Coilla turned to Pepperdyne and hissed, "Bitches? *Cows?*"

"It's what they expected to hear."

"You could have put a bit less bile into it."

"Just playing my part." He stuffed the parchment into his pocket.

"You humans have a high regard for your pieces of paper."

"Too much, if that sergeant's anything to go by. It's not a very good forgery."

"Good enough. It got us through."

"Don't relax yet. We'll have to show it again soon."

The second roadblock was less imposing. It consisted of a farm cart barring the way and a small company of troopers. Perhaps because the wagons had already passed the first checkpoint, scrutiny was casual. The counterfeit papers were given a token examination, and once a lone guard had made a lacklustre inspection of the passengers, the Vixens were let through.

They didn't have to do more than slow down at the third and final roadblock. An apathetic soldier barely looked up from his dice game to signal for them to keep moving.

"That went sweetly," Coilla said.

"Let's hope it's as easy getting out. Assuming we live long enough."

Coilla glanced over her shoulder to see how Brelan was doing on the second wagon. He gave her a cautious nod, working to keep a neutral expression on his face.

Being a restricted quarter, the streets were less crowded than the rest of Taress, and there were more uniforms about. Knots of troopers stood at crossroads and patrols walked the footpaths. Guardposts decorated the roadside.

As they passed, the occupants of the wagons drew stares. Most were dutiful, or idly curious, but it was attention they could have done without.

"This is uncomfortable," Pepperdyne complained.

"Just look as though you've a right to be here. It's not far now."

There were new buildings in the neighbourhood, erected by the invaders at the expense of older structures they requisitioned and tore down. It was to one of these that the wagons were bound.

They saw their goal as they turned into the district's core. In common with many of the buildings put up by the conquerors, hurriedly assembled in the early days of the occupation, it was functional rather than attractive. Standing back from the road, behind a tall iron fence, it was fashioned from plain stone slabs with few windows, set high. It looked robust enough to withstand an all-out assault.

The wagons halted at the gate. While they waited for a pair of guards to amble over to them, Pepperdyne beckoned Brelan. He climbed down.

"You're *sure* you've stopped the cleaning squad they're expecting?" Pepperdyne asked.

Brelan nodded. "They're being delayed by a fake accident a dozen blocks from here."

"Won't these humans be able to tell the difference when a new lot of faces turn up?" Coilla wondered.

"They can't tell us apart. Any more than we can them."

"What about him?" Coilla jabbed her thumb at Pepperdyne. "They'll know *he's* different."

"These details don't always have the same escort." He sounded a little exasperated. "We've been over this a thousand —"

"*Quiet*," Pepperdyne warned. "They're here,"

The guards opened the gates sufficient to squeeze through, and approached.

They were brisk and moderately wary. The false papers came out again. There was the obligatory going over of the wagons, carried out indolently. The guards recited routine questions. Finally they nodded, parted the gates and guided the wagons through.

At the substantial doors of the building itself, the Vixens disembarked, pails in hand. There were worries that Spurral's height would attract attention, but no eyebrows were raised. As the resistance had explained, children were not unusual in work details. Coilla had the uncomfortable thought that the group might be subjected to a body search. But again the fear proved groundless. The humans seemed to have no conception that females could present a threat.

One of the guards rapped on the door with the hilt of his

sword. A panel slid aside and he spoke with someone. Then the door opened and everybody filed in.

The interior was a little grander than the outside. Cool grey marble faced the walls, and there were mosaics. The lofty ceiling had ornate carvings. But the embellishments were unfinished, a work in progress.

"They live a damn sight better than the rest of us," Chillder whispered.

"Surprise," Coilla said.

One of the guards leading the group turned his head and gave them a sour look. They fell silent.

The building was large. Brooms over their shoulders, and clutching their buckets, the Vixens tramped a seemingly endless passageway. They passed a number of doors. Some were open, affording glimpses of humans poring over benches strewn with paper and ledgers; or orcs hauling boxes. One room, bigger than most, held scores of artefacts. Under human supervision, orc servants packed straw-filled crates with gold statuettes, carved wooden relics and ornamental weapons.

"*Damn!*" Brelan muttered under his breath.

"What?" Coilla mouthed.

"Our birthright," he hissed. "Looted to decorate the parlours of empire quill-pushers."

"*Hey!*" the guard yelled. "This ain't a pleasure trip! Cut the mumbling!"

"Too right," Pepperdyne said, stepping in. "Button your lips! And don't dawdle!"

He underlined the point with a hard shove to Brelan and Coilla's backs. When Coilla turned, glowering, he gave her a wink. She didn't return it.

At length they came to a tall pair of double doors. Beyond lay a spacious, hall-like chamber. It contained rows of writing tables with high stalls. The walls were shelved from floor to elevated ceiling, and there were ladders for the upper reaches.

Scroll cylinders, bound volumes and document boxes filled the shelves. Little light entered through the slit windows. Despite being broad day outside, the room was lit by a series of wooden chandeliers, each bearing scores of stout candles, and by a plentiful scattering of lamps.

There were perhaps a dozen humans present, mostly clerks, seated at the tables. Two or three orc lackeys fetched and carried for them.

A stick-thin, gangly human approached. From his dress and bearing he could only be an overseer. The harassed look he wore strengthened the impression.

He clapped his hands like a prissy schoolmarm, his bony palms producing a strangely brittle sound. "Listen to me!" he announced, his tone almost shrill. "You orcs couldn't possibly understand what goes on here in the Bureau of Tallies. All you need to know is that it's much more important than the sum of your miserable lives. Sloppy work will not be tolerated. If you damage so much as a sheet of parchment, you'll be whipped. Is that understood?" He didn't wait for an answer. Which was just as well, given that the Vixens were in no mood for compliance.

Coilla and Spurral caught each other's eye. Coilla nodded, very faintly.

The overseer began issuing orders. Jabbing a lean finger at the ersatz cleaners, he dispensed chores. "And you, you and *you*," he decided, pointing at Coilla, "can take care of the latrines."

"I don't think so," Coilla told him.

The overseer stopped short. He looked to Pepperdyne. "Did that creature address me?"

"Why don't you ask her yourself?"

"*What* did you say?"

"Tell him, Coilla."

"Clean your own fucking shithouse," Coilla said.

The overseer turned scarlet. "How *dare* you talk to your betters like that!"

"I just open my mouth and it comes out."

A vein began pulsing in the overseer's forehead. "This is gross disobedience!" He turned to Pepperdyne again. "Have you no control over this creature?"

Pepperdyne shrugged. "Looks like she doesn't want to clean your latrines."

"I don't believe you're taking the brute's part. Are you drunk?"

"Chance would be a fine thing."

"If this is some kind of joke—"

"Then the laugh's on you," Coilla said. "We might not understand what goes on here, but we sure as hell can stop it."

Alarmed, the overseer backed away and started yelling, "Guards! *Guards!*"

The pair of sentries who accompanied the group on the way in had been watching bemused as the scene unfolded. Now they stirred. The nearest made a grab for Coilla. She deftly swung the bucket she was clutching and struck him square to the forehead. He tottered. She swung again, landing another hard blow, then a third. The guard collapsed. His companion went down under a flurry of punches and kicks from a bevy of Vixens.

The overseer's crimson complexion gave way to pallid. Coilla turned to him. "Now keep your mouth shut and do as you're told."

She bawled an order. The Vixens produced their concealed weapons, and Pepperdyne drew his sword.

"Traitor!" the overseer spat.

Pepperdyne showed him the tip of his blade. "She told you to shut up!"

The Vixens were levering out the false bottoms of their pails and retrieving sealed pots of oil.

"Splash that stuff around as widely as possible," Coilla ordered.

The overseer's eyes widened. *"Louts!"* he shouted. *"Animals! How dare—"*

Pepperdyne drove his fist into the man's jaw. He went out like a snuffed candle.

Coilla nodded approvingly. To the Vixens, she said, "Let's have the tithe detail." Ten females stepped forward. "You know your job. Sniff out the taxes these bloodsuckers have wrung from the citizens. Remember, every coin you find puts another sword in the hands of the resistance. Now get moving."

The group went off.

Coilla looked around the room and saw that the human clerks and their orc menials stood frozen and gaping. She beckoned a trio of Vixens. "Get the civilians clear, and don't let them out of your sight until we're done here."

The onlookers were rounded up and led away, a couple of them dragging the overseer by his heels. As the orcs passed, heads bowed, Coilla needled them with, "We wouldn't have to do this if you had guts!"

"Don't be too hard on them," Chillder said. "They've known no other way."

Coilla shrugged.

"What about the treasures?" Brelan asked.

"What?" Coilla replied.

"Our birthright. The artworks they were—"

"Yeah. What about 'em?"

"We can't leave them here."

"The plan was to grab the loot and torch this place. Nobody said anything about—"

"We *can't* leave them here," Chillder echoed her brother. "It'd be profane."

"We barely have enough hands as it is."

"We don't need your permission when it comes to our heritage," Brelan stated flatly.

Coilla sighed. "All right. You two take care of it." She looked to her depleting forces. "But we can't spare more than four to go with you. We'll meet up on the way out. And if anybody tries to stop you—"

"We know what to do."

The twins quickly picked their helpers and made for the door.

"This we could do without," Coilla grumbled.

Spurral nodded. "It does spread us a bit thin."

"So let's get on with it," Pepperdyne urged.

The Vixens set to trashing the room. Files were torn from the shelves and papers scattered. Furniture was smashed and strewn around. They splattered oil over the debris.

"Right," Coilla said. "As soon as the others get back—"

There was movement farther along the room. A door they hadn't seen, set flush to the wall, sprang open. Three robed men came through it. Coilla recognised the trident-shaped weapons they clutched.

She exclaimed, "*Shit.*"

One of the robed figures pointed his trident.

Pepperdyne yelled, "*Get down!*"

The Vixens hit the deck.

A violet beam cut the air. They felt its heat above their heads. Its glow was so intense it pained their eyes. The bolt struck the shelving behind them, splintering wood and liberating a cloud of fluttering paper. Another blast came instantly. It glanced off a pillar, showering marble chips. A pungent, sulphurous odour perfumed the room.

The Vixens scuttled for shelter. Coilla and Spurral crouched behind an overturned table. Pepperdyne used a nearby heap of wrecked furniture.

As one, the robed humans advanced, tridents raised. A further purple energy shaft crackled past. It punched a wall, exploding plaster and fragments of stone.

"We have to take them out, Coilla," Spurral said. "*Fast.*"

"Tell me about it."

"Why the hell didn't we bring a couple of bows?"

"I've got these." Coilla pushed up the baggy sleeve of her shirt, revealing an arm sheath of throwing knives. She plucked one and handed it to her. "Don't use this 'til I tell you." Coilla turned and attracted Pepperdyne's attention. She tossed him a knife. He caught it deftly. Then she mimed an order, holding up one, two, then three fingers, and indicated the approaching sorcerers. "*Together*," she mouthed. He understood and nodded.

The robed figures kept coming, unleashing beams of dazzling vigour, ravaging wood, stone and glass.

As the trio passed a tangle of wreckage, one of the Vixens popped up from her hiding place brandishing a sword.

Coilla shouted, "No!"

The Vixen made to swipe at the nearest sorcerer. He swung, aiming his trident at her. There was a blinding flash. The Vixen's blade took the brunt and instantly turned as red as a heated poker. She squealed and dropped the searing weapon. The sorcerer made to finish her.

"*Now!*" Coilla bellowed.

She, Spurral and Pepperdyne leapt up and tossed their knives. Coilla's throw was true. The sorcerer who blasted the Vixen's sword took it directly in the chest. Spurral's pitch was good too, though it incapacitated rather than killed her target. The blade struck his face and put him out of the running. Pepperdyne's shot was an honourable miss, but a miss nonetheless. It flew past his mark's left ear and embedded itself in the spine of a tome.

The sorcerer left standing reacted with a wild spray of energy bolts. Grabbed by her comrades, the Vixen who tried attacking was pulled out of sight as the rays demolished desks and gouged walls. The orcs resumed hugging the floor.

"To hell with this," Coilla muttered. She gathered up her

rough peasant skirt, revealing the hatchet in a scabbard strapped to her thigh. Tugging it free, she rose from her hiding place, arm back, ready to throw.

The remaining sorcerer was a dozen paces away. He saw her, and levelled his trident. There was a kind of stasis. It lasted no more than a split second, but seemed to stretch to eternity. His eyes narrowed as he took aim. Her arm came up and over, muscles straining. The axe left her hand.

It tumbled as it flew, end over end, its blade glinting reflected light. The sorcerer followed its path, his head going back, puzzled at the hatchet's unexpected trajectory. Not towards him, but upwards.

Above the sorcerer, and a little ahead of him, hung one of the massive chandeliers.

The hatchet's razor sharp edge sliced through the rope supporting it.

With a tremendous crash the whole affair plunged to the floor, smashing to pieces on impact. Lit candles bounced in all directions. The scattered oil ignited instantly.

A sheet of yellow-white flame sprang up. It engulfed the sorcerer. His wounded companion, on hands and knees, the throwing knife protruding from his gory cheek, was caught too. Their robes blazing, the shrieking men blundered about, spreading the flames.

The fire swiftly followed the trails of oil, probing the length and breadth of the room. It streaked to the shelved walls and began to climb. Where strewn candles came to rest, fresh gouts of flame broke out. Red tendrils snaked to heaps of furniture, setting them ablaze. A pall of smoke rapidly filled the room.

"Get out!" Coilla yelled. *"All of you! Out now!"*

Coughing and wheezing, sleeves pressed to their mouths, the Vixens groped for the door.

"Come on, come on!" Coilla urged, and with Pepperdyne's help shepherded the group out.

In the smoky corridor she undertook a quick head count and judged all present.

"Shouldn't we shut these doors?" Spurral asked, indicating the inferno raging in the chamber behind them.

"No," Coilla said, "let it spread."

There was movement at the other end of the corridor. The Vixens went for their weapons.

"Easy," Pepperdyne cautioned. "They're ours."

The unit Coilla sent to search for the chancellery were returning, along with the three who took away the prisoners. They were carrying four or five wooden chests.

The Vixen in the lead, a pleasingly muscular example of orc femininity, nodded at the fire. "Thought you weren't going to set that off yet."

"Change of plan," Coilla told her. "Any trouble?"

"Nothing we couldn't handle."

"What'd you get?"

They lifted the lid on one of the chests. Gold and silver coins shone in the fire's glow.

"Good." Coilla turned to another of the females. "What about the prisoners?"

"We found a courtyard back there. Shoved 'em into it, barred the door."

"All right. Now let's find Brelan and Chillder and get out of here."

She took the lead, with Pepperdyne close behind.

The corridors grew hazy with smoke as they retraced their steps to the room where the looted art was stored. There seemed to be nobody about. That changed when Coilla, jogging ahead, passed a half-open door.

It was thrown wide, and a sword-wielding human leapt out. Alerted by cries from the Vixens, Coilla spun round while fumbling for her sheathed blade. The man lunged at her, sword raised.

He stopped dead in his tracks. The centre of his chest burst in a shower of blood, the tip of a blade protruding. The stunned human looked down at the flowing wound. Then his eyes rolled to white and he toppled, landing at Coilla's feet.

Pepperdyne stooped and wiped his gory blade on the dead man's tunic.

"Owe you again," Coilla said.

"Forget it."

They carried on, their mood warier, but met no one else until they reached their destination.

Bodies of several humans littered the storeroom floor. Chillder, Brelan and their helpers were placing artefacts in crates.

"Come on," Coilla insisted, "we've got to move!"

"Nearly there," Chillder replied. She was ramming a figurine into a box.

"We can't take it *all*."

"We know," Brelan said. "More's the pity. We've picked the best pieces."

"Well hurry it up."

Three more chests added to their spoils, the group made for the exit. By the time they got to it, the smoke was a lot thicker.

Checking that the street was clear, they quickly loaded the crates on to the wagons, and covered them with sacking. They slammed shut the entrance doors, and once the outer gate had been negotiated, set off.

Pepperdyne, again at the reins of the lead wagon, looked grim. "If that fire's spotted before we get clear—"

"We'll have to hope it's not," Coilla told him. "So let's play it calm and innocent."

"And if it *is* spotted?"

"You know the odds. We'll fight our way out."

It was all they could do to stop themselves from constantly looking back. In their mind's eye a towering column of black smoke formed an accusing finger, pointing their way.

They approached the first checkpoint with trepidation, but in good order. It proved as slipshod as when they entered, and they were scarcely acknowledged, let alone stopped. The second was no different. Jaded sentries allowed them through with hardly a second glance.

At the third and most substantial roadblock there was less laxity. There was no queue to get out, as on the way in, but they were obliged to stop.

The same sergeant they dealt with earlier was still on duty. On sight of them his expression turned chary.

"I wasn't expecting to see you back here so soon, sir."

"No?" Pepperdyne answered.

"The clean-up crews usually take twice as long."

"Do they?"

"Yes, sir."

"Well, this is a particularly hard-working bunch."

"That makes a change for these lazy devils, sir." He fixed Pepperdyne with a hard stare. "What's your secret?"

"Secret?"

"How do you make 'em move their arses?"

"No secret, Sergeant. Just a generous application of the whip."

The sergeant grinned approvingly. "Yes, sir." He glanced at Coilla. She avoided his gaze.

He looked into the back of the wagon. His interest was held long enough to have Coilla suspecting he'd spotted the booty. She began slipping a hand into her folds of clothing in search of a blade.

The sergeant returned his attention to Pepperdyne. "Thank you, sir. You can move out."

Pepperdyne nodded and cracked the reins.

He and Brelan resisted the impulse to speed up. They kept to a steady pace even when the distant sounds of tumult rose behind them in the restricted zone.

Coilla and Pepperdyne exchanged brief smiles.

The wagons trundled past a patch of wasteland on one side of the road, an area where a house had stood before it was destroyed by the incomers. Now the lot was scrubby and overgrown.

An especially eagle-eyed passer-by, or someone particularly receptive to the ambience of magic, might have sensed an anomaly there. A pocket of nothingness slightly out of sympathy with the air around it. Like a transparent bubble which light was not quite capable of passing through. But so muted, so elusive, that an onlooker would likely dismiss it as a mote in their eye.

Wrapped in her cloak of sorcery, the elfin figure of Pelli Madayar observed the Vixens' exploits, and was troubled. There was no doubt that the renegade orc warband was seriously violating the Gateway Corps' precepts. They were playing with fire.

And she knew they had to be stopped.

23

There was a gathering in the grand hall at the fortress in Taress.

The room was crowded. Military top brass were present, along with representatives of the lower ranks. Robed members of the Order of the Helix were in attendance. Bureaucrats, administrators and legislators rubbed shoulders. They had stood waiting long enough to bring on a spate of shuffling feet and stifled sighs.

General Hacher was at the forefront. His aide, Frynt, and Helix luminary Brother Grentor flanked him.

"How much longer?" Grentor whispered. "It's intolerable being treated like supplicants."

"Perhaps you'd care to express that to the Envoy in person when she arrives," Hacher suggested. "She is, after all, the titular head of your order."

Grentor shot him a poisonous look and returned to morose silence.

The sound of approaching footsteps brought on an involuntary stiffening of spines.

With a crash the doors to the hall were thrown open. Two elite guardsmen came in and positioned themselves on either side of the entrance.

Jennesta followed. The hem of her cloak, fashioned from the jet-black, glossy pelt of a beast that could only be guessed at, brushed the timber floor. The clack of her precariously high stiletto-heeled boots echoed throughout the hall.

She swept to the head of the room and climbed the steps to a dais. Then she discarded the cloak, letting it fall from her shoulders in a careless motion. Hacher wasn't alone in thinking of a snake shedding its skin.

Facing her audience, Jennesta spoke without preamble.

"I've been here only a short time," she began, "but long enough to see how this province is run. More importantly, I've seen *who* runs it. Is it the might of Peczan's armed forces? The empire's commissioners, or its lawmakers? The brotherhood of the Helix?" She scanned them coldly. "No. Acurial's true rulers are the very creatures you are supposed to suppress. Rebels. Terrorists. Orc *scum*. How else can it be when the so called resistance strikes at will? When cattle stampede through the streets of the capital, patrols are ambushed and buildings torched. And when *humans* are reported to be aiding the insurgents." She let that soak in for a second. "Discipline is woefully lacking in this colony. Examples need to be set, and not only among the native population." She nodded to the guards at the entrance.

They opened the doors. A pair of Jennesta's undead bodyguards shuffled in. Between them was a terrified looking soldier, his hands chained and his feet in shackles. The bodyguards' appearance, and unsavoury odour, had the crowd willingly parting to allow them through. They looked on in silence as the zombies shoved their prisoner to the front of the room and up to the dais, where he stood trembling before the sorceress.

"The outrage yesterday was the responsibility of many in this administration," Jennesta announced, "but let this man represent all who fail in their duty." She turned her baleful gaze on the accused. He did his best to hold himself erect. "You are a sergeant in charge of a roadblock barring access to the quarter housing the Tithes Bureau?"

"Yes, ma'am."

"And you allowed a gang of orc terrorists to pass your checkpoint and stage an attack?"

"They were accompanied by a human officer, my Lady. I—"

"*Answer the question!* Did you let them through?"

"Yes, Ma'am."

"Then you admit your dereliction and stand condemned. Negligence on such a scale demands punishment equal to the offence. Prepare to pay the penalty."

The sergeant tensed, expecting perhaps to be hauled away and thrown in a dungeon, or even to be struck down by one of his undead captors. Neither happened.

Instead, Jennesta closed her eyes. The keen sighted might have noticed that her lips moved silently, and that her hands made several small gestures.

The accused looked on in troubled bafflement; the audience exchanged mystified glances.

"There," Jennesta said, her singular eyes popping open. She sounded almost amiable.

For a moment, nothing occurred. Then the sergeant let out a groan. He lifted his hands and pressed the palms to his forehead. One of the bodyguards jerked the chain binding his wrists, pulling the man's hands back down. The prisoner moaned, gutturally, and his eyes rolled. He swayed as though about to fall. The groaning became constant and higher pitched.

The area of his temples and up into his hairline rapidly took on a purplish discoloration, as though bruised. His skull visibly swelled, and in the deathly silence a crackling could be heard as the expansion began to split his scalp. Writhing in agony, the sergeant screamed. Just once.

Like an overripe melon dropped from a castle battlement, his head exploded. The discharge scattered blood-matted chunks of hairy flesh, skull fragments and portions of brain. Headless, the stump gushing torrid crimson, his corpse took a faltering step before crashing to the floor. It lay twitching, its life essence pumping out into a spreading, sticky pool.

Many in the front row had their ashen faces and smart dress uniforms splattered by the eruption. An objectionable reek hung in the air.

One of the zombie bodyguards, noticing dully that blood and brain matter covered his bare forearm, started to lick it off with noisy relish.

"Note this well!" Jennesta intoned sternly. "As this man confessed his guilt I chose to deal with him mercifully. Any others who transgress will not be treated with such lenience." She touched a hand lightly to her brow. "The effort has tired me. Go. All of you. Except you, Hacher. You stay."

The spectators began to file out, several dabbing themselves with handkerchiefs. Some hurried, looking as though they sought the nearest privy.

Hacher was wiping the gore from his own face when Jennesta approached, her brace of undead hobbling a few steps behind.

"I trust the import of what you've just seen was not lost on you, General," she said.

He glanced at the sergeant's corpse. Blood was dripping from the edge of the dais. "Hardly."

"Good. Then I expect to see change, *profound* change, in the governance of this colony. Otherwise your administration is going to become acquainted with my less compassionate side. Is that clear?"

"Yes, Envoy. Perfectly."

"I know orcs. And I know the only thing they respect is force. If they raise a seditious hand, cut it off. If they slaughter a single trooper, send ten orcs to the charnel house. If they dare to rise up, grind their bones to dust. Leave them in no doubt who's master. Any less and you imperil our plans for this dependency."

"Which are?"

"Exploiting the land's riches. And in particular, the most valuable resource of all."

"I fear you may be disappointed in that regard. The few deposits of gold and silver we've found are hardly—"

"What I have in mind is worth more than mere gold."

"I don't follow."

"The greatest asset Acurial has to offer isn't to be found under the ground but walking upon it."

"You mean...the natives themselves?"

"Precisely. The orcs have the potential to be the greatest fighting force this world has ever seen."

"But these creatures are meek. Or at least most of them are. The ones who've taken up arms against us are the exception."

"As I said, I know their true natures. I know what they're capable of. *All* of them."

"Even if they do have an inborn aggression, and it could be brought out, why would they fight for us?"

Jennesta indicated her zombie retinue. "They'd have no choice. Subject to my will, their obedience would be beyond question. Imagine it. A slave army, incomparably ferocious and totally subservient."

"And this has the backing of Peczan?"

"As far as you're concerned, Hacher, I *am* Peczan. So why don't you leave the thinking to me and concentrate on instilling some terror in the population?"

Another meeting was taking place in the capital, not far from the fortress, in one of the resistance's many boltholes.

Making a rare excursion from her current hiding place, and having been brought under heavy guard by an elaborate route,

Primary Sylandya was present. She sat at the centre of the small gathering, a goblet of brandy and water to hand.

"You pulled off a great feat yesterday," she said, toasting her offspring and Coilla. "The Vixens acquitted themselves well on their first outing."

"It's time the females got their chance," Coilla replied.

"As I say, the raid was a triumph. The tithes you brought back have swelled our coffers, and I was especially pleased that you recovered those looted treasures."

"Saving trinkets ain't going to win this fight," Haskeer stated.

"Don't undervalue that act as a symbol," Sylandya told him. "It shows the citizenry that their heritage means something."

"And that there are orcs who stand against our oppressors," Brelan added.

Sylandya nodded. "We need to deliver more blows like yesterday's. Who knows? Perhaps if the occupation here is seen to be failing, Peczan's enemies in the east and south will be emboldened."

"The eastern and southern lands are a long way off, Mother," Brelan reminded her, "and they're human realms too. Barbarous tribes, most of them. There's little hope of our enemy's enemy doing anything that might aid our cause."

"I think that's right," Stryke agreed. "You can't rely on help from outside."

"Shouldn't that be *we*?" Sylandya said. "Or do you northern orcs see yourselves as apart from this struggle?"

"We see it as a fight for all orcs," Stryke returned sternly. "It's why we're here."

"Can we get back to the issue at hand?" Chillder asked. "Grilan-Zeat's due in not much more than a week and—"

"*If* it comes," Haskeer said.

"We have to believe it will," Chillder said. "It's a thin hope, but it's all we've got. The question is, what more can we do to hasten an uprising?"

"Take out Jennesta," Coilla replied. "That'd strike one hell of a blow."

"It'd also bring down some heavy reprisals."

"Isn't that what we want? A kick that wakes up the populace and rallies them?"

"We've talked over the assassination idea," Brelan explained, "and we're agreed it should go ahead."

Coilla smiled. "Good."

"But not right away."

"Why wait?" Haskeer grumbled. "Kill her now, I say."

"Our contacts inside the fortress need time to prepare and make us a map of the place. Meantime we carry on harrying the humans. We've got a particular mission in mind that should rock them."

"What is it?" Stryke asked.

"Don't worry, we'll keep you posted. But right now we need to get Mother out of here. She's too rich a prize for the authorities; we have to keep her out of their reach."

"A new hiding place?" Coilla said.

"Yes. But I'm not saying where. What you don't know they can't get out of you."

Brelan and Chillder left, accompanying Sylandya. The couple of other resistance members present went with them.

No sooner had they gone than Spurral and Dallog turned up. Shortly after, Pepperdyne arrived, still sweating from a training session. He had Standeven in tow.

"News," Stryke announced. "They've agreed to us targeting Jennesta."

Pepperdyne was scooping a ladle of water from a barrel. "Really?" He gulped the drink.

"You don't seem too excited about it."

"Just cautious. It's bound to be a dangerous mission, isn't it?"

"That doesn't seem to have worried you up to now."

"We still want revenge on Jennesta," Standeven hastily interjected. "But she's dangerous."

"You're telling us," Coilla said.

Stryke fixed the humans with a steady gaze. "There's something I've been meaning to ask you two. When we ran into you, you said you were seeking Jennesta because she stole your consignment of . . . gems, was it?"

"That's right," Standeven confirmed.

"But we know she hadn't been in Maras-Dantia for years. Why'd it take you so long to go after her?"

"It's a big world," Pepperdyne replied. "Well, the one we came from was." He shook his head, as though clearing it. "You know what I mean. It takes time to mount an expedition, and money. My master here had to recruit a small private army, then we travelled across continents and —"

"Seems to me you do a lot of talking for an aide, or servant or whatever you are. Why can't your master speak for himself?"

"He always had a silver tongue," Standeven explained awkwardly. "I often said he was capable of striking a better deal than I could myself. The words come more naturally to him."

Haskeer eyed Pepperdyne suspiciously. "You weren't a bloody wordsmith, were you? I hate the bastards. Making up stupid stories about us, branding us villains. According to them we're built like brick privies and hate the light. They say we eat babies, and everybody knows we only take human flesh when there's nothing else."

"No, I'm not a storyteller."

"Don't go spreading that talk outside the band, Haskeer," Stryke warned. "The orcs in these parts wouldn't understand it. Let's not give them more reasons to see us as different." He turned back to the humans. "I don't know about you pair. But just don't make the mistake of thinking we're fools."

"Wouldn't dream of it," Pepperdyne replied coolly.

"You're being too hard, Stryke," Coilla protested. "I owe Pepperdyne my life. He's proved himself." It wasn't lost on any of them that she left Standeven out of her reckoning.

"Maybe," Stryke said. "We'll see."

"Now do you mind if we eat?" Pepperdyne asked. Without waiting for an answer he headed for the door, Standeven at his heels.

Once it slammed, Coilla tackled Stryke with, "Why are you so hostile to them all of a sudden?"

"I got to thinking about their story, and it doesn't stack up. Pepperdyne might be straight, but the other one..."

"Yeah, well, no argument there. But I wouldn't be here if it wasn't for Jode."

"Jode?"

"You tend to feel pally to somebody who saves your neck."

"Never thought I'd see the day when you'd count a human as a friend."

"Just go easy on him, all right? He's been useful to us."

Stryke looked to the others present, and Jup caught his eye. "You've not said much, Sergeant."

"About the humans? I've no opinion, beyond not trusting the race much."

"More than that's ailing you," Spurral said, slipping an arm round his waist. "You've been morose for days. Spit it out."

"Well...I'm not likely to play a part in the assassination, am I? Or anything else going on for that matter. It's not as though *I* can go out dressed as a female."

"Why not?" Haskeer ribbed. "It'd suit you."

"Shut it, Haskeer," Jup retorted. "I'm not in the mood."

"I know it's hard on you," Stryke told him, "but your time will come."

"And when's that going to be?"

"There's something you could do tonight."

Jup perked up. "There is?"

"How about a little after hours mission? Part of the harrying."

"What did you have in mind?"

"I thought we might pick a fight. Are you game?"

24

Taress' night-time streets should have been deserted save for patrols enforcing the curfew. But others were abroad.

A group of figures moved stealthily through the capital, slipping from one pool of shadow to the next.

They were ten in number, and Stryke had kept it a strictly Wolverine affair. He led the pack, with Coilla, Jup and Haskeer close behind; Orbon, Zoda, Prooq, Reafdaw, Finje and Noskaa brought up the rear.

Across cobbled lanes and along twisting alleys, the band made its way to a district that would have swarmed with citizens during daylight. Only once did they come close to a watch patrol, a squad of some two dozen uniformed and robed men illuminating their path with lanterns that gave off a violet glow so intense it could only be magical. The Wolverines hid until they passed, pressed into door spaces and the black mouths of narrow passageways.

At length they came to a broad avenue made desolate by the absence of life or movement. Only a gentle breeze disturbed the balmy summer air.

Using the corner of one of the larger buildings as cover, they peered round at their target. Situated on the opposite side of the road, it was a simple one-storey, brick-built structure, typical of many such scattered throughout the city. Serving as both a guard station and barracks, it had a single, robust door and slit windows. To one side stood a hitching rail where four of five horses were tied up. A pair of guards were stationed outside the building's entrance.

"What do you think?" Stryke whispered.

"We've taken better places drunk," Jup reckoned. "Know how many are inside?"

Stryke shook his head. "No idea." He looked to Coilla. "You all right with this?"

"Sure."

He checked that the others were ready. "Then *go.*"

Coilla stepped out from their hiding place and sprinted towards the guard post.

The sentries didn't see her at first. As soon as they did, they instantly bucked up and drew their weapons.

Coilla began to yell. *"Help! Help me! Please help!"*

That threw the guards. They exchanged perplexed looks, and though they kept a defensive stance, it was half-hearted.

Coilla carried on running, still shouting, and waved her arms about in what she hoped was a helpless female kind of way. The sentries stared at her.

Stryke barked an order. Two grunts rushed forward, their bows nocked. Coilla dropped and hugged the ground.

Arrows smacked into the guards. They went down.

As Coilla scrambled to her feet the guardhouse door flew open. Alerted by the commotion, men poured out. Many were minus their tunics or otherwise had their dress in disarray, having been off duty. But they had swords. Coilla drew her own and, bellowing, ran in their direction.

Her war cry was taken up by the Wolverines. Spilling from their hiding place, they charged.

Coilla reached the foremost of the troopers. He made the mistake of trying to bring her down with a tackle. She relied on her sword. As he dived at her, she lashed out, raking his torso. When he doubled, she drove her blade into his back.

A second man immediately moved in. Mindful of the fate of the first, he advanced warily. Coilla powered into him and their blades clashed. An exchange of blows ensued, the pealing of steel on steel echoing through the silent night. His swordplay had a certain finesse. Coilla had the edge in savagery. Knocking aside his incoming sword, she exploited the breach and punctured his lung.

With a roar, the rest of the orcs swept in. The two sides met and a bloody melee erupted. Then it quickly fragmented into a string of discrete fights.

Haskeer laid about him with a two-handed axe. The first human he engaged soon felt its sting. Screaming, he reeled away with a grievous wound that had his left arm hanging by a thread. A charging soldier was the axe's next patron. Swinging fast and hard, Haskeer struck him in the neck, cleanly decapitating the man.

The head bounced several feet and landed in Jup's path. He kicked it aside and faced up to a duo of spear-wielding guardsmen. They were dismayed by their first sight of a dwarf, and startled to see a basically humanoid creature battling alongside orcs. Exploiting their hesitancy, Jup piled into them.

He had the edge as a fighter. The troopers employed their spears by jabbing energetically but with little accuracy. Jup was master of his staff, and used it with greater skill. Some adroit footwork got him past the first spearman's defences to deliver a weighty blow that shattered his skull.

The second man drew back, brandishing his spear to keep Jup at bay. Feigning an advance, then quickly changing tack, the dwarf evaded the weapon and took a swipe at his opponent's head. The human shifted smartly, narrowly avoiding the strike. But Jup rallied instantly. Sweeping his staff low, he cracked it across the man's legs, flooring him; Reafdaw, fighting alongside, spun and plunged his sword into the prone trooper's guts. Dwarf and grunt exchanged a thumbs up and carried on brawling.

Someone started ringing an alarm bell mounted next to the guardhouse door. Its shrill din cut through the night like a hatchet. Zoda lifted his bow and launched an arrow at the bell ringer. It missed, its sharpened tip chipping the guardhouse wall. Zoda groped for another shaft.

Haskeer had fought his way nearer to the building. He brought his axe back over his shoulder, far enough that the head nearly touched the base of his spine. Then he swung it up and over, grunting with the effort of lobbing it. Spinning end over end, the axe flew above the struggling combatants, gathering impetus. It struck the chest of the man at the bell with enough force to pin him to the guardhouse door.

The door opened outwards, with the body still attached, and a couple of stragglers exited. It slammed behind them, the hanging corpse jiggling with the impact.

Stryke was embroiled in grinding combat with a heftily built sergeant. The man's weapon, through choice or hasty necessity, was a long-handled iron mallet, which he managed as nimbly as Stryke plied his sword. Seemingly tireless, the human kept the hammer in constant flight. Several times his swinging passes came dangerously close to Stryke's head, and his greater reach barred retaliation.

Tiring of the cat and mouse, Stryke switched from targeting the man to concentrating on the weapon. As he dodged another swing, he twisted and brought his blade down on the mallet's haft. The steel bit into the wood near the head, but didn't entirely sever it. A brief tussle disengaged the weapons.

Retreating a step, the sergeant grinned and brought up the mallet for another blow. He did it with such force that the weakened head snapped off and flew over his shoulder. It landed on one of his comrades, braining him. Oblivious, the sergeant swept the weapon downward towards Stryke. It has halfway through its arc before he realised the head was missing. While he gaped at the splintered pole he was holding, Stryke ran him through.

The Wolverines had got the better of the guardsmen. Most lay dead or wounded, and the orcs were making short work of the few still standing. Stryke barked an order and the band rushed for the guards' station.

Coilla got there first. Wrenching open the door, with its dead trooper affixed, she stormed inside.

The interior was little more than a long dormitory. Cots lined one wall, lockers and stacked chests were heaped against the other. At the far end was a door ajar, leading to a privy. Coilla judged the place empty of troopers.

She was wrong.

As she walked past the row of cots, a figure leapt up. He had been hiding between two of the beds, pressed to the floor in sly ambush or trembling cowardice, and he hefted a sword.

He came at her fast, yelling something, the sword in motion. Coilla swerved, rapped the blade aside and booted his stomach. He landed on a cot, struggled to right himself, half rose. Then he fell back with a groan, her blade in his innards. She finished him with a thrust to the heart.

He was young, as far as Coilla could tell with humans. She wondered why he didn't try surrendering, though she wasn't sure what she would have done if he had.

The door opened. Jup, Haskeer and Stryke came in, along with several of the others.

"All clear?" Stryke asked.

"Is now," Coilla replied.

They checked the place, to be sure.

"Look at this," Jup said, kneeling by an open chest.

The others gathered round. Somebody snatched a lantern

and held it above the chest. It was neatly packed with military sabres, oiled and wrapped in muslin.

"New issue," Stryke said, "and nice pieces by the look of them. We'll take what we can carry."

They lifted four boxes and hauled them outside. The door and attendant corpse slammed shut behind them.

"Do we torch the place?" Coilla asked.

Stryke looked to the sky. It was lightening. "No. The sun will be up soon. We should be moving." He turned to Jup. "Feeling better?"

The dwarf smiled. "A bit of bloodletting always blows away the cobwebs. It makes for a good—"

There was a commotion from the tethered horses. They shied and pawed the ground. A figure scrambled into the saddle of one and pulled away. As he galloped off, Coilla pitched a throwing knife at him. It fell short, clattering on the cobbled street. A couple of the grunts began chasing the rider.

"*Let him be!*" Stryke ordered, waving them back.

"He looked wounded to me," Jup said.

Haskeer nodded. "Reckon he was playing dead 'til he got his chance."

"Doesn't matter now," Stryke told them. "We did what we set out to do. Let's get out of here."

The rider wore no tunic, and his white combat blouse was stained with blood. Leaning forward in the saddle, in obvious discomfort, he rode hard to get away from the guardhouse.

The streets were still deserted. But dawn was breaking, and soon the curfew would lift.

Without knowing it, the wounded trooper careered past something incongruous. At the side of the road there was a small portion of space at odds with reality. A sachet of non-actuality that denied light.

Pelli Madayar was concealed in the anomaly's embrace. She had something like a crystal in her hand. It was the size of an egg, with markings that made it look like the abstract representation of an open eye, flecked with a mingling of colours resembling oil on water. She held it at arm's length and slowly panned across the scene several blocks distant, where the Wolverines were stealing into the dying night with their crates of plunder.

"You see?" she said, seemingly addressing no one but herself.

"I see," came the reply. It emanated from the not quite crystal, oddly distorted by its passage across innumerable worlds. Warped, but recognisably the voice of Karrell Revers. "And it further confirms that the orcs are interfering dangerously in the affairs of that plain," he went on. "But we knew this, Pelli. You must act."

"I'm aware of what should be done. My fear is that, in trying to prevent any damage the warband may do, we further aggravate the situation. Things are complex here. We have to choose our time with care."

"You're facing the inherent paradox the Corps has to deal with: to prevent interference, we must interfere."

"So how *do* I deal with it?"

"You use your judgement. If I didn't believe you were capable of coping with the present irregularity you wouldn't be in charge of this mission. But be warned, Pelli. The longer you leave intervening, the more events will fester; and when you strike, it has to be decisively."

"I understand."

"Keep one thing in mind. The Wolverines have to be stopped, by whatever means you need to employ."

"I can't help feeling that fate is about to deal them too harsh a punishment. They're starting to seem like no more than pawns in this drama."

"That may well be so. But they are a martial race, and walk with death as a matter of routine. I say again that you must put aside any feelings of consideration you may have for these creatures. Don't go soft on me, Pelli. Because forces of great destruction have been set in motion, and they're on course for a collision."

As the sun rose, there was a bustle of activity around Taress' fortress.

Orc labourers were toiling in the empty moat, clearing out debris that had taken years to accumulate, preparatory to it being flooded again. Crews were beefing up the other defences. New bars of thick metal were being affixed across lower windows. The main gate was reinforced with sheets of iron.

Kapple Hacher stood on the access road, watching the work progress. His aide, Frynt, was beside him, ticking items on a parchment list.

"It's a crying shame," Hacher stated, "that this place was allowed to fall into such a sorry state by the former regime. The defences are a joke."

"They're not a warlike race, sir. I expect they didn't see the need."

"But they saw fit to build the fortress in the first place, whoever long ago that was." He grew thoughtful. "Which makes me think..."

"Sir?"

"Nothing. Will the work be completed on schedule, do you think?"

"It should be if we have them working day and night."

"Bring in more labour if you have to. I want it finished as soon as possible."

"Do you really think the fortress could come under attack, sir?"

"The way things are going, anything's possible. And I don't want to leave us open to the Envoy's displeasure."

"Ah, yes, sir. But is this enough to satisfy the lady Jennesta?"

"In itself, no. I wouldn't expect it to. It's just one measure. The crackdown I'm planning should mollify her to some extent. At least for a while."

"Yes, sir. Let's hope so."

"In that respect..." Hacher looked about, as though spying for eavesdroppers, and his voice dropped. "In that respect there's been something of a breakthrough."

"General?"

"Breathe a word of this and I'll have your tongue. Understood?"

Frynt looked offended at the idea of him being loose with the organ in question. "Of course, sir."

"We've got an informer. Not one of your usual low level turncoats either. This is somebody within the resistance itself. Close to the leadership, in fact."

"Really, sir? May I ask who?"

If Hacher was going to answer the question, it wasn't to be at that moment.

There was a chorus of shouts from the guard detail supervising the workers.

A soldier had arrived on horseback. His shirt was bloodstained and he was yelling. The sentries rushed to him, and he fell into their arms.

25

"Will you stop that bloody row!" Haskeer barked.

Wheam cringed and quit plucking his lute. "I was only—"

"You were only driving me crazy. Now stow the damn thing and follow me."

"Where?"

"Stryke wants you in on something. Fuck knows why. Now move your arse."

Haskeer led him to the rear of the safe house and a closed door. Typically, he ignored niceties and barged in.

The room was the largest in the building, and crowded. It looked as though all the Wolverines were present, along with a number of resistance members and a smattering of Vixens.

Stryke was standing near the door.

"Here he is," Haskeer said. "Though why the hell you'd want him involved—"

"All right, Sergeant. Plant yourself somewhere."

Grumbling, Haskeer went and lounged against a wall, arms folded.

Wheam looked up at Stryke and swallowed. "What do you want me for, Captain?"

"A mission's being planned. We need everybody we can get. That includes you."

"*Me?* But—"

"My band carries no dead weight. It's time you proved yourself."

"I...I wouldn't want to let you down."

"Then see you don't. Now shut up and find a place to perch." He jabbed a thumb.

Wheam spotted Dallog. He weaved meekly through the throng and settled on a patch of floor next to him.

There was a lot of low level muttering. Whatever was going to happen hadn't started yet.

Brelan went to the head of the room and they quietened down. "Everybody here? Good. As you all know, Grilan-Zeat's due to show itself soon. In not too many days' time it'll be at its most visible. When that happens, my mother's going to address the citizenry and the uprising begins. At least, that's what we're hoping. Before that, we need to soften up the enemy, and rattle 'em enough that they'll hit back and rile the populace. We want the pot boiling when the Primary makes her appearance. This is one of the ways we'll do it." There was a crudely drawn map affixed to the wall behind him. He pointed to an area circled in red.

"What is it?" Coilla asked.

"Army camp. A small fort."

"Where?"

"A bit beyond the city limits, to the west. Most of the likely targets here in Taress are better protected since our campaign started, so we're looking further afield."

"What's that wavy line next to it?"

"A river. Fast flowing. And here," he tapped a point near the river's end, "there's a waterfall."

"It might not be as secure as places here in the city," Jup said, "but it's still a fort. Won't it be a tough nut?"

"Which is why we need to muster as big a force as we can."

"So the Vixens will play their part," Chillder explained, "and you too, Jup and Spurral, if you're willing."

The dwarfs nodded. "But what about us being seen?" Jup asked.

"The way we intend going about this, it won't matter. Besides, we'll keep you hidden until we're out of the city."

From the back of the room, Pepperdyne raised a hand. "What can we..." He glanced at Standeven, slumped beside him. "What can I do?"

"Lend your sword arm," Stryke told him. "But we can't pull the uniform stunt again."

"No," Brelan confirmed, "they'll be wise to that by now. Though what we have in mind doesn't call for it. But there's something else you all need to know about the raid. It'll be tomorrow."

"That's one hell of a short notice," Coilla remarked. "Why so soon?"

"Two reasons. First, security. The longer between hatching a plan and carrying it out, the more chance it'll leak."

"You've got turncoats in your ranks?"

"*No,*" Brelan came back huffily. "But it's a rare orc who won't break in one of Peczan's torture chambers."

"What's the second reason?" Stryke said.

"We've learnt there's going to be a changing of the guard at the fort. The new contingent's drawn from the reinforcements we welcomed with the stampede, and they're due to relieve the outgoing company today. Tomorrow's their first full day in a new camp. We'll know the layout better than they do. It's a good time to hit them."

"Makes sense. But you still haven't said how we're going to get in there."

Chillder smiled. "We have a way."

"Think it'll work?" Coilla said.

Stryke shrugged. "What do *you* think? You're our mistress of strategy."

"It's a smart plan, but it's complex. The more parts to a scheme, the more to go wrong."

"What would you change?"

"I'd like us to have a good fallback. You know, a better escape route. Maybe more than one."

"Any ideas on that?"

She nodded. "But it'd take a few fighters out of the front line, and mean some hard work for us overnight."

"Sort out the details soon as you can. I'll talk to Brelan about it."

They were sitting on a weathered, low stone wall in a small inner courtyard of the house the resistance had commandeered. It was one of the few places they were able to find a little privacy.

"Are you sure about Wheam?" Coilla said. "Him coming on the raid, I mean."

"No, I'm not. But we need to make a good show of numbers. Brelan reckons they'll be a couple of hundred humans in that fort. We'll be lucky to scrape together as many on our side. Besides, he's never going to shape up if we don't put him in the field."

"Unsupervised?"

"I'll get somebody to keep an eye on him."

"And tie up a fighter."

"Then I'll put him in some support role."

"Is it worth the risk?"

"Look, if Wheam gets himself killed...well, too bad."

"You mean that? Despite what his father said?"

"Fuck it, Coilla, I won't be cowed by threats from Quoll or anybody else. I thought we got away from all that shit when we left Maras-Dantia. If Quoll ends up with a beef we can settle it with blades. Nobody stops me getting back to Thirzarr and the hatchlings."

"I'd go along with that. But you're being too hard on Wheam. It's not his fault he's in this fix."

"Maybe." He sighed. "Guess I'm feeling a bit snappy."

"Reason?"

"I didn't think things would be this knotty. I want to cut through it all and get to Jennesta."

"You're not alone in that, Stryke. We all want it. But meantime we can help some fellow orcs. That's not bad, is it?"

"Suppose not."

"Tell me something. You've been uneasy about Pepperdyne, but now he's in on this raid. Why?"

"I could say I prefer to have him where I can see him. Truth is, I'm not sure about him. But we need his skills, so..."

"I think you can trust him."

"So you keep saying. I reckon you're a bit partial there."

" 'Cos he's saved my life a couple of times? You bet I am."

"Don't forget he's a human, Coilla. Blood will out."

"Maybe we shouldn't judge others the way we've been judged."

"And maybe some *should* be. Or would you prefer trying to reason with Peczan's army?"

She smiled. "Looking out for tyros and humans you don't trust. You're going to have your hands full tomorrow."

Several hours later, with most resistance members away preparing for the morrow and the shadows lengthening, a human furtively approached the safe house. Despite the clement weather he was bundled in a cloak, and wore an expansive hat with its brim pulled well down to hide his features. Looking to the right and left, he pushed open the door and slipped inside.

There was a room close by the entrance, its door half open. As the intruder crept past, Pepperdyne leapt out of it. They crashed into the opposite wall and a struggle ensued. The man's hat was ripped from his head.

"You!" Pepperdyne exclaimed.

"Take your hands *off* me!" Standeven demanded.

"In here!" Pepperdyne growled, dragging his master into the empty room. Ignoring his protests, he flung him into a chair. "You're lucky I happened to be the one on guard duty. Where the *hell* have you been?"

"I have to account to you for my movements now, do I?"

"You do when you disappear for hours on end without a word. What's going on?"

Standeven dusted himself off with an exaggerated gesture. "I had to get out."

"What, for a stroll?"

"You've seen something of this place. I've only been shunted from one stinking hideout to another."

"My outings haven't exactly been pleasure trips."

"That's your choice. I needed air, and the sight of other faces. I wanted to get away from these creatures you're so fond of."

"So you took a walk in a city full of them."

"*Yes*. And how might that imperil this sordid little enterprise?"

"You fool. What if you'd been picked up by the authorities?"

"They're only interested in orc insurgents. Humans have privileges in this place, I saw that much."

"They know a human's *working* with them!"

"So you can have free run of the outside but I can't. You're not my jailer."

"It seems you need one."

"If we ever get back home, I'll..."

"You still haven't got it through your head, have you? Things are different here. They're different between you and me."

"Which might not last forever."

"You wish."

"And in the event of things going back to the way they were, your fortunes are going to depend on how you behave now. You'd do well to keep that in mind."

"I'm doing my best to keep us alive. Isn't that enough?"

Standeven adopted a conciliatory tone. "And I appreciate it, Jode. I really do."

"You've a strange way of showing it. How do I know what you were up to out there?"

"Wouldn't I be stupid to do anything that might jeopardise my own safety? My wellbeing's tied to this ragtag bunch of rebels, same as you." He spread his hands and added reasonably, "I've nowhere else to go."

"You know the thing about you, Standeven? I can never be quite sure if you're a knave or an idiot."

"On this occasion, probably the latter. I was foolhardy. I'm sorry."

Pepperdyne considered his master's words, and said, "If you ever do anything like this again..."

"I won't. I give you my word. Now forget my stupidity and save your anger for tomorrow."

Pepperdyne expelled a breath and relaxed a little. "Yeah, tomorrow. It's going to be an interesting day."

"I'm sure of it," Standeven agreed.

26

The fort was old. It was built in times long forgotten as part of Acurial's border defences. The pacifistic orcs of the present epoch had allowed it to fall into neglect, and its restoration was undertaken by the human invaders.

It stood on the edge of a rock-face, some thirty to forty feet high, and looked out over an expanse of open land that ran to the distant sea. Below the fort, nestling at the foot of the cliff, was a line of wooden buildings. They were of much more recent vintage, having been erected by orcs of the current era to store grain from nearby farms and to over-winter their cattle. With the coming of the humans these buildings were abandoned and left to rot.

The opposite side of the fort, where its entrance was situated, faced a grassy plain that stretched to the city of Taress. Not that the city could be seen. Even if it hadn't been too far away, a semicircle of squat hills obscured the view, and set the fort in a depression. As a result, the road that ran to its gates was on a slight incline. To the south-west, also hidden, a major river flowed.

A force of orcs, some ninety strong, had approached covertly, and now concealed themselves behind the hill crests. They brought three wagons, the horses' hooves muffled with sacking. The orcs took care to mask their advance. Patrols had been ambushed and lookouts purged.

Brelan commanded the force. Haskeer, Dallog and Pepperdyne were part of it, along with Wheam. Roughly half the Wolverines were present, and resistance members made up the rest.

Peeking over the ridge, Brelan surveyed the fort. It was constructed of stone. There were two towers, and sentries toured the battlements. But there was no moat or portcullis. The road swept straight down to its wooden gates, which were not unlike barn doors, albeit taller and sturdier.

Brelan pulled back and ordered the wagons to be brought up almost to the peak of the hill, where they were still out of sight. The horses were unhitched and quietly led away, and the wagons' shafts were removed. Each wagon carried a stout tree trunk with its fore-end iron-capped. These were hauled forward and securely lashed in place, so that the points jutted from the front.

The wagons had a central lever installed at the driver's end which connected to chains attached to the front axle.

Pepperdyne studied the arrangement. "Clever. But how much control does the lever give?"

"Not a lot," Brelan admitted. "Just enough to steer it a little to the left or right, though it takes some strength to do even that. Which is why we'll have two pairs of hands on each."

"How about braking?"

"There's only the wagon's brake. But we're not sure that'd work, given the weight we'll be shifting. We're relying on the things stopping of their own accord, once the gates and level ground slow them."

"Bit iffy, isn't it?"

"It's the best we could do."

Pepperdyne turned and saw Wheam standing nearby. His lips were silently moving and he wore a look of intense concentration. "All right, Wheam?"

The youngster nodded, and said out loud, "One hundred and four, one hundred and five, one hundred and six..."

"You're doing fine," Pepperdyne told him. "Keep it up."

"One hundred and seven, one hundred and eight, one hundred and nine..."

"Good," Stryke said. "Try to keep to that pace."

Spurral gave him a thumbs up and continued counting under her breath.

They were part of a group, numbering about fifty, cautiously edging their way along the base of the cliff below the fort.

Stryke led them. Spurral, Jup, Coilla and Chillder were acting as his lieutenants. The remainder of the group comprised the balance of the Wolverines, all of the Vixens, and a contingent from the resistance.

They pressed as close to the cliff face as possible, sheltering beneath a narrow overhang to avoid being seen. Their path took them to the first of the derelict buildings.

"We need the third one," Chillder reminded him in a whisper.

Stryke nodded.

He didn't want to take the risk of breaking cover and approaching the building they wanted head-on. So he beckoned a couple of grunts and they set to carefully prising off rotting planks on the side of the first building. When a big enough gap was opened, Stryke began shepherding the group through.

The interior stank of mould, and the floor was strewn with rubble. Just enough light lanced through cracks in the building's fabric for them to see. Stumbling across to the opposite wall, they repeated the process, levering planks off with dagger blades.

Fortunately the buildings abutted each other, which meant no open space between them where the orcs might have been spotted. They had to get through two sets of planks, but they were so decayed it didn't present a problem.

The second building was very much like the first. Except that a mass of fallen timbers blocked the far wall and had to be cleared.

"How we doing, Spurral?" Stryke asked.

"Four hundred and seventy-nine, four hundred and eighty..."

"Right. *Move it,*" he urged the others. "Time's running out."

They got the timbers shifted and attacked the final wall. It was in the same state as the others and they were soon through.

The third building was the biggest so far, with barn-like dimensions and a high roof.

"This way," Chillder said, heading for the rear.

Stryke ordered hooded lamps to be lit and they saw heaps of debris and wood stacked against the back wall.

"Here," Chillder instructed.

They all piled into moving the obstructions and made short work of it. What was revealed was the bare cliff face. But when the lanterns were held close the light showed a large semicircular area that wasn't the same colour as the rock.

"It's just mortar," Chillder explained. "We've already done the work. You've only to break through."

Three or four orcs came forward with sledgehammers that had cloth wrapped around their heads to deaden the sound. They pounded at the mortar and it fell away in great chunks. Dust swirled in the already fusty air, and there was a chorus of coughing and spitting. In minutes an opening like a cave mouth had been excavated.

Stryke had more lanterns lit and torches fired.

"It's a labyrinth in there," Chillder warned. "I'd better go first." She took one of the torches.

They found themselves in a long tunnel low enough that all but the dwarfs had to stoop. It sloped upwards on a steep gradient, and the floor was worn so smooth their boots had trouble gaining purchase.

At last they came to a level. Facing them were the mouths of two more tunnels. Chillder took the one on the right. It was taller than the one they entered by, but much narrower, making its transit oppressive. This led to a circular chamber. On its far side was a stairway carved out of the rock. They started to climb.

The stairs, perhaps a hundred in total, delivered them to a passageway. Along its length were the entrances to a dozen or more tunnels. Without hesitating, Chillder strode to one and entered. It was short.

They came out in a high but constricted gallery. On both sides were ledges of stone reaching to the ceiling. The ledges were packed with skulls. There were bones too. Thigh bones, arm bones, ribs, all neatly stacked and forming solid yellowy-white walls. Every few yards there were complete skeletons, standing to attention as though guarding the house of death.

If an archer had loosed an arrow from where they stood, it would have scarcely reached the far end of the gallery. The skulls and various bones, unmistakably from orcs, numbered in their thousands. Quite possibly hundreds of thousands.

"Welcome to one of the catacombs of Acurial," Chillder announced, a certain awe in her voice.

"How long has this been here?" Coilla asked, taking in the display.

"It's ancient," Chillder explained. "Older than we can guess. At one time, long ago, all orcs were placed in galleries like this when their end came. Our ancestors have slept here for untold centuries."

"The humans don't know about this?" Jup said.

"Most of our own don't know about it. It's just another part of our lost heritage. The resistance discovered it by accident when we were looking for a way into the fortress."

"We should keep moving," Stryke said.

They walked the length of the gallery, their footsteps echoing eerily. The empty eye sockets of the long dead seemed to follow their progress.

At the end of the gallery was another passage and yet more tunnels. Chillder entered the first they came to, and counted as she paced along it. It was so low they could touch the ceiling with ease. Suddenly she stopped and looked up.

"This is the place," she stated.

Their torches showed a white cross marked on the ceiling.

"How we doing, Spurral?" Stryke wanted to know.

"Seven hundred and eleven, seven hundred and twelve, seven hundred and..."

"Let's get on with it."

He called over grunts with picks and shovels.

"*Wait!*" Jup exclaimed.

They turned to see that he was standing with his arms held high and palms pressed to the wall.

"What is it?" Chillder demanded.

"Not here," Jup said. "It's not right."

"What are you talking about?"

Stryke went to him. "What do you sense, Jup?"

"Sense?" Chillder said, obviously bewildered.

"This isn't a good place," Jup replied. "There's a concentration of...I'm not sure. But above this point isn't where we want to come out. There's activity up there. Malevolent."

"Will somebody tell me what's going on?" Chillder demanded.

"Jup has a . . ." Stryke faltered. "He's sensitive to certain things. You're sure, Jup?"

"The farsight works well here. Clearer than I ever knew it in," he glanced at Chillder, "in the north. Believe me, this isn't where we should be. Can we move on a bit? Find another spot?"

"Have you gone insane?" Chillder fumed.

Stryke fixed her with a resolute gaze. "If Jup says it's dangerous for us to break through here, then we'd better listen. He's never wrong about these things. Believe me."

"If you think we're going to change the plan at the last minute on the say so of a—"

"Eight hundred and seventy-one, eight hundred and seventy-two . . . ," Spurral chimed in, glaring at them.

"Trust us, Chillder," Stryke said. "That or stand aside. Only make up your mind now. There's no time for this."

"Gods, you're all crazy," Chillder decided. "This was worked out with care." She jabbed a thumb at the ceiling. "Coming up here puts us behind an outbuilding, somewhere there's less chance of being seen."

"We can't do it. Where else?"

She hesitated for a split second, took in the resolution on his face, and sighed. "I must be damn crazy myself." She turned and looked further along the tunnel. "Let's see . . ."

"Hurry," Coilla urged.

"Let me think!"

Chillder walked the tunnel, staring upwards as though trying to remember or imagine what lay above. They others shuffled along behind her. She stopped, looked as though she was about to say something, then moved on.

The tunnel was a dead-end, and they almost reached it before she halted again. "Here. I think."

"Jup?" Stryke said.

The dwarf put his hand to the ceiling and closed his eyes.

Time slowed to a glacial pace before he opened them again and nodded.

"Move yourselves!" Stryke ordered.

Grunts rushed forward and attacked the ceiling with their picks.

"Nine hundred and thirty-four," Spurral recited, "nine hundred and thirty-five..."

"...nine hundred and thirty-six," Wheam chanted, "nine hundred and thirty-seven..."

"Right." Brelan turned to Haskeer and Dallog. "Get the wagons ready." They went off to relay the order. To Pepperdyne he said, "Clear about the timing?"

Pepperdyne nodded.

"And the archers?"

"Waiting on your word."

"Good. Take your position."

Pepperdyne left him.

"Wheam?" Brelan said.

"Nine hundred and forty-nine, nine hundred and fifty..."

Several dozen orcs were pushing the first wagon to the summit of the hill. The second and third were being readied for their turn. On either side of the road, teams of the resistance's archers were keeping low and looking Brelan's way.

He signalled to the first wagon. It stopped just short of the crest. Fourteen or fifteen heavily armed orcs scrambled aboard.

Brelan looked to Wheam again.

"Nine hundred and seventy-two, nine hundred and..."

Further down the hill, behind the waiting wagons, Haskeer was gathering together the forty or fifty warriors whose job was to provide the motive force, and later be part of the assault on foot. His method seemed to consist largely of swiping at their backsides with the flat of his sword and lots of muttered swearing.

"Wheam," Brelan repeated.

"Nine hundred and eighty-nine, nine hundred and ninety..."

"Keep it aloud."

"Nine hundred and ninety-one, nine hundred and ninety-two..."

Brelan unsheathed his sword and raised it. He could feel every eye on him.

"...nine hundred and ninety-four, nine hundred and ninety-five..."

The pushing crew flowed to the first wagon. Archers nocked their arrows.

"Nine hundred and ninety-seven, nine hundred and ninety-eight..." Wheam's voice strained with tension. "Nine hundred and ninety-nine... *one thousand!*"

Brelan's sword came down in a decisive slash.

The archers leapt up, aimed and fired. Arrows winged towards the fort's battlements. Sentries fell.

The pushing crew shoved the first wagon to the crest of the hill, then over it. Once it reached the downward incline it began to move of its own accord and the crew let go. As it rumbled past Brelan he grabbed hold and scrambled aboard. The wagon picked up speed, bumping and bouncing on the potholed road, with Brelan and a fellow resistance member clutching the steering lever.

Orc archers kept up a steady stream of arrows, pinning down most of the fort's own bowmen. But the garrison had started to return fire. Arrows zinged over and around the careering wagon.

Wheam ran to Pepperdyne, by the second wagon. "Do you think they'll make it?"

"If they don't, we've got two more tries. Now get to your place."

Wheam joined Dallog at the last wagon.

Brelan's party was travelling as fast as a galloping horse and still picking up speed. They hung on grimly as the wagon bucked at every rut it hit. But it was halfway to its destination and still on course. Brelan hoped it would stay that way. He was doubtful they could steer with any accuracy if it deviated.

At the top of the hill the second wagon was trundled into place. Its crew climbed aboard, and Pepperdyne took the steering lever, along with Bhose. The pushers moved in, ready for the off.

"Steady!" Pepperdyne cautioned. *"Wait for it!"*

When Brelan's team started their descent the fortress looked like a child's plaything. Now it filled their world. They could make out the coarse texture of its stonework, the faces of the defenders on its battlements. And as the distance closed, the danger grew. The wagon became the prime target of the fort's archers, and bolts rained down on the orcs' raised shields.

There was a jolt as the road levelled, but no loss of momentum. Nor did the wagon vary its course. It hurtled into the fort's shadow, wheels blurred with speed. The defenders lobbed spears and rocks. Slingshot bounced off the orcs' shields.

Dead ahead, the towering gates loomed.

"Hold on!" Brelan bellowed.

Stryke saw nothing but blue sky.

He hauled himself up and cautiously poked his head through the opening. After a quick look he ducked back down. "We need to move fast," he told the others. "Follow me." He climbed out.

He was near one of the fort's outer walls, on the edge of its parade ground. The gates could be seen on the far side of the square. There were several stone buildings a short sprint from where Stryke stood. He could see men on the battlements above, but as far as he could tell, no one had spotted him.

The others began scrambling out of the hole. He hurried things on, directing them to shelter by one of the outbuildings.

When Chillder emerged he pulled her to one side. "Where would we have come out if we stuck to the plan?"

She got her bearings. Then she pointed to a large building about a hundred paces away. It was plain, with few windows, set high, and could have been a barracks. "On the other side of that."

Stryke sent her to join the others. He kept an eye on the place she indicated until the last of his party came up. Then he hurried after them, keeping low.

"So what did we avoid?" Chillder wanted to know, still doubtful.

"Whatever it is," Stryke told her, "it's behind that barracks."

A commotion interrupted them. They looked to the square. Dozens of soldiers were running towards the gates.

"They've spotted Brelan," Stryke said.

Coilla drew her sword. "Then let's stop 'em."

"I don't like having that at our backs." He nodded at the barracks.

"So what do we do?"

"Split our forces," he quickly decided. "You and the Vixens as one unit; Jup and me take the rest."

Coilla fished out a coin. "Call." She flipped it.

"Heads."

She caught the coin and slapped it on the back of her hand. "Heads it is. What do you want?"

"You get the gate."

She gestured to Chillder, Spurral and the other females. They peeled off from the group and followed her.

Stryke, Jup and the remainder of the party sprinted for the barracks.

They reached its nearest wall and flowed round to the side, lessening the chance of being seen from the square. It was a wonder to Stryke that no one up on the parapet had noticed them yet. But they seemed to be concentrating on whatever was happening outside the fort. He had a couple of his archers keep watch.

Signalling the others to hold their position, he and Jup crept to the corner and peered round it. Some twenty or thirty paces along, in the broad space between the barracks and the fortress wall, there was a large group of soldiers. They stood silently in a wide circle, weapons drawn, staring at the ground.

"That was our welcome," Stryke whispered.

"How did they *know*?" Jup asked.

"Good question."

They stealthily withdrew and rejoined the rest of the group.

With gestures and soft words, Stryke filled them in. Then he divided his force. Half, led by Jup, were sent to one end of the barracks. He took the other half to the opposite end. A lone orc lingered midway, ready to signal when they were in position.

Once he did, the two groups poured around the corners of the building. They charged the startled would-be ambushers from both sides, bellowing war cries, and fell upon them.

The Vixens were halfway to the gates before they were spotted.

Soldiers rushed to engage them. Arrows winged from the battlements.

Coilla, Spurral and Chillder were in the vanguard, and they tore into the humans with savagery. Thirty screaming females, wildly slashing steel, set about the troops like a flock of blood-lusting harpies. A dozen lethal brawls boiled in the middle of the square. More soldiers dashed towards the maelstrom.

There was a tremendous crash. The gates exploded inwards, crushing defenders on either side as Brelan's horseless wagon hurtled through. It ploughed into fleeing troopers, shattering their bones and bouncing over their broken bodies.

The wagon rumbled on across the square, humans scattering in its path. It demolished the corner of a storehouse, but kept going, though its speed reduced. Finally it smacked dead centre into the side of another, sturdier building, where its ram buried itself in the brickwork.

Its payload of bellowing orcs leapt free and charged into the fray.

Then the mayhem started in earnest.

27

"*Now!*" Pepperdyne yelled.

He and Bhose gripped the steering lever. Behind them, the orc attack team braced themselves. The pushing crew shoved the wagon over the lip of the hill and sent it on its downward path.

Pepperdyne could clearly see the damage to the fortress gates, and, on the battlements, more defenders than before. The orc archers sent out another volley, and human bowmen responded.

"We've used up the element of surprise," Pepperdyne said, the wind whipping his hair. "This could be rougher than Brelan's ride."

Bhose nodded grimly.

As they gathered speed, the human gazed at the fortress and added, "I wonder what the hell's going on inside there."

Stryke and his team had made the space behind the barracks block a rat trap. Now it was a bloodbath.

The humans outnumbered the orcs two to one. Stryke's group had the advantage of ambushing the ambushers, and they had orcish ferocity. But with nowhere to run the humans fought with equal aggression.

It seemed to Jup that there was an endless supply of heads to crack and ribs to cave in. Deftly wielding his staff, he obliged. Though his style was somewhat cramped by fighting in such a confined space. He overcame the restriction, and his short stature, by employing a technique that had served him well in the past.

Attacking his opponents' lower limbs, he worked on toppling them. Brought down to his level they were ripe for lethal blows, or quick lunges from the thin-bladed dagger strapped to his palm.

Stryke preferred a sword and knife combination in close quarters combat. When a hulking trooper loomed up ahead of him, he lashed out with the knife, catching him in the chest. Then he used it the way a butcher uses a hook, hoisting the human forward, on to the sword's blade. The man had hardly dropped before another took his place. Stryke felled him too, hacking deep into his neck and letting loose a jet of scarlet.

Venting their hatred for the oppressors, the rest of the orcs toiled as hard, reaping a harvest of rent flesh and severed limbs. In short order the number of dead and wounded mounted. The surviving soldiers retreated, making a last stand with their backs to the wall. Stryke's team pressed in on them.

The fighting was much more widely dispersed on the parade ground. Brelan's group had got clear of their wagon and united with the Vixens. Half of them were archers, and they fell into exchanging fire with the bowmen on the parapets. The rest pitched into the general melee.

Coilla was embroiled with a young officer whose fencing skills were superior to any human she'd so far encountered in Acurial. It was the last thing she needed, and she battled hard to finish it quickly. But she was stymied by his flair for warding off every blow she threw at him.

She spent precious seconds thrusting, feigning, spinning and dodging before her impatience turned to fury. Ignoring caution she turned to brute might. Thrashing wildly, she powered through his defence. Before he got his guard back up she delivered a heavy whack to his sword arm with the flat of her blade. Her reward was a loud crack as the bone shattered. The officer cried out, the weapon slipping from his insensate hand. Coilla instantly followed through, landing a solid hit to his chest.

Internal organs ruptured, he went down spitting blood.

She found herself shoulder to shoulder with Brelan.

"Where's Stryke?" he yelled.

"They had an ambush planned. He's dealing with it."

He looked shocked. "But how—"

"Later, Brelan, later!"

They spiralled off into fresh opponents.

Moments later she noticed he'd gravitated to Chillder, and the twins were fighting in harmony.

Spurral eschewed her usual staff and chose to arm herself with a pair of long knives. Her other weapon was less tangible: the bewilderment of the humans when confronted by a dwarf. Moreover, a female dwarf. If incredulity meant a split second's hesitation she gladly exploited it, and more than one dumbfounded foe paid with his life.

Faced by a couple of troopers less impressed with her otherness, she nimbly plunged her knives into both their torsos simultaneously. Then she spun to avoid a rushing spearman, tripped him as he passed and planted the double blades in his back. The warrior who took his place reeled off clutching an open throat.

Coilla appeared at her side. "We're forgetting the gates!"

Humans were massing there again, intent on closing the breach.

"What do we do?"

"Follow me!"

They weaved through the fracas, gathering as many Vixens as they could. With six or seven in tow they ran towards the gates. That caught the attention of several archers on the battlements. They targeted the sprinting females.

Barely ten paces had been covered when one of the Vixens was struck in the eye by an arrow. She was dead before she hit the dirt.

"*Shit!*" Coilla cursed.

"*Heads up!*" Spurral exclaimed, pointing with a knife.

A mob of troops had spilled out of one of the barrack blocks and was dashing to intercept them.

The small contingent of Vixens stood their ground. With a battle raging behind them, a crowd of troops milling at the gates ahead and knots of soldiers all around, there was little choice.

The fresh troopers swept in. Almost immediately one of the Vixens let out a piercing scream. A spear buried in her chest, she staggered a few steps before collapsing to her knees. Then she toppled, lifeless.

In short order one of her comrades was knocked senseless by a vicious head blow. Another sustained a wound that near severed her arm.

"This is getting hairy!" Spurral yelled. "We need reinforcements!"

There was uproar at the gates. Soldiers went down like scythed corn as Pepperdyne's wagon ploughed through them. Nimbler humans leapt aside when it shot over the square. About halfway across, Pepperdyne applied the handbrake. The wagon skidded, turned almost end on end and came to a juddering halt. But its crew wasn't entirely unscathed. One was dead, and the defenders' arrows had injured a couple more. The rest jumped clear and joined the set-to.

"Looks like we got 'em," Coilla said.

At the top of the hill, the third wagon was launched.

Dallog shared the steering lever with a dour resistance member. Wheam was in the rear with the rest of the attack team.

Turning, Dallog said, "Expect this to be bumpy. Hang on back there." He addressed it more to Wheam than the hardened fighters sitting with him.

The youth gave a weak nod, his complexion chalky.

Having seen off the wagon, Haskeer and the remainder of the force charged down the hill in its wake.

Stryke's group, dealing with the ambushers behind the barracks, had been oblivious to the greater picture. But with the last of the humans quickly and brutally dispatched, their task was done.

"We've wasted enough time here," Stryke announced, jerking his blade from a trooper's lifeless breast.

"Then let's get back to the main event!" Jup replied in a tone that sounded almost gleeful.

They rushed out to the parade ground.

The scene that greeted them wasn't far short of anarchy. There were no defined lines of battle, just a mass of fighting orcs and humans.

"Where to, Stryke?" Jup asked, scanning the confusion.

"Looks like Coilla could use some help." He pointed towards the ruined gates.

"Seems as good a place as any."

Stryke swiftly formed his troop into a wedge formation and led them into the fray.

They traversed the square by the simple expedient of cutting down any humans who came near. Once they reached Coilla's group the wedge broke up and splintered into a dozen separate scraps.

"About time!" Coilla said.

"Been busy," Stryke told her, batting away a soldier's blade.

"Hey, look!" Jup yelled.

Through the gap where the gates used to be they saw the third wagon heading towards the fort.

It was having a rough time. Arrows came down continuously. With the orc archers part of the ground force running behind the wagon, their shields above their heads as though deflecting rain, no one was returning fire.

Apart from their helmets and chainmail, Dallog and his co-driver had no such protection. It proved telling. An arrow struck the co-driver in the neck. He fell heavily against the steering lever, then went over the side. The wagon veered sharply to the right and came off the road. Dallog struggled to control it.

One or two orcs in the back of the wagon managed to jump clear. The rest hung on grimly as it picked up speed. Dallog tried applying the brake. It snapped off in his hand.

Bumping over grassland, the wagon swerved further to the right. It passed the side of the fort, a spear lob to its left, travelling ever faster. Arrows were still raining down on them.

Dallog shouted something, but his words couldn't be heard. Wheam squealed.

Then the wagon ran out of land and plunged over the cliff.

A company of soldiers arrived furtively at the row of ramshackle buildings by the foot of the cliff. They forced the doors, and armed with lanterns poured in to begin their search.

The wagon of bellowing orcs shot over the precipice above. Like a great bird downed by a giant's slingshot, it crashed through the roof of one of the buildings. With a thunderous roar the entire structure collapsed.

The impact sent shockwaves through the unstable buildings on either side. Imitating a line of playing cards swiped by a spoilt child, the ripple effect had them falling into each other. Walls buckled and went down. Roofs caved in. Smoke and flame erupted from the debris, ignited by the lanterns and brands carried by the ill-fated troopers.

They heard the reverberation up in the fort, even above the noise of battle.

"Those *fucking* archers!" Coilla howled.

Stryke nodded. "That's our next objective."

The ground force, with Haskeer in the vanguard, jogged through the gates. Its archers immediately took issue with the bowmen on the ramparts and started swapping bolts with them. The others piled into the battle on the square, with Haskeer taking the lead.

Stryke spotted Pepperdyne finishing an opponent nearby. He left Coilla marshalling her Vixens and went to him.

"Feel like a task, human?"

"What do you have in mind?"

"Clearing those battlements."

Pepperdyne glanced up at the archers. They looked to be at least thirty strong. "I'm game."

"We can't spare many for the job."

"I said I'm game."

"Right." He cupped his hands. "Haskeer! *Haskeer!*" Catching his sergeant's attention, Stryke waved him over.

Haskeer cut down a trooper on the way to keep his hand in. "What?"

"We're going for the archers."

"Good. The bastards."

"We can't take more than six away from this. Grab three. Make 'em Wolverines."

Haskeer's brow creased as he did the sum. "That's five of us."

"He's coming." Stryke nodded at Pepperdyne.

Haskeer scowled but said nothing.

"And get our archers to lay down covering fire. *Go!*"

The sergeant dived back into the melee.

"How do we do it?" Pepperdyne asked.

Stryke pointed to a stone staircase set against the fortress' outer wall. It led directly to the battlements. "Up that."

"Bit exposed, isn't it?"

"Can you see another way?"

Pepperdyne shook his head.

Haskeer soon returned. He had Prooq, Zoda and Finje with him. All were blood-splattered.

"We ready?" Stryke said.

"The archers let rip when we get to the stairs," Haskeer told him.

"All right. Let's move."

They made for the staircase, allowing no opposition to slow them. That meant two or three skirmishes on the way, but nothing they couldn't handle.

A pair of archers were stationed at the base of the steps. When they saw a human with five orcs dashing at them they hesitated. But only for a moment. They loosed arrows. Stryke's crew hit the dirt and the bolts flew overhead.

Haskeer was the first to his feet. As the bowmen nocked afresh he began running at them. He drew back his arm and hurled a hatchet. It struck one of the archers and took him out. The other had his bow taut and aimed directly at Haskeer. A fire-tipped arrow streaked past them and buried itself in the archer's chest. He went down with a cry, his jerkin in flames.

"Nice touch," Pepperdyne said.

Then they were moving again. As they neared the steps the orc archers let go their covering shots, and again the arrows were tarred and burning. A dead human tumbled down the stairs, two flaming bolts embedded in his back.

Stryke at their head, the six tore up the staircase. They were almost at the top before anybody tried to stop them. A sentry came at Stryke with a broadsword, slashing it in a downward stroke. Stryke dodged the blow and kept going. He hunched himself and went for the man's legs. With a heave, he tossed him over the side of the stairway. The human dropped screaming to the ground.

They got to the parapet. Most of the archers were concentrating on the battle below and ignorant of their presence. But several of the nearest turned to defend themselves. There was no time for them to raise their bows so they went for swords. Stryke's crew were on to them instantly, and a short, vicious tussle cut short their resistance.

Stryke knew that the bowmen further along the parapet were the most dangerous, even with orc archers keeping them busy. Unlike the ones just killed, they were far enough away to use their bows and pick off his team.

"We need to get close to them," he said. "Finje, Zoda, Prooq; take these bows and keep 'em occupied."

The grunts stripped the weapons and quivers from the dead humans as Stryke, Haskeer and Pepperdyne set off.

Their first encounter was with two sentries who, seeing the trio coming, charged at them. Stryke and Pepperdyne engaged the pair in swordplay. Haskeer raced on and barrelled into a lone archer in the process of drawing his bow. He battered the man, then proceeded to pound his head against the battlement wall, dashing his brains out.

Stryke and Pepperdyne, having finished the sentries, caught up. The three ran on.

They headed for a knot of four or five archers. Two of them loosed arrows in their direction. One was hopelessly wide of the mark. The other came so close to hitting Stryke he felt the displacement of air as it whistled past his ear.

Before they could take another shot, Pepperdyne, Stryke, then Haskeer hurtled into them. A bloody reckoning with blades, fists and boots left four sprawled on the walkway and one plummeting to the parade ground.

From the rear, Prooq yelled a warning. Stryke and the others dropped. A flight of arrows swept overhead and punched into three fast-approaching sentries. Back on their feet, Stryke, Haskeer and Pepperdyne darted onwards.

They didn't have to work for the next brace of kills. A couple of bowmen in their path succumbed to blazing arrows from orc compatriots below.

Ten paces later half a dozen sentries ganged up on them. Haskeer exposed the windpipe of the first one to venture near his blade. Pepperdyne punctured the second's chest. Stryke ran through the third with a savage thrust, then went on to eviscerate the fourth. Pepperdyne sliced into the fifth's belly, while Haskeer snapped the neck of the sixth.

There was no hiatus. The trio had left just a short trail of bloody footprints before they ran into the next clutch of defenders. And so it went, with a seemingly never-ending cavalcade of human flesh to be carved, stabbed and slashed.

Until at last they stood breathless at the parapet's end, surrounded by a litter of corpses.

Haskeer had hold of the remaining defender. He lifted the dazed, beaten human, with the intention of throwing him from the battlements and down the cliff face. Suddenly he stopped, seemed to lose interest in the man and casually dropped him on to the parapet's flagstones.

"What's going on down there?" he said.

Stryke joined him.

He saw the wreckage of the demolished hovels at the bottom of the cliff, with flames playing over them and billowing smoke. But what really caught his attention was the dozens of soldiers milling about the ruins, and what they must have been doing.

"They were going for the tunnel," he murmered.

"Look at this!" Pepperdyne said. He was standing on the other side of the parapet, staring down at the fighting.

Stryke and Haskeer went to him.

A large number of troops were emerging from a maze of outbuildings and rushing towards the square.

"Must have been holding them back," Stryke realised.

"Set us up," Haskeer growled.

"There's got to be a hundred of them, or more," Pepperdyne reckoned. "Stryke, we can't—"

"I know. *Come on!*"

They sprinted along the parapet to the three grunts, and all of them pelted down the stairs.

The battle was still raging. Stryke spotted Coilla and made for her. He began yelling, "There's a—"

"We see them!"

The first of the reinforcements were spilling into the square, forcing the orcs back.

Brelan arrived, panting. "Look who's with them!" He pointed to a figure striding along in the midst of the troops.

"Who?" Stryke said.

"That's Kapple Hacher. The commander-in-chief himself."

"This ain't by chance," Haskeer stated. "We've been stitched."

"We can't beat these odds," Coilla said.

"No," Stryke agreed bitterly. "Haskeer, sound the retreat."

The sergeant took a curved horn from his belt and pressed it to his lips.

As its strident note rang out, Stryke bellowed, *"Pull back! Pull back!"*

28

The shrill, insistent note Haskeer sent out sparked an exodus.

All over the fort's parade ground, orcs disengaged and headed for the gates. Or at least most did. A few couldn't extricate themselves from overwhelming odds and imminent death. Others lay wounded, or were on the point of capture, and chose to turn their blades on themselves rather than fall into enemy hands. Those who did withdraw were hotly pursued, and rearguard actions were fought across the square.

The retreating Wolverines, resistance members and Vixens clustered at the gates, urging on stragglers and loosing arrows at the humans chasing them.

"Isn't that one of the Ceragans?" Coilla exclaimed, pointing into the heaving scrimmage.

Stryke nodded. "It's Ignar."

"He's in trouble, Stryke."

The raw recruit had almost reached the edge of the scrum when a group of troopers caught up with him. He was trying to beat them off.

"I'm going in," Stryke decided.

"I'm with you," she said.

"Me too," Pepperdyne announced.

With Stryke in the lead they ran towards the mob.

On their way they met the van of the pursuers. Four bawling soldiers blocked their path. Stryke hacked down the leader with a single potent blow. Coilla and Pepperdyne tackled the others as he sprinted on.

Ignar was battling two opponents. He was outclassed, and he was injured. Blood flowed freely from several wounds, not least a broad gash to the chest. It was all he could do to fend off his attackers, and as Stryke approached he slumped to his knees. One of the soldiers lifted his sword to deliver a killing stroke.

Stryke intervened. A powerful swipe of his blade all but severed the human's sword arm. The man screamed and stumbled away, gushing blood. Stryke spun to face his charging companion. Their swords clashed and they furiously hacked at each other. The flurry ended with the soldier taking steel to his belly.

Ignar had fallen. Stryke went to him and found him barely conscious. Coilla and Pepperdyne arrived.

"He's in a bad way," Coilla pronounced as she examined the recruit. "Lot of blood lost."

"We'll get him clear," Stryke said.

He and Pepperdyne half carried, half dragged Ignar while Coilla kept any other would-be attackers at bay. As they neared the gates, orc archers sent out covering fire for them.

They laid Ignar on the ground, and somebody propped his head with a folded jerkin. He seemed unconscious.

Stryke lightly slapped his pallid cheeks. "Ignar. *Ignar.*"

The young orc's eyes flickered open.

"Here," Coilla said, handing Stryke a canteen.

"With a wound like that," Pepperdyne remarked, "he shouldn't drink."

"It doesn't matter now," Stryke told him. He dampened Ignar's lips with a little water.

Ignar tried to speak. Stryke allowed him a drink from the canteen. He coughed, and murmured something. Stryke leaned closer.

"*I'm ... sorry,*" Ignar whispered.

"No need," Stryke replied. "You fought well, and you die a Wolverine."

Ignar managed a faint smile. Then his eyes closed for the last time.

Coilla hissed, "Shit."

"We can't hold here much longer," Pepperdyne said.

"Get 'em moving," Stryke ordered, rising.

"We've got comrades in there," Brelan protested. "We can't leave them."

"We take losses," Stryke said, glancing at Ignar's corpse. "It's part of the price. Linger here and we'll lose more."

"Or all," Coilla amended. She pointed at the mass of humans across the square. They vastly outnumbered the orcs, and they were grouping for an all-out assault. "We have to go. *Now.*"

Reluctantly, Brelan nodded assent.

Stryke turned to Coilla and Jup. "They all know where the rendezvous point is. Any wounded or foot-draggers on the way get left behind. It's every orc for themselves. Pass it on."

They moved off to spread the word.

He looked at Pepperdyne. "Ready for a fast retreat, human?"

"Just say the word."

Stryke signalled Haskeer. The sergeant gave another blast on the horn. Orc archers stepped up their flow of arrows.

The retreat began.

They poured out of the gates and on to the approach road. Shedding excess kit and even some weapons, they headed inland, their pace increasing to a sprint. The tail of the column had barely cleared the fort's precincts when the first of the humans came after them. Orc arrows helped slow the pursuit.

"We're fucked if they've got cavalry," Coilla said, jogging alongside Jup.

"That's right," the dwarf panted, "look on the bright side."

No riders appeared. But more soldiers exited and joined the chase.

The orcs topped a rise and swept down on to the plain beyond. They made for a stand of trees an arrow's flight ahead.

Pepperdyne, next to Stryke at the column's head, glanced back. He saw the pursuing humans on the crest, outlined against the cloudless sky. "Doesn't look like all the garrison. Not by a long shot."

"Good," Stryke replied.

"But why aren't more of them following us?"

Stryke shrugged and upped the pace.

They got to the line of trees and through them. That put them in the first of a series of meadows. They crossed those too, trampling down hedgerows when there was no easier path. Another stretch of open pasture followed, with several copses at its far end.

The humans were still on their trail, but had fallen back some distance.

"Think we might outpace 'em?" Jup asked.

"Wouldn't hold your breath," Coilla said.

"Not a lot left to hold. How much further is it?"

"I reckon we're near. Should see a wood soon. It's past that."

They had a couple more fields to go across before they spotted the wood's edge. Putting on a spurt, they quickly reached it and moved into the trees.

"Be alert!" Stryke warned. "This is a good place to get waylaid. And we've had enough ambushes for one day."

Pepperdyne sidled up to him. "Now I can't see them at all," he said, scanning the open ground they'd just left. "Maybe they've given up the chase."

"Or they're sneaking round to lie in wait for us, like I said. C'mon, and stay awake."

The legion of orcs crept through the woods, keeping vigilant and as quiet as over a hundred hastily retreating warriors could. As they penetrated deeper, dappled sunlight gave way to cool gloom under the leafy canopy. Silence wrapped them, overlaid only by their muffled footfalls on the loam.

After ten minutes of steady tramping they heard something else. A halt was signalled and they listened. It was the unmistakable sound of rushing water, close to hand. They pushed on. The trees began to thin and the light increased. Soon the riverbank was in sight. While the others held back, Stryke and Brelan carried on alone to the water's edge.

The river was wide and fast-flowing. It was thunderous, throwing off spray and spawning white foam where it churned around half-submerged rocks. On the river's far side the wood continued, and beyond it the tops of green hills were just visible.

Brelan cupped his hands over his mouth and gave a passable imitation of shrill birdsong. Further along the bank, five or six of his compatriots came out of hiding.

"Don't ask," Brelan told them as they approached, anticipating their questions about how the raid had gone. Though his expression held all they needed to know.

"We've no time to waste," Stryke said.

Brelan nodded. "Get the others out here."

Stryke gestured to their waiting companions. They started spilling on to the riverbank.

Directed to a spot not far from the rendezvous point, the troop set to clearing away a camouflage of undergrowth. It concealed ten rafts. They were simple but robust, consisting of thick tree trunks lashed together and sealed with tar.

Each raft had a crude rudder, and the minimal protection of a waist-high rope on three sides, looped around several timber uprights.

As they were hauled to the water's edge, Coilla joined Stryke.

"Shame Dallog and Wheam aren't here to see this," she said.

"Or Ignar, or any of the others we lost to deceit today."

"You reckon it *was* treachery?"

"They weren't waiting for us by chance."

"That means somebody in the resistance . . ." She let the implication hang.

"A mission this big, maybe too many knew the plan."

"Not that many knew all of it. Like using the catacombs."

"There were humans down there."

"What?"

"When we were on the battlements I saw soldiers at the bottom of the cliff. They must have been going for the entrance. Looks like it was Wheam and Dallog's wagon that stopped 'em finding it."

Coilla smiled. "So they did some good." She sobered. "But if the humans knew about the catacombs—"

"There's a spy high up in the resistance? Maybe."

"We're in trouble if there is, Stryke."

"There's nothing we can do about it right now. We have to—"

A chorus of shouting broke out. Orcs were heading up the riverbank, towards a group of figures.

Jup ran past, Spurral in tow. Then Haskeer thundered by, with a bunch of grunts in his wake.

Stryke stared at the commotion. "What the—?"

"This I don't *believe*," Coilla exclaimed. "Come on!" She joined the rush.

He followed, and seeing what all the fuss was about, increased his pace.

The advancing figures were orcs. Upwards of a dozen in

number, they were bruised and bloodied, with several needing help to walk. And at the forefront were Dallog and Wheam.

Pepperdyne stared at them. "How the hell...?"

Dallog grinned. "Just sheer good fortune."

Coilla gave Wheam's arm a squeeze. "We thought you were lost."

"So did we," the youth replied shakily.

Stryke elbowed his way through. "Didn't think we'd see you again, Corporal. We'd written you off."

"We were lucky," Dallog told him. "The shanties took the brunt when the wagon went over. Most of us came out with petty wounds. Didn't lose a hand."

"There were soldiers," Wheam piped up. "Did you know there were soldiers down—"

"Yeah," Stryke said, "we did."

"Bit of a shock for 'em," Dallog reported, not without relish.

"And fortunate for us. They'd have ambushed us if we'd left through the catacombs. That or come up at our backs inside the fort."

"But if they knew about the tunnel what's to say they know about this escape route too?"

"All the more reason to get out of here, and fast."

Dallog scanned the orcs crowded round. "I don't see Ignar."

"He didn't make it."

The corporal's face dropped. "No?"

"No," Stryke confirmed.

Wheam looked shocked.

"He died well," Stryke added.

"That's a comfort," Dallog replied. "But I promised I'd keep an eye on those young ones."

"So did I."

Dallog nodded. He said nothing for a second, then added, "But the raid was a success, right?"

No one spoke until Pepperdyne offered, "That's debatable."

"Your crew all right to carry on, Dallog?" Stryke asked.

"We'll be fine."

"Then let's move."

Stryke and Brelan snapped orders and the rafts were readied for launch. Each held twelve or more passengers. Wolverines, Vixens and resistance members boarded randomly. The way it fell out, Stryke, Jup and Spurral found themselves on the same raft. Haskeer and Coilla were together on another; Chillder and Brelan on a third; Pepperdyne, Dallog and Wheam on a fourth.

At Brelan's signal the vessels cast off, pushed clear of the bank with rudimentary paddles. The strong current took hold at once, tossing them about like corks and drawing them into midstream. Before things settled down there was some jockeying, the orcs paddling furiously to avoid collisions as the craft rapidly picked up speed.

The terrain slipped past at a clip. Copious trees and lush pastures. A glimpse of a small lake ringed with jade hills. Fields with flocks of sheep and startled shepherds. The sight of distant cerulean cliffs, shimmering in sunlight.

They rounded a bend. The river became wider and faster. They were drenched with the spume, rafts bouncing on the surge, bow and stern see-sawing.

"Hey!" Spurral yelled.

"What?" Stryke bellowed.

"Back there!" She pointed to the rear.

He squinted through the vapour and made out oblong patches of white. The mist cleared a little and he realised they were sails. They belonged to an armada of boats coming round the bend after them.

As they drew nearer they were noticed by the occupants of other rafts.

On Coilla's, she turned to Haskeer and said, "Now we know where they disappeared to."

"The bastards are on to our every move."

"There's gotta be a spy."

Haskeer snarled, "If I get my hands on him—"

"We've more pressing problems. Hold tight!"

On the raft carrying Dallog, Wheam and Pepperdyne they were counting the pursuing craft.

"Twenty-one," Dallog said.

"Twenty-*two*," Wheam corrected. "You missed one."

"The number's not important," Pepperdyne interrupted testily. "Outrunning them is."

"They're gaining!" Wheam cried.

Brelan and Chillder's raft was at the back of the orc flotilla. Close enough to the boats chasing them to see who stood at the prow of the leading vessel.

"It's him all right," Brelan confirmed, shading his eyes with his palm, "Kapple Hacher."

"It was no fluke him being here," Chillder reckoned. "This whole thing stinks, brother."

The river meandered for a mile or two, the turns and curves taming its pace. That slowed the rafts, dependent on current, and forced the orcs to work their paddles. The boats trailing them, under sail, began to close the gap. And even when the river straightened and flowed quickly again they continued to catch up, until the foremost were within an arrow's flight.

The humans proved the point by loosing a salvo. Arrows zinged over the orcs' heads, or fell short, cutting into open water. Orc archers returned fire. Their footing was unsure on the heaving rafts and the results were ragged. But the exchange carried on, and there were hits. Through skill or luck, two orcs were struck by bolts. One plunged overboard and was lost. The other fell wounded into the arms of comrades.

A human paid with his life, taking an arrow to the chest. Another was injured and dragged clear of the rail.

By this time the boats had closed in. But the rafts had a small advantage over the larger craft. They didn't have sails to tack, giving them a bit more leeway to manoeuvre. That kept most of the boats clear, though some got in close enough to engage. Spears were lobbed. Arrows, throwing knives and slingshot clattered against raised shields on both sides.

The speed of the river's flow hampered ramming attempts by the boats. Instead they tried to get alongside the rafts and board them. Others did their best to outpace the rafts, hoping to block their way. The orcs fought to stop them.

In this way the two small fleets played cat and mouse along the river. Harrying and assailing, bumping and swerving, hurling weaponry back and forth.

At length, a change came over the river. It flowed even faster, and up ahead it seemed to disappear into a boiling cloud. A deep rumbling could be heard.

"What the hell's that?" Jup said.

"Must be the falls," Stryke explained.

"So what do we do?" Spurral asked, a little uneasily.

"Brelan's got it worked out. I hope. Just be ready to hold on tight."

Every rudder operator on the orc rafts was a resistance member, briefed on what to do and when. As the chase progressed they steered nearer to the left bank and stayed alert for a signal.

The roar of water grew louder, the misty cloud loomed higher. Several boats were neck and neck with orc rafts.

On the bank, perilously close to the deafening lip of the falls, stood a cluster of mature trees. They were taller than any others on that stretch. From high up on the tallest there was a spiky flash of light. It repeated a number of times, proving it to be a confederate holding something reflective.

As one, the rafts veered sharply towards the bank. The orcs braced themselves. At the same time bands of archers ashore, some hidden in trees, peppered the human's boats.

The well chosen spot was shallow near the bank, and the majority of the rafts simply ground to a halt. Their occupants leapt off and splashed to shore. Some rafts were barred from quite reaching the shallows by the clutter of vessels. They tossed anchors of iron and rock overboard, then their passengers waded waist high to the riverbank.

The suddenness of the move confused the humans, though they must have known the orcs had no plan to go over the falls. A number of them tried copying the move and beaching in the shallows. But the deeper hauls of their bigger craft ran aground far short of the bank, leaving the troopers loath to brave the fast-flowing water.

Other boats dropped anchor in full flow, but had no benefit. There was such force in the tide that rather than holding, the anchors were dragged along the riverbed by the swiftly drifting boats. Some struggled to turn away from the attraction of the falls and head back the way they'd come. All the while, arrows rained down on them.

One boat, losing all control, slowly spun like a child's paper toy in a gushing stream as the river pushed it past the chaos of vessels and towards the falls. Men jumped from its decks, only to find that the river had as powerful a hold on them as their abandoned craft. Boat and men, black dots in a torrent of foam, rolled into the vast cloud of water vapour. The boat, dark outline showing through the mist, tipped, and for a second seemed to stand on its nose before plunging out of sight.

The last of the orcs swarmed ashore and into the trees. Humans who made it to the bank met a hail of arrows that kept them pinned down at the water's edge.

The resistance had horses waiting, along with a couple

of wagons for kit and the wounded. Everyone quickly mounted. In minutes they were on a trail and heading out of the woods.

Their path took them to a rise that ran parallel with the river, so that they could look down to the tangle of vessels, and the humans milling on the bank. One figure was unmistakable. Kapple Hacher stood apart from his men, his fists balled. He looked up and saw the escaping orcs. Even from that distance they could sense his impotent rage. The orcs spurred their mounts and pushed on.

A while later, well clear of the river, they allowed themselves to slow down.

Riding next to Stryke and Brelan at the column's head, Pepperdyne had a question. "Does that count as a rout or a success?" he wondered.

"Bit of both," Stryke replied.

"I'd say that's a generous way of seeing it."

"We did damage. And the way the humans tried to spring their trap could have been handled better, lucky for us."

"I'm wondering if it was worth upward of forty of our lives," Brelan said.

"And now we've got a traitor to contend with," Pepperdyne added.

"We don't know that," Brelan came back irately. "It could have been chance."

"Oh, come *on*."

"Maybe Hacher was doing a snap inspection or something, and—"

"And at the same time they just happened to find the entrance to the catacombs minutes after we went in? Listen to yourself."

"Face it, Brelan," Stryke said. "The odds are somebody informed on us."

"The resistance are loyal," Brelan stated indignantly. "You'll find no betrayal in our ranks."

"Didn't say there was."

"What *are* you saying then? Because if there is a spy, and it wasn't an Acurial orc, that doesn't leave much scope, does it?"

"I'm as sure of the Wolverines as you are of your comrades."

"Can you speak for all of them?" He glanced at Pepperdyne. "Even those not of our kind?"

"I vouch for them all," Stryke replied, unswerving.

"I hope you don't need to eat those words. I've things to do." Brelan turned his horse and rode back down the column.

Pepperdyne looked to Stryke. "Thanks."

"I'm trusting you to deserve it. If I'm wrong...well, you'll know about it."

Before the human could reply, Coilla galloped alongside.

"What's wrong with Brelan?" she asked. "He shot past me with a face like a corpse."

"He's pissed off about the way it went," Stryke said. "Only natural."

"And he's tetchy about the idea of a traitor in his group," Pepperdyne added. "But I guess that's natural too."

"What is it, Coilla?" Stryke wanted to know.

"I finished checking the wounded, like you asked. We've got two likely to lose limbs. The rest's all minor stuff. Not bad, considering."

"No. I need to talk to you, Coilla. Alone." He gave Pepperdyne a pointed look.

"Don't mind me," the human responded. He dropped back along the column.

"Have you got it?" Stryke said.

Coilla's expression was blank. "What?"

"The *star.*" He looked pained at her not immediately knowing what he meant.

"Oh. Course I have." She slipped a hand into her jerkin and brought out the instrumentality just enough that only he could see it.

"Good. Guard it well. Above all else."

"You know I will." She stuffed it back. "Really, Stryke, you're obsessed with this thing. Relax, and trust me."

29

The resistance let a week pass to lie low and regroup before renewing their harassment of the occupiers. In turn, the authorities bore down ever harder on the occupied.

With the possibility of a spy in their midst, the rebels trod warily, conscious that they could be exposed at any time. Stryke wasn't alone in thinking that the humans and dwarfs in his group were looked on with suspicion. A feeling strengthened perhaps when Jup's power of farsight had been revealed to Chillder, for all that the Wolverines tried to brush it off as mere "intuition."

The band found itself fully employed helping to put pressure on the humans. The Vixens, too, played their part in stirring things up. As reward, the first signs of disobedience by the general populace showed themselves. The hoped-for revolution started to look like more than a possibility.

Adding to the tension, and assuming the prediction was true, the comet Grilan-Zeat was expected almost hourly.

But for Stryke and his band one mission was paramount.

The plot to assassinate Jennesta was known to very few, even within the Wolverines. Stryke kept his team small, picking only Coilla and Haskeer, with Eldo and Noskaa as back-ups. A sufficient number as the plan depended on stealth, not force of arms. Equipped with a rough map of the interior, supplied by sympathisers working as menials in the fortress, Stryke and the others set out on the first cloudy night.

Like all old castles, Taress fortress was large and rambling, having been added to and refashioned over centuries. Such an acreage meant many walls to protect and doors to be kept barred. One particular annexe, projecting from the fort's eastern side and unprotected by the older moat, was where the daily needs of a garrison were most obvious. The kitchens and food stores were there, alongside the heaps of vegetable waste, stripped carcasses and other flyblown detritus waiting to be hauled away. It was the province of servants, and welcome to it.

There were guards, as everywhere on the perimeter, but they were few and Stryke had been told their routine. Furtive blades easily dealt with them, and their bodies were hidden in piles of refuse.

Finding a recessed door, Stryke softly knocked. The response was so long coming he was about to rap again when the sound of drawing bolts was heard. The door creaked open a crack and anxious eyes surveyed the group. Then it was pulled wide to usher them in.

The orc who admitted them was aged and crook-backed. He wore a once-white apron, grubby from toil and bloodstained.

"You know what you have to do?" Stryke said.

"It's little enough," the servant replied. "I get you in. After that you're on your own."

"What about you?"

"I'll go missing as soon as you're in, and I won't be the only one tonight." He stared at the group with rheumy eyes. "I don't know who you are, but if you're here to put paid to that...hell cat, I pray the gods are with you."

"You mean Jennesta."

"Who else?"

"It'd be better if you didn't know why we're here. For your own safety."

The old one nodded. "I hope it's her. The bitch. You wouldn't believe the depravity since she got here."

"I think we would," Coilla told him.

"Time's pressing," Stryke reminded them. "It won't be long before those sentries are found and—"

"Follow me," the servant instructed, reaching for a glowing lantern on a shelf by the door.

He led them through corridors and twisting passageways, up small flights of steps and down deep staircases. Until at last they reached a heavy door, which he unlocked with a brass key. There were more steps inside, going down to a dim passage.

"This is one of the tunnels we use to service our betters," he all but spat the word, "without them having to suffer the indignity of looking at us."

"We seem to spend a lot of time in tunnels these days," Haskeer observed.

The tunnel proved as ill-lit as they expected, and damp ran freely on the walls; a reminder that they were passing under the moat.

They came to another door.

"Beyond that, you're in the castle proper," the old menial explained. "That's when your map comes into play. Take this." He thrust the lamp into Haskeer's hands. "My eyes are used to the gloom down here. Now go! The door's unlocked, we've seen to that. And good luck." He turned and shuffled off into the shadows.

They approached the door cautiously. On the other side was a corridor. It was unlit, but there were hangings and items of heavy wooden furniture against the walls, indicating that they'd moved from the world of servers to the served.

With Haskeer holding up the lamp, Stryke got out the map and laid it on an ornately carved half moon table. He'd already done his best to remember most of it, and what he saw confirmed his recollection.

"We should be here," he said, tapping a finger on the parchment. "Our quarry's high up. Five flights. So we need to go ... that way." He pointed to the right.

The corridor was long and branched off in various places. But they kept straight on to the end and a twisting stone staircase.

"This is only for servants too," Stryke said, "and if we've been told right, they'll not be using it tonight."

"What about guards?" Coilla asked. "There have to be some."

"The map shows where the permanent ones are stationed. They're where you'd expect; the governor's private quarters and the like. We don't know about patrols."

"Which are likely to be random, right."

"So stay sharp."

They began to climb.

A few hundred steps took them to the first landing. Two doors were there, both firmly shut. They crept past them. The next floor was the same; closed doors, no sign of anyone. Things were different on the third. Here the landing opened directly on to a corridor. It was richly carpeted, and they caught glimpses of fine paintings as they stole by. The fourth level was again open, like the one below. On the fifth they found a door unlike any other. It was lavishly ornamented, too much so, though its decoration was old and beginning to fade.

"Remember," Stryke reminded them, "it's a sharp turn to the right then two passages down." He looked to Noskaa. "You're guarding this door. If we're not back soon, get out. Fast."

The grunt nodded.

"Now let's see if this door's unlocked," Stryke said, reaching for the handle.

"And if there's magic?" Coilla wanted to know.

"We trust our blades to better it." He turned the handle.

The door opened on to a corridor that spoke of the status of those who walked it. Brightly lit, it was sumptuously carpeted and exquisitely embellished.

"You won't need that," Stryke whispered, indicating Haskeer's lantern.

The sergeant gratefully dumped it on a nearby cushioned chair.

They took the right turn and padded along to the second corridor on their left.

"You're stationed here, Eldo," Stryke ordered, strengthening his line of escape. "Same as I said to Noskaa; if we're not back, or you think we're lost, get yourself out. Otherwise, if anybody comes near, drop 'em."

"Got it, Captain."

Strykc, Coilla and Haskeer entered the corridor. It was as handsome as the other, but there were no doors. Ahead of them, about as far as Haskeer could throw an enemy's leg, it turned sharply to the right.

When they got to the corner, Stryke whispered, "We think they'll be a couple of them. It'll have to be quick, and true."

Coilla nodded and plucked a throwing knife from her arm scabbard. She gave it to him and drew another for herself.

"Ready?" Stryke said.

She nodded.

"*Now.*"

They swiftly rounded the corner. They were in a short corridor that stretched to a set of imposing double doors. Two sentries stood by them.

Coilla, the better thrower, was first to get a bead. She tossed her blade and brought down one of the guards cleanly. Stryke's throw hit home, but it wasn't fatal, his target catching the blade near his shoulder. Coilla quickly grabbed a second knife, lobbed it and finished the job.

"Thanks," Stryke mouthed.

Joined by Haskeer, they moved towards the doors. About halfway there, they noticed an opening on their right, which turned out to be a passageway. Its entrance was askew, the right side protruding further than the left, so that it was hard to make out until almost on it.

"Shit," Coilla hissed, "that wasn't on the map."

As she spoke, the sound of muffled boots came to them. Before they could react, a guards patrol came out of the hidden passage. They looked as surprised to see the orcs as the orcs were to see them. But the spell was not long breaking.

The guards charged. The trio met them, steel on steel.

"We'll handle this!" Coilla yelled. "Go! *Go!*"

Stryke dodged a swinging blade and sprinted for the double doors. He struck them at speed and they flew inward, nearly putting him on the floor of the room he tumbled into. Then by some agency the doors slammed shut behind him. He spun, gripped the handles and pulled, but they wouldn't be moved.

Jennesta's suite was extensive and opulently appointed. It also seemed empty. There was a grand bed, draped in sheerest silks and dotted with gold-tasselled cushions. But there was no sign of anyone having used it.

Stryke was about to try one of the two doors in the room when the nearest opened.

Kapple Hacher strode in.

"I don't think we've met," he stated evenly.

"I know who you are," Stryke said.

"Then perhaps you also know that no one enters this citadel uninvited. Not if they want to live."

"My business isn't with you, and you won't stop me."

"We'll see."

"Just you, is it? No platoon of troopers to back you up?"

"You're not worthy of it. Besides, I need no help dealing with your kind."

"Bigot."

"*Liberator*, if you don't mind. We invaded this land to stop them using weapons of magical destruction against us."

"That's bull. Orcs don't have a way with magic. Where were they, these weapons?"

"We haven't actually found any yet, but—"

"Lies. A ploy to invade. And who the hell were you liberating?"

"Those many orcs who wanted to avoid the consequences of their masters using their hidden magic against us. You could say we were invited, in an unspoken kind of way."

"You can't believe that. You've seen the orcs here. They're placid. They'd never have threatened you."

"Not all your kind are placid, it seems. Are you not from here?"

"You're right. Not all orcs are placid, not at heart. They're aggressive, tough. Warriors far greater than humans."

Hacher laughed scornfully. "Not on the evidence I've seen. And a few freaks of nature like you won't change it."

"So why waste words?"

"Why indeed?" Hacher drew his sword.

Stryke pulled free his own and they set to.

For Hacher, old enough and high ranking enough to have been taught in a classical style, fighting was *fencing*. To him, a scrap was a duel. As far as Stryke was concerned, a scrap was a scrap.

It came down to undoubted skill and stylishness versus seasoned brute determination.

Hacher fenced, Stryke hacked. Hacher blocked passes with dexterity and put together complex attacks. Stryke battered away and thought only of skewering his opponent's lungs.

In the end an orc's fury and stamina proved the better. Bludgeoning the general's defences, he found a breach and sent his blade through it. The sword pierced Hacher between breastbone and shoulder. It wasn't a deep wound, but enough to offset him and he fell, losing his sword.

Stryke moved in to finish the task. Then stopped.

A presence had entered the room. Somebody who didn't have to speak to command attention. He turned from Hacher and stared.

Jennesta was dressed in black, with leather playing a major part in her ensemble. She wore a choker bristling with glinting spikes, and smaller versions on her wrists. There was something unnameable and almost palpable about her. It was a kind of allure, mixed with equal parts of revulsion. She exuded a power, and there was very little light in it.

Stryke couldn't quite stem a feeling of awe. He had a hint, deep down, of an emotion orcs found alien. Fear.

"It's been a long time," she said, her tone surprisingly mild.

"Yes," he said, tritely and feeling like a hatchling.

"You know, you should really bow to me. After all, technically you're still in my service. I never released you from it."

"We don't bow and scrape since we took our freedom."

"That wasn't all you took, was it?"

Stryke stopped himself from sending a hand to the pouch he carried the stars in. He said nothing.

"But we're going to put that right at last," she told him. "We're going to—"

Hacher groaned.

She swung her head to him, furious. "Oh get out, you useless wretch. Go and have that seen to. Though why I don't let you bleed to death..."

"Will you be safe with him?" Hacher asked.

"You certainly weren't! There's nothing here that's beyond me. Now *get out!*"

The general climbed to his feet and limped to the door, a hand pressed against his bleeding wound.

When he left she refocused on Stryke. "Where were we? Oh,

yes, the instrumentalities." Her face screwed with wrath. "They were rightly *mine*. I searched years for them and you've added years more. That's not something I tolerate."

"They're not for the taking," Stryke informed her.

"Oh yes they are. The taking, and a lingering death as reward for your insolence."

"Then you won't mind a condemned orc's last request. How did you escape? After you —"

"After my dear father consigned me to the vortex, you mean, in the hope that I'd be torn to pieces? No, I won't. I don't grant wishes. You can die wondering."

"And you've climbed high in the world of humans. I'd like to know how."

"Humans are scum. I've nothing but contempt for them. They're just a means. How I rose among them is something else I won't trouble you with. But it was absurdly easy, I'll say that."

"Ever the conniver."

"Realist." Unexpectedly, her tone became even, almost conversational. "You know, it's a pity things worked out as they did. You were a good slave once. I might have given you a high position in my service. And when I think about it, we do have something in common, don't we?"

"What in hell could that be?"

"No home. No realm in my case," she added bitterly. "Neither of us has roots, somewhere we can have allegiance to. But at least you have your own kind. There aren't many like me."

"I believe it. What are you saying, Jennesta?" He felt a little flip in his stomach for using a term other than "Your Majesty." "That you want me back in your service?"

"Gracious, no. I was just dangling something you couldn't have in front of you. No reprieves."

Stryke lunged at her, bringing up his sword. She quickly moved her hands in some unfathomable way.

He froze. Try as he might, not all his strength could make him move. He stood like a statue, sword outstretched, body tensed for the thrust.

She laughed at him. Then she called out in some guttural, arcane tongue. Half a minute later two of her lumbering zombies shambled in.

"You know what to do," she told them without bothering to look their way.

They shuffled to Stryke and began pawing at his clothes. Their soft, bony fingers probed his pockets. Yellow skeletal hands searched for his belt pouches. This close, the foul smell of the creatures was overpowering. But Stryke was powerless to shift, no matter how hard he struggled.

Inevitably one of the goons found the pouch of stars. When he upended it and they tumbled to the carpet, Jennesta's face lit up with an awful fire. She rushed to the spot, clouting aside the zombie who tipped the bag, as though in penalty for his disrespect. Kneeling, she took up the stars with reverence. If she was disappointed at finding only four, she didn't show it. Which some small part of Stryke's writhing mind found strange.

"These will give me a power you can't imagine," she boasted, flaunting the stars at Stryke. "I won't have a mere realm. I'll have *realms*. The dominance of not one but many worlds. And it starts with an orc army as obedient as these two." Jennesta nodded at the undead. "Pity you won't see it." She lifted a hand.

The double doors crashed open. Haskeer charged in, carrying a wooden bench, which he casually tossed to the floor. Coilla was right behind him, sword and dagger in hand.

The intrusion threw Jennesta, and for an instant her attention wandered, breaking whatever hold she had on Stryke. Freed, he carried through with the suspended thrust, no matter that Jennesta was no longer in front of him, and almost fell. Shaking himself, he made ready to strike again.

Coilla got there first. As Stryke thawed she sent a knife Jennesta's way. It struck her, hilt first, on the temple. The sorceress cried out, part in pain, mostly in fury. There was something like blood on her forehead, had it been blood's colour. Drawing back from what may well have been the only physical blow she had ever received, Jennesta called out in the secret tongue.

The pair of zombies immediately became animated. Moving surprisingly fast, they obeyed their mistress and attacked. Haskeer ran to meet them, straight off plunging his blade into the nearest one's chest. The tip erupted from the zombie's back, but in a plume of dust, not a surge of blood. Haskeer wrenched the sword free. The zombie, still standing, swayed for a second. Then he carried on as though nothing had happened. Haskeer tried again, and this time his sword went well into the belly. The zombie hardly broke step.

"We can't kill 'em!" Haskeer roared.

"Depends how you do it!" Coilla shouted back. Rushing at the next goon she gave a swipe that completely severed his arm. The limb fell uselessly to the floor, the zombie kept coming.

"Chop 'em into bits?" Haskeer queried.

He didn't get an answer. There was a commotion outside the wrecked double doors. Men shouting and running feet, heading their way.

More of a threat as far as Coilla was concerned, Jennesta seemed to have gathered herself, if the twisted expression she wore and the gestures she was making with her hands meant anything.

Coilla saw a route out. It was risky, and could have killed them as easily as staying here. But it was a chance. She grabbed Stryke and Haskeer's arms and drew them to her.

"Window!" she yelled.

"Huh?" Haskeer grunted.

"Window!" she repeated, pointing to the floor-to-ceiling framed glass doors at one end of the room.

Haskeer got it. "Right!"

They began to run as shouting guards spilled into the room. Stryke, between Coilla and Haskeer, and as much propelled by them as his own efforts, was still woozy. His head cleared instantly when he saw the windows rushing towards them.

He managed to yell, "She's got the sta—"

A cacophony of breaking glass and snapping wood drowned him out.

Then they were in silence. Falling. Seeing flashes of stars through cloud in the night sky. Followed by the tops of other buildings and the dark ground.

They landed in the moat quite close together, all things considered. The fall hurt them, but didn't irreparably harm them, though the water was cold and foul enough to instantly sober them. They swam to the edge and scrambled out. Eldo and Noskaa were waiting tensely nearby. All five melted into the night.

They left Jennesta playing with her toys.

"I can't believe you left it here!" Stryke grumbled as they were let into the current safe house, their clothes still wringing.

"*I* can't believe you took yours *with* you!" Coilla snapped back. "Talk about a lion's den."

"I thought carrying the stars was the best way of protecting them. I was wrong. But that doesn't excuse you putting yours at risk."

"Stryke, if I'd had it on me back there she could have got them all. I thought hiding it was the safest."

"And didn't tell me."

"You only would have got...the way you are about it now. You need never have known."

Moving into the house, they heard a commotion. Resistance orcs were hurrying to and fro, and there was a crowd in a side room.

"Oh, no," Coilla groaned.

"What?" Stryke said, alarm rising.

"Better find out." She headed for the crowded room, Stryke right behind her.

Elbowing in, they found Brelan, Chillder and Jup at the heart of it. They were staring at a small strongbox lying on the floor, its lid wrenched open.

"How did you fare?" Jup asked expectantly.

"We didn't," Coilla admitted.

There were groans and words of sympathy from the crowd, which was increasing.

"What's going on here?" Stryke said.

"Oh," Jup replied, "yes, it's strange, and disturbing."

"What happened?"

"It seems somebody broke in and cracked open this strong-box."

"Got in? In this place? With so many around and all the security?"

"There's signs. Stove-in window at the back. Lock broke on this door." He nodded to the entrance. "What we're trying to figure out is who the box belongs to."

"It's mine," Coilla said.

"Don't tell me," Stryke pleaded in an undertone.

Grim faced, she gave him a tiny nod.

"Yours?" Chillder said.

"I had it hidden behind that loose brick over there." Coilla indicated the spot where the brick had been discarded, next to its empty hollow.

"Whoever it was, found it," Brelan said. "But they don't seem to have taken anything else. Was there something valuable in it?"

She paused for a moment, then answered, "No, just some keepsakes. Junk mostly, but I was fond of it."

"Why should anybody steal junk?" Chillder asked, her gaze fixed on Coilla.

"More important," Brelan said, "is *how*? If somebody can get in here this easily our security needs beefing up. A lot."

"If it *was* somebody from outside," Stryke offered.

"What?"

"There's another possibility."

Brelan frowned as realisation dawned. "Not that again, Stryke. I've told you the loyalty of our group is—"

"I'm just saying it's possible. So would it hurt to check everybody here?"

"*Search* them? Even if that wasn't repugnant it can't be done. There's been a steady stream in and out today, and I would have thought a thief wouldn't linger. But *search* them, for what Coilla's says is junk? Get a grip, Stryke. Making this place secure comes first. So if you don't mind, I'd like to hear about tonight's failure, but—"

"It could have been treachery again," Stryke told him.

Brelan gave him a hard look and said, "You might dry yourselves," as he walked out.

The onlookers were largely silent now, and craned curiously. Stryke felt like he was in a zoo. He gathered Jup and, along with Coilla and Haskeer, went to find a quiet place. When they found it, round a table at the back of a noisy room, with a fire to steam their wet clothes, Stryke broke the news to Jup.

"Damn it, Stryke," the dwarf came back, "that's a blow."

"You must hate my guts, Stryke," Coilla said.

He shook his head. "No. I gave you the responsibility, and you acted as best you could. I'm the greater fool for handing her the stars on a plate."

"Do you think she's got the other one, my one?"

"Amazed if she hasn't."

"Jennesta with all five instrumentalities," Jup muttered. "Doesn't bear thinking on."

"And us stuck here," Haskeer put in.

"It's going to be fun telling the rest of the band," Coilla remarked.

"Oh, *no*," Haskeer moaned. "Does it mean we're stuck with those two humans?"

Standeven could be seen on the other side of the room, sitting alone and sipping something from a tumbler as more productive work went on around him.

"I'm getting the stars back," Stryke vowed darkly. "They're going to be back in our hands if it kills me."

"A good prospect with Jennesta," Jup reckoned.

"So we're fucked," Haskeer said.

"Oh, I don't know," Jup replied. "Look at it objectively. This is a fair land, nothing like Maras-Dantia. I don't know about Ceragan, but is that any better?"

"It isn't occupied by humans," Coilla informed him.

"That won't last. There's a revolution brewing, and we helped fire it. So there's prospect for fighting, seeing the orcs in these parts right, which is what we set out to do, and a comely home at the end of it. Could be worse."

Coilla smiled, not broadly. "Nice try. Though I wonder how you and Spurral would feel in a world of orcs."

"I'd be honoured."

She raised her cup of wine to toast him for the compliment. "Perhaps you're right and we'll have to make the best of it."

"We'll have the stars," Stryke promised. "I meant it when I said—"

"*Sssshhh!*" Coilla had her finger to her lips. She nodded towards the door. Chillder was hurrying their way.

"It's here!" she beamed. "Grilan-Zeat. The *comet*. It's arrived! Come and look!"

They got up and followed her. Everybody else in the room was heading for the doors.

Outside the farmhouse there was a silent, growing crowd of resistance members. All had their heads back, staring at the sky. Stryke and the others followed their gaze. They saw a light in the heavens. It was small, about the size of the smallest coin held out at arm's length, and had a misty, watery aspect. But it gave out light of a kind unlike anything else in the night sky, and it seemed somehow to have a purpose.

"Wonderful, isn't it?" Chillder said, sidling up to them. "Now my mother can issue her call to arms. Then we'll see what the orcs of Acurial are made of."

Stryke feared that might be the case.

"If they got this right," Haskeer announced, "maybe the heroes bit's true, too." He sounded hopeful.

Stryke spotted Wheam in the crowd, looking up enraptured. Dallog was nearby, and most of the recruits from Ceragan. Staring. Transfixed by the wonder and mystery of it. He knew orcs all over Taress, all over the land, would be seeing the same, and he wondered what they'd make of it.

"It'll grow!" Chillder promised. "The nearer it gets, the bigger."

Coilla had drifted apart from the others. She found a stretch of low wall and sat to watch the sky. She felt contrition for her carelessness, but strangely that wasn't the major thing on her mind. As she gazed at the comet and heard the droned conversations from the crowd, she realised how different this land was. Not in big ways, but in small differences that were enough to throw you off. She felt drained, and very tired.

Jup had spotted her sitting alone and, guessing she might need cheer, left Spurral and made for her.

He hauled himself up next to her, his feet not quite scraping the ground, and said, "It's not the end of the world, you know."

"No," Coilla said, "but you can almost see it from here."

THE ORCS RETURN IN:

ORCS: ARMY OF SHADOWS

Stan Nicholls

A sojourn in their idyllic homeworld left Stryke and the Wolverines lacking purpose. So when an opportunity for bloodletting arose, Stryke seized it. Utilizing mysterious artifacts, the Wolverines are transported to Acurial, a world where the indigenous orc population is cruelly subjugated by human invaders.

Upon their arrival, Stryke's band joins with Acurial's emerging resistance movement. As the revolution gathers pace, the Wolverines are forced to embark on an odyssey through outlandish parallel dimensions—a chase that would see Stryke and his comrades pursued by both their most ruthless enemy and a mysterious troop hell-bent on their destruction.

Coming in 2010

Available wherever good books are sold

extras

meet the author

Peter Coleborn

STAN NICHOLLS is the author of more than two dozen books, most of them in the fantasy and science fiction genres, for both children and adults. His books have been published in over twenty countries. Before taking up writing full-time in 1981, he co-owned and managed the West London bookstore Bookends and managed the specialist SF bookshop Dark They Were and Golden Eyed. He was also Forbidden Planet's first manager and helped establish and run the New York branch. A journalist for national and specialist publications and the Internet, he was the science fiction and fantasy book reviewer for the London listings magazine *Time Out* for six years and subsequently reviewed popular science titles for the magazine. He received the Le Fantastique Lifetime Achievement Award for Contributions to Literature in April 2007.

introducing

If you enjoyed
ORCS: BAD BLOOD,
look out for

THE DWARVES

by Markus Heitz

*For countless millennia, the dwarves of the Fifthling Kingdom have
defended the stone gateway into Girdlegard. No man or beast has ever suc-
ceeded in breaching it. Until now...*

*Abandoned as a child, Tungdil the blacksmith labors contentedly in the
land of Ionandar, the only dwarf in a kingdom of men. Tungdil has never
even set eyes on another dwarf. But all that is about to change.*

*Sent out into the world to deliver a message and reacquaint himself
with his people, the young foundling finds himself thrust into a battle for
which he has not been trained. The life of every man, woman, and child
in Girdlegard depends upon his ability to embrace his heritage. Tungdil is
certain of one thing: no matter where he was raised, he is a true dwarf.*

And no one has ever questioned the courage of the Dwarves.

Glandallin's gaze swept the front line of monstrous beasts, shifting back to survey the second, third, fourth, fifth, and countless other grunting rows, all poised for the attack. He glowered from under his bushy eyebrows, forehead furrowing into a frown.

Giselbert lost no time in reversing the incantation. At the sound of his voice, the gates submitted to his authority, swinging back across the pathway but moving too slowly to stop the breach. Giselbert strode behind his troops, laying a hand on each shoulder. The gesture was a source of solace as well as strength, calming and rallying the last defenders of the gates.

Trumpets blaring, the riders ordered the attack. The orcs and ogres brandished their weapons, shouting to drown out their fear, and the army advanced with thundering steps.

"The path is narrow. Meet them line by line and give them a taste of our steel!" Glandallin called to his kinsfolk. "Vraccas is with us! We are the children of the Smith!"

"The children of the Smith!" the fifthlings echoed, feet planted firmly on the rocky ground beneath.

Four dwarves were chosen to form the final line of defense. Throwing down his shield, the king took an ax in each hand and led the surge toward the enemy. The dwarves, all that remained of Giselbert's folk, charged out to slay the invaders.

Ten paces beyond the gateway, the armies met. The fifthlings tunneled like moles through the vanguard of orcs.

With only one ax with which to defend himself, Glandallin struck out, slicing through the thicket of legs. He did not stop to kill his victims, knowing that the fallen bodies would hinder the advancing troops.

"No one gets past Glandallin!" he roared. Stinking blood streamed from his armor and helm, stinging his eyes. When his ax grew heavy, he clasped the weapon with both hands. "No one, do you hear!" His enemies' bones splintered, splattering him with hot blood. Twice he was grazed by a sword or a spear, but he battled on regardless.

The prize was not survival but the closing of the gates. Girdlegard would be safe if they could stave off the invasion until the passageway was sealed.

Until this hour his ax had defended him faithfully, but now the magic of its runes gave out. Glancing to his right, Glandallin saw a comrade topple to the ground, skull sliced in half by an orc's two-handed sword. Seething with hatred, and determined to fell the aggressor, Glandallin lunged once, twice, driving his ax into the creature's belly and cleaving it in two. A shadow loomed above him, but by then it was too late. He made a last-ditch attempt to dodge the ogre's sweeping cudgel, but its rounded head swooped down and struck his legs. Bellowing in pain he toppled against an orc, severing its thigh as he fell, before tumbling onward through the army of legs. He lashed out with his ax until there were no more orcs within his reach.

"Come here and fight, you cowards!" he snarled.

The enemy paid him no attention. Fired by an insatiable hunger, they streamed past him toward the gateway. They had no need of stringy dwarf flesh when there were tastier morsels in Girdlegard.

Trembling with pain, Glandallin rose up on his elbows. The rest of his kinsfolk were dead, their mutilated bodies strewn on the ground, surrounded by scores of enemy corpses. The diamonds on Giselbert's belt sparkled in the sunlight, marking the place where the fifthling father had fallen, slain by a trio of ogres. At the sight of him, Glandallin's soul ached with sorrow and pride.

The sun rose above the mountains, flooding through the gateway and dazzling Glandallin with its light. He raised a hand to his sensitive eyes, straining to see the gateway. *Praise be to Vraccas! The gates were closed!*

A blow from behind sent pain searing through his chest. For the duration of a heartbeat the tip of a spear protruded through his tunic, then withdrew. He slumped, gasping, to the ground. "What in the name of...?"

The assassin stepped round his body and knelt beside him. The smooth elven face was framed by fine fair hair that shimmered in the sunlight like a veil of golden threads. But the vision bore a terrible deformity; two fathomless pits stared from almond-shaped holes.

The creature wore armor of black metal that reached to its knees. Its legs were clad in leather breeches and dark brown boots. Burgundy gloves protected its fingers from grime, and its right hand clasped a spear whose steel tip, sharp enough to penetrate the fine mesh of dwarven chain mail, was moist with blood.

The strange elf spoke to the dwarf.

At first the words meant nothing to Glandallin, but their morbid sound filled him with dread.

"My friend said: 'Look at me: Sinthoras is your death,'" a second voice translated behind him. "'I will take your life, and the land will take your soul.'"

Glandallin coughed, blood rushing from his mouth and coursing down his beard.

"Get out of my sight, you pointy-eared monster! I want to see the gates," he said gruffly, brandishing his ax to ward away the beast. The weapon almost flew from his grip; his strength was ebbing fast. "Out of my way or I'll cut you in two like a straw, you treacherous elf!" he thundered.

Sinthoras laughed coldly. Raising his spear, he inserted the tip slowly between the tight rings of mail.

"You are mistaken, my friend. We are the älfar, and we have come to slay the elves," the voice said softly. "The gates may be closed, but the power of the land will raise you from the dead and from that moment on, you will be one of us. You know the incantation; you will open the door."

"Never! My soul belongs to Vraccas!"

"Your soul belongs to the land, and you will belong to the land until the end of time," the velvety voice cut him short. "Die, so you can return and deliver Girdlegard to us."

The spear's sharp tip pierced the flesh of the helpless, dying dwarf. Pain stopped his tongue.

Sinthoras raised the weapon and pushed down gently on the battered body. The final blow was dealt tenderly, almost reverently. The creature waited for death to claim its prey, watching over Glandallin's pain-ravaged features and drinking in the memory.

Finally, when he was certain that the last custodian of the gateway had departed, Sinthoras ended his vigil and rose to his feet.

VISIT THE ORBIT BLOG AT

www.orbitbooks.net

FEATURING

BREAKING NEWS
FORTHCOMING RELEASES
LINKS TO AUTHOR SITES
EXCLUSIVE INTERVIEWS
EARLY EXTRACTS

AND COMMENTARY FROM OUR EDITORS

WITH REGULAR UPDATES FROM OUR TEAM,
ORBITBOOKS.NET IS YOUR SOURCE
FOR ALL THINGS ORBITAL.

WHILE YOU'RE THERE, JOIN OUR EMAIL LIST
TO RECEIVE INFORMATION ON SPECIAL OFFERS,
GIVEAWAYS, AND MORE.

imagine. explore. engage.